MY HEART
REMEMBERS

A NOVEL

Books by
Kim Vogel Sawyer
FROM BETHANY HOUSE PUBLISHERS

Waiting for Summer's Return
Where Willows Grow
My Heart Remembers

MY HEART
REMEMBERS

A NOVEL

Kim Vogel Sawyer

BETHANY HOUSE PUBLISHERS
Minneapolis, Minnesota

My Heart Remembers
Copyright © 2008
Kim Vogel Sawyer

Cover design by Brand Navigation

Scripture quotations are taken from the King James Version of the Bible.

Published by Bethany House Publishers
11400 Hampshire Avenue South
Bloomington, Minnesota 55438

Bethany House Publishers is a division of
Baker Publishing Group, Grand Rapids, Michigan.

Printed in the United States of America

ISBN 978–0–7642–0493–7

In memory of
Tantie

O Lord, thou hast searched me, and known me. . . .
Thou hast beset me behind and before, and laid thine hand
  upon me. . . .
Whither shall I go from thy spirit? Or whither shall I flee
  from thy presence?
. . . Thy right hand shall hold me.
    —Psalm 139:1, 5, 7, 10b KJV

PART ONE

CHAPTER ONE

Maelle
New York City
March, 1886

Maelle Gallagher sat straight up, careful not to bump Mattie, who slept sideways in the bed, his head near her hip. An odd yellow glow lit the tenement's bar-covered window, making shadows dance on the far wall. Maelle frowned. Light came from sunshine, but Ma and Da in their bed across the room meant it must still be nighttime. She rubbed her eyes, then looked again at the glowing window.

She smelled something that reminded her of the fireplace back at their cottage in Ireland. The smell made her throat tighten and her stomach feel full. She tugged at the buttoned collar of her nightshirt, covering her mouth and nose. Her heart pounded in fear, although she wasn't sure why she was frightened.

She scratched her short-cropped hair—oh, how she missed the long curls Da used to tug when teasing her—and slipped from the bed. Tiptoeing, she crossed the room and peeked out the window.

The light was brighter there, making her squint. Sounds she hadn't heard in the city before—like dry grass crunching under someone's feet and the far-off roar of a river—came through the open window, increasing her confusion. The fireplace smell was stronger by the window, and she coughed.

"Who is it?"

She sucked in her breath, realizing she'd roused her father. She whispered, "Me, Da."

"My . . . elle." Her name split with his yawn. "Lass, what're ya doin' up in the middle o' the night?"

The gently scolding tone made Maelle shrug her shoulders and look down in shame. Suddenly he leapt from the bed and let loose a string of language of which Ma did not approve. Da only cursed when angry. Maelle shrank against the window frame.

"Lass, wake yer brother!"

Maelle stared stupidly at her father as he raced to the bureau, yanked open the top drawer, and withdrew a cloth bag. She watched him throw several items into the bag and then spin toward her. "D' ya hear me, Maelle?" He shoved the bag into her arms. "Wake yer brother 'n get out!"

Maelle's fuzzy brain could not comprehend the strange order. Get out? Why would Da pack her a bag and send her away? And why make Mattie leave? Mattie still slept like the good boy he was. He had done no wrong. She remained rooted in place with the bag in her arms, shivering although the night was unusually hot.

"I'm tellin' ya, lass. Get out!"

Da's hollering woke baby Molly, and she wailed from her basket on the floor. Ma sat up then, as did Mattie. Still Maelle stood by the window, watching, listening, her breath coming hard and fast as fear made a foul taste in her mouth. Screams pierced the night, adding to the crackling and roaring that seemed to grow louder by the minute.

Rubbing her eyes, Ma said, "Angus, what—?"

Da snatched up the wailing Molly. "A fire, Brigid!"

"Fire?" Ma leaned into the corner, pulling the sheet to her chin. Her eyes looked wild. She began to moan. "Oh, saints in heaven, save us!"

Da stood for a moment, staring at Ma. Then he shook his head and whirled toward the bed Mattie and Maelle shared. Holding Molly against his shoulder, he grabbed Mattie by the arm and jerked the boy from the bed. Mattie cried out as Da shoved him in Maelle's direction. Mattie fell against her, nearly knocking her down. Maelle caught him, holding him up, though her limbs quivered. Da had never been so rough.

"Out! Out!" Da yelled in Maelle's face, and finally Maelle found the ability to obey. Clutching the bag Da had given her, she took hold of Mattie's hand and stumbled behind Da to the hall-way. Molly's high-pitched screams carried over all other sounds, the baby's red face furious as it bounced on Da's shoulder.

Smoke hung heavy in the hallway, stinging Maelle's eyes. People milled in a jumbled stream toward the stairway that led to the lower floors, their feet pounding, voices calling out to hurry, hurry. At the top of the stairs, Da shoved Molly into Maelle's arms and then stepped away from her. "Follow the others, lass, 'n get yerself 'n the wee ones outside. I'll get yer mither 'n some more o' our things, 'n then I'll follow. Take care o' the wee ones. Don' let them out o' yer sight. D' ya hear me, lass?"

"I hear ya, Da," Maelle gasped. Then Da touched her hair—her short hair—and gave a little pat. A gentle pat. The kind Maelle expected. His smile flashed, and he turned and disappeared into the smoke.

Gagging against the horrid smell that cut off her breath, Maelle struggled to keep hold of Molly. The baby bucked and cried in her arms as they made their way down the stairs. "Hold tight t' me, Mattie!" She felt his hand grasp a fistful of fabric at her back. Others, all set on escape, pushed past them, and Maelle feared they would be separated. But Mattie's hand held tight to her nightshirt, and finally they burst through the outside doors and sucked in great gulps of night air.

Clanging bells and horse hooves on cobblestone sounded above the voices of frightened tenants. Men in blue uniforms with sticks in their hands pushed in front of the building, forcing people away from the entrance. "Get back! Get back now! The fire wagons are comin'! Make way!"

Maelle led her brother across the street, where they could watch the doors for Da and Ma. She sat cross-legged, the sack at her feet and Molly in her lap. Mattie stood beside her, his hand clamped on her left shoulder. Mattie and Molly both cried, but Maelle didn't cry. Blinking to clear her vision, she squinted across the street. She didn't want to miss seeing her parents come through those doors.

She would show Da she'd done just as he'd asked—she'd looked out for the wee ones. Remembering his hand on her hair, she smiled. He'd be so proud of her.

"Maelle? Maelle . . ."

Something shook her arm, and she grunted in displeasure, unwilling to surrender her sleep. She jerked away from the intrusion, pushing a bulky weight from her lap. A baby's cry brought her fully awake. Opening her eyes, she saw little Molly sprawled across the sidewalk and Mattie leaning over the baby.

"Maelle, ya should be shamed. Ya threw poor Molly onto the ground."

Her brother's tone reminded her of Da's. She scooped up Molly and patted her. "Sorry I am, wee one. I meant no harm to ya." She continued rocking Molly, who sucked her fist and complained. Looking around, she realized they were on the sidewalk across from their apartment building. Confusion dizzied her mind.

She pressed her memory—the last thing she remembered was watching streams of water from the fire wagon shoot over the building and hoping Ma and Da wouldn't get a soaking. Although she'd meant to stay awake until her parents came out, tiredness must have overtaken her. The noisy milling crowd from last night had cleared, although people still stood in small clusters outside of their building, and some stretched on the sidewalk near where she and Mattie sat.

"Do ya see Da or Ma, Mattie?"

Mattie shielded his eyes with a dirty hand, peering across the street. Then he shrugged and squatted beside her, putting his hand on Molly's tangled curls. "Maybe they went to work?"

Worry made her tummy tremble. If Da and Ma had already left for their jobs at the manufactory, they wouldn't be home until late. Maelle was accustomed to caring for Mattie and Molly

13

in her parents' absence, but she was always instructed to stay in the flat. Da would not be pleased if they spent the day outside.

She struggled to her feet, her movements awkward due to Molly's uncooperative bulk. "Pick up the bag, Mattie, an' come with me."

"Where're we goin'?"

"To the flat. We canna be outside in our nightclothes." Maelle looked both ways, then dashed across the street, wincing when her bare feet encountered rocks. Mattie followed her as she made her way to the concrete steps leading to the doors of their apartment house. But before she had taken two steps upward, a stern voice froze her in place.

"You there, boys! Where do you think you're going?"

Maelle turned and spotted a scowling man in a blue uniform, pointing a stick at her. Confused by the term "boys," she raised her eyebrows high in query. "Is it us ya're speakin' ta, sir?"

"Yes, you." He clomped closer and propped his elbow on the iron baluster. "Where are you goin'?"

Maelle wanted to shrink into her grubby nightshirt. Mattie scuttled behind her, obviously frightened by the man. "To me flat, sir, as me da would expect."

The man shook his head. "You can't go into that building, young man."

Young man? Maelle scowled, then realized he must think her a boy with her short hair and Da's old shirt. Shame engulfed her again as she recalled being shorn at the Ellis Island station due to the nits that had taken hold of her head during their journey. Da had soothed her with the promise her hair would grow back in time. She wished it would hurry. To the man, she said, "Why can I na go in?"

"It ain't safe. There was a fire last night."

Maelle looked at the building. Although the smell from last night remained strong, she could no longer see the yellow glow. "Is the fire na gone, then?"

The man looked at her as if she'd gone daft. "Well, sure it's gone, but it burned out several floors. If you go in, you could be hurt." He plucked Mattie from the stairs, placing him on the sidewalk, then reached for Maelle. "You come down from there, now."

Maelle scrabbled down the two steps to stand beside the cowering Mattie. Her heart pounded, too, but fear of disappointing Da was greater than fear of this stranger. She peered up at him and argued, "But I have to go in. Me baby sister needs a nappy change."

"Well, you won't find no nappies in there. They'll be all burned up."

Maelle's gaze jerked to the building. An image of their cottage's fireplace appeared in her mind, the flames licking at the peat Da layered in. When the flames died out, nothing of the peat remained except char. The fire last night was bigger than a fire in a fireplace. Everything in their flat must be char now, too.

She shivered and sat on the step, cradling Molly in her lap. Mattie perched beside her, hugging the bag Da had packed. He leaned against her arm, and she took comfort from his presence. She thought the man would leave now that they weren't trying to get inside the building, but instead he squatted in front of her.

"Do you have folks?"

Maelle nodded. "Yes, sir. Me da is Angus, and me ma is Brigid. Angus an' Brigid Gallagher."

"Where do your folks work, son?" He'd sounded gruff before, but his tone was now kind.

Although still bothered by the "son," Maelle answered with pride. "Da an' Ma make lanterns at the manufact'ry."

"The Geist manufactory?"

Maelle nodded. "Da says it's not like havin' 'is own shoein' shop, like in County Meath, but it is good honest work."

"I'm sure your da is right." The man pushed to his feet. "But we can't leave you sittin' here on this stoop all day. Your baby sister there needs attention. Let's go to the manufactory and see if your ma or da can be with you."

Maelle considered the man's suggestion. Would it upset Da to be pulled away from work? He was lucky to have the job, he'd said, and he must never be late or he might lose it. "I'm not knowin' if we should . . ."

"But you haven't had your breakfast, have you?" The man's question caused Maelle's stomach to clench as she recognized her hunger.

Breakfast—and seeing Ma and Da—sounded good, but still Maelle hesitated.

The man leaned forward, propping his hands on his knees. "Listen, son, I'm a police officer. My name is Officer Jorgens. My job is to help children, and you and your brother and sister need help right now."

Maelle couldn't argue with that.

"It'll be all right." Officer Jorgens straightened and held out his arms. "Here. Let me carry your sister, an' we'll go find your folks."

She'd been warned by Da to never let anyone take belongings from her. The city was full of thieves, he'd said, and one must always be careful. She would never allow a stranger to take Molly. She tightened her hold on her sister. To Mattie she said, "Carry our bag."

The walk to the manufactory was only four blocks, but on bare feet and with little sleep, it seemed much longer. They reached the metal doors, and Officer Jorgens stopped.

"I'll go in and ask about Angus Gallagher." His expression turned stern. "You wait right here for me."

Maelle nodded to indicate she would follow his order. She bounced Molly, who complained softly, while Mattie rocked from foot to foot. After a few minutes, the doors opened again, and Officer Jorgens came out followed by a man who wore dirty pants and a sweat-stained shirt. His face was all shiny from sweat—the way Da looked when he came home at night—but it wasn't Da.

The man looked from Maelle to Mattie, then shook his head at the police officer. Without a word, he headed back inside, closing the doors behind him. Officer Jorgens stared at the closed door for a few moments, and Maelle saw his shoulders rise and fall with a big breath. Finally he turned around, and the look in his eyes made her heartbeat quicken.

But then he smiled. "Well, let's go get you some breakfast."

The suggestion of food should have made her hunger increase. But it didn't. A funny weight filled her belly—the same feeling she'd had last night when she'd awakened and thought the sun was shining through the window.

This time she knew what the feeling meant. Something was wrong.

Chapter Two

Bits and snatches from the past hours cluttered Maelle's mind in a confusing mosaic. The frantic rush from the tenement; Da and Ma allowing her, Mattie, and Molly to sleep unattended on the sidewalk; the officer's odd look when he stepped out of the manufactory.

"It's na hungry that I am, sir. Please . . . where is me da?" Maelle heard the panic in her voice, but she couldn't control it. Mattie stared, wide-eyed, at the officer.

Maelle was certain she saw pity in the man's eyes. His gaze flitted to Mattie and Molly before returning to her. Her heart pounded hard in her chest, making it hard to breathe.

"It might be best for us to talk alone—man to man. Can we do that?"

Her breath came in little spurts through her nose. She nodded and turned to Mattie. "Hold tight to Molly. I'll be talkin' to the officer over there."

Mattie sat on the ground and cradled Molly. Maelle followed Officer Jorgens to the sidewalk, where he crouched down in front of her and put his hand on her shoulder.

"What's your name, son?"

"My-elle." It came out in a strangled gulp.

"Michael," the man repeated. "I can't know for certain, Michael, but I'm afraid your da might not have made it out of the tenement."

The softly uttered words, so gentle, struck Maelle as if delivered with a sledge hammer. "You . . . you mean you think me da is . . . burnt up?"

The hand on her shoulder tightened. "Now, we don't want to lose hope, son, but he didn't come to work today. Nor did your mother." He took a deep breath. "Did your folks ever miss work before?"

Maelle shook her head wildly. Never did Da miss work, and he always made sure Ma went, too. He expected Maelle to be dependable in looking after her brother and sister. She looked at Mattie and Molly cuddled together. They looked so small and alone.

Alone . . .

Tears pricked her eyes. No matter what Officer Jorgens said, there was no hope. Her da wouldn't have left them on the sidewalk all night, unattended. He wouldn't have missed work, either. He must be char. He and Ma, they were char, burnt up in the fire. She, Mattie, and Molly were alone.

"I . . . I must be goin' back to me brother an' sister. I promised me da I would—"

Officer Jorgens held her arm. "Wait, Michael. I need to know . . . do you have any relatives here in New York?"

Maelle blinked, holding back tears. "No, sir. Me da an' ma was all we had. We have an uncle back in County Meath, but no one here."

"Friends, then, who might be able to take care of you?"

Maelle's chin began to quiver. She set her jaw. "No, sir. Me da an' ma worked all the day. They had no time for makin' friends." Da's last words had been to look out for the wee ones. Maelle would do that. Squaring her shoulders, she declared, "But it ain't needin' anyone we are, sir. I'll be takin' care of Mattie an' Molly meself."

The officer's head lowered for a moment as he heaved a sigh. "Now, that's a brave lad, but it can't be done."

"It can." Maelle stuck out her chin. "Me da trusted me to take care of me brother an' sister. I won't be lettin' 'im down."

"Of course you won't." Officer Jorgens squeezed Maelle's shoulder. "But staying on your own in a big city isn't a good idea. You're just a boy—you need help."

Maelle grimaced. She needed to tell him that she was not a boy, but there was a bigger argument to be won. "I need no help. It's takin' care of Mattie an' Molly I been doin' ever since we came, an' even before, with me ma bein' sick in the heart from her own ma's passin'. So I cared for Mattie an' Molly. An' I'll still do it. I'll get a job at the manufact'ry, makin' lanterns like me da, an' I'll work, an'—"

"And who'll care for Mattie an' Molly while you're away at work?"

The question brought her up short. "Well . . . Mattie can look after Molly."

"What about school?"

"School?" Maelle puckered her lips.

"Sure, school. You should go to school. Mattie should, too." Officer Jorgens shook his head, his eyes sad. "It's a good thing you want to do, Michael, to take care of your brother an' sister, but . . ."

The lump in Maelle's throat strangled her words, making them come out in a harsh whisper. "I promised me da."

Officer Jorgens gave her shoulder a pat, then dropped his hand to his knee. "Did that promise mean you had to take care of them all by yourself? Don't you think your da would understand if you asked someone to help you?"

Maelle considered the question. Back in Ireland, the villagers worked together, each one using his or her skill for the good of the community. Da hadn't thought it weak to rely on the Carmichaels for bushels of corn or the Delaneys for fabric Ma sewed into shirts and aprons. And of course Da did the shoeing for everyone in Dunshaughlin.

Slowly, Maelle shook her head. "No. It's fine to be lettin' 'em help, me da would say."

The officer broke into a smile. "And that's what we'll do— we'll find someone to help. I know just who to ask."

A small weight lifted from Maelle's chest at the realization she would not have to carry this burden alone. "Thank ya, sir."

"You're welcome." He rose and held out his hand. Maelle hesitated for a moment before placing her hand in his. "Let's go get some breakfast now. You'll need a full belly to get you through the morning."

Although the officer's hand wasn't as calloused as Da's, the width and strength gave Maelle a small reminder of how it had felt to walk hand-in-hand with her strapping father. As they returned to Mattie and Molly, she closed her eyes for a moment and allowed herself to pretend.

❧

"So nothing is left of their belongings?"

The young woman who spoke sounded dismayed. Officer Jorgens had hired a carriage to cart himself and the children to a large building far from the tenement Maelle had shared with her parents. As the horse had clopped along, carrying her farther and farther from their familiar neighborhood, her panic had risen higher and higher. Officer Jorgens had assured her the people at this big red-brick building would help her, but it didn't sound as though this woman wanted to help.

Officer Jorgens replied, "No, I told you, their tenement burned last night. If there's anything that wasn't burnt up, it will be ruined by smoke an' water. All they have is that little sack."

The woman's dark eyes looked to the sack. "Do you have clothes in there?"

Maelle shook her head. She'd peeked in the sack earlier, hoping for a clean nappy for Molly, who must have a terrible rash by now. "No, mum. It has only our ties to home."

The woman's thick brows came down. "What?"

Maelle slipped the sack behind her back. "Our Bible, a picture o' me family, an' some letters me ma wrote to me da when they was young. Ma called 'em our ties to home."

The woman's expression cleared. "Well, it's nice, I'm sure, that they were saved, but some clothing . . . There are so many needs here. . . ." She pursed her lips.

Officer Jorgens reached into his pocket and removed a coin purse. Snapping it open, he dug his fingers around in the little purse and withdrew a few coins. "Here." He thrust the coins at the woman. "Buy them something to wear. They can't be standing around in nightshirts the rest of the day."

His abrupt tone caused the woman to shrink back for a moment, her hands fluttering in front of her chest. "Oh no, Officer, I wasn't asking for money. Miss Agnes handles all of our donations . . ." Her cheeks turned a bright pink. "Of course I'll find something for the children to wear."

Spinning away from the officer, she reached toward Maelle. "Give me the baby now, and I'll see that she gets cleaned and changed."

Maelle looked at Officer Jorgens. At his nod she allowed the woman to bustle away with Molly.

As the first lady left, a second one approached—this one older, wearing a flowing black dress with a crisp white collar. Her hair, streaked brown and gray, was swept away from her face into a neat bun like Ma wore back in Ireland. The lady's whole face smiled, and at once Maelle sensed she could trust her.

The lady held her hands out to Officer Jorgens, who took both of them. "I was told some children orphaned by last night's fire were being delivered. Thank you for thinking of us." It seemed this lady didn't mind that Maelle and Mattie had brought no clothes.

Officer Jorgens turned his smile on the children. "I knew I'd be leavin' 'em in good hands with you, Miss Agnes." Touching Maelle's shoulder, he added, "This is Michael Gallagher and his brother, Mattie. Their baby sister, Molly, was already taken by one of the keepers. She was . . . wet."

Miss Agnes laughed softly. "A clean diaper will do the baby much good, I am sure." She clasped her hands beneath her chin. "What handsome children—such pretty red hair . . ." She stroked Mattie's dirty head with her work-worn hand. He leaned against Maelle, his brown eyes fearful.

Officer Jorgens chuckled. "These two don't have nothin' on red compared to that baby sister of theirs. Her hair is as red as the paint on a fire wagon."

The woman shot the officer a sharp look. "You don't say?" She seemed to think deeply, her lips sucked in. Then she gave herself a little shake and fixed her gaze on Maelle. "And you have had a rough night, haven't you, Michael?"

The kindness in the woman's tone, as well as the genuine concern in her eyes, made Maelle wish she could throw herself against those voluminous black folds of fabric and cry the hurt away. But before she could move or say anything, the woman turned back to Officer Jorgens. They spoke softly, and then Officer Jorgens turned to Maelle and gave her shoulder a pat.

"I've got to get back to my beat, Michael, but I'm leaving you in good hands. Miss Agnes will take care of you and your brother and sister. You be good for her, will you?" He gave one more smile, the flash of his teeth reminding her of Da's last smile, then he turned and strode out of the building. Maelle watched him go, a weight building in her chest.

"Now, then . . ." Miss Agnes's voice captured Maelle's attention. "We need to find you two something to wear and get you settled."

Maelle found her voice. "Can't I be seein' me sister?"

Miss Agnes's eyes twinkled. "Well, now, Michael, here at the Good Shepherd Asylum we have three sections. The babies go to the nursery, the girls go to their floor, and the boys to theirs. Since your sister is a baby, she goes to the nursery, but you're a fine big boy. You won't be able to stay there."

Panic filled Maelle's breast. "But can't she stay with me?" She started to explain that she wasn't Michael but Maelle, a girl like Molly, so they could be kept together. But Miss Agnes spoke.

"Now, didn't I just tell you the babies, boys, and girls are separate?"

Maelle considered the woman's kind yet firm reply. If what Miss Agnes said was right, then Molly would be in one place, Mattie in another, and Maelle in yet another. None of them would be together. Babies and girls were kept apart, so she couldn't be with Molly even if she explained she was a girl. But if she went on being Michael, she could at least stay with Mattie. She would let the lady think she was Michael.

"Yes, but . . ." Maelle struggled for a way to still see Molly. "Me da told me to be keepin' watch over her."

"And a good boy you are to obey your da," Miss Agnes said in a warm tone. "He would be proud of you. But you must trust me when I say Molly will be well cared for, and you may visit her every evening. How will that be?"

Maelle preferred to see her sister now, but she would not shame her father's memory by arguing with an adult. She said dully, "Fine that will be, mum. Thank you."

"Good." Putting her hands on the backs of their heads, Miss Agnes herded Maelle and Mattie down a long hallway. "Now let's go get changed, shall we?"

Changed? Maelle's heart began to pound. Her secret might be revealed far too soon.

❧

"Michael! Michael Gallagher!"

Maelle groaned at Miss Agnes's stern call. She released Jimmy's shirt front with a shove, sending the boy onto his backside in the dirt. Bending over him with her clenched fist under his nose, she hissed, "Leave me brother alone or ya'll know what ta expect from now on."

Just as she straightened, Miss Agnes took hold of her ear and marched her to the edge of the play yard. The woman shook a finger in Maelle's face. "This fighting must stop. This is the third time this week you've been caught fighting. What am I to do with you?"

In the three weeks since Officer Jorgens had deposited her at the orphans' home, Maelle had been involved in more fights than she could count. And she'd won nearly all of them. Her da hadn't taken much with fighting, but Maelle felt she had little choice. She stuck out her lower lip, which she could tell was beginning to swell from the clop Jimmy had delivered, and said, "I'll na be lettin' them torment me brother." She waved her hand toward the cluster of boys gathered near the fence, offering sympathy to Jimmy. "They pick on Mattie, callin' 'im *mama's boy* an' *sissy*. He ain't none o' that—he's just a little boy who still misses his ma." Maelle's voice rose with passion.

Mattie raced to her side, tucking himself beneath her sheltering arm. He peered upward at Miss Agnes, his expression pleading. "Don't be mad, mum. Sorry we are."

As always, Mattie's big brown eyes under his mop of reddish curls did the trick. Miss Agnes's countenance softened, the frown lines giving way to a gentle smile. "I know you are, dear boy, but words must be followed with action to be truly sincere." She gave Mattie's hair a stroke before putting her hands on her hips and adding, "Which means I can no longer accept your apology unless I see a change in behavior. No more fighting, for either of you. Do you hear me?"

"*D' ya hear me, lass?*" Da's voice rang in Maelle's memory. Automatically, she nodded. "Yes. I hear ya."

"Good." Miss Agnes crossed her arms. "Now, since you have misbehaved in the play yard, you've given up your privilege of free time today. Instead, you'll go to the kitchen and ask to wash tables."

Maelle and Mattie exchanged looks of disgust.

"Go now."

The stern tone spurred them to action. Maelle took hold of Mattie's hand, and together they dashed across the play yard and into the building. Inside, Mattie giggled. "Yer a good fighter for a girl."

Maelle sent a frantic look up and down the hall. She heaved a sigh of relief when she realized no one was around. Taking hold of her brother's shoulders, she gave him a firm shake. "Hush now, Mattie! Are ya wantin' to get us split up? Don't ya ever be callin' me a girl!"

Mattie's lower lip trembled. "Sorry I am, Maelle—I mean Michael. Sometimes I forget."

"Well, ya can't be forgettin'. Not unless ya want me sent to the other side of the building. I told ya: it's careful we must be." She frowned, her heart constricting. "We hardly see Molly as it is. I couldna be standin' it if they took me away from ya, too."

Mattie barreled against her chest. "I won't be sayin' Maelle ever again."

Maelle kissed the top of Mattie's head. "Okay it is if you slip, Mattie. Maelle an' Michael sound enough alike, no one will be questionin'."

But Mattie shook his head fiercely. "No. I'll na be makin' that mistake. Ya'll always be Michael. I promise."

Tightness pressed at Maelle's chest. How long could she continue to be Michael? It was hard to keep the secret—to find a private time for bathing and dressing with so many boys around. She'd kept anyone from looking inside the family Bible where the birth of Maelle Gallagher was recorded in Da's neat penmanship. Yet she knew the day would come when she'd be found out. And as soon as it happened, she and Mattie would be separated. Who would protect Mattie then?

Swallowing, Maelle said, "An' I promise to always be lookin' out for ya, just as I told Da I would."

They hugged, Maelle's hold on her brother desperate. The echoing squeak of the door to the play yard intruded, and they broke apart.

"Miss Agnes is comin'." Mattie's eyes were wide. "Let's go!"

Hand-in-hand, they ran to the kitchen.

CHAPTER THREE

Snuggled together in Maelle's cot that night in the dark, Mattie nudged his sister and whispered, "Mae—Michael?"

Maelle snuffled. "Aye?"

"Is yer lip still hurtin'?"

Maelle touched the swollen lip with her fingertips, grimacing at the tenderness. It hurt, but she'd learned to take the punches without crying. "Fine I am. Ta sleep wi' ya."

Cots squeaked as boys shifted. Footsteps echoed in the hallway outside the closed door of the room. One of the boys coughed. Then Mattie's voice came again.

"Michael?"

"Aye?"

"I'll be fightin' me own battles from now on."

Maelle propped herself on one elbow and peered down at her brother. In the dim light, she could barely make out his features, but she could tell his eyes were huge in his thin face. "Ya'd be pounded to pieces by the bigger boys."

"But then ya won't be in no more trouble." Tears welled in Mattie's eyes and spilled over. "Maybe they won't send ya away."

Maelle frowned. "What?"

"I heard 'em, Maelle. The ladies talkin'. They said ya'd be better off in the country, away from the city an' all the fightin'. They said—"

Mattie's voice rose in volume. Maelle put her hand over his mouth to stop his words. "Hush, Mattie. No one's goin' ta send me away."

Mattie's head bobbed up and down, making the cot creak. "On a train. I heard 'em say so." He whispered, but his tone was shrill with near hysteria.

Maelle wrapped Mattie in her arms as she lay back down. She stroked his tousled hair, thinking about what he'd said. Sent away on a train . . . Her heart pounded as she realized Mattie could be telling the truth. She'd heard the others talk about trains that carried orphans to western states. Was it possible Miss Agnes would send her to the West, away from Mattie and Molly? Tears gathered in her eyes, but she blinked to push them away.

She'd promised Da to look after the wee ones—how could she do that if she was far away? The more she thought about it, the more frantic she became. She knew she wouldn't be able to sleep until she'd spoken with Miss Agnes.

She tipped her ear toward Mattie. His even breathing told her he'd drifted off to sleep. She eased out of the cot, slipping the pillow down for Mattie to snuggle against. On stealthy feet, she crept to the door, opened it wide enough to allow herself to slip through, then closed it behind her without a sound.

In less than a minute she stood breathlessly outside Miss Agnes's office door, her heart pounding so hard she was sure it would break through her chest. The woman's eyes widened as Maelle stepped into the room. She put down a pen and fixed her with an unsmiling look. "Michael Gallagher, you should long be asleep. Why are you prowling the hallways at this hour?"

Maelle dashed forward and grabbed the edge of the desk with both hands. "Mum, will ya be sendin' me away?"

Miss Agnes leaned back sharply, her chair creaking in protest.

"Me brother said it's so. I told him he need na worry, that ya surely wouldn't be makin' me go away. But I couldna sleep." Maelle held her breath, waiting for Miss Agnes to assure her Mattie was mistaken.

But the woman sighed, closing her eyes for a moment. "Ah, that Mattie . . . Such a bright lad. He misses little, that one. . . ." She opened her eyes and looked steadily at Maelle. "Although I do not like to make announcements until the time of departure, it is true. I plan to send you on the next train. It leaves for Missouri in a few weeks."

Maelle's knees went weak. She slid into the sturdy seat of a nearby chair while clinging to the edge of the desk for support. "But . . . but . . . I canna be leavin' me brother an' sister."

Miss Agnes rose and came around the desk, knelt, and placed her hand on Maelle's knee. "You're all going—you, Mattie, and Molly. None will be left behind."

Maelle shrank into the seat, relief nearly toppling her. "You said . . . Missouri?"

"That's right. A western state with many opportunities for a bright lad like you. Families there are eager for children." For a moment, the woman's eyes seemed to dim, her face pinching into a pained expression that frightened Maelle. But then she relaxed her expression. "I worry for you here, Michael. The fighting . . ."

Maelle touched her lip, wincing. "I do na like the fightin', and I would na fight if I had no reason. The others, they bother Mattie, an' they try to take me things."

Miss Agnes tipped her head. "You mean the bag you brought?"

Maelle nodded, scowling as she remembered tussling for the bag. "Those things're mine. Ma treasured 'em. Da saved 'em from bein' turned to char. I can't be losin' 'em to some dirty orphans." She spat the last words.

Miss Agnes clicked her tongue against her teeth. "Michael, you mustn't speak that way. You've changed, my boy. This is why I want you to go west. You're a good boy, but the city is turning you into one like so many others who fight and scrabble for survival. You're far too fine a boy to be allowed to go that cynical pathway. I believe better things await you out west."

So sending her away wasn't a punishment? It was a reward? Pride welled in her chest. She stood. "I thank ya, mum. If I go, I'll do me best to be a better . . . boy." She hesitated. "An' ya're sure Mattie an' Molly will be comin', too?"

That odd look returned to the woman's eyes, but she nodded. "Yes, Mattie and Molly will go west, too."

Maelle stuck out her hand. "We'll go then, mum, an' gladly. Together, we'll find our better things in the West."

❧

Grand Central Depot, New York City
May, 1886

Maelle planted a kiss on Molly's plump cheek, unable to hold her sister close enough. How she had missed the little dumpling in the weeks at the orphans' home! But Maelle had been allowed to carry Molly to the train station. Maelle was thrilled to have her sister back in her arms, and she determined that was where Molly would stay the whole journey to Missouri. She'd never let anyone take Molly from her again.

Molly looked so sweet in a lacy white dress and matching bonnet. All the children had been given new clothes this morning for their journey. Maelle had come close to divulging her secret when she'd seen the lovely frocks being offered to the girls. Wool dresses with bows and ruffles and matching capes . . . Oh, how Maelle would love to own even one such beautiful dress!

But instead she'd been issued a white shirt, brown wool trousers, and a matching jacket. She and Mattie had gotten haircuts, too, and it had taken all of her strength to keep from shedding tears at the loss of her hair again. Would she ever be able to grow back the tumbling curls Da had so admired? At least a little billed tweed cap covered her shorn head, hiding her shame.

With pudgy fingers, Molly tugged at the tag pinned to Maelle's jacket front.

"No, no, sister," Maelle scolded, shifting the baby's fingers away. "The tag must be stayin' in place or our new parents won't be knowin' us."

Tags crinkled on every child's chest. Miss Agnes had told the twenty-six children who were boarding the train that they would journey four days and three nights, and they must keep their tags intact. Maelle thought it foolish to put the numbered tags on so soon. She hoped she could keep little Molly from tearing loose not only her own tag but Maelle's and Mattie's, as well. The year-old baby considered everything a play toy.

"Michael!" Mattie charged across the station's marble floor and skidded to a stop in front of his sister. He swung their bag in excitement, his eyes wide and glowing. "Did ya see the train? It's black an' shiny, with so much smoke comin' from a gray chimney. Did ya see it?"

"Mattie, ya've already scuffed yer new shoes," Maelle chided. "An' yer tag is loose. It's settlin' down ya must be or we'll never get ya to Missouri in good form."

Mattie looked down at the black boots he'd been given only that morning, his face falling as he noticed the dull scuffs across the toes. "Do ya think our new folks will na take me with scuffed shoes?"

The worry in his voice pinched Maelle's conscience. He was just a wee boy, excited at the prospect of a train ride. She shouldn't be so harsh. "Of course our new folks won't be thinkin' the less of ya just because of scuffed toes." She took heart when his smile returned. "But all the same, we must be stayin' as nice as we can. I'll have enough keepin' Molly neat. Can ya mind yer own manners?"

Mattie beamed. "For sure, I can."

"Good."

"Children! Children, gather close!" Miss Agnes raised her arms and gestured to the milling throng. The children, some with babies bouncing in their arms and some with bags bumping against their knees, formed a snug circle in front of Miss Agnes. Maelle kept a firm grip on Molly, who leaned forward and tried to grab the hair bow of a little girl in front of her.

"Children, this is Miss Esther." Miss Agnes put her arm around the shoulders of a thin, bespectacled woman with a long face and wide mouth. "She will be your escort to Missouri. She has already visited Severy, informed the town of your coming, and knows of several families eager to meet you and make you their own."

Cheers went up from several children, and Mattie and Maelle exchanged smiles of joyful anticipation.

"I trust you will obey Miss Esther on the journey and will show all the people on board what wonderful children you are." Tears sparkled in the woman's eyes as she finished. "Now, let us have a word of prayer before you board the train."

She closed her eyes, folding her hands in front of her. All the children followed suit, except Maelle, who needed to keep her eyes on Molly.

"Bless these children, Lord, as they venture forth. Keep your hand of safety over them, and lead them to the parents who will nurture them and raise them in the knowledge of your love. Amen."

"Amen," echoed the children.

Miss Esther clapped her hands. "Form a line now, children! Quickly!"

With giggles and shoves, the children fell into a makeshift line with Maelle and Mattie somewhere in the middle. Maelle whispered, "Get behind me, Mattie, an' hold on ta my jacket."

Molly's wiggling form in her arms and Mattie's hand on her back reminded Maelle of the night they had escaped the tenement. A wave of homesickness for Ma and Da hit her so hard tears spilled from her eyes. But she blinked bravely and marched in line with the others to their waiting railroad car. *Boys do na cry,* she told herself fiercely. Yet she heard sniffling behind her, and even without looking she knew the sound came from Mattie.

Peeking over her shoulder, she gave her little brother a quavery smile. "Do na cry, Mattie. Do ya na be rememberin' what Miss Agnes said? We're goin' to better things. . . ."

Severy, Missouri
May, 1886

Maelle stood on a raised platform at the front of the sanctuary of the Presbyterian church, flanked by Mattie and a chubby boy named Pat. A splash of color from a stained-glass window high and to her left fell across baby Molly's head, highlighting the red curling wisps of her hair. Although her shoulders ached from her sister's constant weight, she held Molly so she faced outward, her tag easily seen. Mattie fidgeted, standing on one foot, then the other. Maelle hoped he didn't need to use the outhouse.

After four days of sitting on a hard bench, with only brief marches around the train at watering stops for exercise, it felt good to stand. Her heart pounded with hope, even as an odd worry pressed her chest. This was the moment for which they had waited—the moment of meeting their new parents. Before leaving the train to walk to the church, Maelle had asked Miss

Esther if parents had already selected her, Mattie, and Molly, but Miss Esther's reply had been less than satisfying.

Maelle retrieved the words from her memory. "You will all be cared for, Michael. That is what is important." Then she had raised her shrill voice to address the entire car of children, cautioning them all to be on their best behavior since parents would not choose an ill-mannered child.

Out of the corner of her eye, she glimpsed Mattie's continued wiggling, and she gave him a light bump with her elbow to settle him down.

Now Miss Esther marched to the double doors at the front of the sanctuary and opened them wide, calling out, "We're ready. You may come in."

Maelle pasted a smile on her face and prayed Mattie was doing the same.

The pounding of feet on the wooden floor of the church vibrated through Maelle's shoes and into her legs as couples poured into the sanctuary. She kept her smile in place as she searched faces, her heart pounding, wondering which of the couples entering the building—if any—had come for her, Mattie, and Molly.

A well-dressed couple approached, the woman's eyes scanning tags. When her gaze fell on Molly's, her face lit and she rushed forward. "Reginald, look! There she is—number twelve!"

Before Maelle could react, the woman snatched Molly from Maelle's arms and held her out to the man. Mattie looked at Maelle, his eyes wide, and she shrugged in response. The woman exclaimed over Molly, touching the baby's curls and smoothing her plump cheek with her fingers. The man leaned in close.

Molly grasped his chin with her dimpled hand, and he and the woman laughed.

"Oh, Reginald, look at her!" The woman beamed up at her husband. "As red-haired and green-eyed as my mother. Oh, she's just as I imagined her to be!"

Maelle carefully examined the couple. Older than Da and Ma, and wearing fancier clothes than she'd ever seen, they seemed nice enough. Though not as pretty as Ma, the woman's face was pleasant, her blue eyes shining. The man had thick whiskers growing on both sides of his face leading to a mustache that grew over his upper lip. At first glance, the facial hair gave him a gruff appearance, but when Maelle looked into his eyes, she saw a tenderness there. Surely they would be loving parents.

The woman kissed Molly's cheek, and finally her gaze drifted to Maelle. She flashed a quick smile. Then the man put his hand on the woman's back and they turned toward the front doors. Molly blinked at Maelle over the woman's shoulder.

Maelle picked up their bag and took Mattie's hand. "C'mon, then." They followed the couple.

Halfway to the door, the man glanced back, and his brows came down. "Boys, you go back to the stage."

Maelle and Mattie exchanged startled looks.

The woman stopped, turning to face the children. Molly leaned toward Maelle, reaching to be held. Maelle dropped the bag and stretched her arms toward her baby sister. But the woman pulled Molly against her shoulder. Molly began to cry.

"Take the baby outside, Rebecca," the man said, and his wife swept toward the doors while soothing Molly, who continued to wail. When Maelle tried to follow, the man placed his hand against her chest. "No, boy. You stay here."

"But . . . but . . ." Maelle swallowed, her heart pounding so hard she could hardly catch her breath. "That's me sister she's takin'."

"We are adopting the baby." Though firm, his voice was not unkind. He started to turn away, but Mattie jumped forward and gave the man a kick on the shin.

"You canna take me sister!" Mattie pulled his foot back, ready to kick again.

Miss Esther rushed over. "Matthew Gallagher, I'm ashamed of you!" She glowered at Mattie briefly, then turned to the man. "I apologize, Mr. Standler. I will explain the situation to the children. You and your wife have a safe journey home."

The man nodded, sent one more frowning look at Mattie, and left the building. Miss Esther hauled Mattie to a corner, where she shook her finger under his nose and scolded. Maelle took advantage of the moment to snatch up her bag and run after the couple.

She slid to a stop in the sunny churchyard, frantically looking both right and left. She spotted the man climbing into a fancy enclosed carriage. Dashing across the grass with the bag banging against her leg, she cried, "Wait! Mister, please wait!"

The man folded his arms as she came to a panting halt beside the carriage. "Young man, I am sorry, but my wife and I are only adopting the baby."

Tears stung behind Maelle's nose. Although she had considered begging them to take her, the look on his face immediately silenced her pleas. Instead, she drew a deep breath and made a request she hoped would be honored. "Please, sir, can I kiss me sister good-bye?"

39

For long moments the man stared down at her while she held her breath, silently pleading with her eyes. Finally he gestured toward the carriage with a sweep of his hand. Maelle pulled herself onto the little step leading to the carriage and leaned in. The woman kept hold of Molly's waist, but Maelle hugged the baby as best she could and kissed both of her cheeks, forehead, and nose.

"Good-bye, Molly. I love ya, wee one." Tears distorted her vision, and she jumped free of the carriage, determined not to let this couple see her break down. Her foot bumped the bag, and she spun toward the man. "Please, sir, one more minute?"

The man blew out an impatient breath, but he waited while Maelle flopped open the bag and removed the Bible. After slipping the photograph free, she held out the book.

"Will . . . will you take me family's Bible . . . for Molly?"

The woman called through the door, "Take it, Reginald, and let us be off."

Silently, the man took the Bible and then closed the door behind him with a snap. The driver brought the reins down across the backs of the horses, and the carriage rolled forward. Maelle remained in the churchyard until the carriage turned a corner and disappeared from sight.

She closed her eyes for a moment, willing the name to memory: Mr. Standler. Standler. Standler. Her chest ached so badly she feared her heart might be crushed. Molly . . . gone. And Mattie—

With a start, she realized she didn't know what had happened to Mattie. Grabbing up her bag, she raced for the church, weaving between couples who were heading toward wagons, most with children in tow. Had Mattie been taken, too?

She careened through the door, and she nearly wilted with relief when she spotted Mattie in one of the wooden pews. He sat with his head bowed, tears creating rivers down his pale cheeks. She slid in beside him and dropped the bag in her lap.

"Miss Esther says nobody will be wantin' me now that I kicked that man."

Mattie's sad words made Maelle's chest ache even more. She feared he might be right. Unable to answer, she simply nodded.

"But I had to do somethin'. They took Molly away." He squinched his eyes closed, and tears spurted. "Miss Esther . . . she let 'em take Molly away. We won't be seein' her again. Just like Ma an' Da . . ."

Maelle swallowed her own tears. Reaching into the bag, she pulled out the photograph and pressed it into Mattie's hands. "Ya hold on to this. Ya can look at Molly an' Ma an' Da whenever ya're wantin' to."

Mattie held the picture in his limp fingers while tears continued to roll down his cheeks and plop onto his wool pants, leaving speckles behind. Maelle put her arm around his shoulders, blinking to keep her tears back. Crying wouldn't change anything.

She now understood Miss Agnes's funny look and Miss Esther's careful wording. They'd planned all along to give Molly to that couple. Never had they planned to let Maelle and Mattie go, too.

She envisioned the couple in their fancy clothes, riding in their fancy carriage. Rich people. Hadn't Da always said you couldn't trust rich people? And now rich people had Molly. At least they had seemed to like the baby. They probably couldn't have wee ones of their own. Wouldn't they treat the baby like a princess? She hoped so. And she knew their name. *Standler.* She'd find Molly again. She would!

She and Mattie sat on the pew while, one by one, the children left with couples. Eventually only Miss Esther and a man who leaned against the far wall remained. The man pushed off from the wall and approached Miss Esther.

Maelle heard their mumbled voices, but she ignored them until they crossed the floor to stand beside the pew. Miss Esther touched Maelle's shoulder. She looked up, and she hoped the hatred she felt didn't show on her face.

"Michael, this is Mr. Richard Watts. He's looking for a boy to travel with him and help him in his business."

Out of the corner of her eye, Maelle looked Mr. Watts up and down. Dressed in a brown suit with a string tie beneath his chin, he looked like many of the other men who'd come to the church that day. He needed a shave and haircut, though. The man's gaze bored into her. Maelle turned her face away.

Suddenly a hand curled around her upper arm and pulled her from the pew. Mattie's cry of fear brought Maelle to life. "You needn't be grabbin' at me! I can stand on me own."

The man laughed and squeezed her arm. "Feisty, huh? Well, that's good. Need a boy who's got some fight in him."

His fingers bit into Maelle's flesh, hurting her, but she couldn't pull loose. She glared at Miss Esther, who stood to the side. "I won't be goin' nowhere without me brother. You can tell him so!"

Miss Esther gave Watts an apologetic look. "Although arrangements had been made prior to our leaving New York for the youngest Gallagher child, I assured the proprietress of Good Shepherd the brothers would not be separated."

Maelle felt a small lift of hope at Miss Esther's words. Mattie scooted out of the pew to stand beside her. He slipped his hand in hers and clung.

"Well . . ." Watts scratched his whiskery chin with one hand while maintaining his hold on Maelle with the other. "As I told you, I've got a good business going with my photography equipment, but my home is a box wagon. It would be a might crowded with two boys. Don't know as I can take both of them."

Miss Esther raised her chin. "I'm sorry, sir, but it's both or neither."

Watts gave Maelle's arm another squeeze. He worked his jaw back and forth as he looked at her. "Tall boy, seems to have some muscle in that arm. Appears to have some intelligence, too, even if he does talk like a mick. The kind of boy who could learn the trade."

Miss Esther nodded. "It would be good for Mattie, as well, to learn a trade."

Suddenly Watts released Maelle's arm. She stumbled against Mattie. Rubbing her arm, she looked directly into the man's face. "I ain't goin' without me brother. An' that's that."

The man threw back his head and released a laugh that echoed to the rafters. "That's that, huh?" Still chuckling, he turned to Miss Esther. "All right, then, lady. I'll take 'em both."

CHAPTER FOUR

The man called Watts dragged Maelle toward the only remaining wagon in the churchyard. Mattie trailed behind, lugging their bag. Stopping in front of the wagon, Watts gestured proudly toward it with his hand.

"Well, here you are, boy. Your new home." It was a big box with some words painted on the side in dark green, square letters. "Drop the back hatch and climb in, but mind you don't bump any of my equipment. We'll hunt us up some lunch, then find a dry goods store and get you some gear. That suit'll be fine for shoots, but you need some traveling clothes." He pulled himself up on the high seat and picked up the reins.

Maelle wasn't sure what a back hatch was, so she and Mattie remained on the ground, peering upward.

Watts scowled down at them for a moment, then shrugged. "Okay, then, follow me." He slapped the reins onto the horses' backs, and the animals trotted forward. Maelle grabbed the bag from Mattie and caught his hand. Together they dashed after the wagon. They came to a panting stop when Watts reined in next to a saloon.

Watts hopped down from the high seat. "Well, at least I know you can run." He didn't apologize for making them trot behind the wagon like flea-ridden curs. Pointing toward the doors of the saloon, he said, "Let's go."

But Maelle held back, clutching Mattie's sweaty hand. "Me ma would not approve of us goin' into a place where spirits is sold."

Watts glowered at her, his brows low, and for a moment she feared he would force her inside. But then he shrugged and straightened the lapels of his jacket. "Suit yourself. But it'll be a long time to breakfast tomorrow."

In reply, Maelle sat on the edge of the boardwalk. Mattie sank down beside her. Without another word, Watts pushed the swinging doors to the saloon open, calling, "Get me a bowl of stew and biscuits."

Maelle's stomach growled as she thought about Watts eating a bowl of hot, meaty stew. On the train, the children had been given cold sandwiches and tinned milk—filling, but flavorless. Mattie's whimpers weakened Maelle's resolve, but memories of her mother's admonitions about demon rum kept her planted on the boardwalk.

After a long while, Watts emerged. "Here." Leaning forward, he dropped a dry biscuit into each of their hands. As he straightened, Maelle glimpsed a slim tin canister in his shirt pocket. Her thank-you died on her lips with the sight of that little flask. "Now, let's go."

Once more, Watts climbed onto the wagon's seat, and Maelle and Mattie chased the wagon down the street to a dry goods store. Without speaking, Watts gestured for them to precede him into the store.

Something good greeted Maelle's nose as she stepped into the store—a malty, yeasty, tangy smell that made saliva pool in her mouth. Maelle sniffed deeply, as did Mattie. A grin of delight split her brother's face when he spotted rows of candy jars. He dashed forward and, resting his fingertips on the wooden counter edge, raised up on tiptoe for a closer look at the jeweled gumdrops, striped peppermint sticks, and long ropes of licorice.

Watts stomped over and gave Mattie a cuff on the back of the head that sent his hat askew. "Get away from there."

Maelle clamped her jaw against the protest that formed on her tongue. How dare that man hit Mattie? Holding his head, Mattie stayed close to Maelle as they followed Watts to the shelves of trousers and shirts.

Maelle wondered what Watts would say if she suddenly blurted out she was a girl and not a boy. He'd put her back on the train and disappear with Mattie, she was sure. She tightened her grip on Mattie's hand and kept silent.

Watts held items against Maelle's front and eventually built a short pile of two pairs of britches—one brown, one tan—and three shirts in different plaids. He plopped the stack into Maelle's arms. "Come over here." He led the children to a shelf that held folded pairs of long johns, and he added two pairs to her arms after shaking them out for inspection.

"Well, that's that, then." He turned toward the counter.

Maelle sent a startled glance at his retreating back. Trotting up beside him, she said, "Aren't ya gettin' somethin' for me brother?"

Watts barely glanced at her. "He can wear hand-me-downs." Grabbing the clothes from her arms, he thumped them onto the counter and told the merchant, "Figure my tab."

The dry goods door opened and a family entered. The wife and two little girls remained close to the door, but the man removed his battered straw hat and came to the counter. "Excuse me, sir," the man said, his gaze on the merchant. "The missus and I came into town to meet up with that train carrying orphans. We went to the church, like the printed flier said, but nobody's there."

Maelle's heart rose into her throat. She looked at the woman beside the door. Plain-faced and simply dressed, she cupped the shoulders of the two little girls who leaned against her skirts. Her hands, although work worn, seemed gentle in the way they stroked the children's shoulders. She was a good ma—Maelle could sense it.

She jerked her attention to the man. His clothes, too, were those of a working man, more like what Da had worn. Oh, why hadn't this couple been at the church earlier? Maybe she and Mattie would have been taken by them!

"Far as I know, mister," the merchant said, "all them orphans have been claimed. Train pulled out just a bit ago, and that city lady who brung 'em was on it."

The man turned to his wife. "We're too late, Martha."

Tears winked in the woman's eyes, her chin quivering. "How we was hopin' . . ."

Moving to his wife, the man patted her shoulder. "Now, don't fret. There'll be other trains. We'll leave earlier next time. We'll get us a boy, don't worry."

Watts frowned at the couple. "You there. You said you were wanting a boy?"

The man faced Watts. "That's right, mister. We drove all the way from Shallow Creek, thinkin' we'd choose us a new son. Our own Titus died of the fever last winter. Me an' the missus have missed havin' a boy around the place."

Watts caught Mattie's collar and hauled him forward. "This boy came off the train. He needs a home."

Maelle leaped to Watts's side, the betrayal stinging like a slap. "He ain't needin' a home! He's got one—with you!"

Watts clamped a hand around the back of Maelle's neck and squeezed, silencing her. "I took both of these 'cause they were all that was left, but I really only want the one. You can take the smaller boy, if you want. I was gonna leave him in the orphanage in Springfield, but it'd probably be better if he went with a family."

Maelle watched in mute horror as the man went down on one knee before Mattie.

"What's your name, boy?"

Mattie's Adam's apple bobbed in his skinny neck. "Matthew Gallagher, sir." The words came out in a hoarse, quavering whisper.

"Matthew. Good strong Christian name."

The wife leaned forward, her hand stretching out to touch Mattie's cheek. Mattie shrank away, and the woman's fingers trembled. "Got brown eyes, just like our Titus."

Without another word, the man scooped Mattie into his arms. Mattie let out a squawk of protest and began to kick, reaching for Maelle. The man didn't even seem to notice Mattie's actions.

He headed for the door, his wife and the little girls scuttling ahead of him.

Maelle wrenched free of Watts's grasp and charged after them. "Come back here! You canna be takin' him! You canna be takin' me brother!"

The man swung Mattie into the back of a weather-worn wagon. Mattie made as if to scramble out again, but the man said in a low tone, "Stay put." He turned and caught Maelle's shoulders, crouching to her level. "Don't make this harder'n it needs to be."

Warm tears splashed down her cheeks. "But . . . but . . . please take me, too!"

The man gave her a shake. "Can't afford to feed you. We can only take one. I'm sorry. I can see you're a fine boy. But we'll take good care o' this'n."

The woman crowded close, her linked fingers beneath her chin. "Please don't carry on. I need that little boy. Got a ache in my heart that can't be filled no other way."

Maelle knocked the man's hands away from her shoulders and swiped the tears from her cheeks. "You'll be lovin' me brother?" The words were more demand than question.

The woman nodded. "Like he was my own."

Miserably, Maelle turned to the man who still hunkered before her. "Can I at least be sayin' a proper good-bye?"

Catching her beneath the arms, he lifted her into the wagon bed. Mattie sobbed as she pulled him snug against her chest. His hat fell off, and Maelle stroked his rumpled curls and murmured soothing sounds.

Eventually she pulled back and took Mattie's face in her hands. "Ya got the photograph, Mattie, don't ya?" She waited for his nod. "You'll always be rememberin' Ma an' Da an' baby Molly an' me. An' someday I'll be findin' ya. We'll be together."

Tears coursed down Mattie's pale cheeks. "Ya promise me?"

Maelle hugged him again. "I promise ya." She choked on her words. "No matter how long it takes or how big ya get."

His face pressed to her neck, Mattie asked, "If I get big, how will ya be knowin' me?"

Maelle pulled loose and forced a smile. "By the photograph. Just as I'll be knowin' Molly by the Bible. An' you'll be knowin' it's me when I show ya Ma's letters tied up in the pink ribbon."

Mattie nodded.

"Be good for these people," Maelle instructed, using her best big sister voice. "Don't be shamin' our da, ya hear?"

"I'll be good," Mattie promised.

Just as she had Molly, Maelle kissed her brother's cheeks and forehead. She whispered, "I'll always be lovin' ya, Mattie Gallagher."

The man stepped to the edge of the wagon. "Come on now." He lifted Maelle from the back. "Scoot on into the store." Although his words were gruff, she saw kindness in his lined eyes. She moved to the boardwalk but didn't step up on the wood walkway.

The man pulled himself onto the seat and then looked at Mattie, who stood in the bed of the wagon opposite to where the little girls huddled together. "Matthew? You want to help yer pa drive the team?"

Mattie's eyebrows shot up. He touched his own chest with a questioning finger.

The man smiled. "Yes, I mean you. C'mon up here, boy."

Mattie scrambled to the front of the wagon, and the man settled him between his knees. He placed the reins in Mattie's hands, curling his own large hands around Mattie's much smaller ones. The man guided Mattie's hands into flicking the reins. "Giddap!" The horses lurched forward.

The wagon rolled down the street. Mattie's face appeared briefly as he leaned out and craned his neck to look backward. But then the man shifted his shoulders, shielding Mattie from view.

The intense pain in Maelle's heart made her legs feel weak. She longed to chase after the wagon, to cry, to scream, to storm at the unfairness of having Molly and Mattie taken away. But a part of her recognized no amount of protest would change a thing. They were gone. Her sister and brother were gone, and she—

"Mike?" Watts called from the doorway of the dry goods. "I bought these britches extra big so they'd last longer. You'll need suspenders to hold 'em up. Come choose a pair."

Maelle cared nothing about suspenders. Where was the family taking Mattie? She squeezed her eyes closed, and then she remembered: Shallow Creek. She added the name to her memory bank. Standler. Shallow Creek. Then, opening her eyes, she took a step farther into the street for a last glimpse of the wagon.

A hand clamped around the back of her neck, yanking her onto the boardwalk. She yelped, swinging her arms. Watts let go with a shove that sent her sideways. Maelle regained her footing and glowered at the man.

Hands on his hips, he growled, "Mike, I'm a mild-mannered man, but when I tell you to do something, I expect you to obey. I got hundreds of dollars worth of photography equipment you'll be learning to use. One misstep because you didn't follow directions, and something gets ruined? I'll cut me a switch and leave tracks on your legs that'll be there 'til next Christmas. Do you understand me?"

Maelle clenched her jaw so hard her teeth hurt. She sucked air through her nose to keep from crying. Reaching back to rub her neck where his fingers had dug in, she gave a single nod of her head in reply.

"Good. And one more thing . . ." He bent forward, bringing his face level with hers. "I'm sorry I couldn't keep your brother."

She searched his eyes. Was he being honest with her?

"I don't have room for him in the wagon, and I don't have need for more than one apprentice. Besides, he's with a family. Isn't that what you'd want for him?"

Maelle considered his words. A family was best for Mattie—a ma and a da, and even sisters. Her heart skipped a beat. Mattie would have sisters. Would those new sisters replace her and Molly?

He straightened. "Well, you're a quiet one, now. Seem to have lost that fire you had in the church." Arching one brow, he mused, "I figure it'll come back, though. When the hurtin's done in your heart."

Maelle swallowed. He'd sounded . . . kind.

Then he grabbed her shoulder and turned her toward the dry goods door. "Get in there and pick out some suspenders. In time, you'll be so busy you'll forget you had a brother."

Maelle did as she was told, but she made a promise to herself. She'd never forget she had a brother in Shallow Creek. Or a sister with a family named Standler. And someday she'd find them. Like she'd told Mattie, she'd know them by their ties to home.

PART TWO

CHAPTER FIVE

Maelle
Dunbar, Louisiana
December, 1902

Y ou there, boy!"

Maelle "Mike" Watts retained her casual pose—elbow propped on top of the camera case, right leg bent with the toe of her boot pressed into the dirt—and waited for the boy she'd called to pause in his scurrying journey toward the weighing shed. His dirty bare feet stirred dust as he stumbled to a stop. He turned, the full buckets in his hands swaying with his movements. Squinting, he sent her a puzzled look. He couldn't be more than eight years old.

"You talkin' to me?"

Maelle nodded in reply.

"Gotta get these weighed." An air of importance underscored his statement. The child attempted to heft the buckets, but his scrawny elbows splayed outward with no discernible lift to the galvanized steel.

"Want to stand there long enough to get your picture taken?" Maelle had learned over the years that children, regardless of their station in life, couldn't refuse the opportunity to pose in front of her camera.

The boy licked his lips, his wary eyes darting toward the line of shucking sheds where a flurry of voices and clanking of buckets could be heard. "Will it take long?"

Maelle quickly stepped behind the camera and wrapped her hand around the bulb. "As long as it takes to make a smile."

Immediately the boy curved his lips into more of a grimace than a smile. Maelle pressed the bulb, and the child jumped at the *pop*, but he held his pose until she said, "That's it! Thanks."

He scuffled forward a few steps, his expression curious. "Do I get to see it?"

Maelle grinned over the top of the wood case. "It'll take me a day to process it. Will you be here tomorrow?"

The boy nodded, his grimy hair bobbing. "Always work here. Ever' day."

The blithe statement made Maelle's heart ache. The child obviously had no idea tomorrow was Christmas. "I'll bring your photograph by tomorrow, then."

"Thanks!" He turned to hurry off.

"What's your name?" Maelle called to his retreating back.

He didn't even pause. "Georgie!"

"See you tomorrow, Georgie."

A bob of his shaggy head gave acknowledgment, and Maelle packed up her camera. She wanted to stick around the oyster shucking dock and take a few more pictures, but she'd learned over the years brief stops were best. She'd created many a photograph at mills and docks and factories, and she always feared the little workers would suffer the bosses' wrath if she overstayed her welcome. So despite her desire to capture a few more barefooted, dirty children wielding knives too large for their hands or carrying buckets too heavy for their skinny shoulders, she carefully loaded her camera into the back of the wagon and headed toward town. She'd return tomorrow and give Georgie his photograph.

᪥

Maelle stopped at the first hotel she encountered—a rather rundown two-story building facing the town. If it weren't for Georgie's photograph, she'd keep driving until she reached one of the larger cities and something more . . . welcoming. The only night she offered herself the luxury of a hotel was Christmas Eve, keeping with the tradition established by Richard, and she hated to waste her night of extravagance in a place like this one. But getting that photograph to Georgie—undoubtedly his only Christmas gift—would make it worthwhile.

She tethered Samson and gave the horse a loving neck rub before picking up her carpetbag and camera box and entering the hotel. To her relief, the interior was cheerier than the outside, the floral wall coverings, thick carpets, and velvet-upholstered furniture providing a touch of elegance. Perhaps the humid weather had aged the wooden structure, she surmised. Behind a tall, paneled desk, a man in a black suit smiled and said, "Welcome to Hartling Hotel, sir."

"Thank you." Maelle dropped the carpetbag but bent over to place the camera box with care on the floor beside the bag. Her long braid swung over her shoulder as she leaned forward, and she observed the clerk's face flood with red. "I'd like a room with a private bath, if possible."

"Of . . . of course, m-miss."

The stuttering had no effect on Maelle. She'd grown accustomed to people's reaction to her masculine mode of dress. She signed the guestbook—*Mike Watts*—tucked the key into the pocket of her shirt, and picked up her belongings. Before turning away from the desk, however, she asked the question she always asked: "Do you know of any Gallaghers in town? Mattie or Molly?"

The clerk frowned, tapping his chin with a narrow finger. "Gallagher . . . I don't believe so." His brows quirked. "Kin o' yours?"

"Yes." She didn't elaborate. "Thank you." She strode away from the desk. A porter met her at the bottom of the stairs and offered to take her bags, but she shook her head. She was capable of carrying her own items, and she wouldn't relinquish her camera to anyone.

Jerking her chin toward the front doors, she said, "If you'd have someone see to my horse—out front, the wagon has Watts Photography painted on its side—I'd be obliged." The porter bustled off.

In Room 106, she placed the camera box in the corner farthest from the window, then moved toward the bed. Her boots clumped against the wood floor, creating a hollow thud. A louder thud sounded when she dropped the carpetbag. Seated on the edge of the creaky mattress, she tugged off the boots but left her thick wool socks in place. Opening the battered carpetbag, she rummaged for her nightshirt. She thought she detected a slight essence of bay rum caught in the fabric of the bag, bringing with it the bittersweet memory of her surrogate uncle.

Maelle's eyes drifted shut. He'd been gone almost nine years now, and she still missed him. In many ways, he'd been less than ideal. His penchant for visiting saloons, his gruff tone when speaking, and his expectation for perfection were sometimes difficult to abide. But she'd grown to love him.

An unwilling chuckle built in her chest as she remembered her third Christmas with him. As had become their custom, he'd rented a hotel room for Christmas Eve night.

The hotel was a fancy one, with a view of the Gulf of Mexico and a private bathing room right off the bedroom. Uncle Richard had told her to bathe before bed. She'd eagerly filled the elongated tin tub with steaming water straight from a brass spigot and climbed in.

The once-a-year comfort of hot water up to her armpits had lulled her to sleep, but she'd startled awake when Richard pounded on the door and then stepped in. Shocked by the unexpected intrusion, she'd leapt to her feet, slipped on the slick bottom, and then fell backward with a splash that displaced half the water in the tub. Richard had discovered her secret.

She could still see his look of open-mouthed surprise and hear his hoarse yelp, "Mike? You—you're a *girl*?" The word *girl* had exploded like a curse word, and she'd hunkered in the tub, quivering with fear. He'd spun, presenting his back. His neck glowed bright red, the way it did when he was very, very angry. She'd stared at the thin band of exposed crimson skin between his shirt collar and thick hair. Her tightly held breath made her chest ache. It seemed hours passed before he finally stomped toward the doorway.

Her stiff fingers clutched the rolled tin lip of the tub. "W-what're you goin' to do?" she asked.

He came to a halt, his face aimed away from her. Her heart pounded as she waited to hear him say he was throwing her out or taking her to an orphanage.

"Gettin' a second room for you for tonight. And tomorrow I'll put up some kind of privacy barrier in the wagon. Clean up the water on the floor before it leaks to the room below." The slam of the bathroom door ended their conversation.

And Maelle had melted into the remaining tepid water with a sigh of relief. Despite the harsh tone, his message had let her know he was keeping her, girl or not. She knew why—he'd spent three years training her, trusting her, molding her to take over the photography business. Even at the tender age of twelve, she'd known it wasn't affection that made him keep her, but a need for her services as apprentice and assistant.

It wasn't until five years later that she discovered he'd grown to love her. His death had proved it.

A series of hard knocks on the hotel room door jerked her from her reverie. She jumped up and crossed the floor with a wide stride. Swinging the door open, she discovered the hotel clerk in the hallway.

"Sorry to bother you . . . miss." His gaze drifted briefly down the length of her wool trousers, then bounced up again, his cheeks stained pink. "If you're interested, the First Baptist Church is having a Christmas Eve service. It's for the whole community. There'll be singing, and the preacher'll speak, and then we'll have cookies and hot apple cider. It's always a real good service."

Maelle's heart twisted with desire. Uncle Richard had spent Sundays sleeping off his Saturday evening binge, which had left her to her own devices. So she'd visited churches, searching faces, always hoping for a glimpse of Mattie or Molly. And in a little church in Spring Arbor, Michigan, Maelle had met someone who would never be taken away from her. Since then, her reason for church attendance had become two-fold. She still sought her brother and sister, but she also sought to grow in her knowledge of Jesus.

"Where is the church?" she asked.

"Seventh Street." The man gestured. "You go west on Cyprus Street, then turn north on Seventh. You can't miss it. Church has a real nice steeple and cross, and there will be candles burning in the windows." He paused, his attention once more jerking from her britches to her eyes. "We all . . . uh . . . put on our Sunday best for this particular service." His glowing face rivaled the bulb dangling from a twisted cord overhead.

Maelle's lips quirked. "Thanks for your kind invitation, but I've got a photograph to develop. Good night." She closed the door on his repentant expression and headed directly for the private bath to enjoy a leisurely soak.

Later, listening to the crunch of wagon wheels rolling past the hotel, Maelle regretted her hasty decision. She sighed, rubbing a soft cloth over the finished image of Georgie standing proudly on shell-scattered ground with buckets dangling from his dirty hands. Loneliness smacked hard. Maybe she should get dressed and go to church, after all. But then, remembering the clerk's comment about "Sunday best," she shook her head, causing her still-damp tumbling curls to spill across her shoulders.

She set the photograph aside, gathered the errant waves of her waist-length hair, and deftly formed a loose braid. As she braided, her gaze drifted to the carpetbag and she envisioned the contents. For a woman, "Sunday best" meant a dress. There were no dresses in her bag. There was one dress in the wagon—wrapped in tissue and resting in the bottom of a wooden box beneath her bunk—but she'd never put it on. Not again.

❧

Maelle awakened Christmas morning with a dream hovering on the fringes of her mind. A familiar dream, one in which she, Mattie, and Molly played together in the New York flat while Da watched from his chair, his chuckle rumbling in response to their antics, and Ma stirred a pot on the little stove in the corner. She smiled, allowing the images to linger for as long as they would remain, until finally—like smoke drifting from Da's corncob pipe—they faded away into nothingness.

Ignoring the lonely wrench of her heart, she threw back the light covers and stood, stretching. A glance out the window told her it was still early, the sun a rosy glow on the horizon, but she surmised little Georgie and his fellow shuckers were already at work. She would pack everything and head out from Dunbar after she delivered the photograph. "Maybe I'll head north—toward Missouri," she told her image in the mirror as she splashed her face with cold water to wash the sleep away.

Every year since his death, she had continued Richard's yearly travel course that led across the United States, visiting states during times when the climate was mild and conducive to life in a box wagon. Missouri had never been a winter destination, so why even consider it?

With a sigh, Maelle spoke the reason out loud. "Because Missouri calls to me."

It didn't matter how many years had passed. It didn't matter that Richard told her she was mooning for something that could never be. It didn't matter how many times she'd spotted a head of auburn hair and felt a leap of hope only to have it crushed with the realization that she'd made a mistake. The last time she'd seen Mattie and Molly had been in Missouri. And revisiting the state offered a sense of homecoming that nothing else could.

It had occurred to her after Richard's death that she could travel to Missouri any time she wanted. But Richard had lectured her severely on the importance of keeping the camera from excessive heat or cold. Maintaining a working camera held great importance. Not only was it her livelihood, it was her inheritance from Richard. No matter how hard the tug of Missouri, she would protect her equipment.

Grabbing her shirt, which she had draped over the back of a chair, she announced, "Missouri will still be there in the spring, and with people out on the streets instead of holed up in houses, I'm more likely to spot Mattie or Molly in a crowd."

Just speaking the names of her younger siblings brought a stab of pain, but she pushed it aside as she'd learned to do. A familiar prayer formed in her heart. *Lord, be with me brother and sister. Be bringin' them back to me again.*

Dressed in her usual trousers and flannel shirt, topped by a light tan jacket, Maelle gathered up her belongings and headed for the stairs. Less than half an hour later she had her horse hitched to the wagon and held the reins, ready to guide Samson toward the oyster shucking company. Once more the desire to head to Missouri pressed at her, and her fingers twitched on the reins.

"I could wrap the camera in quilts," she muttered to herself, "and keep it protected from the cold that way . . ." But then another of Richard's admonitions played through her head: *"Folks're less likely to want a picture made when they're uncomfortable. And who's comfortable when it's too hot or too cold?"*

With a snort, Maelle acknowledged the absurdity of heading to Missouri in the middle of winter. She'd wait until spring, just as Richard had always done. She flicked the reins. "C'mon, big boy," she called to Samson's broad back. "Let's get this photo delivered, and then you and me will be headin' toward Texas. Richard always said it was a good place to make a few dollars. But come spring, I'll expect you to remember the roadway to Missouri. . . ."

CHAPTER SIX

Mattie
Spofford, Texas
January, 1903

N ow, Matthew, you take care of yourself."

Matt took Mrs. Smallwood's wrinkled hand and gave it a gentle squeeze. "You, too, ma'am. You'll be all right here in town?"

She offered a wavering smile. "Well, it's a might snug compared to the ranch, but I couldn't stay out there without my Hud. Just doesn't feel right without him."

Matt agreed. Hudson Smallwood was the finest man he'd ever worked for, and there'd been plenty of bosses in his short life.

"I'm just sorry the new owner brought in his own men, Matthew. Hud would turn over in his grave if he knew you'd been cut loose like that."

"Aww, think of it this way . . ." Matt searched for a way to ease the old woman's mind. "It's a new year, a new beginnin' somewhere." Her dubious look told him she wasn't assured. He gave her hand one more squeeze before stepping back and slapping his hat on his head. "Don't worry about me, ma'am. I'm like a cat. I always land on my feet."

Her husky chortle made him smile. "I will miss you, son."

Son . . . That simple word propelled Matt forward three feet. He wrapped his long arms around Mrs. Smallwood in an impulsive hug that she returned with a strength that belied her advanced age and diminutive size. When he pulled back, he glimpsed tears in her eyes and knew he'd better get moving. Quick good-byes were always best.

But before he could turn away, she caught his coat sleeve. "Matthew, you keep walkin' with your Savior, you hear? You might be leavin' Spofford, but you aren't leavin' your faith."

"Yes, ma'am, I know." Of all the things he'd learned from Mr. Smallwood, leaning on Jesus was the best. He'd never lose sight of that. "I got the Bible you an' Mr. Smallwood gave me, an' I'll read some on it every day, just like I promised him."

Mrs. Smallwood smiled her approval. "You're a fine man, Matthew. I pray you'll find a special girl and settle down somewhere. You need a family."

Matt's heart lurched. If Mrs. Smallwood only knew how much he longed to find the two special girls who could give him all the family he needed.

With a final wave of his gloved hand, Matt spun on his heel and thundered down the street. It hurt to leave kind Mrs. Smallwood. Hurt to pull up stakes. Again. He set his jaw against the sting behind his nose. By now he ought to be used to moving on—after all, he'd been shuffled from pillar to post since he was no taller than a hitching rail. "Well, Lord," he mumbled as he stepped onto the boardwalk fronting the city's business district,

"I'm just gonna have to trust that you got a place waitin' for me. Sure would appreciate it if this time it could last long enough for Maelle to find me. She said she'd be lookin', but I don't make it easy for her, movin' from hither to yon like I do."

He reached the post office and stepped inside the small, dry building. Doffing his hat, he held the door for two women and then strode to the large board at the back corner where job opportunities were listed. He examined each in turn, scowling as he dismissed the ones seeking a cook, a wet nurse, a barkeeper. His finger paused at the advertisement for a stable boy, and he gave the sheet several thoughtful taps before releasing a sigh and lifting the bottom edge of the final listing, which was stuck by itself in the lower right hand corner of the board.

He straightened his shoulders, jerking the paper free of its tack and reading eagerly. *Ranch hand needed for thriving ranch in Ralls County. Wages commensurate with experience, starting at 35 dollars/month. Every third weekend off. Only reliable applicants need reply. Contact Mr. Gerald Harders of Rocky Crest Ranch, Shay's Ford, Missouri.*

Missouri! His pulse quickened. He'd left Missouri almost ten years ago, and he'd vowed never to go back. Too many bad memories were associated with Missouri. Losing Molly and Maelle, losing the Bonhams, working for Jenks . . . Sweat broke out across his forehead. What if he returned to Missouri and Jenks found him? But there were no other positions listed for ranch work, and what else did he know?

His hands began to tremble. Then he noticed the date at the bottom, scrawled by the postmaster to indicate when the listing was posted. He whispered, "October second, 1902."

Matt nearly sagged with relief. The decision was taken from him. Surely by now the position had been filled. The postmaster had probably just forgotten to take it down. He wadded the paper into a ball and turned to toss it into the brass spittoon beside the door.

"Hey!" a voice barked. "What do you think you're doing, destroying government property?"

Matt's hand froze midthrow. He looked over his shoulder at the angry postmaster. Turning slowly, he glanced at the ball of crumpled paper. "It's just an outdated posting."

The man's scowl deepened. "Give me that." He snatched it from Matt's hand and flattened it on the wood counter that separated his office from the main floor of the post office. His brows knit together as he ran his fingers over the wrinkled paper. "This is not outdated. If a position gets filled, I put the word 'filled' and the date right under the date of posting. Then I file it." He glared at Matt. "I'll thank you not to tinker with my system."

Matt blinked rapidly, snatching his hat from his head. "I apologize, mister. I just figured with that date of October—"

"Well, don't figure, just ask." The man pounded his finger against the paper three times. "As far as I know, this position's open, and it'll stay on that board until I hear otherwise." He charged through a narrow doorway to the right of the counter, muttering under his breath.

Matt watched the man yank a tack free and impale the paper. With the stab of the tack into wood, Matt felt as though something stabbed through his heart. He needed a job. A ranching job. And right now, the only job he knew about waited in Missouri. He took a great breath and said, "Take it back down, mister."

The man spun, giving Matt a fierce glare. "Didn't you hear anything I said? I told you—"

"I know." Matt twisted his hat in his hands. "But I . . . I'm wantin' to fill the position."

"Oh." The man lost his crusty tone. "That's different, then. Come over here." He returned to the office area behind the counter and slapped the paper onto a desk in the back corner. Seating himself, he called, "That'll be ten cents to send a telegram to this"—he looked at the paper—"Mr. Harders. Might take a day or two to get a response if he lives out away from town."

Matt withdrew a dime from his pocket and placed it on the counter. He had nowhere to go or anyone waiting for him. "I got a day or two to spare." *Maybe another job will turn up in the meantime.*

The postmaster picked up a pencil, licked its point, and aimed it at a pad of paper. "What do you want me to tell Mr. Harders?"

Matt sucked in a deep breath. "Keep it simple. The name's Matthew Tucker, I'm reliable, and I'm . . . available."

A few clicks on the telegraph machine sent Matt's message winging across the country from Texas to Missouri. After the postmaster instructed him to check back the next day, he headed toward the livery where he'd boarded his roan, Russ, after Mr. Smallwood's funeral last week. He could bed down with the beast until he received word on a job—whether it was the one in Missouri or someplace else. It didn't bother him to sleep in a stable. Truth was, he'd slept in worse places.

The worst of all was in Missouri.

Russ greeted his master with a snort and nuzzled Matt's shoulder with his moist nose. Matt wrapped his arms around the beast's massive neck and pressed his face to the warm tawny hide. Eyes closed, he silently pleaded, *Lord, I'm so tired of this movin' around. I need a home—one that'll last longer'n a year or two. I might've sent that telegram, but . . . Missouri, Lord?* He swallowed, his hand convulsing on Russ's neck.

A snippet from his Bible reading sifted through his mind. He repeated the words aloud. " 'Thou has beset me behind and before, and laid thine hand upon me.' " Lifting his gaze to the rafters overhead, he said, "Does that mean you'll go ahead of me, preparing the way . . . even back to Missouri?"

CHAPTER SEVEN

Molly
Kansas City, Kansas
January, 1903

Isabelle Standler rested her head on the brocade back of the parlor settee and stared at the plaster ceiling. The crystal teardrops dangling from the chandelier sent out dozens of dancing rainbows. Her attention flitted from one splash of color to another, a feeble attempt to cheer herself as she had ever since she was twelve and Papa had installed the ostentatious light fixture.

With the thought of Papa came a rush of sorrow so intense tears spurted into her eyes, making the miniature rainbows swim. Closing her eyes, she brought up her hand to cover her mouth and stifled a pained moan. Oh, how she missed Papa and Mama!

"Isabelle?"

Randolph's query straightened her in the seat. "I'm in here," she called in a weary voice, watching as her older brother strode through the wide doorway and crossed the carpeted floor to stand in front of her. He had not yet removed his mourning armband for the evening, and the black crepe band seemed to shout the reminder of what she'd lost. She forced herself to look into her brother's face, and a chill went down her spine. Randolph's expression was stern, as always, but today it seemed particularly grim.

"There you are." His tone indicated he believed she'd deliberately hidden from him. "We need to talk."

"All right." She linked her hands in her lap. "What is it?"

Randolph perched on a wing-back chair near the settee, his dark brows pulled into a frown. "As you know, Father made me executor of his will."

Pain stabbed. Isabelle swallowed, staring at her hands. How pale her skin appeared against the black of her full skirt. She knew they needed to discuss Papa's will, but she wished it could be delayed. The longer they waited, the more she could pretend it was all a dream—that Mama and Papa were simply away for their annual New Year's celebration and would be coming home with smiles and hugs and presents, as they had every year for as far back as Isabelle could remember.

"I know," she contributed in a strained voice, raising her face to meet his gaze again. "Papa believed it was your responsibility as firstborn, and I trust his judgment."

Randolph's scowl deepened. "I'm more than the firstborn."

Isabelle pinched her brow at his harsh tone, but she offered a nod of agreement. "You're also the only son. Of course, I—"

"I *mean*," he interrupted, his eyes narrowing to mere slits of snapping black, "that I'm the firstborn and the only true heir to the Standler fortune."

Isabelle bit her lower lip. Although she'd longed for a close relationship with her brother her entire life, she had come to accept he wished to remain distant. His resentment of her was as familiar as Mama's tender care and Papa's gentle guidance, but she wished he could set it aside. "Randolph, I don't understand why—"

Without warning he thrust something at her. A book. A small leather-bound volume, with a worn cover and curled pages. "This should help you understand. Open it."

Isabelle's heart jumped into her throat. "W-what is it?"

"I said open it." Her brother's icy glare demanded obedience.

With trembling fingers, Isabelle turned the first page, bringing into view a record of births and deaths. Randolph leaned forward, pointing to the third name in a list. "This, *my dear little sister*"—the disdain in his tone made her scalp prickle—"is your true heritage. Molly Gallagher, born of Irish descent in County Meath, Ireland. You aren't a Standler. And you'll be receiving no inheritance."

Isabelle shook her head, a new sorrow striking. How could Randolph's resentment carry him to the extreme of purchasing a used Bible and trying to convince her she had been born to some other family? She closed the book and held it out to him. "It won't work, Randolph." When he made no move to take it from her, she went on in a soft, pleading tone. "I'm sorry I've never pleased you—heaven knows I've tried—but this is cruel. Please . . . can't we set aside our past differences? We're all the family we have left."

"I have no family left." Randolph grated out his harsh words through clenched teeth. Rising, he paced to the fireplace, where he stood, his back to her, seeming to examine the portrait that hung in prominence over the mantel. Suddenly he snatched the portrait from the wall and threw it into the fire. The glass shattered as the frame struck the brick of the inner hearth, exposing the picture to the fire's licking tongues.

"Randolph, no!" Isabelle tossed the Bible aside and raced to the fireplace, reaching to retrieve the picture taken only three years ago of her with her parents and brother. Before she could grasp the frame, Randolph caught her arms and flung her backward. She fell into a table, knocking a lamp to the floor. It crashed into slivers of rose-colored glass.

"See what you've done!" Randolph stood over her, his angry face only inches from hers. "You ruin everything, Isabelle; you always have! You took Mother's love, Father's attention. . . . You won't take my inheritance!" Grabbing her by the arms, he shook her violently. "No longer will I continue the pretense of you carrying the Standler name! I want you out, Isabelle! Today, do you hear me? Out!"

He released her with another shove. She stumbled but didn't fall, clutching her arm where his fingers had bruised her flesh. Tears coursed down her face. "But . . . but this is my home. Where will I go?"

Randolph spun around and stared into the fire as the last bit of the photograph was consumed by greedy flames. "That isn't my concern." The cold tone chilled Isabelle thoroughly. "I just want you gone." Glancing briefly over his shoulder, his gaze dropped to the settee where the Bible lay, open, its curled pages seeming to invite examination. "And take that book with you. I need no reminder of you in my house."

Isabelle stared at his back for several moments, unable to believe he truly meant what he said. When he remained as if planted in front of the fireplace, she moved carefully past the shattered lamp—the sharp shards an ignominious picture of her shattered heart—and lifted the Bible. Clutching it to her breast, she walked out of the room, her steps measured, with the grace and dignity her mother had taught her.

By the time she reached her bedroom, hurt had grown to anger. How dare Randolph treat her in such a reprehensible manner? Papa would be appalled—he would never allow her to be cast from her home. She would see that Randolph was taken to task and forced to apologize. She knew just who would accomplish it, too.

Picking up the little brass bell that sat on her bedside table, she rang it furiously. In moments, her personal maid appeared in the doorway.

"Yes, miss?"

By the girl's bright red cheeks, Isabelle knew she'd heard every bit of Randolph's tirade. She swallowed her humiliation and assumed a tart tone. "Pack me a bag, Myrtle. I'll need clothing for a stay of perhaps a week. Be sure to include all of the personal effects from my dressing table, as well as this Bible." She held out the Bible, and Myrtle took it with both hands. "Then have Toby bring the carriage around."

Suddenly Randolph stepped into the doorway. "Myrtle, do not instruct Toby to bring the carriage. She can hire a cab. Here." He threw a handful of bills and coins onto the carpeted floor of the bedroom. One coin rolled past Isabelle's feet and disappeared under the bed. He swung around and disappeared down the hall.

Myrtle looked uncertainly at the money flung across the floor. "Do . . . do you want me pick this up an' put it with your belongings, miss?"

Isabelle shook her head, her curls bouncing against her tear-stained cheeks. "No. I want nothing from him. Just pack my bag as I've asked. I'll be back after I've arranged transport." With her chin held high, she swept from the room.

She paused for a moment in the hallway, looking at the closed door of her parents' bedroom. Randolph would never have dared to behave so high-handedly if Papa were alive. The pain of her loss struck again, bringing a new rush of tears. But she swished them away with trembling fingers and vowed in a whisper, "You'll pay for this, Randolph. How dearly you will pay. . . ."

❧

Isabelle swung herself from the cramped area beside the hansom cab driver, then reached to retrieve the bag she'd wedged in at her feet. Shivering from the cold wind that lifted her cape and sent little particles of snow down the back of her dress, she dropped a few coins into the man's outstretched hand. He gave no nod of acknowledgment, merely slapped the reins down on the horse's back, forcing her to leap backward against the curb.

Her heel caught in the hem of her dress, and she heard the fabric rip. Sucking in her breath in aggravation, she resisted the urge to check the damage. It was cold and dark—she needed to get inside as quickly as possible. Lifting her skirt with one hand and holding the leather handles of her bag with the other, she made her difficult progress along the dim, shadowy sidewalk that led to the Heatons' stately home.

Facing the eight concrete steps that led to the receiving porch, she chose to leave the bag behind. One of the Heatons' servants could retrieve it after she'd been allowed entry. She climbed the slippery steps and twisted the brass key that sounded the bell. In moments the door swung wide and the Heatons' butler invited her in.

Her spine straight and chin angled high, she said, "I need to speak with—"

"Isabelle!"

Glenn Heaton approached in long, eager strides. Isabelle almost began to cry when she saw his sweet smile of welcome. Her proud posture dissolved. She needn't maintain the façade of strength now that Glenn was here. She stretched her hands toward him, relishing the secure feel of his long, cool fingers wrapped around hers.

"Mother will be so disappointed. She's already retired for the evening. What brings you out on such a frosty night?" Then his brows thrust downward, and his blue eyes narrowed in concern. "My dear, something is wrong." With an arm around her waist, he guided her to the parlor and assisted her to a chair. He knelt and grasped her hand. "What is it, darling? Are you missing your parents terribly?"

She sniffed, blinking hard against more tears. "Yes, but it isn't that."

"What is it, then?"

Isabelle's chin quivered from the effort of containing both anger and grief. "It's Randolph. He—"

Glenn's father entered the parlor at that moment, crossing quickly to the pair. "I was told we had a guest, but I didn't expect to see you out at this hour unescorted, Isabelle. Your father—God rest his soul—would be distraught by your wandering the city alone at night. I trust you have good reason for this late visit."

"Father, my fiancée is the one who is distraught," Glenn said, his tone severe. "Something is wrong. Perhaps you should sit down and listen."

Mr. Heaton harrumphed but seated himself on the edge of the sofa without another word.

Glenn turned back to Isabelle, his expression attentive. "Now, there. Tell me. What has happened to Randolph?"

"Nothing has happened *to* Randolph, but . . ." Isabelle explained as best she could the odd discussion that had taken place between herself and her brother. Glenn's face changed from concerned to puzzled to indignant as she finished. "The Bible he gave me is outside in my bag, at the base of the porch stairs with the few belongings he allowed me to bring from my home. I . . . I don't know what to do, Glenn." Her voice broke on a sob.

"You did the right thing, coming to me, Isabelle." The sweet brush of his knuckles on her cheek was as intimate as a kiss. "I'm sure Randolph is merely so distressed by your parents' untimely deaths he is not within his right mind. He'll come to himself in a few days and invite you back."

Isabelle blinked away her tears. "Are you certain?"

"Of course," Mr. Heaton inserted. "People do odd things in times of grief. In the meantime, we will put you in one of our guest rooms." He rose and called for a servant. The butler immediately appeared and received directions to retrieve Miss Isabelle's bag and carry it to the Yellow Room. Turning back to

Isabelle, Mr. Heaton said, "Now, no more worrying, my dear. Everything will seem brighter in the morning."

"Oh, I do hope so," Isabelle murmured as the man strode out of the parlor.

Glenn patted her hand. "See? You're all taken care of now."

Isabelle fell into his arms, nestling her head on his shoulder. "Oh, Glenn, I was so frightened. And angry! Randolph and I have never gotten along, but I never dreamed he would disown me." Still within the circle of his arms, she added, "Where could he have gotten that Bible? Why would he concoct such a story?"

"Now, Isabelle, you're upsetting yourself for no reason. Didn't we tell you things will be all right?"

Isabelle lifted her head, looking into Glenn's eyes. "But you didn't see or hear him, Glenn. He was so . . . *cold*."

"Miss Isabelle, your room is ready," the butler said from the parlor doorway.

Glenn rose, pulling Isabelle to her feet. "You go on upstairs, Isabelle. Sleep well." He kissed her forehead, his lips lingering against her skin. "No worries. I'll put everything to right."

She released a breathy sigh and thanked him.

After allowing Mrs. Heaton's personal maid to assist her into her bedclothes, Isabelle snuggled against a pile of pillows. Her scalp still tingled pleasantly from the brushing delivered by the maid. Her thick tresses, plaited into a shimmering red braid, fell across one shoulder.

She held a teacup beneath her chin and frowned at the well-worn Bible lying open in her lap. Warm and snug beneath the downy comforter, the honey-sweetened tea soothing her from the inside out, she tried to set aside the odd sense of discomfort the Bible's family record caused within her breast.

A wedding date for Angus Gallagher and Brigid McCue on the first page led to a list of children's names and birthdates on the second. She read the names written in a neat, slanting hand—Maelle Gallagher, Matthew Gallagher, Molly Gallagher. Isabelle's brow pinched as she stared at the final name in the birth register. The youngest Gallagher would be her same age—eighteen—and the child's birth date was only a few weeks from her own. It gave her a small, unexplained sense of connection with the name on the page.

The discomfort grew.

Closing the Bible with a snap, she set the book on the marble-topped table beside the bed. Staring at it, she blew out a dainty breath. What a lot of effort Randolph had gone to in order to convince her she wasn't his sister. He must have searched every used bookstore in Kansas City to find that Bible. What a cruel, heartless trick.

Cradling the teacup between her palms, she turned her attention to the amber liquid in the porcelain cup. Her heart ached. All her life she'd longed for a loving big brother, one like her schoolmates had, who would alternately protect and tease her. But instead, she'd had Randolph, who had tormented her, openly despised her, and broken the toys Papa brought home to her from his travels.

Why, she wondered again, had Randolph always been so spiteful? Her heart pounded. Was it because, as he'd said this evening, she wasn't truly his sister? Her hands began to shake, and she feared she would spill the remaining tea. She set the teacup on the little tray on the bedside table and pulled the covers to her chin.

Ridiculous. Of course she was his sister. Hadn't Mama and Papa always loved her? Hadn't they called her their darling, their precious lamb, their sweet gift? Hadn't they always said she looked just like her grandmother? Never, in all of her lifetime, had they given her reason to question her position in the family. She took a great breath, calming herself. Randolph's nonsensical ranting was nothing more than jealousy.

She'd come along later in Mama and Papa's life, and they had spoiled her. She acknowledged that truth without a hint of compunction. Their doting had simply caused Randolph to feel left out.

Propping herself on one elbow, she leaned toward the table and twisted the little key on the lamp, plunging the room into darkness. Rolling sideways, away from the table and the offending book, she closed her eyes. As Mr. Heaton had said, everything would look brighter in the morning. Randolph would receive his comeuppance.

She fell asleep with a smile on her face.

Chapter Eight

A light tap roused Isabelle. She stretched and yawned and opened her eyes. For a moment she lay there bewildered, and then she remembered her escape to Glenn's home last night. The tapping came again, and she offered a sleep-raspy invitation. "Come in."

Leaving the door open behind him, Glenn strode across the Persian rug and stopped a few inches from the edge of the carved walnut bed.

Isabelle peered at him from beneath a rumple of covers, offering a flirtatious upturning of lips. "Good morning. I expected the maid, not the master of the house."

Technically, Glenn was not the master of this house, but he would be one day. His father's wealth matched that of the Standlers'. It was only one of the reasons she and Glenn were such a perfect match.

His muttonchop whiskers twitched, his eyes twinkling. "Ah, but why should a mere maid be given the privilege of the first glimpse of your morning loveliness?" He clasped his hands behind his back, assuming a formal air. "Did you sleep well?"

Isabelle offered a delicate yawn, covering her mouth with slender fingers, then nestled into the jumble of pillows. "Oh yes, wonderfully well. Thank you." Lowering her eyelids to half-mast, she gave him a contented cat smile. "I'm so glad I came here last night. I love you, Glenn."

"As I do you." Glenn took a backward step. "I wanted to check on you before I left. I am, of course, visiting Randolph this morning."

Sitting upright, Isabelle clutched the covers to her chest to hide her ruffled nightdress. "I wish to go with you."

"Isabelle . . ."

Ignoring the warning in his tone, she said, "I have a right to be there. Randolph is trying to rob me of my inheritance. Why should I not be a part of seeing him brought to task?"

Glenn bit down on his upper lip, surveying her with heavy lids. Finally he released a sigh and nodded. "Very well. If you can be dressed and ready to leave in—" he consulted his pocket watch—"twenty-five minutes, I shall allow you to accompany me."

She released a squawk. "Twenty-five minutes?" Then she looked into his unyielding face. With a huff, she said, "Very well. Twenty-five minutes. Now remove yourself from my bedroom and send in the maid!"

❧

"See for yourself." Randolph's smug grin as he dropped the thick packet of papers onto Reginald Standler's cherry desktop made Isabelle wish Glenn would put his fist through her brother's nose. "I found all of that in Father's safe, tucked in the back. Of course, I removed the Bible and gave it to Molly. It does belong to her."

Glenn lifted the leather packet and opened the flap. Leaving the pages inside, he thumbed through them, glancing at the documents. "How do I know you didn't manufacture all of this to cheat Isabelle"—he emphasized the name—"out of her share of your father's estate?"

Randolph glared across the desk. "I have no need to manufacture anything. Take the papers with you. Show them to your father, to your lawyer, to whomever you please." He swung his arm wide. "I don't care. It will be proved *Isabelle* is the only forgery." Striding to the window, he stared across the lawn and rose gardens. "For seventeen years I've tolerated the presence of that . . . intruder . . . in my home. Well, no more. The truth will come out now."

How dare Randolph speak of her as if she didn't sit in the room? His discourteous tone and attitude were reprehensible! Isabelle looked at Glenn, begging him with her disbelieving expression to speak in her defense.

"The real truth, or your version of it?" Pushing himself from the brocade-upholstered chair, Glenn crossed his arms and stared at the back of Randolph's head. "For as long as I've known you, you've resented Isabelle." He slapped the packet onto the desktop. "This all seems to be a well-constructed scheme of revenge."

Without turning from the window, Randolph chuckled. "Oh yes, a well-constructed scheme. Of course, I managed to pull all of this together in the week since Mother and Father's deaths. Or I was wily enough to know they would be killed when a boiler exploded on the paddleboat so I had everything in place, waiting to spring it the moment they were in the grave."

Isabelle's heart pounded. As much as she hated to admit it, Randolph made a good point. She turned to Glenn. His pensive expression sent a chill down her spine. But she was cheered somewhat when he goaded, "I can see you putting something like this into place and biding your time, waiting for the moment you could get even with Isabelle for the affection your parents lavished on her instead of you."

Randolph spun around, his eyes sparking with anger. "Yes, they lavished affection on that Irish spawn. Yes, I've resented her. I'll never forget the day my parents returned from their lengthy 'business trip.'" Storming back and forth in front of the wide window like a caged animal, Randolph spewed a hatred that made Isabelle shrink into her chair. "Eighteen months they'd been gone, leaving me in the care of an indifferent staff at an unbearable boarding school. Then they return and offer their surprise. Oh, how Mother beamed as she held out that redheaded brat. 'Look, darling, you have a baby sister. Aren't you pleased?'"

Randolph stopped beside the desk and slammed his fist onto the solid surface, his cold glare boring into Isabelle. "Pleased? Wasn't I *pleased*?" A mirthless burst of laughter emphasized his words. "Certainly, I wasn't pleased! I'd been without my parents for well over a year, and it was clear from the way they fawned over that mewling scrap of humanity that I would never have them again!"

He took up his pacing once more as Isabelle watched, silent, amazed by the amount of revulsion expressed in Randolph's words and actions. She had never suspected his resentment went so deep. Certainly this kind of dark emotion could compel him to create a wild tale of foundlings. Her hopes rose.

"Mother raved on and on about the baby's similarity in appearance to her dead mother. Her praises made me feel ashamed of my own brown hair and eyes—as if I were second best. She had eyes only for the child, not for the son she'd borne. Did it matter to her that I'd been left motherless and unattended for such a length of time? Of course not—all that mattered was she now had her arms filled with a red-haired, squirming, squalling brat."

Randolph stopped and pressed his palm to the window casing, the muscles in his back twitching with the force of his fury. "When Mother took the baby upstairs, I asked Father where he'd found the child. I knew she didn't belong to Mother—that red hair didn't fool me for one moment. If Mother had been expecting a child before they left, Father would never have taken her on an ocean journey. Mother was fragile—Father wouldn't have risked the loss of a baby. So I knew they'd found or purchased the child . . . somewhere."

Randolph pushed off from the casing, his focus still aimed outside. His voice dropped to a grating whisper. "Father nearly wrenched my arm from the socket as he told me I was to never ask such a question again. Isabelle was my sister. I would acknowledge her as my sister, or I would suffer the consequences." Randolph rubbed his shoulder, seemingly lost in thought. "I did as he commanded. I kept silent. For seventeen years, I kept silent . . ."

Then he spun, facing Glenn. Not even a flicker of a glance found Isabelle. His voice rose. "But no longer. My parents are gone. I have no need to continue the charade. I *won't* continue it. Isabelle is not my sister. And that is the untarnished truth."

Isabelle remained in the chair, deliberately keeping her face clear of all expression while underneath her stomach churned at the bitterness she'd witnessed. Standing beside her chair, Glenn placed his hand under her elbow and drew her to her feet.

Glenn lifted the packet. "Very well." Quirking one brow, he added, "Of course, you won't mind if I have this all substantiated by legal authorities?"

Randolph offered an arrogant shrug. "As I told you earlier, feel free to share those documents with anyone you choose. I have nothing to lose . . . except a *sister.*" The last word hung in the air like a bad stench.

Glenn tucked the packet beneath his arm. He escorted Isabelle to the doorway of the den, but before leaving the room he paused and turned back. "You do realize one thing, Randolph . . ."

Isabelle held her breath, wondering what Glenn would say in parting. Randolph's brows pulled down into a scowl, which Glenn seemed to find more amusing than threatening. With a smile, he said, "Even if Isabelle is not your biological sister, the law does recognize adoption as binding. You can disown her as your sister, but she can't be disowned as your father's heir."

A sly smile crept up Randolph's cheeks. "Oh, certainly I'm aware of the legalities of adoption. We'll see how cocky you are when you've finished with the legal authorities. My parents never adopted her. They simply expected everyone to believe she was their own."

Glenn's fingers clamped around Isabelle's elbow, and he propelled her from the house, hissing through clenched teeth, "I'm taking you back to the house. I'll go see my family lawyer. We'll get to the bottom of this!"

His ominous tone made her glad Glenn was on her side of this issue.

❦

"Duped . . . We have been unequivocally duped!"

The rancor in Glenn's tone caused Isabelle's heart to beat at twice its normal rhythm. She had paced beside the parlor window for almost four hours, waiting for his return—and her vindication. When the Heaton carriage had pulled up, she'd rushed to meet Glenn at the door, but he'd pushed past her as if she didn't exist and charged straight to his father's den. Although he hadn't invited her to join them, she had crept down the hallway and now stood outside the pocket doors, listening, her pounding heartbeat nearly covering the men's voices.

"How could we have been so stupid?"

"For what reason would we have checked into Standler's background?" Mr. Heaton sounded more perplexed than angry. "When the man approached me and suggested a union between you and Isabelle, he sounded like any other loving father, interested in pursuing the best position for a beloved daughter."

"And I eagerly entered into the bargain, fully anticipating all I would gain from the dealing." His words held an undertone of bitterness. "What if the Standlers hadn't perished in that paddleboat accident? What if Isabelle and I had exchanged wedding vows prior to their demise? Reginald would have given Isabelle's share of his estate to us as a wedding gift, foster child or not."

His tone rose in volume as Isabelle shrank against the wall. Had his interest in her been a farce? Her breath came in little huffs, her chest heaving, as she battled to accept the words pouring from the man she thought she loved. The man who claimed to love her.

"I could be in possession of that wealth right now were it not for bad timing. But as it stands, I can't possibly follow through on our plans." His regret-laden sigh brought tears to Isabelle's eyes. "Not even her beauty is enough to compensate for all I would have to give up."

Suddenly Mrs. Heaton bustled around the corner, her mouth pursed. She spotted Isabelle and paused outside the den doors, touching Isabelle's sleeve with her fingertips before speaking. "Glenn, I could hear you in the kitchen, as could every servant in the house. What's going on?"

Glenn stepped into the wide doorway. His gaze bounced from his mother to Isabelle, who cowered next to the doorjamb. He looked at Isabelle when he spoke, but she felt certain the words were meant for himself. "I can hardly bear to think of that arrogant Randolph having the victory, yet what else can I do?"

Mrs. Heaton shook her head. "What are you talking about?"

Glenn drew in a deep breath, disappointment appearing in his eyes before his expression became stony. "Legally, there is no Isabelle Standler. Therefore no agreement exists between Reginald Standler and Father. There can be no wedding."

CHAPTER NINE

"W-what do you mean there won't be a wedding? Of course there will be a wedding!" Though Isabelle implored Glenn with her tone and fervent gaze, he did not look at her.

"Glenn . . . Garrett . . ." Mrs. Heaton looked from her son to her husband as Isabelle stared in horror. "Will someone please explain what is going on?"

"This." Glenn snatched up a paper and held it out. The paper crinkled within his clenched fist. "It's a statement of agreement—signed by Reginald Standler—transferring responsibility from the Good Shepherd Asylum for Orphans and Half Orphans of one-year-old Molly Gallagher to the Standlers." His jaw muscles bulged. "Of course, we've been introduced to that child as Isabelle Standler."

Isabelle stared at the paper. Although she recognized the boldly scribbled signature at the bottom as belonging to her father, she still raised her voice in argument. "This simply must be counterfeit. Why, Mama and Papa never intimated I was not born to them. Mama showed me pictures of her own mother. She said I looked just like my grandmother!"

Mr. Heaton lifted another page from those scattered across his desk and offered it to Isabelle. "As you can see from the copies of correspondence, Reginald went to a great deal of trouble to secure a child who would resemble Rebecca's mother. That letter was sent to four different organizations that sent orphans west. You were selected specifically because of your physical appearance."

Leaning back in his chair, Garrett Heaton fixed Isabelle with a hooded gaze. "Reginald Standler was wily. He carefully planned, well in advance, so he and Rebecca could be gone from the community an adequate length of time to fabricate the duration of a pregnancy and allow for your age when you were received. No one had reason to suspect you were anything but their biological daughter."

Isabelle shook her head. This couldn't be true. Her parents wouldn't have kept this a secret from her. "I refuse to believe it."

"You have no choice," Glenn said harshly. "There is no birth certificate for Isabelle Standler. There is no adoption form that proves you are Isabelle Standler. On the contrary, all of the evidence points to the fact that you are, indeed, Molly Gallagher."

Isabelle blinked rapidly, holding back tears. Was it possible Glenn's statement was true? And what if it were? Would it change that she had been raised by Reginald and Rebecca Standler? No. Did it mean she hadn't been loved by her mama and papa? Certainly not! Did it erase the opportunities she'd been given to be educated, groomed, and taught to be a lady? Of course not. It was merely a name. A name that, in a few months, would change again when she became Mrs. Glenn Heaton.

Her racing pulse calmed. She raised her chin and forced a quavering smile to her lips. "All right, then. Fine. I was born Molly Gallagher." Flipping her wrists outward, she said, "However, I prefer to use the name with which my parents gifted me—Isabelle Standler." She placed her hand on Glenn's arm, giving him a smile. "At least until April."

Glenn jerked away from her. The abrupt motion sent a chill down Isabelle's spine. "As I've already stated," Glenn said, "there will not be a wedding."

The chill was chased away by a burning heat that rose from Isabelle's middle.

"Isa—Molly . . ." Mrs. Heaton twined her fingers together, placing both hands against her own heart. "Surely you understand that the wedding must be cancelled. Why, this entire agreement was based on a foundation of lies. We have a certain standing in this community. Glenn must marry a woman of wealth, of breeding. Nothing else is acceptable."

Isabelle looked again at Glenn's stiff profile. His stern expression, lowered brows, and tense muscles did not invite communication, yet she set aside her own pride and said timorously, "Glenn, none of this changes how I feel about you. I . . . I love you. Do you not love me?"

He aimed an icy stare across the room. "Love . . . has nothing to do with it." His emotionless words pierced Isabelle. "Ours was an agreement based on financial advancement for both of our families. I must consider what is in the best interest of my future heirs. Marrying a woman with no dowry, with no social status . . ." He swallowed, his Adam's apple bobbing visibly in his taut neck. "It can't be done. It simply . . . cannot . . . be done."

The tears Isabelle had held back now spilled forth. The room swam through her distorted vision, but she managed to stumble down the hallway. She clamped her jaw against the sobs until she'd fled up the stairs to the Yellow Room, but the moment she closed the door behind her they burst out in harsh, wracking gasps that crumpled her to the floor.

Discarded . . . Glenn had discarded her, just as Randolph had. Perhaps even as her birth parents had. After all, how did she know for sure she was an orphan? She'd heard of parents abandoning babies, selling babies. Who was to say she hadn't been left on the doorstep of an orphanage by parents who chose not to care for her any longer?

Certainly her heart had shattered, so great was her pain. She lay on the thick carpet, wailing until every tear was spent. And even then, when all that was left was dry, shuddering sobs, she remained on the floor, her mourning dress wrinkled and sodden from the tears.

A nightmare . . . Surely it was all a nightmare. She would close her eyes, slip away to sleep. When she awakened, Mama and Papa would be alive. She would be in her childhood home, anticipating her upcoming wedding and the establishment of a new home as Glenn's wife.

Hugging herself, she coiled into a ball and drifted into unconsciousness.

*

A firm knock jolted Isabelle awake. She sat up, then grimaced as pain sliced between her shoulder blades. She blinked, squinting against the deep gray shadows of midevening. Where was she? Her fingers pressed the plush Persian rug beneath her, and suddenly realization swept over her.

It hadn't been a nightmare. Fresh tears stung her raw eyes. "Oh, Mama and Papa, I need you . . ." The words groaned out on a low note of despair.

The pounding came again, followed by a voice. "Isabelle? Are you in there?"

Glenn. Her heart leapt into her throat. Surely the shock of discovering her true birthright had ended. Surely Glenn had come to his senses and realized he couldn't throw away their plans based on something that had happened seventeen years ago. Everything would be all right now.

She scrambled to her feet, tripping on her skirts as she staggered toward the door. Twisting the crystal knob, she flung the door open and fell into Glenn's arms. "Oh, I knew you'd come to me!"

He held her, his hands contorting on her back, before clasping her upper arms and setting her aside. "We must talk."

Although his tone was terse, Isabelle believed she glimpsed compassion in his eyes. She allowed him to guide her to the bed, where she seated herself on the edge and smoothed her hopelessly wrinkled skirts over her knees. Glenn snapped on the bedside lamp, which sent out a gentle yellow glow. She blinked in the sudden light, meeting Glenn's gaze.

He shook his head, his brows low. "Gracious, you're a mess." Reaching inside his pocket, he withdrew a handkerchief. "Clean your face, please."

Isabelle followed his directions, then held the handkerchief in her lap, continuing to peer up at him. Questions hovered in her mind, but she held them back, eager to hear what he would say.

"I've been thinking. . . . Despite Standler's duplicity in misrepresenting you as his biological child, he and my father maintained a business relationship as well as a friendship. Out of respect for their long-standing relationship, I—"

She sprang from the bed and threw her arms around his neck. "Oh, I knew you wouldn't be able to call off our wedding." Pressing her face to his cologne-scented collar, she released a sigh of relief. "It was just the shock of it all. I understand, and I forgive you for your hasty words downstairs. All will be well now."

"Isabelle." He caught her wrists and tugged her arms away from his neck, then pushed her back onto the mattress. "Allow me to finish, please."

Isabelle's heart raced once more. She licked her lips, her mouth dry. "A-all right, Glenn. Please proceed."

Glenn seated himself beside her on the bed, his knees brushing her skirts. "It's no secret I find you attractive. When Standler first approached my father with the suggestion we begin courting, I was not opposed. Of all the marriageable women in our families' circle of acquaintanceship, you are by far the most desirable. I could envision a lifetime of your face across the breakfast table, of you serving as hostess for dinner parties, of squiring you to operas and having you accompany me on business trips to England. Having you on my arm is a pleasure I have long anticipated."

His breath stirred her hair as he continued. "I still greatly desire to have you on my arm." His face twisted into a scowl of displeasure. "Of course, many of the places I mentioned wouldn't be a possibility, given the fact that there can be no marriage. Your lack of dowry and absence of social status create an impenetrable barrier to marriage, but that doesn't mean—"

Isabelle gasped and leaped from the bed. Spinning to face him, she stared at him in horror. "Are you suggesting I become your . . . your . . ." She couldn't bring herself to say the word.

Glenn held out his hands in supplication. "It isn't uncommon." His lurid tone caused Isabelle to break out in a cold sweat. "Consider the positive aspects. I would purchase a little house for you, give you an allowance. You'd be able to travel, as I would take you on business trips outside of Kansas City. I could even locate someone to come in and clean and cook for you. In view of your background, I'd say it's a fine opportunity."

In view of her background? Isabelle quivered from head to toe with indignation. How dare he assume that simply because she had been taken in and raised by parents other than her own she had no scruples? Did the humbleness of her birth eradicate every remnant of the previous seventeen years?

Straightening her shoulders, she raised her chin and pinned Glenn with a smoldering glare. "I shall never degrade myself by becoming intimately involved with a man other than my own husband! It's morally repugnant, and I am appalled you would even suggest something so distasteful!"

He pursed his lips and lowered his head. Isabelle took a step backward, putting more distance between them. She had loved this man, but now she viewed him as nothing more than a lecher. Had he hidden his true character from her all this time? Perhaps her parents' early demise had saved her from a life of heartache. . . .

At last Glenn raised his face and looked at her. "Suit yourself. It was merely a compromise." His eyes seemed devoid of all feeling. "Father has a suggestion, as well, if you'd care to hear it."

Isabelle hugged herself and waited for him to continue.

"He could arrange transport to Shay's Ford, Missouri, where he has a business acquaintance—a Mr. Mason Drumfeld. The man will house you, clothe you, and see to your immediate needs until which time you believe you can care for yourself."

Isabelle pressed a hand to her throat. Her pulse pounded beneath her shaking fingertips. Fear nearly made her swoon. How would she manage on her own in a strange community? Perhaps she should consider Glenn's compromise. . . .

She stared into his unemotional face, imagining a life of waiting for his visits, spending time in secret, having the community point and whisper behind her back, calling her "the mistress." Isabelle's mother had spoken with disdain of such women. Despite her fears, she could never lower herself to such depths.

Glenn rose from the bed and slipped his hands into his pockets. "Shall I tell Father you choose to travel to Shay's Ford?"

Isabelle could give only one answer. "Yes."

"Very well." Glenn's calm response showed no evidence of the magnitude of the conversation that had taken place between them. He barely glanced at her as he said, "I'm sure a train will be leaving yet this evening given the busyness of the station. It will take you to St. Louis, and from there you will travel by barge on the Mississippi River. Of course, Father will purchase the necessary tickets since you are without resources. Prepare your bag. I'll send the driver for you when the carriage is ready."

He crossed the room without looking at her and closed the door behind him. Isabelle stood in the middle of the floor, her gaze on the wooden door, her heart in pieces at her feet.

Chapter Ten

Mattie
St. Louis, Missouri
January, 1903

T hank you, boy." Matt tossed a quarter to the pock-faced teen who handed off Russ's reins. He could see at a glance that Russ had been well cared for in the cattle car, which eased his mind considerably.

It had pained him to be separated from the animal for the past week. He and Russ had boarded the new Burlington–Rock Island train to cut some time off their journey from Spofford to Shay's Ford. Although he'd visited Russ at each stop, it wasn't the same as their usual sunup to sundown togetherness. But Russ didn't seem to hold a grudge for having to ride in that slatted car with three cows and a bawling calf. The loving nuzzle on the back of Matt's neck told him Russ still considered him a friend.

Throwing the saddle over Russ's broad back, Matt shivered. The temperature was considerably cooler in St. Louis than what he'd become accustomed to over the past few years in Texas. Or, he acknowledged with a quick glance over his shoulder, maybe it was a fear-shiver rather than a cold-shiver. Ever since he'd crossed the border into Missouri, he'd had trouble shaking the worry that Jenks might be lurking around the corner, ready to grab him and insist he work off his debt, or worse.

Russ snorted, blowing steam into the air. Matt gave a final yank to tighten the saddle's flank cinch, buckled it, and swung into the seat. Russ nodded his head as if eager to get going. With a pat on the horse's thick neck, Matt said, "Easy now. We'll get movin' soon enough. I gotta make a quick stop, though, an' pick up a few supplies for the trail. Be at least three days yet to Shay's Ford."

As Russ clopped down the street toward the business area, Matt patted the hidden pocket inside his jacket. He'd spent a sizable portion of his money on the train ride. Judging by the snow that dusted the ground, he might need to purchase some warmer work clothes. He hoped he had enough money left to cover his needs. It'd be a while until he received his first pay from Mr. Harders.

In his saddlebag, he carried the telegram giving him approval to join the crew at Rocky Crest Ranch. The reply had come four days after his inquiry. By then Matt had decided the position was no longer open and had reconciled himself to taking the stable hand job until something better came along. Even with the approval in his hand, he'd considered working at the stable rather than traveling to Missouri.

But the wording of the telegram had changed his mind. He'd read it so many times he had it memorized: *Mr. Tucker, please plan to make Rocky Crest your home.*

Home. Hadn't he prayed to God for a home? Must be God had something planned for him here in the state he'd done his best to avoid for the past ten years.

Bringing Russ to a stop in front of a place called Dave's General Store, Matt murmured, "I'm trustin' you to know what you're doin', Lord, bringin' me back here. . . ." He wrapped the reins around the rail, gave Russ's nose a brief rub, and then stepped up onto the rickety walkway fronting the store. As he pushed open the door, he heard a noise that chilled him from his hairline to his toes.

A woman stood behind a dusty counter, counting coins, while wails and a repetitive *swish-whack* filled the small room. The woman seemed oblivious to the sound that made Matt tremble like a willow branch in a Texas norther. Unpleasant memories tried to surface, and Matt slammed the mercantile's door, chasing them away.

With the bang of the door, the woman looked up. "Howdy. What can I do for you?" She raised her voice to be heard above the pained cries carrying from somewhere beyond Matt's sights.

Matt crossed the floor in three long strides. "Who's makin' that ruckus?"

The woman grimaced, glancing toward a planked door at the far left corner of the store. "Petey. That boy's not worth the clothes Dave puts on his back, but Dave keeps tryin' to whip some sense into him."

Even before she finished speaking, Matt stomped to the door and pushed it open. His stomach churned at the sight of a man— Dave, he assumed—with a strap in hand, holding a small, squirming boy over a barrel. Matt cringed as the strap landed squarely across the boy's back. He felt the sting of a lash and had to resist releasing his own yowl of pain with the child's.

Dave's arm lifted for another blow, but Matt strode forward and caught it midswing. The strap dangled uselessly from the man's hand. "Hey!" Dave jerked his arm free, spinning to face Matt. "What do you think you're doin'?"

Matt balled his hands into fists. He kept his focus on the man, although the boy's shuddering sobs made it hard. "Stoppin' you. What right've you got to be whalin' on that boy?"

Dave snorted, looking Matt up and down as if deciding whether or not to start a tussle. "Got every right, for as much good as it does. Kid's absolutely useless."

Matt glanced at the boy, who remained draped over the barrel. His little body jerked with hiccuping sniffles. The total defenselessness of the child raised a wave of empathy Matt couldn't ignore. "Nobody's got the right to beat a child." Glaring at Dave, he added, "There're better ways to teach him whatever it is you're wantin' him to do."

Dave released another derisive snort. He grabbed the boy's arm and yanked him to his feet. The boy cried out, flinging his free arm upward to shield his face. Dave gave a shove that sent the boy scuttling sideways into a stack of lumpy, well-filled burlap bags. "Go finish stacking those boxes, like I told you, an' don't you drop another one"—he brandished the strap—"or you'll know what to expect!"

The boy dashed out the back door into the cold. Without a jacket, Matt noted. As soon as the door slammed, Matt faced Dave. "That your son?"

"Ha!" Dave headed for the door leading to the store. "No. I took him in about six months ago. Caught him rummagin' through my lean-to, lookin' for food. He said his folks kicked him out—had too many mouths to feed and it was time for him to take care of himself." Hanging the strap on a nail beside the door, he said, "I can see why they didn't want him. Never met such a worthless boy."

The boy's story made Matt's heart ache. He followed the man back into the main part of the store. "Then why keep him?"

The man huffed. "I need somebody to unload goods an' clean up." With a shrug, he added, "One of these days he'll figure out I'm not gonna spare the strap until he does the jobs right. He'll straighten up."

"You ain't got no right to beat him," Matt muttered.

Dave glowered at him. "You come in here just to pester me, or did you need somethin'?"

Although the last thing Matt wanted to do was give business to the man whose treatment of the hapless Petey had conjured too many painful reflections of his own childhood, he said, "I need supplies for a three-day journey." If he kept the man occupied for a few minutes, Petey would get some peace.

"Just for yourself?"

Matt hesitated. A plan formed of its own accord in the back of his mind. "Me an' my . . . partner." He hoped the good Lord would forgive him for stretching the truth.

"You travelin' on horseback?"

"That's right."

Dave nodded. "I'll set ya up. Give ya a good price, too—better than the big mercantile down the block."

"Fine." Matt ambled toward the front door. "I'm gonna go check on my partner, make sure he's finishin' his dealings."

"Gimme ten minutes," Dave said.

"Ten minutes is just fine." Matt hitched his collar around his jaw and stepped out the door. He took a moment to take a few calming breaths and let Russ nuzzle him before slipping behind the building. He located Petey easily—there was only one small boy in the alley.

The sight of that miserable child—in tattered clothing, his nose red and eyes watery, moving very gingerly—was like looking into a mirror. It took great self-control not to rush forward, snatch the boy up in his arms, and run off with him. But if he did that, he'd only frighten the child. First he had to earn Petey's trust. Then he could help him.

Petey lifted a crate from the lowered hatch of a wagon. He stumbled backward with the weight, but surprisingly, he didn't fall. Turning, he shuffled into a lean-to attached to the back of the store. A *thud* let Matt know the crate had been released. Then the boy stepped back into the alley. He came to a halt when he spotted Matt. His eyes grew wary, and he rubbed a finger along his nose.

"I ain't doin' nothin' wrong." The words could have been an accusation.

Matt twitched his lips into a grin. He rested his elbow on the side of the wagon. "Appears to me you're doin' fine, but I've got a few minutes to spare. Wondered if you could use a hand."

The boy's eyes narrowed. "Why?"

Matt raised one shoulder in a lazy shrug. "Why not?"

Petey stared at him silently for several seconds before he imitated Matt's one-shoulder shrug. "Suit yourself."

Matt and the boy worked in silence, unloading and stacking the last few crates. Then, without a thank-you, Petey brushed his chapped hands together and headed for the back door. Matt called, "Hold up there."

Petey turned around and folded his arms across his chest, shivering. "I gotta get back in. Got sweepin' to do."

Matt crossed the hard ground to hunker on his haunches in front of the boy. "You like workin' here?"

The boy shook his head.

"If you had the chance to live someplace else, would you take it?"

Petey blinked several times. "Dave says I owe 'im."

Matt's chest constricted. "I reckon Dave's got his due from you." He straightened. "I'm headin' on to a place called Rocky Crest Ranch. I can't take you there, but I know of a home in Springfield where you could stay. You want to, I'll take you to a train station an' send you there."

Petey glanced over his shoulder. "An' I wouldn't have to work for Dave no more?"

"No more."

Without a moment's hesitation, Petey nodded, his shaggy blond hair bobbing with the movement. "I'll go."

Matt gently turned Petey toward the lean-to. "Wait for me in there. I'll get my supplies, and then we'll head out." He waited until Petey trotted to the lean-to before heading around the building and through the front door. As promised, Dave had a bundle waiting.

"I put in salt pork, beans, coffee, cornmeal . . ." The man recited the list and named the cost.

Matt removed his money purse and plopped the coins into Dave's waiting hand. Hefting the bag, he clumped to the door, but halfway there he stopped and turned back. "You got coats for boys?" His heart pounded. Would Dave figure out what he was up to?

"What size?"

Matt didn't have any idea. "Need it for a boy about six or seven years old." He hoped he'd guessed correctly.

Dave pulled a brown wool coat off of a wooden hanger and held it out. "This do?"

Matt looked it over. He suspected the coat would be too big for Petey's slight frame, but bigger would last longer. He nodded. "That'll do. How much?"

"Three dollars."

Three dollars was about half of what Matt had left in his purse. He slipped the purse out and unsnapped it. "I'll take it."

Minutes later, astride Russ, Matt doubled back through the alley and reined in beside the lean-to. "Petey?"

The boy's blond head poked out. Matt threw him the coat. Eagerly, Petey pulled the coat over his shirt and buttoned it to the collar. He peered up at Matt with wide, trusting eyes.

Matt leaned down, offering his hand. "Okay, partner, grab on." With a slight tug, he swung Petey behind him. The boy weighed next to nothing. "Now hold tight," he advised, and he felt Petey's arms grip his waist. "C'mon, Russ, let's go."

Riding over the hard-packed road leading away from St. Louis, Matt was very aware of the small boy snuggled against his back. The child had to be cold and—as the afternoon wore on—tired, but he never complained. He didn't ask questions, either—just slipped his hands into Matt's pockets, pressed his cheek to Matt's back, and clung in silence.

Matt asked himself plenty of questions as he guided Russ across the bleak countryside. What did he think he was doing, sneaking off with a child who didn't belong with him? Would Dave send the law for him—accuse him of stealing his property, as Jenks had done all those years ago? Would he have enough money to buy a ticket for Petey to get to Springfield when he reached a train station? It'd been a long time since he'd been to Springfield—what if that orphanage he'd told Petey about wasn't even there anymore?

Lord, I acted so quick, I didn't think things through, Matt prayed, breathing in the crisp winter air. *But I couldn't leave him there to be treated bad by Dave. I did the right thing . . . didn't I?* As a young boy, suffering under Jenks's hand, he'd wished for someone to come along and rescue him. Surely rescuing Petey couldn't be wrong. Still, he worried about the legalities of his choice. *I hope I don't end up regrettin' this. . . .*

Behind him, Petey suddenly loosened his grip and slipped sideways.

"Whoa!" Matt drew up on Russ's reins with one hand and caught the boy with the other. Craning his neck around, he asked, "You okay?"

Petey nodded, grinning sheepishly. "Must've fallen asleep. Sorry."

"No need for apologizin'." Matt paused, surveying the landscape. A few scrubby trees about a quarter mile off the road would provide shelter for the night. "Sun's gettin' heavy. Time for us to be finding us a sleepin' spot, anyway. You ready for rest?"

A yawn provided Petey's answer.

"All right, then. We'll stop." Matt tugged Russ's reins. "C'mon, big boy."

Later, their bellies filled with salt pork, beans, and corn pone, Matt and Petey lay back-to-back beneath Matt's saddle blanket. Petey faced the campfire. Matt figured the scrawny child needed the warmth more than he did. He blinked into the inky darkness, breathing in the cold air and releasing it in clouds of condensation. Overhead, stars winked blue and white. Russ snorted contentedly from his spot beside the scrub trees, providing a familiar lullaby.

Petey shifted, his elbow banging Matt between the shoulder blades. Matt scooted forward an inch or two to give the boy more room, but then a small finger tapped his back.

"Yeah?"

"Just wanted to say . . ." The child's voice seemed smaller in the surrounding blackness. "Nobody's ever been as nice to me as you. Thank you, mister."

Matt reached back awkwardly to give the boy's leg a pat. "You're welcome, partner. Now sleep, huh? Long way to go tomorrow."

Another shuffling and a few bumps let Matt know Petey had rolled over. Silence reigned once more. But the boy's simple words lifted Matt's heart. *Yeah, I did the right thing.*

CHAPTER ELEVEN

Shay's Ford, Missouri
January, 1903

Hey, Petey, end of the trail."

Matt urged Russ forward while Petey held tight to Matt's shoulders and leaned sideways to peer at the town. According to Mr. Harders' telegram, Shay's Ford was the closest town of size to Rocky Crest Ranch. Laid out along the Mississippi River, it looked to be well established. Trolley tracks cut down the center of the cobblestone streets, and several buildings were constructed of brick with mortar medallions. The businesses built of clapboard all sported whitewashed fronts with fancy trims in bold, eye-catching colors. Matt liked the look of this town.

But one thing seemed lacking. A train station. After riding up and down the business district twice, Matt reined in and called to a man on the wooden walkway. "Excuse me, sir?"

The man's determined stride halted. "Yes?"

Matt shifted his hat to the back of his head. "I'm lookin' for the train—need to buy a ticket to Springfield."

The man stepped to the edge of the boardwalk. "Well, you're looking in the wrong town if you need a train. We send out goods from the docks, so the railroad hasn't come to Shay's Ford. The closest train station is at Paynesville, about fifteen miles southwest of here."

Matt stifled a groan. Southwest was opposite the direction he needed to go to reach Rocky Crest. And he hoped to be at the ranch before nightfall.

The man slipped his hands into his jacket pockets and raised his shoulders. "There is a stagecoach that runs once a week, on Friday mornings, to several towns, including Paynesville. You could make use of that."

Friday? Matt couldn't hang around that long. And he couldn't leave the boy in town without supervision. Plus, he was pretty sure he didn't have enough funds to cover a stagecoach plus a train ride. He mumbled a thank-you, which the man acknowledged with a tip of his hat before heading into a tall brick building with a square brass plate embedded in the brick bearing the words *Logan and Tyler Law Offices*.

Petey tugged at his sleeve. "Mister, I gotta use the outhouse."

Matt caught Petey's arm and lowered him to the ground. He pointed to a white-painted facility at the edge of a park area across the street. "Go ahead. I'll get directions to the ranch. Reckon I'll just hafta keep you with me for—" He let the sentence die as Petey zigzagged between passing carriages to the outhouse, heedless of Matt's worries.

He slipped out of the saddle and stretched. It felt good to stand after the long days of riding. But his destination was near. A nervous excitement filled his belly as he thought about the ranch ahead: a new start, a new opportunity to settle in. For good this time? In his ride up and down the streets, he'd spotted at least three churches but no saloons. And with no railroad, it was unlikely Jenks would have any need to come to Shay's Ford.

Yes, it appeared Matt's choice to pack up and leave Texas for Missouri would work out after all. Now if he could just figure out how to get Petey to that orphanage in Springfield, his problems would be solved.

He scowled. Where was that boy? He'd been gone long enough to take care of business. After looping Russ's reins over the rail in front of the law office, he crossed the street and jogged to the outhouse. He tapped on the door. "Petey?" No response. He tapped a little harder. "You okay in there?"

When he still got no reply, he peeked in. The outhouse was empty. Frowning, Matt headed back into the park area. Surely the boy hadn't gotten confused and gone the wrong way when he came out. Cupping his hands beside his mouth, he hollered, "Petey!" He looked right and left, but no tousle-haired boy in a new jacket came running.

Matt searched for nearly an hour, one eye looking for Petey, the other watching the sun slowly dip closer to the bare tree-tops. Dusk would fall soon, and he needed to reach the ranch while he could still see to travel. With a heavy heart, Matt returned to Russ. Climbing back in the saddle, he looked up and down the street for a sheriff's office where he could report a missing child. But then it occurred to him that it would take some fancy footwork to explain how he'd brought Petey to Shay's Ford in the first place.

"Lord, where did that child go?"

Russ pawed the ground, snorting, as if he were concerned, too. Matt patted the animal's neck, contemplating spending the night in a livery and searching again for the boy in the morning.

At that moment, the same man who had suggested taking a stagecoach to St. Louis stepped out of the lawyers' building. His gaze landed on Matt, and he strode to the edge of the boardwalk. "Did you decide to remain in town and wait for the stagecoach?"

Matt shook his head, sliding down from the saddle once more. "No. I don't have the time to wait. But I got a bigger problem than that now."

"Oh?" The man seemed genuinely interested.

"Yeah." Matt scratched his whiskery chin. "That little boy I had with me? He was kicked out by his folks, and I wanted to send him to an orphanage in Springfield—that's why I was asking about the train. But he went to the outhouse over an hour ago and must've got lost. I can't find him now, and I'm needin' to leave town. Got a job waitin', but I can't leave him behind."

The man curled his hands over the hitching rail. "Would you say he is accustomed to fending for himself?"

"I'd say so." Matt understood Petey. He, too, had been self-sufficient by necessity far too young.

The man pulled his lips to the side, twitching his mustache. "It grieves me to say it, but Shay's Ford has its share of street waifs. They come in on the barges and spend their days picking pockets, working on the docks, or selling newspapers or rags to survive." The man shook his head. "My guess is he's met up with a pack of our boys and joined their ranks."

Matt frowned. He hated to think Petey would just take off without saying good-bye after the help he'd given him. "You really think so?"

"That's my best guess." The man gave the railing a slap. "If you'd like to tell me your name and where you're staying, I'd be glad to send you a telegram if I spot him. I'm acquainted with a local couple who look out for the street boys. If your little friend has joined the gang, they'll meet him eventually."

"Much obliged." Matt pulled his purse from his pocket. "Let me pay you for your trouble."

The man waved his hand in dismissal. "That isn't necessary. I'm interested in helping out these street children in whatever way I can." Removing a small leather book and pencil from his jacket pocket, he said, "Tell me your name and where you're staying so I can reach you."

With a nod, Matt put his purse away. "Name's Matthew Tucker, an' I'm headin' to take a position at the Rocky Crest Ranch."

The man's head shot up. "Rocky Crest? With Gerald Harders?"

"That's right."

"Well, I'll be . . ." The man stepped around the railing and held out his hand. "I'm Jackson Harders. Gerald is my father, so I imagine our paths will cross again whether I locate this boy of yours or not."

Matt blew out his breath. "Nice to meet you. An' thank you again for keepin' a look out for Petey. I'd hate to see him come to harm."

Jackson Harders released a deep sigh. "Unfortunately, harm can come." He gave Matt's shoulder a hearty pat. "But I'll say a prayer for your young friend. God knows where he is right now—even if we don't."

Matt experienced a rush of comfort with Jackson's words. He was still fairly new at learning to put things into God's hands, but Jackson reminded him of his need to trust and let go, the way Mr. Smallwood had taught him.

"I'd best be on my way. I'm expected." He pulled himself into his saddle. As much as it pained him to leave the boy behind, he felt better knowing Jackson Harders would be watching for him.

∽

Rocky Crest Ranch

Matt whacked his hat against his leg and turned from the sign. Although the sun had nearly disappeared, there was enough light to make out the letters formed from molded lengths of iron. But he still wondered if it was some kind of joke. He'd traveled almost one thousand miles to find sheep? He might be better off running with that pack of street urchins in Shay's Ford!

Astride Russ's back, he looked across the graying landscape dotted with woolly critters. Disappointment hit hard. *Lord, what'm I doin' here?* How he'd dreamed of that ranch up ahead where he'd have a bunk to sleep in, the company of other humans, the chance to settle in and be home. But he hadn't counted on sheep. According to Jenks, sheepmen were lower than a snake's belly. Even gentle Mr. Smallwood had indicated the country would be better off without those woolly baa-ers.

113

At the end of the lane, a big rock house waited. Lights glowed in every window, beckoning to Matt. Yet he sat in the saddle, debating with himself. He'd told Mr. Harders he was reliable, but what he was considering was far from reliable. He wanted to turn tail and head back down that trail all the way to Texas.

With less'n three dollars in your pocket? He'd also, of course, told Jackson Harders he could send information about Petey to the ranch. Matt groaned. Like it or not, he was stuck.

"On a sheep ranch," he blasted, giving his leg another mighty whap with his hat before plopping it on his head. He sighed, watching his breath hang on the evening air. "Come on, Russ." Russ trotted obediently across the dusty ground, stopping in front of the rambling rock house.

As Matt swung down from the saddle, one of the wide double doors opened to reveal a big-boned man wearing brown britches and striped suspenders over a tan shirt. The man's face widened into a welcoming smile. "Good evening. Are you Matthew Tucker?"

Matt twisted Russ's reins around the wooden hitching post in front of the porch and gave a nod. "Yes, sir."

"I've been expecting you. I'm Gerald Harders. Welcome to Rocky Crest."

Matt clomped across the porch to shake the man's hand. He forced his lips into a smile he didn't feel.

"Come on in here." Gerald directed Matt to enter the house with a sweep of his broad hand.

Shrugging out of his jacket, Matt stepped over the threshold.

The owner closed the door and gave Matt another smile. "Follow me."

Matt trailed him down a long, paneled hallway that was lit by gas lamps mounted high on the walls on either side. They entered a wood-paneled den, and Matt couldn't stop the whistle of approval that came from his lips. The rustic exterior of the house offered few clues to the fine interior. He stood for a moment, taking in everything from the huge desk and bookshelves that dominated one corner, to the massive stone fireplace on the opposite wall. An oil painting hung above the carved mantel, a landscape with sheep grazing and a stone house in the background. *This* house, Matt realized. The family must have been on this land for many years.

He felt a stab of loneliness as he contemplated the difference between the Harders' history and his own background. Turning from the fireplace, he spotted Mr. Harders seated in a black leather chair.

Mr. Harders pointed to the matching sofa that faced his chair. "Have a seat."

Matt rounded the sofa and, aware of his dusty clothes, perched on the edge of the thick cushioned seat. He draped his jacket across one knee and held his hat between his widespread knees, meeting the man's friendly gaze.

"I'm sorry you had to arrive at night, Mr. Tucker. It's hard to see the layout of the ranch without the sunshine. But there will be time for that tomorrow."

Matt cleared his throat. "Um, Mr. Harders, I have to admit somethin' here. . . ." He scratched his chin, wishing he'd had a chance to shave and clean up before meeting his new boss. "I was under the impression this was a cattle ranch, but ridin' in . . ." He let out a short, rueful chuckle. "Well, sir, to be truthful, I've never worked sheep before."

Mr. Harders leaned back and rested one ankle on the opposite knee. "Now, I don't want you to worry about those woollies out there. Sheep are pretty easy to care for—a lot easier than cattle, I can tell you! The dogs do most of the work."

Matt's lips twitched. "Then what do you need me for?" He was only half joking.

Mr. Harders released a guffaw, although Matt sensed it was forced. "Well, I suppose I gave the dogs too much credit. You'll have a few responsibilities the dogs can't meet. Shearing happens once a year, lambing never more than twice. Those are busy times, but nothing you can't learn." He leaned forward, resting his elbow on his knee. "I've got three other hands. The best one is Clancy Parks. He's been with me for twenty-seven years."

Twenty-seven years? Matt stared bug-eyed at that. Matt had never stayed anywhere for more than twenty-seven *months*.

"Clancy can teach you anything you need to know, and he'll do it willingly." His eyes narrowed as he gave Matt a serious look. "Do you have any smarts?"

Matt blinked a couple of times, taken aback by the abrupt question. He hadn't had much schooling, but he'd sure learned a lot over the years. Giving a nod, he answered honestly. "Yes, sir, I reckon I do."

"Then you'll be fine." Mr. Harders slapped his thighs and rose, his knees cracking. "As my advertisement promised, you'll have room and board on top of your salary. You'll share a cabin with Clancy. It has two bedrooms, so you'll have privacy, and you'll take your meals here at the big house with me."

"A cabin?" Matt's heart lifted with pleasure at this news. He slipped a hand beneath his jacket and stood. "I was expectin' a bunkhouse."

Mr. Harders chuckled mildly. "With sheep, you don't need as many hands. A bunkhouse would be a waste. Besides, a cabin feels more like a home, don't you think?"

Something filled Matt's chest at that question. How many times had he prayed for a home? A place to stay, find acceptance, and give up the wandering ways that had driven him since he was a youngster? God sure did work in mysterious ways.

Matt cleared his throat, gratitude at this man's confidence in him giving him more pleasure than he could explain. "Mr. Harders, I appreciate you still keepin' me on even though I told you I'm without experience in sheep ranchin'." He paused, drawing a deep breath. "I'd be proud to give it a try."

Mr. Harders pumped Matt's hand, smiling broadly. "Well, then, Mr. Tucker, let's get you settled."

"You can just call me Matt."

"Will do. And you call me Gerald."

Matt shook his head. "Oh no, sir. You're the boss, an' I wouldn't feel right about that. I'll have to stick with Mr. Harders for you."

The man smiled. "You know, Matt, I think you and I are going to get along real well."

CHAPTER TWELVE

Molly
Shay's Ford, Missouri
February, 1903

"M iss Hoity-Toity, you're as worthless as they come."

Isabelle's muscles stiffened at the familiar nasal voice of Patsy, the cook's helper. Stifling the sigh that longed for release, she asked, "What, pray tell, am I doing wrong now?"

Patsy shoved a pot under Isabelle's nose. "See this? Still has gravy on the rim. If you wasn't so worried about those lily white hands o' yours, you'd be able to get dishes clean the first time." Patsy plopped the pot into the large sink, splashing Isabelle's apron with sudsy water.

Wandering back to the food preparation counter, the woman muttered, "Can't even wash a pot . . . Don't know how she made it through life this far . . ."

The cook's soft words only added to Isabelle's shame. In all her life, she'd never suffered such abuse as she had in the past six weeks at the Drumfeld residence. Although Glenn had intimated she'd be housed as a guest, Mr. Drumfeld had shown her to tiny servant quarters and informed her she'd be working to earn her keep.

The household staff's censure left bruises on her heart nearly as deep as those Randolph had administered. Never having had to make beds, wash or iron clothes, clean up in a kitchen, or dust furniture, Isabelle was ill-equipped for the position of house maid. And no one seemed interested in teaching her the skills. They preferred to berate and humiliate her. So she learned what she could by observing the others. Unfortunately, most of the time, she failed dismally.

Reaching to the bottom of the tin sink basin, she located the rag and scrubbed again at the pot she had been certain was clean the last time. The steamy water formed little sweat beads on her upper lip and forehead. Strands of hair slipped from her shabby braid and stuck to her moist skin, tickling her jaw. Her shoulders sagged in defeat. She couldn't even form a braid that would hold longer than an hour or two.

When she returned home, Isabelle would shower appreciation on Myrtle, the personal maid who had seen to so many of her needs over the years. Had she ever really thanked Myrtle for her service? Praised her for her diligence? Those who worked for a living deserved more than the meager salaries they usually received.

"Ain't you done with that yet? I need it to soak peas!" Patsy shoved in front of Isabelle and snatched the pot from her hands.

Isabelle bit down on her tongue to hold back words of protest. She'd learned the first few days here that any protests only earned more verbal abuse. Staying silent was the best course of action. Yet as Patsy marched off, drying the pot with her stained apron, Isabelle reflected on her previous thoughts. Myrtle had deserved words of commendation, but not all servants did. Patsy deserved a tongue-lashing the likes of which Isabelle was fully capable of delivering. But for now she must restrain herself. She had nowhere else to go.

She drained the sink and washed it, her heart aching with desire for Randolph to come to his senses and call her home. Despite the documents he had located, she held to hope that there had been a horrible mistake. She didn't fit here. No matter what the Bible's register said, she could not possibly be Molly Gallagher. When would she be allowed to go home?

"Got that sink clean?" The cook's gravelly voice carried from the opposite side of the kitchen.

Isabelle wrung out the rag and draped it over the edge of the basin. "Yes, ma'am."

"Take your break, then. Come back when the three-o'clock chimes sound. I'll need you to scrub potatoes for tonight's supper."

Isabelle plodded up the servants' stairs tucked into the front corner of the kitchen to the tiny attic bedroom of her new home. She shivered as she entered the room. No radiator warmed the third floor. After the steamy heat of the kitchen, the room felt especially frosty. Flopping onto the lumpy mattress, she left her feet dangling over the edge and covered her eyes with her arm. Tears stung, but she kept them at bay. If she went down to the kitchen with red-rimmed eyes again, she'd never hear the end of it. "Crybaby" was the mildest of the terms the other servants had thrown at her.

Fearful she'd fall asleep and neglect to go back downstairs, she forced herself to sit up. On a slatted crate beside the bed, the Bible Randolph had thrust into her hands less than two months ago waited, inviting her attention. She had picked it up on countless occasions, tempted to pitch it into the waste bin, but each time she'd returned it to the crate. What was the strange pull that book had over her? To distance herself from it, she rose and crossed to the tiny, grime-encrusted square window that faced out over the side yard.

When she'd arrived at the Drumfeld home, she had cheered herself by peering out this window. The sparkle of sunshine on unblemished snow had reminded her of making snow angels in her own backyard with Papa when she was a little girl. But today's brown, brittle grass below brought no tender memories to her heart. Loneliness made her heart ache, and she returned to the bed, wrapping the worn patchwork quilt that served as a bed covering around her shoulders. Once more her gaze drifted to the Bible.

Her fingers stretched out and picked up the book. She placed it on the mattress next to her hip and flopped it open. At the top of the page it said *Psalms*. Although they hadn't attended regularly, her parents had taken her to church. The minister sometimes read from the book of Psalms. Psalms were like poems, she recalled. Mama had often read poetry aloud when tucking Isabelle in at night.

Eager to find a poem that might lift her spirits, she glanced across the columns of small type. She read, *"Thou has beset me behind and before, and laid thine hand upon me."* The psalmist was writing of God, Isabelle surmised, but she had little understanding of what it meant to have God surround her or lay His hand on her.

Closing the Bible, she shut her eyes and imagined what it would be like to feel God's presence on all sides of her. The longing to experience such a thing took her by surprise. She'd never been interested in religion. But, she acknowledged, she'd never had cause to pursue it. Up until Mama and Papa died, she had been happy and fulfilled.

At least, she'd always thought she was.

Her eyes popped open. From where had that thought come? Before she could ponder the source of the unbidden notion, the bell from the chapel a few blocks away tolled. Three o'clock. She tossed off the quilt and scurried to the door. As she touched the brass doorknob, she glanced at the Bible. The book seemed to hold secrets—secrets she suddenly longed to unravel.

She headed down the stairs, the melodic ring of the chapel's bell vibrating in her chest, beckoning her to come to Sunday service.

&

Lyndon Hill Chapel, Shay's Ford
March, 1903

Isabelle scurried up the front walk of the simple chapel, her head low and arms crossed tightly over her ribs. The shawl she'd thrown over her mourning dress did little to hold the damp air at bay, and she slipped inside the double doors with eagerness to escape the drizzling mist and chill breeze.

Lanterns glowed cheerily from opposite walls of the rectangular foyer. Wide open doors led to a sanctuary lined with wooden pews, but no lights shone in the larger room. Was no one here at all?

A shuffle sounded, followed by a sharp clank, the noises seeming to come from beneath her. She frowned, glancing around, and spotted a door in the far left hand corner of the foyer. She walked to the door, her sodden skirts dragging on the wide planked flooring. Catching the iron doorknob, she eased the door open, revealing steep wooden stairs leading to what must be the cellar. A fusty smell filled her nostrils, and she sneezed.

"Hello? Is someone there?"

The deep voice from the depths of the cellar caught her by surprise. She jerked backward, her shawl slipping from her shoulders. Feet pounded, and a man burst through the doorway. He was tall, his broad shoulders encased in a faded tan jacket, and he had thick, dark hair and eyes the same color as the Mississippi River when viewed from a distance—a vibrant blue-green. Energy emanated from him, and even though they were the only two people in the foyer, the room suddenly felt crowded.

She took another step backward, and her wet skirts tangled around her ankles, causing her to stumble. He leapt forward and captured her elbow.

"Easy there. Don't want you to slip."

Isabelle's face burned at his familiarity. She yanked her elbow free. "I'll thank you to unhand me!"

He gawked at her, his thick lashes shielding his eyes. "I wasn't meanin' to be rude. I was just—"

"I am capable of standing on my own." She drew herself to her full height and fixed him with her sternest glare.

A brief scowl marred his brow, and she heard him mutter, "'Whatsoever ye do in word or deed . . .'"

"Excuse me?"

"Nothin'. Just remindin' myself of something."

Isabelle yanked her shawl back where it belonged. "Do you work here?"

The man's chest seemed to expand, and he rocked back on the worn heels of his scuffed boots. "Yes, indeed. I'm just a common laborer, but I find great satisfaction in my tasks here. Might not be the chapel's minister, but I figure I minister through keepin' the chapel clean and comfortable for its parishioners."

Isabelle crinkled her nose. Clean and comfortable? The musty cellar smell clung to him, and a chill filled the air. She hunched into her shawl and shivered.

His brows puckered in concern. With rapid movements, he yanked free of his jacket and held it out to her. "I just got the furnace to blastin', but it'll take a while for it to warm up in here. Why don't you slip this on an'—"

"I am perfectly fine, thank you." Isabelle shrank away from the worn jacket. No matter how cold the room, she could never wear a frock still bearing the warmth of another's body—especially the body of a stranger.

The man lowered his arms.

"When does the service begin? The bell tolled nine times over a quarter hour ago. I assumed it was a call to service."

The man swallowed, the sound loud in the otherwise quiet foyer. "I rang the bell at nine o'clock, like I do every day at nine, noon, three, and six. The service will begin promptly at ten." He took two sideways steps away from her, shrugging back into his jacket. "I have quite a bit to do to be ready for it, so if you'll excuse me . . ." He turned toward the sanctuary doors.

Isabelle slumped in frustration, releasing a sigh.

He glanced over his shoulder, and it seemed his eyes located the Bible she hugged to her ribs. For a moment he stood still, worrying his lower lip between his teeth. Then he lifted his gaze to meet hers. "Miss, even though the service won't be startin' for a while, you can go on in and have a seat in the sanctuary next to one of the registers. It'll be warmer."

"I . . . I don't wish to inconvenience you." Isabelle tried to maintain a haughty tone, but her voice quavered with uncertainty.

He offered a lopsided smiled. "I got to clean up the puddles you left anyway, an' I can't do that if you're standin' over 'em."

She glanced at the floor and then covered her mouth with her fingers. Guilt assailed her as she realized what a mess she'd left behind. "Oh! Gracious, I had no idea. Perhaps I should mop this floor."

He shook his head firmly. "That's my job, an' I pleasure in it. Go ahead an' sit." Pointing to the pews, he said, "You can do a little readin' or prayin' while you wait for the service to start."

Isabelle stared at him in amazement. He found pleasure in mopping? What an odd sort of man. . . . Then, realizing her jaw hung slack, she clamped her lips together and moved forward, lifting her skirt slightly to avoid dragging her hem through the wet spots. She seated herself at the end of a pew near the back, across the side aisle from a black iron vent.

Allowing the Bible to flop open in her lap, she leaned over the book, hoping she gave the illusion of reading so he wouldn't suspect she was listening to his cheerful whistle as he cleaned up her mess.

CHAPTER THIRTEEN

After much fumbling in the Gallagher Bible, Isabelle managed to locate the section the minister was reading. It was about Jesus calling Lazarus from the grave days after his death, and it made her wish the same could happen for her parents.

Sadness washed over her, and she glanced around the simple sanctuary in an attempt to dwell on something else. The man who had offered her his jacket that morning sat in the pew directly behind hers, at the opposite end. The rapt interest on his face captured her attention.

She'd seen him slip into that spot just as the minister stepped behind the lectern. Another few seconds, and he would have disrupted the start of the sermon. A niggle of remorse had struck at his last-minute arrival; she hoped his time conversing with her hadn't put him behind in his duties. At the Drumfelds', any delay in finishing assigned tasks resulted in a temper tantrum by Mr. or Mrs. Drumfeld, the butler, or the cook. The man in the pew, however, did not appear stressed or unhappy.

His interested, intelligent look contrasted with his otherwise common appearance. Despite the morning hour, he already possessed a light shadow on his cheeks and chin, as if shaving had taken place many hours ago. Plain brown trousers, a white shirt with no tie, vest, or suit coat to cover it, and brown work boots made up his Sunday attire. Isabelle considered the three-piece pinstriped and tweed suits worn by the cologne-scented men in Kansas City who attended Sunday service. Hadn't Papa always said the clothes made the man? Perhaps no one had ever mentioned that to this man.

Still, she supposed if his duties were to keep things clean in the chapel, his clothing was appropriate for the task. It did seem, however, that a suit coat would not be amiss. The other men in the congregation at least wore two-piece suits with a tie, and a few had vests. She wondered if this man's garb reflected a casual attitude toward convention or if he simply did not have the funds to purchase a suit.

With a start, Isabelle realized she now had limited funds for clothing, as well. When the year of mourning was over, she would need to rebuild her wardrobe. On the meager salary she received as a servant, she would no doubt be forced to dress simply, too.

Suddenly his gaze shifted, meeting hers. Her face flooded with heat when he offered a gentle upturning of his full lips. Turning forward, she did her best to stay focused on the minister for the remainder of the service. After the final prayer, she fell into the line of parishioners passing by the minister. When she reached him, the minister greeted her warmly.

"Good morning. I don't believe we've met. I'm Reverend Leonard Shankle."

"Isabelle Standler." The other name—Molly Gallagher—haunted her thoughts, but she knew even if she came to believe Randolph's claim about the origins of her birth, she would never be able to think of herself as anything other than Isabelle. Molly Gallagher seemed a stranger, a stranger Isabelle had no desire to know.

Reverend Shankle smiled warmly. "It's so nice to have you with us at Lyndon Hill Chapel, Miss Standler. I trust you enjoyed the service?"

Isabelle offered a demure nod. "Yes, sir." Several questions pressed her mind, most notably how a man who had been dead for several days could emerge from a grave, but she set the questions aside. She could read more from the Bible when she returned to the Drumfelds'. She had little else to do for entertainment.

"Do you live nearby?"

Shame—and anger—washed over her as she considered her humble attic space, so different from the lovely bedroom back home. Instead of answering, she posed a question of her own. "Do you know of a small apartment or cottage available for rent? My current dwelling is . . . unsuitable, yet I'm unfamiliar with the area."

The minister nodded. "As it happens, my brother Albert owns several rental properties in the city. I'm certain he would be able to assist you. What are your needs?"

Isabelle swallowed the laugh that threatened. Her needs were well beyond her means. Or, perhaps, she corrected herself, her *wants* were well beyond her means. She had learned, against her will, how to live simply in the past weeks. "My . . . needs . . . are modest. Something . . ." She licked her lips, seeking appropriate words. How did one delicately admit financial woes?

Suddenly a voice from behind Isabelle interjected, "Cheap?"

Her cheeks filling with heat, she spun to face the speaker. A portly man in his midfifties stood at her elbow. He stared directly into her eyes, his broad face friendly.

"Miss Standler," Reverend Shankle said, "please meet the Rowleys—Ralph and Helen."

A short, round-faced woman angled around Mr. Rowley to take Isabelle's hand and give it a squeeze. Her face beamed in a sweet expression of hello.

Reverend Shankle continued. "They own Rowley Market on the corner of Parks and Second. Have you shopped there?"

Isabelle faced the minister again. "I've only been in Shay's Ford a few weeks. I've done little exploration."

"You have employment?" the minister asked.

Her parents would have considered his question inappropriate, yet looking into his open, honest face, Isabelle realized he did not intend to be offensive. "Yes, sir, but the current situation is . . . unpleasant." That seemed an understatement considering the verbal abuse heaped upon her by the staff members. Yet she would not lower herself to sharing something so personal with strangers—not even a man of the church.

"I see . . ." Reverend Shankle scowled thoughtfully. "Perhaps—"

"Reverend?" Mr. Rowley held out a big, calloused hand. "My missus an' me have that room in the back of the shop we've let workers use before. Mary moved out a week ago when she and Tim married. So . . ." His gaze flitted briefly to Isabelle. "Maybe the little miss could live there?"

Reverend Shankle's eyes lit. "That could be a good solution for you, Miss Standler. A young woman alone in the city is not the best situation." He looked pointedly at her black dress. "I assume you are alone?"

How that question stabbed! Swallowing, Isabelle managed a brief nod.

A sympathetic smile crossed the minister's face. "Staying in the market would ensure some chaperonage since the Rowleys reside in the upper floor of their business. You wouldn't feel quite so alone."

Tears stung her eyes at the man's kindness. The lump in her throat kept words from forming.

Mr. Rowley clasped his rough hands across his thick middle. "With Mary's leave-takin', we also have need of a hand."

Isabelle looked from Mr. Rowley to Mrs. Rowley. Though simple in appearance with their worn yet clean clothing and gently lined faces, they seemed an honest couple. And ever so much kinder than the Drumfelds. Her parents would be appalled to learn their Isabelle was working in such a menial position as shopkeeper, but it couldn't possibly be any lower than that of house servant. *Oh, Mama and Papa, how I wish you were alive and things were as they have always been. . . .*

Forcing aside the bubble of sorrow that threatened to reduce her to tears, Isabelle interjected as much enthusiasm as she could muster into her voice. "I greatly appreciate your kind offer, Mr. Rowley. When . . . when might I be able to assume the position?"

The man looked at his wife, his wide shoulders rising in a shrug. She smiled and gave a nod. He turned back to Isabelle. "Soon as you need to. Tomorrow, if you'd like."

Tomorrow! Isabelle's head spun. Never would she have anticipated such a quick turn of events—and all because she answered the tolling of a bell! Clutching the Bible, she said, "Thank you. I shall make arrangements immediately."

The minister laughed, the sound filled with delight. "It seems Albert won't be needed after all."

The couple joined Reverend Shankle in a brief chuckle, and then Mr. Rowley spun around, cupped a hand beside his mouth, and called, "Aaron!"

From the end of the line, the man who had earlier directed Isabelle into the sanctuary trotted to the older man's side. "Yes, Pop?"

Mr. Rowley beamed. "Miss Standler, here, is goin' to come work at our market. She's takin' Mary's place. You go on with her now an' help her gather her things." He turned another bright smile on Isabelle. "This is our son, Aaron. He'll carry your things to the market for you."

Isabelle swallowed. This man . . . was the Rowleys' son? She gaped at the tall man—at Aaron Rowley—while her mind whirled.

Aaron tipped his head to the side, his lips twitching. "That all right with you, Miss Standler?"

Willingness to please shone clearly in his eyes. Although she little understood such desire to assist a stranger, and although it shamed her to have anyone see the room in which she currently resided, she knew she would require assistance. She owned very little, thanks to Randolph's insistence that she leave her belongings behind, but her only means of transport was her feet. In the rain, even a distance of a few blocks was unpleasant—as she had discovered this morning making her way to the chapel.

She took in Aaron's broad shoulders and thick-muscled chest. If Mr. Drumfeld created a scene, Aaron's mere presence should be enough to keep him from coercing her to stay. Aaron Rowley would be of help in more ways than one.

Swallowing her pride, she said, "I would greatly appreciate your assistance. Thank you."

CHAPTER FOURTEEN

Maelle
Near St. Peters, Missouri
March, 1903

The breeze coming off the Mississippi River sent a shiver down Maelle's spine. Shifting the reins to one hand, she folded the collar of Richard's brown tweed jacket up around her jaw. The jacket was still a bit damp from yesterday's rain, but it provided more warmth than no jacket at all.

She glanced to her right, smiling at the beauty of the wide, smooth river. Richard's normal route through Missouri started in Kansas City and cut east. But Maelle had now experienced a new view of the Midwest by traveling north from Arkansas. Keeping the Mississippi in her sights, she'd known she would encounter Missouri eventually. And she was right—four days ago she crossed the border. She'd been pushing Samson hard, only pausing long enough in the towns she encountered to ask whether anyone knew Mattie or Molly Gallagher rather than staying over to solicit photograph opportunities. There'd be time for that once she reached her destination. Of course, other than Missouri, she hadn't quite decided on her final destination. She shrugged. She'd know it when she saw it.

The song of the river filled her ears, and she gave Samson his head, leaned back, and absorbed the sight. Over the past week, she'd seen plenty of paddleboats and barges on the water, but this morning no boats were in sight, giving Maelle an uninterrupted view of the "mighty Mississipp'," as Richard had called it. Just as it had when she glimpsed the river for the first time from the high seat of Richard's wagon as a child of nine, the breadth and beauty of the river created a fullness in her chest. Back then, the sensation had made her feel small and insignificant; now it filled her with a sense of God's presence.

"What a good job you did in creatin' that river," she said, allowing a hint of her long-forbidden Irish brogue to creep through. As always, Samson perked his ears at his mistress's voice and released a soft snuffle of acknowledgment. Maelle laughed, lifting her face to the sky. "See, God? Even Samson here is agreein' with me!"

Traveling alone often brought waves of melancholy, but on this particular morning she felt far from dismal. Who could be gloomy on such a glorious day? Overhead, fluffy clouds floated lazily in a brilliant blue sky. The early spring rain had ignited an abundance of fresh scents as well as brought a touch of green to the landscape. If she squinted she could make out tiny buds on the tips of bare trees. It wouldn't be long before wild flowers would be making an appearance.

Some people would scoff at her appreciation for nature's beauty, given her mode of dress. Yep, the britches certainly hid her feminine side. But skirts got in the way of her work. To get the best angle on a picture, sometimes she had to trek over rough terrain or climb on a ladder or get into an unusual position. Trousers were better suited to her job. And, she thought with a shudder, they were safer.

Beneath the male trappings, Maelle held the womanly dreams of a home, a husband to talk with and work beside and pray with when things got tough, children . . . But she no longer believed those dreams would come true. There would be no husband in her future. No husband . . . and no children.

At the thought of children, images of Mattie and Molly tried to appear in her mind, but the passing of years had dimmed the edges until all that remained were fuzzy pictures of a nondescript little boy and red-haired baby girl. A pang of guilt accompanied the realization that she'd lost the memory of her siblings' faces—Da had instructed her to look after the wee ones, but she'd failed him.

Other pictures crowded her mind—of other children she'd encountered in her travels. How many photographs had she taken of children hiding their sad, hopeless situation behind a forced smile? Each time she'd tried to coax a genuine smile, she'd thought of her brother and sister and prayed the same despondency didn't exist in their eyes, wherever they were.

Suddenly, from the bushes along the riverbank, a bird burst into song. Maelle's heart gave a leap at the happy notes of praise. She pushed the negative images away. She didn't want to dwell on anything gloomy today. Not on this gorgeous spring day with the beautiful Mississippi guiding her through the state that represented homecoming. Today she would smile and sing and laugh.

Shay's Ford, Missouri

"Whoa, there, Samson." Maelle pulled back on the reins, bringing her wagon to a halt. The sight of a sizable crowd gathered in the center of the Shay's Ford City Park created a tingle in her scalp—a signal she had learned to heed. There was a photograph waiting here.

Hopping down, she brushed the travel dust from her tan trousers and marched to the rear of the wagon. Her box of blank plates and her camera were at the back, ready for quick use. She set them on the ground, took a moment to fasten the padlock that secured the wagon, then scooped up her gear and headed across the grass.

The crowd congregated beneath a towering elm tree that provided dappled morning shade. As she neared, Maelle picked up bits of the introduction being shared by a short, balding man who stood on a wooden platform with his hands raised high. " . . . originates from our own fair state . . . earned degree from . . . esteemed lawyer . . . so without further ado, I present Mr. Jackson Harders. Please offer your warm welcome."

Applause from indifferent to enthusiastic broke out from various areas in the crowd. Maelle listened with half an ear while she scoured the area for a good place to set up her camera.

"Thank you, ladies and gentlemen, for your attention and your concern. As you know from recent newspaper accounts, the number of impoverished in Shay's Ford is becoming alarming. . . ."

Maelle, her gaze wandering, thought it couldn't be worse than any other city—and she'd certainly seen her fair share of cities over the years of traveling with Richard. She spotted a slight incline in the landscape to the west of the crowd. It would provide a natural perch for her camera. Giving a satisfied nod, she trotted to the spot and set up the tripod.

"Many of these impecunious souls are children, left to fend for themselves in a harsh, ruthless, apathetic world. . . ."

Maelle nearly rolled her eyes at the man's dramatic presentation. She peered through the viewfinder, adjusting the camera box until she could see the speaker's face above the heads of the gathered crowd. She slid in a plate and took the shot.

" . . . six years old, yet working ten hours a day to bring home less than fifteen cents for his endless, daunting efforts. . . ."

Maelle propped her arm on the camera box, smiling to herself. She'd give this Jackson Harders one thing—he knew how to milk a crowd. Several people shook their heads in dismay, a murmur of protest rolling like a wave across the group.

" . . . must be done to salvage these children's childhoods. They should be in school, receiving an education. Education, not employment, is key. These children must be given the opportunity to discover ways to better themselves so the cycle of poverty might be broken!"

To one side of the group, applause broke out. Maelle quickly put in a second plate and focused on one man who stood with arms crossed, a scowl on his face, while those around him cheered. After taking the shot, she leaned on the camera, watching the sullen man as the speech continued.

"Legislation is needed to change the laws pertaining to child labor. Right now, in the state of Missouri as well as the majority of the states in the Union, it is perfectly legal for children to spend their days in backbreaking labor rather than at a school desk. What kind of future awaits these unfortunate boys and girls as they enter adulthood without a proper education?"

Maelle shifted her shoulders within the loose bounds of her chambray shirt. The words "proper education" struck hard. Her education was far from proper, but at least she could read, write, and cipher thanks to Richard's tutelage. Many of the children this man referenced could not. He was right—what kind of future would they have?

"I need your signatures on this petition to change the laws that dictate the number of hours these youngsters can legally spend at a place of employment in our fair state of Missouri. With your support—"

"Now wait a minute, mister." The man with the crossed arms stepped forward.

Maelle got another plate ready, just in case an altercation broke out.

"Before anybody signs anything, I got a question. If you make some law that says children can't work, what's to keep my sons from telling me they don't have to do their chores anymore? You're putting too much power in the hands of children who still need to be told what to do."

An answering mumble rose, and Jackson Harders held up his hands. "Wait, wait. Let's not jump to the wrong conclusion. This legislation has nothing to do with chores assigned by parents in a home. It has to do with children outside of their own homes working like a full-grown adult."

"But will the children know the difference?"

The shrill question came from a thin woman at the edge of the crowd. The panic in the woman's voice amused Maelle. Before she could stop it, her laugh rang out.

Immediately several in the crowd turned, their stares boring into her. Still chuckling, she raised one hand in defeat. "I'm sorry. I really am." Sliding her hands into her pockets, she ambled down from the rise and approached the crowd. "It's just such a funny question. The children knowing the difference, I mean."

"I don't see any humor in it, young . . . woman." The man who'd started the argument looked Maelle up and down, clearly confused by her waist-length hair and feminine voice packaged in trousers and a man's shirt.

Maelle ignored the look and shrugged. "I guess you have to look at it from my viewpoint."

The shrill-voiced lady said, "Which is . . . ?"

The crowd parted, giving Maelle the opportunity to step onto the wooden platform beside the speaker. Although he raised his eyebrows, he stepped back and allowed her the floor.

"The lady over there"—Maelle pointed, and the woman's face turned scarlet—"asked if the children would know the difference. I think what she's asking is, if this legislation is passed, will a child instructed to perform a chore at home understand that the law doesn't give him the right to say 'No, Ma, I ain't gonna do it.'"

A titter of laughter sounded from somewhere in the ranks, followed by a firm "Shh!"

Maelle held out her hands. "Parents, this is what you have to ask yourself. Have you taught your children to respect you? Do they understand being part of a family means contributing to the family, and that means chores? If so, no child is going to point to a law written up by politicians and use it as a weapon against his parents."

Low-voiced murmurs came again, and Maelle jerked her thumb toward Jackson Harders, raising her voice to be heard over the mumbling. "What this man says is true—children all over the country are working in jobs that should be held by grown-ups. I know. I've seen it."

A muscular young man in a snug-fitting pin-striped suit stepped forward. "What have you seen?" The crowd seemed to press behind him, straining toward Maelle like vultures around a fresh kill.

She wouldn't sensationalize it for them. Straight facts—that's all they'd get. She closed her eyes for a moment, gathering her thoughts, images appearing behind her lids. Only these were real-life, full-color, breathing children instead of black-and-white replicas . . .

Picture by picture, she shared what she'd witnessed—small children standing long hours on a cold, damp floor shelling oysters for pennies a bucket, twelve-year-old boys with permanent humps in their backs from leaning over breaker boxes to pick out the lumps of slate that trundled down the chutes with the coal, little girls with missing fingers because their tiny hands got caught in the workings of a mill treadle. . . .

"And then, of course, there are those newsboys who offer their papers on the street corners every day, who go home to a box or an alley corner with no supper in their bellies, to wake before dawn the next morning and begin it all again." Maelle held her audience spellbound. Finally she released a sigh, raising her shoulders in a gesture of futility. "They need your help."

She hopped down from her perch and headed back to her camera with long, sure strides, while behind her Jackson Harders' voice rose again.

"My helpers are passing around the petitions, folks. Do the best thing for these children—sign your name. Give these hapless little workers your voice in our government."

Behind her camera again, Maelle took shots of people signing petitions and speaking in small, animated groups. She reached into her box for another plate and realized there was only one left. Her hand on the remaining glass plate, she heard the familiar voice of Jackson Harders.

"You were an unexpected boon."

Her head shot up to find him standing not more than three feet from her camera, a smile lighting his face. She placed the plate back in the box and straightened to meet his gaze. "I didn't say anything that wasn't true."

"I know. You've certainly done your research." He stood with his weight on one hip, one hand in his pocket. His jacket gapped, and Maelle got a glimpse of a flat vest front stretched taut across a well-toned torso. This was a lawyer who didn't spend too many hours behind his desk.

"Research?"

"Yes. Study for a specific purpose." He pointed at her with a blunt, smooth finger. "Your anecdotes perfectly matched my own reading."

She released a huff of laughter. "I didn't read about it, and I didn't go around *studying* those children—I just happened to be there while they were working, and it isn't the prettiest thing to see." She lifted her brows, giving a one-shoulder shrug. "But I gotta say, you're the first fancy pants I've found who really cared. That's in your favor."

He grinned, one side of his lips tipping higher than the other. His dark eyes sparkled. "Well, I'm pleased to know I find favor."

She frowned. "Don't let it go to your head."

He laughed out loud.

Turning away from him, she put her hand on top of her camera. "I've got one slide left. Would you like your picture taken? Just a follow-up to the others I shot this afternoon."

"I noticed you snapping away back here. What, may I ask, are you planning to do with the photos you took?"

"Hopefully talk the newspaper into buying them for use in a feature story."

Jackson heaved a sigh. "I hope they will, but so far no one's given this effort a great deal of attention."

"Well, as I said, one left . . . You can get your picture taken or not."

Jackson stroked his chin, examining her as if seeking hidden motives. "May I invite others to join me in that picture?"

"Sure." Maelle lifted the plate and got her camera ready.

Jackson turned his back on her and cupped his hands beside his mouth. "Aaron! Petey! Would you come here, please?"

The husky man who had asked Maelle to share what she'd seen removed himself from a small gathering. He held out his hand to a little boy with thin cheeks, shaggy blond hair, and enormous blue eyes, and the pair joined Jackson.

"We're going to have our picture taken by—" Jackson turned a puzzled expression in Maelle's direction. "I didn't get your name."

"You can call me Mike," Maelle said.

"Mike?" The tone used by the young lawyer indicated amusement. "And that is short for . . . ?"

"Michael."

Jackson's laughter boomed. *"Michael?"*

Being laughed at normally offended her, but Maelle fought a smile. She sensed no insult was intended. "My uncle wanted a boy, so he called me Mike."

The other man—Aaron—said, "Well, Mike, you did us a great service here today. We got twenty-two signatures!"

"That's wonderful!" Jackson clapped Aaron on the back. "So a photograph is a perfect way to celebrate our success." Looking at Maelle, he held out his arms in query. "Where do you want us?"

Maelle rounded the camera and took control. When it came to shooting people, Richard had taught her composition was everything. Balance. Shadows. Filled spaces and open spaces. All of these ideas flitted through her mind as she angled Jackson so the sun glinted off his raven hair and brought out his chiseled features. Pointing to a spot in the grass, she instructed Aaron and Petey to position themselves opposite Jackson, as if prepared to engage in conversation, with little Petey in the center of the group.

Rather than having the trio look at the camera, she put a petition in Jackson's hand and said, "All of you, look at the paper." When they followed her direction, she smiled in satisfaction.

The contrast of white paper against the framing background of dark clothing pleased Maelle's artist-eye, and she snapped the shot without another word. Slipping the plate from the camera, she put it in the box with the others. Then she picked up her camera and headed for her wagon.

Footsteps pounded behind her. "Wait! Wait!"

She didn't slow her pace, just glanced over her shoulder. "What?"

Jackson Harders charged to her side. "I didn't get a chance to find out where I can retrieve my finished photograph."

Maelle stopped. "Maybe you can help me with that. I need to park my wagon somewhere. I sleep in it."

His gaze went briefly to the boxy enclosed carriage with *Watts Photography* painted on the side. "That's your home?"

Maelle gave a shrug in response.

He stroked his mustache with two fingers. "You're welcome to park it behind my office building. There's an alley that doesn't get much attention. No one will bother you. If you need water, I can give you a key to the back door."

Maelle backed up a step. "You're awfully trusting with someone you've just met."

"Well, I don't make that offer to just anyone, but . . ."

She tipped her head. Her braid swung across her shoulder, and she pushed it back with a flip of her wrist. "But?" she prompted.

He met her gaze. "But I believe you're trustworthy. As a lawyer, I've learned how to read a person's character by looking him in the eyes. I'd bet my last dollar you won't let me down."

Traveling with Richard, never making friends, always being looked at as an oddity with her strange mode of dress and gypsy way of living, she'd never heard such kind words. She cleared her throat. "Well, you're right. I'm not a thief. And I appreciate the offer." Taking in a deep breath, she asked, "So . . . where's your office?"

He pointed to the towering brick building where she'd parked her wagon. "Here."

CHAPTER FIFTEEN

Molly
Shay's Ford, Missouri
March, 1903

A strange buzzing sound crept through Isabelle's mind, rousing her from a restless sleep. Eyes still closed, she scrunched her brow and listened, attempting to recognize the odd noise.

Over the past several days, she'd become accustomed to the mournful call of foghorns, the street noises, the clanking pipes, and the scurrying feet of little creatures in the storeroom beside her tiny bedroom. But this sound—an odd whistle offset by a discordant buzz—was new. The only correlation she could find in her memory was the grinding of chain gears on an elevator.

There was no elevator in Rowley Market.

As she tried to reason another source for the sound, something moved at the foot of the bed, bumping against her toes. A rat? Her eyes popped open and she sat upright. Blinking, she stared at a lump not made by a rat, but something much larger—a shifting lump, with appendages flopping in various directions. The whistle-buzz emanated from the lump.

Her sleep-fuzzy brain awakened in a burst of terror. Some sort of animal had found its way to her bed and now slept at her feet! Isabelle let out a screech and curled herself against the iron headboard, the blankets crushed to her chest like a shield.

The creature's appendages—four of them—shot straight outward from its body, and it released a yelp. Then the creature seemed to pull itself together and sit up, and finally Isabelle's eyes adjusted enough to the murky darkness to make out a head, body, arms, and legs. The creature was a child!

She nearly melted with relief. But what was a child doing in her bed?

"Who're you?"

Had she heard correctly? Was this child questioning her? Tugging the blanket to her chin, she assumed a haughty tone. "Who am I? Perhaps you should explain who you are!"

A hand came up to scratch the head. "I'm Petey, o' course."

Although Isabelle was greatly relieved she wasn't under attack by a wild animal, she still resented the interruption of her sleep. Her words snapped out. "And what are you doing in my bed?"

The little head tipped. "Sleepin'."

At that moment the door flung open and light spilled into the room, illuminating both Isabelle and her uninvited guest. In the yellow glow from the lantern, she now saw that Petey was thin, blond-haired, and had a spattering of freckles on his dirty face. When he scratched his head again, she emitted a huff of worry. No doubt this scruffy child was infested with lice, and now her bed would need to be completely deloused. What a chore!

Turning to the holder of the lantern, she launched a complaint. "Mr. Rowley, I was not aware my bed would be a stopping point for street urchins. I've had quite a fright."

Instead of addressing her, Mr. Rowley aimed his gaze at the boy. His round face shone with pleasure. "Petey, the missus an' me have been prayin' you'd come back. Where've you been, son?"

Isabelle gawked as the child sprang from the bed and raced across the short expanse of floor to wrap his skinny arms around Mr. Rowley's bulk.

"I got stuck on the other side o' town. Ol' Blackie snatched me up, but I wiggled away. Come back here. I can stay, right?"

"'Course you can!"

As touching as she found the reunion, Isabelle worried about the quick agreement. *Where* would this child stay? Not at the foot of her bed!

"We'll fix you up a little pallet in the storeroom."

Isabelle sighed, relieved. From the looks of the child, he'd fought off worse things than rats. He'd do fine in the storeroom.

Mr. Rowley turned his attention to Isabelle. "Miss Standler, I apologize for Petey slippin' in on ya. I'll see that he don't bother ya again. An', Petey"—he raised one eyebrow as he looked at the child—"you spread the word that no others are to come creepin' in here an' botherin' Miss Standler. Tell 'em the sleepin' room is closed."

The child nodded, his smile bright. "Yes, sir, I'll tell 'em!"

Isabelle shook her head. How many people had access to this room? She would need to spend a bit of her earned money and purchase a lock for the door. The fragile sense of security she'd built in her few days here was now shattered, thanks to the intrusion of one small street urchin.

"We'll leave you to get back to sleep, Miss Standler." Mr. Rowley nodded his head in her direction. "Come along, Petey." Holding the child by the hand, he slipped out and closed the door behind him, sealing her in darkness.

Isabelle lay back against the single pillow and flopped her arms outside the blankets. Although tired, she couldn't get back to sleep. Worry that someone else might come sneaking in while she slept kept her eyelids wide open. She stared at the ceiling and listened to the mumbled voices of Mr. Rowley and the child, scraping sounds of boxes being dragged across the floor, and finally the click of a door latch. Shortly, the same whistle-buzz that had wakened her came again, muffled by the plaster-and-lath wall separating her room from the storeroom.

She sighed. How she wished the child would cease his annoying snore so she could sleep. Lying awake gave her too much time to think. And thinking always led to sadness. Which led to anger.

Her days, thanks to the Rowleys' offer of employment, were full, busy, and less discordant than those spent in the Drumfeld household. No one scolded or criticized. Even when she made mistakes, such as dumping a fifty-pound sack of potatoes onto the floor, Mr. Rowley merely laughed and helped her put things right again. These employers were certainly different from the Drumfelds, and Isabelle appreciated their gentle spirits.

But as much as she liked them, she still wished desperately she were at home in Kansas City with Mama and Papa. How she missed the life she had left behind, and her heart still ached for her parents. Parents . . .

As had happened too frequently in the past weeks, the thought of parents immediately led to the Bible and the names penned inside the cover. Was it possible Angus and Brigid Gallagher were her true parents?

"No!" She moaned the word aloud. Reginald and Rebecca Standler were her parents. Wouldn't Mama have told her if it weren't so? Of course she would have! Isabelle could not understand where Randolph had secured all those false documents and the Bible, but she would never—*never!*—believe she was anyone but Isabelle Rebecca Standler, child of Reginald and Rebecca. And she would find a way to return to her home in Kansas City someday. That was her rightful heritage.

Rolling onto her side, she curled her body into a ball and pinched her eyes closed. The nighttime noises continued, and she pressed the now-familiar sounds to the back of her mind, allowing them to become a dissonant lullaby. Slowly drowsiness took hold, easing her closer to dreamland. But hovering on the fringes of consciousness were the names Angus and Brigid.

❧

"What I don't understand," Isabelle said, lifting a spoonful of oatmeal to her lips, "is why a child Petey's age is creeping around at night, unattended."

Across the table, Aaron released a sigh. "Petey spends days *and* nights unattended."

Isabelle shot him a sharp look. "Days? Shouldn't he be in school?"

"Of course he should!" Mr. Rowley's booming voice filled the tiny kitchen. "But when you don't got parents to provide for ya, ya have to take care of yourself. An' that's what the little paperboys like Petey do. Provide for themselves."

Isabelle plunked her spoon back into the bowl, her appetite gone. "Do you mean to tell me there are more of these children wandering the streets? But why?"

Mrs. Rowley put down her coffee mug and fixed Isabelle with a serious look. "Lots of reasons. Some of them are orphans—their parents are gone, and there's no one to care for them. Some have been put out by their parents—there are more children in the family than the parents can afford, so they push the biggest ones out. That's what Petey says happened to him."

Isabelle's jaw dropped. "Petey? But . . . but the child can't be more than five years old!"

"He's seven," Aaron put in, "but small for his age."

Isabelle shook her head. "Five, seven—either way, he's far too young to be left on his own."

The warm look Aaron sent her made her heart skip a beat. She quickly turned to Mr. Rowley. "Last night when Petey . . . invaded . . . my bed, he mentioned he'd wiggled loose from Old Blackie. What did he mean?"

Mr. Rowley swallowed a bite of cinnamon bun before answering. "Ol' Blackie is a man who lives t'other side of the river. He owns a ferry, but he doesn't work much. Uses it mostly to transport his gang of boys to the city, where they collect rags an' bottles an' do a little stealin' on the side. The boys' efforts feed Ol' Blackie. He's always lookin' to add another to his flock. Petey, bein' new in town, as well as small an' defenseless, probably got grabbed up by some of the bigger boys. His newspaper sellin' would be a good source of income for Ol' Blackie."

Isabelle cringed, envisioning some grimy old man forcing Petey to hand over his wages. And, according to Mr. Rowley, Petey had parents who should be caring for him. It made no sense at all! Her voice sounded shrill as she turned to Mrs. Rowley and asked, "What kind of parent simply pushes a child out the door?"

Mr. Rowley cleared his throat and reached for another bun from the plate in the middle of the table. "Lots of 'em are from immigrant families. They come to America for better opportunities, an' what they find is crowded cities an' jobs that don't pay enough to feed the family. So the youngsters have to get out on their own. Or they go to work, too, an' give the money to their folks to help out. Either way, the little 'uns have it rough."

The word "immigrants" taunted Isabelle. Randolph had indicated she was the child of Irish immigrants. If that were true, and if the Standlers hadn't taken her in, would she have been like one of these vagrant children, selling papers or matches on a street corner to survive? She pushed the thought aside.

"In these enlightened times, children shouldn't spend their days running wild, fending for themselves, or toiling at a job." She sat back and crossed her arms. "Something should be done."

Mrs. Rowley shrugged and lifted her coffee mug for a sip. "Well, there's orphanages, but they can't meet all the needs. We used to—" She jerked, shooting a panicked look across the table.

Isabelle glanced at Mr. Rowley. The man's brows pulled low and his eyes sent a warning to his wife. When she looked at Aaron, he appeared uncomfortable, his head down, his lips set in a firm line.

Her heart pattered. Swallowing, Isabelle prodded, "You used to . . . ?"

Mrs. Rowley seemed to beseech her husband with her eyes. Mr. Rowley gave a nod, and the woman took a deep breath before answering. "For several months we allowed the homeless boys to sleep in the market at night an' gave them a warm breakfast of buns an' coffee or tea."

An odd feeling wiggled down Isabelle's spine. She spoke slowly. "Other than Petey, I've not seen any children here in the market."

Mrs. Rowley sent her husband another sidelong glance before continuing. "Well, Mary never seemed to mind havin' the children underfoot, but we weren't sure about you, so . . ."

Heat filled Isabelle's face. The Rowleys had stopped providing shelter to the children because of her. The moments of panic when Randolph had told her she must go away replayed themselves. It had been horrible to know she had no home— no one who cared. And now, because of her, children who'd previously at least known the comfort of a pallet were sleeping out on the streets.

She pressed her palms to her chest. "I never meant for you to . . . Why would you assume . . . ? Oh . . ." She choked out, "P-please excuse me." And she fled the table.

Closed in her tiny room, she sank down on the bed and fingered the brass lock she'd selected from the market shelves only that morning. She had intended to ask Aaron to install it to ensure her privacy. Suddenly she had the urge to throw the lock across the room. But how ridiculous would that be? It would change nothing for the children.

Rising, she crossed to the little bureau that held her few belongings. On top rested the Gallaghers' Bible. She touched it with trembling fingertips. Biting down on her lower lip, she lifted the cover and slid her finger along the list—Angus, Brigid, Maelle, Matthew, Molly . . . A family. An immigrant family.

According to the documents Randolph had given her from the orphans' home in New York, the Gallagher parents hadn't willingly thrust their children into the cold. The children had gone to the orphanage because their parents had died.

But no! She was *not* Molly Gallagher.

Squaring her shoulders, she made a decision. She was a Standler, and a Standler gave to charity. Hadn't Mama and Papa preached that those who were blessed were duty-bound to share with the less fortunate? These little children who sold newspapers to survive were certainly in need of charity. If no one else was going to help them, she would. She had nothing of value of her own to offer, yet after watching Mama gather items for the destitute, Isabelle knew what to do.

She counted her paces across the room, gaining a rough measurement of the width and length. Standing in the middle of the room, she plotted out the available space. If she pushed her bed and bureau along one wall, it would open up the opposite wall to store boxes of clothes, shoes, bedding, and food staples. She cringed—it would be dreadfully crowded, but she could bear it for the sake of the children.

Tonight she would ready her room, and tomorrow she would begin visiting local businesses. She would also go door-to-door through the prestigious housing districts of Shay's Ford and solicit assistance. People like the Drumfelds had more than enough. It wouldn't hurt them to share. Those little street urchins would have warm clothing, blankets, and full bellies by the time she was finished.

Charging out the door, she called, "Aaron? I need your help."

Chapter Sixteen

Mattie
Rocky Crest Ranch
March, 1903

H ey, Matthew, I thought you was goin' to the cabin."
Matt turned from the ewe he'd been treating to an ear
scratch. Clancy ambled across the hay-scattered floor of the barn.
The openings at either end of the huge barn allowed anyone to
come and go without squeaky door hinges sending an advance
warning of their presence. More than once he'd been startled
by one of the other hands who'd quietly moseyed in.

"Your turn fer church service tomorrow. Carriage leaves
early."

Clancy's reminder made Matt smile. The wiry, leather-faced
sheepman had assumed a fatherly role toward Matt after learning of his orphan status. Matt had grown very fond of Clancy,
despite the older man's crusty tone.

"Oh, I'll be up an' ready." Matt had only attended one worship
service since he'd arrived at Rocky Crest, and that was with an

itinerant circuit preacher. Tomorrow Mr. Harders was driving the distance to Shay's Ford to attend a chapel with his son. Matt looked forward to worshiping in a real church building rather than in the circuit rider's tent. He also aimed to thank Jackson Harders for sending word about Petey. Apparently the little boy had joined up with some newsboys who were allowed to sleep nights at a shop in town and then were given breakfast each morning. It had eased his mind considerably, knowing the boy at least had some care.

"What'cha doin' out here, 'sides keepin' that ewe from sleepin'?"

Matt glanced around the barn, pulling in a deep breath. "Just came out to . . . I don't know . . . relax, I guess. It's peaceful out here." The truth of his statement took him by surprise. Who would have thought he'd find sheep preferable to cattle? Yet the woolly bleaters had grown on him. Rocky Crest had grown on him. He liked Clancy, he liked Mr. Harders, he liked his cabin . . . and he even liked the sheep. Smiling to himself, he turned back to Clancy. "I could ask you the same question. Quittin' time came and went quite a while ago."

Clancy shrugged and sauntered forward to drape his bony elbow over the wooden rail that separated two stalls. "Monday is hoof-trimmin' day. Thought I'd come out, peek at a few feet, get an idea on how many'll need attention."

Matt knew how to shoe a horse but not how to trim a sheep's hoof. He stepped forward, eager to add to his knowledge. "How's it done?"

As Matt had come to expect, Clancy gave a deep bob of his gray head and said, "Lemme show ya." He bent over, lifted a rear foot on the ewe, and rested it between his knees. "See, first you check for hoof rot. Hoof rot can be real contagious, so you have to treat it right away."

Matt nodded. When he'd first arrived, he'd expressed surprise at the open barn. Clancy had explained the lack of doors provided cross ventilation, keeping things more dry, which helped prevent hoof rot. Of course, those wide openings also made it easy for the sheep to take a mind and wander off. A fellow had to keep a close eye on the critters.

He returned his focus to Clancy's tutelage. "How do you know if it's there?"

The older man worked his grizzled jaw back and forth for a moment, as if deep in thought. "Wal . . . there'll be soft spots on the hoof—you hafta cut 'em off. Most likely they'll bleed afterwards, so you follow that up with chloroform to keep it from gettin' infected."

"Chloroform?" Matt crunched his eyebrows. "Isn't that what's used to put people to sleep for surgery?"

Clancy smirked. "Yep. But like lots of things, it's got more'n one use."

"Okay." Matt shrugged. Interesting the things he'd learned from Clancy. "What else?"

Clancy shifted his gaze to the ewe's hoof. "The hoof has to be trimmed at the tip—see how it's stickin' a-way out here? That makes walkin' uncomfortable. So you trim that part off. You also trim the weight-bearin' part of the hoof"—he skimmed his hand along the bottom—"so it's flat. Then you clean around the edges, tuggin' loose any dried grass or thorns. Then you give the ewe a nice pat"—which he did—"and let it go. All done."

Clancy straightened and brushed his palms together while the ewe did a little shifting dance at his feet. "An' now that you know, ya oughtta head on to bed. That ride to Shay's Ford is pert near an hour. Gerald don't hold with leavin' late."

Matt chuckled. "Clancy, I've been risin' early for as many years as I can remember. I won't miss my ride."

Clancy grimaced. "Heaven knows you're a capable man an' I got no need to fuss over ya. But . . ." He rubbed the underside of his nose with a weather-aged finger. "Never had me a family to fuss over, y'know."

Matt's heart turned over at the sincere words muttered in the familiar terse voice. *Lord, thank you for sendin' me here. I do feel at home.*

"Yeah . . ." Clancy's voice sounded distant—even a little sad. His gaze aimed somewhere beyond Matt's shoulder. "All the hands that've come an' gone . . . Fellers just don't seem to cotton to our woollies fer some reason. Makes it hard on a body, gettin' used to someone new all the time. But you, Matthew?" He looked Matt in the eye. "You got stick-to-it-iveness, an' I gotta say I'm proud of the way you been jumpin' in, doin' whatever's asked without complaint. Gerald hired himself a good'un when he hired you."

Clancy's approval made Matt's chest feel as if it expanded. He grinned, backing up and lifting his hand in a wave. "I'll head on to the cabin now. Don't wanna oversleep an' miss my ride to church. See you tomorrow."

Walking through the dusky twilight, Matt sucked deeply of the evening air. Even the smells were different on a sheep ranch, he acknowledged. Sheep were more . . . He pinched his brow, trying to find a description. He settled on musky. Not unpleasant, he realized. *The smell of cows could curl a man's nose hair.* Then again, a person got used to it over time.

Just like he'd gotten used to the sheep.

He entered the cabin he shared with Clancy. A long, narrow sitting room opened into two ten-foot-square bedrooms that each contained a rope bed, a small table for a lantern, and a trunk to store belongings. Nothing fancy, but dry, clean, and all his own.

Matt lit the lantern, closed the door, and stripped down to his long johns. Stretched out on his bed, he stared at the soft shadows dancing on the thick ceiling joists. It was quiet without Clancy's rattling snore coming through the walls. Funny how a person got used to certain sounds. Without the snore, he didn't feel like it was time to sleep.

Sitting up, he reached for his Bible, which waited on the small table beside his bed. Holding the book, he remembered Mr. Smallwood's delight when Matt had shared his decision to ask Jesus into his heart. The old man had embraced him, told him he'd been praying for Matt to do that very thing, then hauled him into the mercantile to buy him his very first Bible.

"You read that every day, Matthew," Mr. Smallwood had said as he'd placed the Bible reverently into Matt's hands, "and you'll grow ever closer to your Savior. You strive to follow Him, and you'll find joy." Flicking the edges of the pages, Matt suddenly remembered a preacher calling Jesus the Good Shepherd. The remembrance stirred pleasant feelings in his chest.

Opening the cover on the black book, he removed a faded photograph. He held it toward the yellow lantern glow to better see the sober faces. Ma, Da, Maelle, baby Molly, and himself, all lined up in front of their little cottage. With a rough finger, he touched each face, the loneliness swelling as it did every time he took out the picture. *Lord, be with 'em, wherever they are.*

He placed the Bible back on the table and propped the creased photo against it.

He eased under the quilt and rolled to his side, facing the table. The coarse sheet covering the straw mattress smelled dusty, but it sure beat a bedroll on the ground. "Dear Lord," he prayed aloud, "thank you that I'm no longer movin' on. Do you reckon now that I'm settled Maelle'll finally be able to find me?"

❧

Maelle
Shay's Ford, Missouri
March, 1903

Maelle held a match to the lantern's cloth wick. The bright flare made her blink rapidly. She adjusted the dial, bringing the flame under control, and then lowered the globe into place. A pleasant yellow glow lit the wagon's interior. With a puff, she extinguished the match and dropped it into a bowl of water. She smiled at the hiss of the match as it hit the soapy liquid.

What a gift Jackson Harders had given her by allowing her access to his office building. Running water less than twelve feet from the back of her wagon! And she didn't have to boil it before using it. Just splash it from the bucket into the pitcher or the washbowl. Her skin tingled pleasantly from the recent bath. How good it felt to be clean.

She drew her finger through the cool water in the bowl, creating swirls in the soap residue. Her imagination took flight, and she envisioned clouds, then creamed coffee, and a man's curling white beard. The thought of a beard made her frown, and she turned from the bowl, wiping her finger dry on her pant leg.

Somewhere in the distance, a bell began to toll. She paused, her head tilted, counting the resounding bongs. Over the week she'd spent in Shay's Ford, she'd become accustomed to the bell tolling out the hours of nine, noon, three, and six o'clock each day. Before she left, she'd have to locate and take a photograph of the bell's source. She imagined a quaint chapel—one bearing a deeply steeped roof, stained-glass keyhole windows, and a high cupola graced by a wooden cross.

Opening a small cupboard, she withdrew a loaf of bread and jar of jam. Her fold-down bunk served as a table when she rolled the pallet aside and perched beside it on a stool. As she leaned forward to smear jam on a thick slice of bread, her hair swung into her way. She caught the thick waves and gathered them into a tail at the base of her neck, nimbly twisting the strands into a loose braid. Closing her eyes, she relished the feel of her fingers in her hair. The auburn locks hadn't felt a scissors' blades in more than a dozen years. If she had her way, they never would.

Her hair temporarily restrained, she ate her simple breakfast in the dim lantern light. Glancing around the shadowy, stuffy space, she once again wished the wagon had a window. Just a small one to let in the morning light and air.

The only opening in the wagon was the back hatch. But opening it exposed the entire interior to the public. When she parked in the countryside, she left the hatch open, but never in town. Even here, parked in an alley, the back of the wagon faced a side street—a busy side street, since it intersected with Main Street. And an open hatch invited curious gawking. So, despite the confined feeling, she kept it closed.

She finished the last bite of her bread and pushed to her feet, prepared to transform her bunk-turned-breakfast-table into a work surface to develop the portraits she'd shot of area families during the past week. Just as she reached beneath the bunk for her box of chemicals, a banging on the back of the wagon startled her.

Frowning, she took the two steps necessary to reach the drop-down door, released the pins, caught the rope, and allowed the door to fold outward a few inches. Buttery sunlight and a sweet-scented breeze poured through the narrow gap. "Who's out there?"

"Jackson Harders."

Her heart lurched. What could he want? "Step out of the way—I'm dropping the hatch." She waited a few seconds before letting the rope slide through her hands until the hatch caught on the side chains. With the hatch fully open, the morning sun nearly blinded her.

She shielded her eyes with her hand and peered down at Jackson, who stood to the side, grinning upward. She scowled. "Have I worn out my welcome?"

His grin faded at her solemn greeting. "What?"

"Did you come to tell me it's time to move on?" A week was about as long as she and Richard had ever stayed in any community, but based on the contacts she'd made in the past several days, she knew she could stay busy here for at least an-other week—maybe longer. According to the townspeople, a photographer hadn't been through in quite some time. If Jackson sent her away, she'd find a camping area close to town.

Jackson removed his bowler and held it against his thigh. "I have no intention of asking you to leave. You may stay as long as you like."

Relief washed over her.

163

He flashed a bright smile. "The photographs you sold to the newspaper, and the subsequent interview the reporter offered me, have generated much interest in my cause to end child labor. You, Miss Mike Watts, are my new hero."

A flutter of nervousness diminished the feeling of relief. His gaze was a bit too attentive for comfort. "Oh. Thanks." The chains groaned in protest as she crept out onto the hatch. "Then, what did you need?" She looked him up and down, taking in his three-piece pin-striped suit and newly polished shoes. Instantly she felt dowdy in her wrinkled shirt, trousers, and unraveling braid.

Slapping the hat back over his dark, brilliantined hair, he grinned. "My father is coming in this morning. Would you like to accompany me to church service?"

Maelle nearly laughed. The idea of attending a formal service certainly appealed to her, but he must be daft to think she'd go with him. "No, thank you."

"Why not?"

His innocent query stirred Maelle's frustration. Her primary reason was to keep her distance from him. But she didn't care to communicate that to Jackson. So she chose an excuse he would certainly understand. Her eyebrows high, she silently gestured to her clothes.

He gave her a glance, and understanding dawned. "Ah . . ." Then he shrugged. "Service doesn't start for nearly an hour. Change."

Change. As if it were that simple. Temptation to go—not necessarily *with* Jackson, but to just go to a church service—tugged hard. Taking in his fashionable appearance, she was certain the members of whatever church he attended would not appreciate having a trouser-wearing female in their midst. She shook her head, strands of hair slipping loose from her braid and tickling her cheeks.

"Sorry, but I have a lot of photographs to develop today. I promised Monday delivery. So . . . I'll stay here." Stooping down, she snatched up the knotted end of the rope. "Enjoy the service."

He opened his mouth to speak, but she stepped into the wagon and gave the rope a firm pull, sealing off his words.

CHAPTER SEVENTEEN

Mattie
Shay's Ford, Missouri
March, 1903

Mister! Mister!"

At the high-pitched voice, Matt turned from the carriage. He recognized the small boy running pell-mell across the churchyard, and he braced himself. Petey threw himself against Matt's legs and clung, his head back, grinning upward. "I never thought I'd see you again!"

"Me neither, partner." Matt stooped down and gave the child an awkward hug, aware of people staring from the sidewalk. Not having been given many hugs, the contact felt alien yet strangely pleasing. He hoped his face wasn't as red as it felt.

Gerald Harders looked on, his lips twitching in a grin. "Who's your little friend?"

Matt pulled loose of Petey's grip. "This is Petey. I—" Should he tell his boss he'd taken the boy from a store in St. Louis?

Mr. Harders might not approve. What he'd done wasn't exactly legal.

Petey, his fingers still gripping Matt's jacket tail, chirped, "He saved me from Dave, an' now I live here, an' I came to church with Aaron an' Mr. an' Mrs. Rowley, but Isabelle—she didn't come 'cause she said she had work to do."

Matt wouldn't have guessed the quiet kid he'd hauled across the state on the back of his horse had that many words in him. Apparently the boy liked being in Shay's Ford. The boy prattled on about storerooms and newspapers and dodging Ol' Blackie. Matt understood little of it, but he listened, his heart light, enjoying the child's enthusiastic report.

"Father!" The eager call interrupted Petey's chatter.

Matt looked up to see two men approach from the chapel porch. One was Jackson Harders. The moment Jackson neared, Mr. Harders stepped forward and embraced his son, delivering several enthusiastic thumps on his back. The sight made Matt's chest feel tight. How many years had passed since he'd known the warmth of a father's arms around him? He turned away to see the man who had accompanied Jackson Harders curl his hand around the back of Petey's neck.

"Petey, it's time to head in and sit down. The service is going to start." Although the words could be considered a command, the man's voice sounded kind.

Petey puckered his face. "Aw, Aaron, I wanna talk to my friend." Pointing at Matt, he added, "He's the one I tol' you about who saved me from Dave."

The man called Aaron sent a brief smile in Matt's direction. "And you'll be able to talk to him after the service. But come on now. We don't want to be late, and you don't want to make your friend late."

For a moment it appeared Petey would argue, but then he sighed. "Okay." Peering up at Matt, he waved. "Bye, mister. I gotta go now."

Petey took Aaron's hand. The pair headed up the sidewalk and stepped into the chapel. Mr. Harders said, "We better head in, too. We'll have lunch following the service and get caught up."

Matt followed Mr. Harders and his son into the chapel, and they slid into a pew just as the minister stepped behind the simple lectern. Reverend Shankle delivered an excellent sermon based on a passage from Jeremiah. Matt listened intently, filing away bits and pieces to chew on later. He liked the idea that God had made plans for His children, and that the plans were to give His children hope.

Hope . . . A beautiful word. He held hope that one day he would be reunited with Maelle and Molly. He held hope that he'd have his own place, his own family. Leaning forward, he listened carefully to the minister's next words.

"How do we discover God's good plans for us? By seeking Him. Just as the Good Book says, we will find Him if we seek Him with all our hearts."

Matt nodded. Sure enough, the moment he'd followed Mr. Smallwood's prompting and sought God, he'd found Him. Now he was a part of God's family—an adopted son, Mr. Smallwood had said. Glancing at Mr. Harders and Jackson, seated side-by-side on his right, he felt a twinge of regret that he couldn't sit in a church service with his father. How he missed Da. . . .

When the sermon ended, he rose for the final hymn and the reverend's closing prayer, and then he followed Jackson and Mr. Harders into the churchyard. People milled in small groups, visiting, and he looked for Petey. But to his disappointment the boy seemed to have disappeared.

Mr. Harders clapped his shoulder lightly. "Shall we go get some lunch?"

Matt faced his employer. "I was hopin' to talk to Petey before we left."

Jackson scanned the crowd. "I don't see the Rowleys. I'm sure Petey went with them. If Father has time, I could take you by their market before you head home. It's likely Petey will spend the afternoon there."

Matt shook his head. "I don't want to hold anybody up. I got to see the boy is doin' well. That's all that matters."

Mr. Harders hauled his bulky frame into the driver's seat of the carriage, and Matt and Jackson climbed into the back. Once they were seated, Matt asked, "How long has Petey been livin' with the Rowleys?"

The carriage hit a rut, bouncing the seat. Jackson grimaced, but Matt wasn't sure if it was due to the road condition or the question he'd asked.

"He's not exactly living with the Rowleys."

Matt frowned. "Then, where is he living?"

Jackson shrugged. "Petey spends his nights at the market. The Rowleys have set up several pallets in their storeroom for some of the street children, and Petey is there nearly every night. He eats one meal at the market each day, but most of his time is spent on the street, selling newspapers."

When Matt had seen the boy walking hand-in-hand with Aaron Rowley, he had assumed the child was being cared for. The realization that he was still without a home generated an uneasy feeling in the pit of Matt's stomach. "He's just running wild?"

"I'm afraid so."

The carriage rolled past the business district, and Matt turned to watch the passing buildings. Despite Petey's cheerful appearance, he wondered if the boy were any better off in Shay's Ford than he'd been in St. Louis. Then he thought of Dave's strap, and he decided at least he wasn't being abused. Turning back to Jackson, he said, "You said the Rowleys take care of several boys like Petey?"

"That's right."

Blowing out a frustrated breath, Matt growled, "Well, at least somebody's tryin' to do *something* to help."

Mr. Harders glanced over his shoulder. "The Rowleys aren't the only ones trying to help the street children, Matt. Jackson here has quite a campaign going to find a way to get those kids off the streets and into school."

Matt shot Jackson an interested look. "Oh yeah?"

Facing forward, Mr. Harders continued. "He wants to change the laws that allow children to work all day. If the laws change, then it will be illegal for people to hire boys like Petey to sell newspapers. He believes the children need to be in school if they're to have any chance for a decent future."

Matt swallowed. A decent future . . . Matt hadn't had much schooling. He'd spent most of his growing-up years working all day. Oh, the Bonhams had sent him to school, but they'd only had him those two years. And there was a little schooling at the orphanage, but after that, Jenks had made sure his days were filled with hard work. And hard knocks.

Without conscious thought, he zipped a glance over his shoulder. Of course Jenks was nowhere in sight. Jackson's voice pulled his attention back.

"As long as laws allow employers to hire children, the childhoods of countless youngsters will continue to be lost. We've got to get these children out of jobs and into classrooms. And we've got to do it now."

Matt nodded thoughtfully. He knew why children were hired in place of adults. Children worked for lower wages, and often they could be bullied into continuing longer hours. During his years with Jenks, he'd rarely gotten more than six hours of sleep a night. Jenks hadn't been concerned about working him to death—he could just go to the orphanage and pick out another worker. But if Jackson managed to change those laws . . .

Mr. Harders drew the carriage to a stop in front of the Riverside Hotel and Restaurant. He set the brake and then turned in the seat to face his son. "We're doing our part, son. We'll make people listen. But for now, let's eat." With a smile in Matt's direction, he added, "You're in for a treat. The cook here sears the best steaks in the state of Missouri."

During the meal, Matt sat quietly while Mr. Harders and Jackson visited. The restaurant's wide windows faced the Mississippi River, providing a beautiful view. The décor inside was fancier than anything Matt had ever seen. But he couldn't really enjoy the surroundings. His thoughts were too jumbled.

He replayed Jackson's words about changing the laws concerning children's labor. What if laws had been in place when he was still a boy? What might he be doing now if he'd had the chance to finish school? Would he still be a ranch hand, or might he be something else—even a lawyer like Jackson Harders? He almost chuckled at that thought. No, being a lawyer meant college. College cost a lot of money, and orphans didn't have money for college.

Money . . . His fork paused on its way to his mouth. It was rich folks who had taken his baby sister away all those years ago. Had baby Molly been given the chance to go to school? Probably. But not Maelle. The photographer had said he wanted an apprentice. He lived in a wagon. Maelle probably hadn't gotten any more schooling than he had. He hoped Maelle had at least been treated okay. The food lost its appeal, and he put his fork on his plate.

"Matt, are you finished?" Mr. Harders' voice cut into Matt's thoughts.

Matt pushed his reflections aside. "Yes, sir. I'm finished."

The older man dropped several bills on the table and rose, sending a smile at Matt. "I hope you don't feel ignored." He flung one arm around Jackson's shoulders and the other around Matt's and began guiding them toward the outside doors. "Jackson and I see one another so seldom since he went away to college, we tend to forget anyone else is around when we are together."

"I'm just fine," Matt assured him, "but I was thinkin' on what Jackson said. About changing the laws?"

The three men paused on the wooden walkway outside the restaurant. A cool breeze that smelled of rain curled around the building, filling Matt's nostrils. The clean, fresh scent seemed to awaken something inside of him.

"I'd like to do my part, too, in gettin' those laws changed. Kids like Petey"—and *Maelle and me*— "they deserve a better chance at life."

Jackson grinned. "I can use your help next month, Matt, if you'll still be at the ranch."

Matt looked from one man to the other. Clancy had indicated Mr. Harders had a hard time keeping hands—the sheep ran them off. But it took no effort to promise, "I'll be around."

"Father is planning to run for a seat in the Missouri House of Representatives. If he's elected, he'll be our voice for the children. But it takes a great deal of financial support to fund a campaign."

Matt raised his shoulders in a shrug. "How can I help?"

The three walked together toward the carriage as Jackson continued. "I'm hosting a meeting in Shay's Ford the eleventh of April to discuss Father's candidacy. I could use an extra pair of hands that day, handing out information and collecting pledges."

Matt nodded. "If your father can spare me, I'd be proud to give you a hand."

Jackson formed a fist and punched the air in excitement. "It should be a rousing meeting! I've invited every influential rancher in the state to attend." He released an exultant whoop before climbing into the carriage. "And nearly all of them have accepted my invitation."

Matt's mouth went dry. Every influential rancher in the state? His hands began to tremble. Then that meant Lester Jenks would be coming to Shay's Ford.

CHAPTER EIGHTEEN

Molly
Shay's Ford, Missouri
March, 1903

Isabelle heard a shuffle outside her door and glanced over her shoulder. Aaron stood framed in the doorway, a wide box in his arms and a helpless expression on his face. She put her hands on her hips and chided, "That box is more narrow than long. Turn sideways and come on in."

With a sheepish grin, Aaron angled his body perpendicular to the opening and eased through. The moment he entered the room, she said, "Set it on top of the one marked *soup*. That will prop it high enough for me to sort through the contents easily."

Aaron followed her instruction. Isabelle's chest puffed up in satisfaction at the stacks of crates lining the wall. Over the past two weeks, she'd worked tirelessly and accomplished a great deal. It gave her heart a lift when she thought about making the lives of the newsboys a little brighter. Aaron's willingness to aid in her efforts had been a great help, too.

Last Tuesday she had convinced him to squire her all through the Lyndon Hill area, holding an umbrella over her head to protect her from the drizzling spring rain while she solicited contributions from every household in the neighborhood. His smile of approval as she'd valiantly presented her case to the wealthy families of Lyndon Hill, arguing the advantages of keeping the children healthy and well fed so the city would not be burdened with medical expenses or losses to thievery, had spurred her onward.

Aaron popped open the top crate on the stack and then turned to face her, brushing his palms together. "Are you finished with me now?"

Isabelle crinkled her brow, thinking aloud. "If that crate of shoes arrives, as Mr. Wallace promised, I shall require your assistance in constructing a shelf where I can arrange them by size. But we can do that tomorrow afternoon."

A scowl marred Aaron's normally placid face. "Tomorrow's Sunday."

"I am aware of that."

"So you're intendin' to work tomorrow instead of comin' to chapel service?"

Isabelle swallowed a sigh. She hadn't gone to a service since the day she'd met the Rowleys and moved into this humble room. Mrs. Rowley had spoken with her about the importance of keeping the Sabbath day holy, but when else did Isabelle have time to herself? "Yes, I'll be working here." She rested the tips of her fingers on the crate's edge and gave a dismissing nod of her head. "But you're free to go, as I have no further need of your assistance right now."

Aaron stood beside the stack of crates, arms folded and eyebrows high in silent query.

Isabelle stared back. "Did you need something else?"

"Well . . ." He scratched his chin. "I was hopin' maybe you'd give me a thank-you."

Her cheeks flamed, and she turned sharply away, biting down on her lower lip. Odd, the feeling of remorse his simple statement created. She hadn't been raised to express gratitude for every act of servitude offered by those in her family's employ, so conveying appreciation made her tongue stiff and awkward. Yet she realized Aaron had given up his free time and often delayed completing his own tasks to assist her. She battled with herself, seeking appropriate words to offer thanks for the endless help he had cheerfully given.

Suddenly he chuckled.

She fixed him with a pointed look. "You find something amusing?"

He leaned his elbow on the top crate. "Oh, I s'pose not. I was just thinkin' maybe instead of you thanking me, I should be thanking you. After all, you've been the busy bee on behalf of our newsboys." His eyes shone with admiration, creating a flutter in her heart. "Why are you doin' it, Isabelle?"

Raising her chin, she answered honestly. "I was raised to understand the duty of caring for the less fortunate."

A frown creased his brow, bringing a hint of apprehension to his eyes. "So you're doing all this"—he swept his arm, indicating the stacks of crates—"out of duty?"

"Of course."

"You do confuse me sometimes, Miss Standler."

She tipped her head, and a strand of hair slipped from its knot to curve beneath her chin. She pushed the errant coil back into place. "I confuse you?"

"Yes. You were working as a house servant when I met you, but you don't act like any servant I've met before. You just said you were raised to look out for the less fortunate, but there are some who would say you're part of the less fortunate, considerin' this room an' the job you've got. So . . ." He lifted his hand in query. "How do you explain all that?"

Aaron's question dredged up unpleasant reminders of how much her life had changed. She set her lips in a grim line and began digging in the crate.

Taking a step forward, Aaron touched her arm. "And why do you only wear black dresses, Isabelle? What are you mourning? The loss of a person . . . or the loss of somethin' else—like a way of life?"

Her gaze jerked to meet his. Heat climbed her cheeks, and she wished she could hide. "You're prying, Aaron."

He stepped back, slipping his hands into his trouser pockets. "I s'pose I am. I apologize if I offended you."

Turning away once more, she sighed. "You needn't apologize. Sometimes I . . . I'm not sure what I mourn the most." Her final words came out in a pained whisper.

"Isabelle . . ."

Before he could ask anything else, she took in a quick breath, clapped her hands together, and announced, "Well, I have much to accomplish here. I *thank you*"—she forced a teasing smirk to her face—"for your kind assistance, but as I said, you may go on to your own duties now. I intend to have these long johns organized by size before suppertime. I told Petey to bring every homeless boy in town to the storeroom at dusk so they may each be issued a warm pair."

Aaron headed toward the door. "Well, it's a kind thing you're doin'."

Isabelle, her hands full of long johns, raised her brows at him. "Yes, I know."

Something flickered in Aaron's eyes—not approval, certainly, but something unreadable. Almost a worry. But before she could question it, he stepped out of the room.

CHAPTER NINETEEN

Maelle
Shay's Ford, Missouri
March, 1903

Maelle sat cross-legged just inside the hatch of her wagon and munched her simple lunch of cheese and crackers. Rain fell softly outside the opening, bringing in the odors of moist earth, new grass, and a hint of fish. The rain had held off until she'd finished her morning deliveries of portraits—the last pictures she intended to take in Shay's Ford. From the looks of the gray sky, the rest of the day would be wet, which didn't make for pleasant traveling. But for now she was dry inside her wagon, and Samson was dry inside the livery down the street, so she wouldn't complain.

She popped another cracker into her mouth as thunder gently rumbled in the distance, sounding to Maelle like wooden wheels on cobblestone. Moments ago she'd watched Jackson's surrey pull around the corner. Every day since she'd arrived in town, she'd seen him walk to and from the law office. The sight of him in that surrey had drawn her up short. She supposed she should have guessed from his stylish clothes and his position as a lawyer that he was a man of wealth, but it had taken the leather-covered surrey to classify him as rich in her mind.

In her years of traveling with Richard, she'd photographed more wealthy families than she could count. And she'd never learned to like them. Every one of those families reminded her of the callous couple who had snatched her baby sister from her arms and driven away. She scrunched her eyes closed, searching her memory for the name of the family. Shambler? Stamber? She huffed in frustration.

Although she'd determined to remember it, her inability to write it down—and Richard's refusal to allow her to talk about it—had erased the name from her mind. She opened her eyes and stared at the cheese in her hand. She couldn't remember their name, but she remembered their attitude when they'd taken Molly away. Heartless. The wealthy were heartless.

She bit off a chunk of cheese, her thoughts returning to Jackson. He was certainly wealthy, but could she call him heartless? He seemed very concerned about children caught in terrible situations. The speech he'd given at the park had been flowery, but he'd also sounded sincere. And he'd given her a safe place to park, allowing her the unlimited use of his office building. Maybe she shouldn't call him heartless.

Finishing the last bite of cheese, she reached for her jacket. She held it over her head as she slid out of the wagon and walked to the front of the law office, where she could look across the street to the park. Through the light veil of rain, she spotted the wooden platform where Jackson had eloquently lectured his audience. Her memory replayed an image from her viewfinder:

Jackson's fervent face, his brow creased in concentration, his hands raised in supplication. Yes, he certainly cared about the children of whom he spoke. He wanted to make a difference in their lives.

Dashing across the street, she made her way to the rise where she had set up her camera. A smile tugged her cheek as she remembered the grumpy man and the shrill-voiced woman. It had felt good to stand on that wooden stage and let them know how ridiculous they were being. If they'd seen what she'd seen over the years, maybe they'd set their petty concerns aside and join Jackson in his fight.

"Take care o' the wee ones."

Her pa's voice from long ago still echoed through her heart. Maelle closed her eyes for a moment, battling the tears that always accompanied the memory. Hadn't she tried to take care of the wee ones? How many fights had she gotten into, protecting smaller kids from bigger ones? She hadn't kept count, but surely she'd set some record for pounding bullies into the dust. Richard never approved of her fighting—especially after he'd discovered her true gender—but she'd felt obliged to follow her father's last directive.

Now Jackson's words seemed to be pulling her into another battle for the wee ones. A battle with legislation and politicians. She chuckled ruefully. A sock in the nose wouldn't do much good there. It would take something more. It would take many people working together. It would take evidence of the harm being done.

She straightened her shoulders. She had evidence. Photographs. Dozens of them snapped at various work sites across the United States. She'd kept them in one of Richard's discarded cigar boxes and had gotten them out now and then to pray for the children projected on the paper. But now she could do more than pray. She could put the photos into the hands of someone who could use them for a greater good.

❧

Maelle gave Jackson a half hour to settle in before she entered the law office and marched to his door, the cigar box under her arm. Without asking permission from the scowling secretary, she raised her fist and banged on the paneled door.

"Come in." His aggravated voice barked the invitation.

She pushed the door open and crossed quickly to the desk where Jackson sat blotting several ink-splattered pages with a stained handkerchief. "Accident?"

He snorted. "Well, I certainly wouldn't do something like this on purpose."

She resisted the urge to laugh. "No. I suppose not." She tipped sideways to peer at the papers. "Looks like you'll be redoing those."

A noisy breath whooshed out of him. "Yes. As if I have time to redo these. Ah, well . . ." Tossing the handkerchief aside, he leaned back in his chair and crossed his arms. "What can I do for you this dismal afternoon?"

She plunked the cigar box on the desk right in front of Jackson. "It would be better to ask what *I* can do for *you*."

"All right, then . . ." He glanced at the worn box, his lips quirked in puzzled query. "What can *you* do for *me*?"

Reaching across the desk, she flipped open the lid on the cigar box and waited expectantly.

Jackson looked into the box, his eyebrows jerked up, and he sat upright. "Mike . . ." He lifted out the top photograph, which showed a little girl with bare feet and a dirty apron, stretching her tiny hand toward the thread bobbin of a massive machine. His gaze slowly followed the photo as he set it aside; then his chin jerked as he turned again to the box. He reached for another, which showed a boy slumped, asleep, in a narrow patch of floor between machines.

"You took these?"

She nodded. "From Maine to the Carolinas to California . . . My uncle allowed me to practice on whatever I chose as he taught me to use the camera. Since I was a kid, I picked kids to photograph."

He held up a picture of a row of young boys leaning over some sort of chute and tapped the photo with the backs of his fingers. "Breaker boys?"

Maelle gave a grim nod. "They sit there all day, watching the coal come out of the chutes. Their job is to pick out the rocks. Somewhere in that box is a picture of a foreman striking one of the boys on the back with a club because he dared to take his eyes off the box and stretch." She didn't mention the same foreman had chased her away, waving the club.

She shook her head, staring at the picture. "Can you imagine sitting like that for ten hours at a time? Some of those kids have permanently humped spines from it." With a shrug, she added, "But at least those boys are in the fresh air. A lot of kids work inside the mines, inhaling coal dust. That's a lot less healthy than a curved spine."

Jackson looked at every picture, clear to the bottom of the box, then leaned back and stared at her in wonder. "These are unbelievable. And I thought our little newsboys had it rough! But this . . ." He gestured toward the stack of photographs. "This is beyond imagination. Children should not spend their childhoods like this."

"I agree." Maelle rested the heels of her hands on the edge of the desk. "I spent my childhood working as my uncle's apprentice. But I had it good—I was never overworked or mistreated. He taught me to read and write, and I learned a trade that lets me take care of myself now that my uncle's . . . gone. I've carted those pictures around for years. I used them as reminders to pray for the kids. But I think you could put them to better use."

Jackson let out a whoop as he came out of his chair. Rounding the desk in three bounds, he captured her in a hug. "You're marvelous!"

Bile rose in her throat. With a cry of alarm, she shoved her palms hard against his chest. He released her abruptly. She stumbled but quickly regained her footing and made a show of adjusting her shirt, refusing to look at him even though she sensed his confused stare.

A few tense moments ticked by while she fingered the buttons of her shirt and he remained motionless beside his desk. Then, finally, he walked slowly behind the desk and stood there, his fingertips resting on the wooden surface.

She lifted her chin slightly and peered at him through her fringe of lashes. "Kindly keep your hands to yourself." Deliberately, she maintained an even, almost friendly tone, but she felt certain the warning came through.

"I apologize. I just wanted to thank you for . . ." His hoarse voice drifted off, and he shook his head. "I didn't mean any harm."

She sucked in a deep breath and released it by increments, bringing herself under control. She offered a nod of acknowledgment before pointing to the scattered photographs. "Will those speak loud and clear to the politicians who need to change the laws?"

Jackson's brows pulled down. "Mike, are you sure you want to part with these?"

His penetrating gaze sent a buzz of awareness down her spine. Backing up, she said, "I'm sure. Like I said, I just used them as a reminder to pray. But those images . . ." She tapped her forehead. "They're in here, too." Along with other images, other memories, that were just as difficult to dislodge. She swallowed. "I can pray without the pictures."

Jackson nodded. Putting the photographs down, he offered a hesitant smile. "Thank you, Mike."

"You're welcome." She turned toward the door. "I best be heading out now. Take care, Jackson, and thanks again for your hospitality."

"Wait!" He started to come around the desk, then stopped. "You're leaving town?"

Her hand on the doorknob, she gave a slow nod. "Yes."

"But you've only been here . . . what? Three weeks?"

"Yes."

"But aren't there more pictures to take?"

Maelle sighed. "Jackson, I live in a wagon because I'm a *traveling* photographer. Well, the time has come to travel."

"But if you leave now, you'll be missing an opportunity to capture history in the making."

His impassioned tone made her pause. "What opportunity?"

He took two steps closer but still maintained several feet's distance. "On April eleventh, approximately thirty ranchers are meeting in Shay's Ford to discuss providing financial backing to a potential new member of the Missouri House of Representatives. If elected, this candidate plans to use his position to change the labor laws of our state to exclude the employment of children."

Jackson snatched up one of her photographs and waved it. "If things go the way I plan, these pictures will be a memento of the past rather than a current-day happening. And you could be the one to record it for history."

The familiar tingle in her scalp signaled her interest. She licked her lips, considering Jackson's words.

Apparently he took her silence for a lack of interest, because he threw his arm outward and implored, "At the very least, wouldn't you like another opportunity to be published in the *Shay's Ford Progress*? You do keep a portfolio of your work, don't you?"

A slight grin trembled on her lips. Jackson would be stunned by her "portfolio." She cleared her throat. "Oh yes. I've made use of several cigar boxes."

Jackson chuckled. "Quite the filing system."

"Simple, but effective."

"And in the meantime," he went on, "surely there are more families in town who could benefit from your services."

Jackson was a good lawyer—he'd managed to change her mind, which was no mean feat. She sighed. "All right, Mr. Fancy Pants. I'll stick around for your meeting. A follow-up in the newspaper would make a nice addition to my cigar box of articles. And there is one section of town I haven't visited yet." *The wealthiest section* . . .

Jackson smiled. Her hand on the doorknob, Maelle nodded toward the desk and the cigar box, which sat open on top of the ink-stained pages. "Take good care o' me wee ones," she said, and then she slipped out the door.

CHAPTER TWENTY

Molly
Shay's Ford, Missouri
April, 1903

Isabelle stared with longing at the remaining bit of cinnamon-laden bread on her plate. The delectable flavor of spices on her tongue made her want to snatch up the last bite and eat it. All of the Rowleys cleaned their plates at every meal. Mr. Rowley even used a piece of bread to mop up any crumbs, leaving his plate looking as though it hadn't been used.

Mrs. Rowley reached for Aaron's empty plate. "Are you finished?"

"Yes, ma'am, and thank you."

Isabelle glanced up to watch Aaron rise and deposit a kiss on his mother's plump cheek. The familiar, affectionate gesture sent a second, more intense spiral of longing through her chest.

Mrs. Rowley then turned to Isabelle. "You done, too?"

Isabelle sighed, giving her plate a little push. "Yes. Your cinnamon buns are the best I've ever eaten."

Mrs. Rowley's hand fluttered at her throat in pleasure. "Why, thank you. Don't you want to finish it?"

Isabelle drew herself straight in the chair and rested her hands in her lap. "My mother taught me that to completely clean one's plate appears gauche and gluttonous."

Mr. Rowley choked on his coffee, and Aaron quickly patted him on the back. Mrs. Rowley's face mottled with red. She smacked Isabelle's plate on top of Aaron's. "Well, around here, dear, we try not to waste food. So don't worry about appearing gluttonous. If the food tastes good and you're hungry, eat."

Isabelle licked her lips, peering at Mrs. Rowley with her head low. "I . . . I shall try to remember."

The older woman's face relaxed into a gentle smile. Setting aside the stack of plates, she touched Isabelle's shoulder. "I'm sorry I scolded. It's clear you was raised a bit different than my scamp here." She sent a teasing grin in Aaron's direction, which he returned with a wink. "We're all learning to put up with each other, and with God's help, we'll manage fine."

Isabelle's lips twitched into a half-hearted smile. "I suppose."

Mrs. Rowley gave a bright smile. "Maybe later this morning, if things are slow, we can come up here and I'll show you how to make the buns. Then, when you have your own house, you can still enjoy them."

Pushing back her chair, Isabelle said, "I appreciate your offer, but I don't see the need. I am certain I shall have a cook to see to the baking in my home." The moment the words were out, she recognized how ungrateful and superior they sounded. Heat filled her cheeks. Sinking back into her chair, she covered her face with both hands and released a muffled groan.

Warm, sturdy arms surrounded her, and Mrs. Rowley's tender voice whispered, "Tell us what's troubling you, Isabelle. We'd like to help, if we can."

Her face still hidden behind trembling hands, Isabelle shook her head. "There—there's nothing anyone can do."

A gentle tug brought her hands away from her face, and Isabelle found herself under the sympathetic scrutiny of the entire Rowley family.

Aaron leaned forward. "Isabelle, why are you in Shay's Ford? What brought you here?"

She straightened in her seat, disengaging Mrs. Rowley's embrace, and fixed him with a fierce glare. "Nothing *brought* me here. I was *forced* here against my will!"

"Forced?" Mrs. Rowley asked. "To Shay's Ford?"

Isabelle grabbed the older woman's hand. "My brother kicked me out of our home after our parents were killed. My fiancé broke our engagement and trundled me away in disgrace. They say—they say I'm not Isabelle Standler. They say I'm an orphan named Molly Gallagher, but I'm not! I tell you, I'm not!"

Mr. and Mrs. Rowley looked at each other. Mr. Rowley shook his head and emitted a puzzled chuckle. "You're gonna have to slow that down a mite. I'm not so sure we follow ya."

Tears flooded Isabelle's eyes. She brushed them away with an impatient swipe of her hand. "I was raised in Kansas City, in the Chesterfield area." From their blank expressions, she could tell they knew nothing of Chesterfield. She offered a simple explanation. "My father co-founded the Western-Continental Railroad."

Mrs. Rowley plunked back into her seat. "Railroad tycoon?" she clucked, pressing a hand to her bodice. "Why, little wonder you carry yourself like a princess."

Isabelle grimaced and hurried on. "When he and my mother were killed in a paddleboat explosion, my brother, Randolph, took ownership of the business. At the same time, he disowned me."

Her chin quivered, but at that moment she couldn't decide if she felt more distraught or indignant. "He gave me a Bible, which originally belonged to a family named Gallagher. Randolph insists I am one of the Gallagher children listed in the Bible's record. He also displayed a packet of papers he asserts prove I was not born to my parents but was taken in as a baby. I'm certain all the documents are forgeries, concocted by Randolph to lay claim to my share of the inheritance, but no one believes me. When my fiancé learned I no longer had my promised inheritance, he cancelled our wedding plans. Then he—" She paused, pursing her lips. "He suggested something immoral in lieu of a marriage." Her chin shot up. "I refused."

"Good girl." Mrs. Rowley gave Isabelle's shoulder an emphatic pat.

Drawing in a deep breath, Isabelle continued. "The only other option given was for me to travel to Shay's Ford and assume the position of house servant for a business associate of my fiancé's father. I had no place to go, so I accepted the position with great reluctance." She shuddered. "It was a deplorable situation. You all saved me from that, but . . ." Tears stung again.

From below, a banging erupted. They all jumped, and Mr. Rowley shot to his feet. "Customers thumpin' the door. Gotta open up."

Aaron started to follow. "I'll help you, Pa."

But Mr. Rowley waved a big hand. "No. You stay here—get Isabelle taken care of. I can handle things for a while."

Aaron sat back down and gave her an encouraging smile. "Go ahead. We're listening."

One tear spilled down Isabelle's cheek. "But I don't belong here." She pressed her palms to her heart, her expression fervent. "I'm certain I'm Isabelle Standler, but the Bible mocks me with the idea that perhaps I'm Molly Gallagher. I miss my home in Kansas City so much it is a constant ache in my heart, yet I can't return to that life until my brother relinquishes his allegation that I'm not his sister. And the only way he'll do that is with irrefutable proof. Yet how do I prove it?" A deep sigh escaped. "It's all so very hopeless."

"It isn't hopeless," Aaron said. "I think I know how you can prove it."

Isabelle gaped at Aaron. "How? How can I prove it? Tell me." She heard the command in her tone yet refused to apologize for it.

Aaron shrugged. "I have a friend—Jackson Harders—who's a lawyer. He could look at those papers you were talking about and figure out if they're real or not."

Isabelle lowered her brows. "You have a friend who's a lawyer?"

"Is there some reason I shouldn't know a lawyer?"

She had insulted him, but that was the least of her worries at the moment. "Do you think he would be available to speak to me today?"

Aaron's frown deepened. "Maybe. But you're working today, remember?"

Isabelle ducked her head. Of course. She had things to do. Her parents had taught her to honor her responsibilities. Regardless of how desperately she wanted answers now, she couldn't simply leave the Rowleys shorthanded.

Her head still down, she admitted, "You're right, Aaron. I am working." She stifled the sigh that longed for release and lifted her gaze. "Perhaps when you see him next, you might inquire about a convenient time for us to meet?"

He offered an approving nod. "Yes, I can do that. I meet with him every Friday afternoon."

Isabelle couldn't imagine what business a storekeeper's son would have with a lawyer—especially business that required weekly contact—but she wouldn't resort to nosiness. Friday was only two days away. She could wait that long. "I thank you." Pushing herself to her feet, she squared her shoulders. "I apologize for burdening you with my personal troubles. I assure you I will not do so again. I will allow this lawyer friend of yours"—she forced herself to smile—"to take care of things from this point forward."

Aaron and Mrs. Rowley exchanged glances. Isabelle was sure she read sadness in their eyes, and her heart contracted with the knowledge of their genuine concern for her.

Mrs. Rowley reached out and brushed her fingertips down the length of Isabelle's arm. "Honey, I have to tell you . . . you need more than just a lawyer."

Isabelle stiffened. She didn't care to be reminded of the number of things she needed. A lawyer, yes—but also her home, her place in her family restored, a return to the life she had led in Kansas City. The warmth of the previous moments swept away, and she opened her mouth to protest the woman's callous remark.

"You need a Savior."

Mrs. Rowley's simple statement sent Isabelle's heart to clamoring, but she didn't know why.

Aaron rose and met Isabelle's gaze. "Isabelle, before you go downstairs, can we pray for you?"

Isabelle stepped away from her chair and took hold of the spindled back. Ministers prayed in churches, and of course Mr. Rowley prayed before meals, as had her own father on occasions such as Christmas or when important guests were present. To pray in the middle of the morning felt uncomfortable . . . yet she did, for some reason, want Aaron and Mrs. Rowley to pray for her.

Aaron walked around the table and stood between the two women. Taking his mother's hand, he offered his free hand to Isabelle. After a moment of hesitation, she placed her hand in his. Then Mrs. Rowley caught hold of her other hand, and they formed a small circle. Both Rowleys bowed their heads, and Isabelle followed suit, closing her eyes and listening as Aaron petitioned the Lord on her behalf.

"Dear Heavenly Father, thank you for bein' a God who cares about all of our needs. Isabelle needs to know the truth of her past. You know the truth, God, so I ask that you help her learn who she is and . . . where she belongs."

Did she hear a catch in his voice? She fought the urge to peek at him, to see if he looked as troubled as he sounded.

"You have a perfect plan for Isabelle's life, God. I ask you to help her find her plan an' then give her the wisdom to follow your leading. Amen."

Isabelle's heart pounded. God had a plan for her life? God cared . . . about *her*? She raised her head and offered Aaron a puzzled smile. "You truly believe God has made a plan for my life?"

Aaron nodded, his expression eager. "'Course I do. Psalm 139 talks about how all the days ordained for us were in His book before one of them came to be. He has a plan for every life."

"He surely does," Mrs. Rowley put in, giving Isabelle's hand a squeeze. "And, honey, He's just waiting for you to recognize He wants what's best for you. That's His greatest desire for all of us—for us to follow His ways."

Isabelle nibbled her lip, her brows crunched in confusion. All of these ideas were so new . . . and strange. It almost felt wrong to think of God dictating where a person should go and what he should do. Yet, at the same time, she yearned for someone wiser to give her direction, to put her on a proper pathway.

She shook her head. "Well, I thank you for your prayer, Aaron." She suddenly became aware that he still held her hand, and she pulled it loose, pressing it to her thumping heart. "But for now, I believe my pathway is the stairs leading to the market. Mr. Rowley can surely use my assistance by now."

Mrs. Rowley clapped her hands to her face. "Oh my, yes! We've left poor Ralph down there alone far too long!" She waved both hands at the pair. "You two go down. I'll get these dishes washed up."

Aaron gestured toward the stairs, and Isabelle preceded him to the lower level, keenly in tune with the sound of his feet on the risers behind her, the gentle swish of his calloused hand on the rail. She recalled the rough calluses against her own smoother palm when they'd held hands to pray, and the fine hairs on the back of her neck prickled with awareness, making her want to hurry her steps and escape the feeling. But at the same time a part of her wanted to slow her pace and more fully examine the sensation. Why was she always so filled with mixed emotions these days? Aaron's prayer—the request that God give her wisdom to discover His leading—tickled her mind. If God answered, where might she be taken next?

She reached the bottom of the stairs and turned the corner to enter the market, allowing Aaron to step past her. She watched him head straight to his father's side, and for a moment she observed the pair, at ease with one another and their tasks.

Never, in all of her growing-up years, would she have envisioned herself in this setting. Yet, despite everything, she had discovered a sense of purpose here—assisting the homeless newsboys. Was it possible God had led her to this place?

With a shake of her head, she pushed that thought away. Randolph's jealousy and Glenn's greediness had been the force behind her coming to Shay's Ford. Nothing more than two men's selfish choices brought about this change in her life. But as she slipped a work apron over her mourning dress, Aaron clinked two glass jars together, reminding Isabelle of the church bell's toll. The sound had beckoned her to the Sunday service, where she had met the Rowleys and been offered a job here in the market. Her hands fumbled with the apron ties. Had God orchestrated that series of events, or was it simply chance? Her breath came in little spurts as thoughts tumbled through her mind. The family had offered her a home and a job, and now Aaron had offered to speak to a lawyer for her—to help her discover a way to regain her home and social status. She might soon be going back to Kansas City!

She finished the bow and smoothed the apron over her hips as she slipped behind the counter. After work, she would read Psalm 139 in the Gallagher Bible.

But when her gaze fell upon Aaron leaning down to hug Petey, who must have slipped in for a cup of coffee, she felt her heart lurch. Suddenly the thought of leaving Shay's Ford lost some of its appeal.

CHAPTER TWENTY-ONE

"I thank ya, miss, for these long johns."

The boy beamed up at Isabelle. The bruise on his cheekbone appeared even deeper in hue now that his face was clean, thanks to Isabelle's scrub bucket and rag. Isabelle watched the boy, who couldn't be more than ten years old, rub his hands up and down the soft cotton fabric covering his thin ribs. The sight of those ribs made her chest feel constricted, and she turned away, speaking briskly. "Yes, well, mind you don't sell them to someone." She'd already heard of two boys letting their fine new clothes go for the price of a dinner. "If you're hungry, you come here to the market. I'll see you're given something."

The boy nodded, his smile showing one missing tooth. "Oh, I won't be sellin' 'em, I promise ya that! First gift I ever got that I c'n remember. I won't be sellin' 'em, no, ma'am!"

The first gift he ever got . . . a pair of long johns. Isabelle followed the boy to an open pallet, thinking about all the wonderful gifts her parents had lavished on her during her childhood.

Had she ever considered how fortunate—how spoiled—she was while growing up? These children made her view the world in a different way, and she wasn't sure she liked it. She determined that even after she returned to Kansas City and her rightful home, she would continue to seek out children such as these and help them.

The boy stretched out on the pallet, and Isabelle draped a thick wool blanket over his lanky form. He yawned, pulling the blanket to his chin. "Thank ya, miss."

Isabelle watched him for a few moments, wondering where he'd gotten that ugly bruise. When she'd asked, he'd changed the subject. Wasn't it enough that he lived on the streets—must he also suffer abuse?

Snores and snuffles filled the room as the nearly dozen boys settled down to sleep. Most of them Isabelle had seen before, and a few, like Petey, were regulars since she'd put out the word about the availability of a warm, safe sleeping room. She recognized Petey, Johnsey, Hank, Anders . . . Her gaze drifted back to the boy with the bruise. His eyes were closed, his mouth hanging slack. Sound asleep already.

She turned to leave and noticed Petey's bright eyes following her. Crouching by his pallet, she resisted the urge to smooth his shaggy hair away from his eyes. There was no sense in getting too attached to any of these children since she would be leaving soon. Instead, she pointed to the new boy. "Petey, do you know that boy's name?"

Petey nodded, his hair flopping with the movement. "Uh-huh. He be Matt."

Matt—short for Matthew. . . . Isabelle's heart set up such a thrumming she found it difficult to breathe. Jolting to her feet, she wished Petey a quick good-night and left the room, closing the door behind her. In her crowded room, she picked up the Bible and sat down on the edge of her bed. She didn't need to open the book to remember the names listed inside the cover.

Matthew Gallagher, born in Dunshaughlin, County Meath, Ireland, in 1880 . . . Where was that boy now? Had he grown up on the streets, too, selling newspapers to survive? Had he been smacked and bruised and forced to sleep in the cold? Had anyone shown him a hand of kindness?

Standing, she paced the narrow slice of floor between her bed and the crates of goods. If she was truly Molly Gallagher, somewhere out there she had a brother and a sister. At least, she supposed she did. According to the documents the Heatons had shown her, the parents had died in a fire. Nothing was said about the children named Maelle and Matthew. They could still be alive—perhaps even together somewhere.

Isabelle stopped in front of the bureau and examined herself in the round, cracked mirror that hung on a nail pounded into the plaster wall. Green eyes, red hair . . . According to the letters penned by Papa, that was why she had been chosen—for her looks. Did that mean her sister and brother didn't have red hair and green eyes?

A sudden desire welled up inside of Isabelle, nearly closing off her throat. It wasn't a new desire. Often, as a child, she'd experienced it when Randolph was particularly unkind. She'd longed for the protective love of an older brother. Would she have had that if she'd been allowed to remain with Matthew?

Releasing a groan, Isabelle threw herself across the bed. She must stop torturing herself. Hadn't she decided she wasn't Molly

Gallagher—that it was a mistake, one which she intended to right?

Suddenly, the words she'd read the day the chapel bells had encouraged her to attend service flitted through Isabelle's mind. *"Thou hast beset me behind and before . . ."* How she wished to know the security of family, of a protector, maybe even of God.

"Who am I?" she whispered to the quiet room. "Are Maelle and Matthew out there somewhere? Do they know about me?"

Although she listened for a long time, no answer came.

♣

Isabelle wove her fingers together and pressed her hands to her lap. Aaron, in the horsehair chair on her right, sat quietly, just as he had while she had explained the course of events that led her to Shay's Ford and employment with the Rowley family. Now they waited while Jackson Harders examined each document by turn, his thick dark brows pulled into a thoughtful scowl. He opened the cover of the Gallagher Bible and slid his finger down the list of names. Isabelle's heart pounded hopefully. Surely her deliverance was near.

Jackson let the cover slip closed, and he set the Bible on top of the stack of papers. He met her gaze and quirked one brow. "Well, Miss Standler, if these documents are forgeries, your brother found an expert to create them. Even the ink in the Bible has the appearance of age, lending credence to the names having been recorded several years ago."

Isabelle's heart sank to her stomach. Her hands began to tremble. "Then you—you believe all of these are authentic?"

201

The ebony-haired man gave a slight shrug. "Well, at first glance, they appear to be in order. I would like to show them to my superior and get his opinion."

Aaron placed his hand over her clenched fists. Although her mother's friends back home might have considered the touch inappropriately intimate, Isabelle welcomed the comfort it provided. She focused on Aaron's work-roughened hand joined with hers and swallowed, fighting the sting of tears.

"However," the young lawyer continued, "regardless of their authenticity, there could be some legal recourse for your abrupt displacement from your home. I would need to see a copy of your father's will to determine whether at least a portion of your inheritance could be recovered."

Bringing up her chin, Isabelle stared at Jackson. "You think . . . even if it's proven that I am not . . . Isabelle Standler by birth . . . I might be able to receive my inheritance after all?" If that were true, she needn't stay in Shay's Ford. She would have money to travel wherever she pleased, purchase a home, and regain her former status as one of the elite.

Jackson held up both hands, palms out. "I don't want you to get your hopes too high. I said there *could be*. It will depend on how the document is phrased." He folded his hands together and rested his elbows on the desktop, fixing her with a querying expression. "Would it be possible to receive a copy of your father's will?"

Isabelle bit down on her lower lip. Would Randolph send a copy? Probably not—he wouldn't wish to assist her in any manner. But, she thought with a rush of hopefulness, her father's lawyer might forward a copy, if he were paid well for the service. Immediately her elation crumbled. She had little money to offer.

Aaron asked, "Isabelle, who would we contact for a copy of your father's will?"

Isabelle once again read genuine concern in Aaron's expression, and her heart turned over in her chest. Even if everything else was falling apart, she had Aaron's friendship. Turning back to Jackson Harders, she admitted, "I am quite certain my father's lawyer would be willing to submit a copy were he given . . . monetary incentive. However, I—" Swallowing, she took in a deep breath. "I find myself with limited financial resources, and I am unable to—"

"Don't worry," Aaron cut in, giving her hands a pat. "We can work something out. Can't we, Jackson?"

Jackson raised his shoulders, his jacket pulling taut. "Certainly. You just need to give the go-ahead, Miss Standler."

Isabelle offered a nod, hoping she didn't appear too eager.

"Very well, then." Jackson slid a sheet of paper and gold fountain pen across the desk. "Write down the name of your father's lawyer, and I will proceed. I believe a telegram would be the quickest means of communication."

Isabelle wrote the name with a trembling hand.

"Now," Jackson said briskly, setting the address aside, "I will confer with my superior and send a messenger when I have his opinion as to the genuineness of these documents. Perhaps I'll have information for you by the end of the day."

Filled with hope, Isabelle nodded. "Thank you very much."

The lawyer rose. "You are quite welcome, Miss Standler. I hope the situation will rectify itself with the proper motivation."

Isabelle looked at the stack of papers on the desk and the Bible prominently on top. Jackson had indicated he needed to show the documents to his superior, but she wondered . . . "May I take the Bible with me?" *I didn't realize I'd formed such an attachment to that little book.*

"Of course." Jackson handed it across the desk. He looked at Aaron. "Will I see you this evening?"

Aaron nodded, his thick hair falling across his forehead. He smoothed the locks back in place with a brush of his hand. "Eight-o'clock sharp."

Isabelle looked from one man to the other. They were such an incongruous pairing. Curiosity swelled, but she kept the questions to herself.

Putting his hand beneath Isabelle's elbow, Aaron escorted her out of the lawyer's office and onto the street. They walked briskly over the boardwalk toward the market, their feet squeaking on the damp wood. The rain that had fallen over the past week had blessedly ceased, and the yellow sun cast its golden light, but the moist ground cooled the air. Isabelle hugged the Bible to her chest to help ward off a shiver.

Aaron glanced down at her. "Cold?" The single word query managed to convey concern.

"I'll be fine," she said, giving him a quick smile. His dimpled grin in return made her heart skip a beat. Confused by her odd reaction, she posed a blunt question. "Are you cleaning for Mr. Harders this evening?"

One eyebrow shot skyward. "Cleaning?"

"Yes." She lifted her skirts slightly as they crossed the street. Aaron's hand cupped her elbow. The brief gentlemanly contact pleased her. "You said you'd see him promptly at eight. Do you clean for him as well as for the church?"

Aaron chuckled. "No. We're workin' together on legislation to get the children off the streets an' into school, where they belong."

"Legislation?"

"Yes. Children like Petey who work all day won't have much of a life if they never learn to read or write. Jackson is tryin' to get legislation passed making it illegal to hire children. He hopes that'll make business owners pay adults a decent wage so they don't need to send their kids out to work, and will put the children in school instead."

Isabelle came to a stop and stared up at Aaron. "I had no idea you were . . . Why haven't you ever said anything?"

"You didn't ask." He touched her arm, his expression serious. "Isabelle, what you've been doing is wonderful. Givin' the children warm clothes, feeding them, providing shelter . . . Those are good things, but they're temporary fixes. If the children are going to care for themselves as adults, they need schooling. That's what Jackson and I are workin' toward."

Isabelle blinked rapidly, absorbing the truth of his statement. He was right—she'd worked valiantly to care for the children, but they needed more than what she'd offered. "It is very commendable, Aaron. Is there anything I can do to help?"

"You really want to help?" He sounded incredulous.

She set her feet in motion and her tone turned tart. "Of course I do."

"Good. You come with me tonight. Jackson will put you to work."

The warmth in Aaron's blue-green eyes gave her the courage to ask something she'd long wondered. "Aaron, I understand why you're trying to help the children. But why are you so kind to me?"

His laugh startled her, and she frowned. "You find the question amusing?" Her cheeks burned as she hurried her steps, weaving past a street vendor and his circle of shoppers.

Aaron caught her elbow again, slowing her down. "Now, don't get uppity on me, Miss Isabelle," he said with a teasing grin. "I just wondered if you thought there was some reason I shouldn't be kind to you?"

Isabelle calmed herself with a deep breath. "I find it perplexing, that's all. Your parents offered me a job when they had only just met me. No matter how many times I blunder, no one ever berates me. And now, knowing that recovering my inheritance and my standing in my family would mean losing an employee, you still assist me." She stopped, peering into his serious face. "Why do you do it, Aaron? Why are you so kind?"

Someone pushed past the pair, forcing Aaron to move closer to Isabelle. His breath brushed her cheek as he answered quietly. "The Bible instructs us to treat others as we'd like to be treated. If I were in need of help, I'd hope somebody would hold out a hand. That's all I'm tryin' to do for you."

But something in his fervent expression made Isabelle wonder if there was something deeper—something more personal—that motivated Aaron. The thought brought another rush of heat to her face, and she shifted her focus to the plaid fabric stretched across Aaron's broad chest. She became aware of the worn leather cover of the Bible in her hands. Standing on the busy sidewalk with Aaron's sweet gaze warming her from the inside out, she held out the Bible and allowed herself to voice another question. "Could you show me where those words are found? I . . . I would like to read them for myself."

Aaron's face lit with pleasure. "Why, sure I would! As soon as we get back to the market, I'll look it up for you."

"Thank you."

Isabelle trotted along beside Aaron, taking a step and a half to each of his long-legged strides. Her skirts swished across the walkway, and she kept her gaze on her toes to avoid stumbling on a warped plank. As they neared the market, Isabelle became aware of a change in the tone of the street sounds. There was a sense of urgency that made her look to Aaron in concern, although she wasn't sure what had prompted the sudden rise of worry.

His brows pulled low and his mouth twisted, Aaron was focused on something ahead, and Isabelle turned to what held his attention. A bustle of activity on the curb outside the market made her heart leap to her throat.

"Aaron, what—?"

His fingers wrapped firmly around her elbow, he propelled her forward. "Come on!"

Isabelle's skirts tangled around her ankles, making rushing impossible. She jerked loose of Aaron's grasp. "Go ahead. I'll catch up."

Without hesitation, he broke into a run, pushing his way to the center of the circle. Even over the other sounds, Isabelle heard his cry of distress. Disregarding propriety, she snatched up her skirts and raced forward, pushing her way to his side. And when she saw what lay on the dirty street, her heart nearly stopped beating.

Chapter Twenty-Two

Maelle
Shay's Ford, Missouri
April, 1903

Maelle pulled back on Samson's reins. A chattering circle of people stood in the street, blocking her passage. Her scalp prickled. Setting the brake, she leapt over the side of the wagon and dashed to the back to retrieve her camera. After her week of portrait shooting, her supply of plates was low, but if she could manage to push her way to the inside of that circle, she might capture one or two worthwhile photographs.

"Excuse me, excuse me," she murmured, crushing the camera to her chest and working her way slowly through the throng. When she reached the center, her throat felt tight, and for a moment she forgot about operating the camera.

A small, white-faced boy lay on the cobblestone street. A gray-haired man knelt on the ground beside him, holding a bundle of rags against the child's leg—a leg that was notably shorter than its mate. A young, distraught couple hovered over the man's shoulder. She read in their expressions the same horror that gripped her, and her gaze returned to the child. He lay perfectly still, his mouth open in a silent cry of agony. Newspapers scattered across the ground identified him as one of the many little newsboys of the city.

Suddenly she realized the opportunity that lay in front of her. Right before her eyes existed inarguable proof of the danger these children faced on the streets. The voices of the crowd faded into the distance as Maelle swung her camera into position. She centered the boy and his benefactor in her viewfinder. But she didn't push the shutter.

The picture, although telling, fell short of expressing the whole story. Her mind raced as she processed the best way to reach the hearts of those who would view this photograph. A close-up of the child's pale, motionless form might repulse some people, but empathy could be achieved by capturing the genuine distress on the faces of the onlookers. She needed a broader view.

"Please . . . back up for a moment," she directed, looking right and left. But no one budged, their focus on the child rather than her.

Someone in the throng yelled, "I hear the ambulance comin'!"

The crowd shifted, people turning to peer down the street. Maelle dashed into a narrow opening between onlookers, aimed her camera, and shot. There was only time for the one picture, but the glimpse through the viewfinder sent a quiver of awareness from her scalp to her toes. If the picture turned out, it would be a masterpiece of emotion.

The child, arms outflung, helpless in the street. The older man, his chin quivering in despair, his bloodstained hands cupping the boy's bloody stump. The younger man, leaning forward, his hands fluttering uselessly over the boy's still frame. And the young woman, her red hair disheveled, tears raining down her cheeks, her fingers covering her lips, appearing to be holding back a scream of anguish. The woman even wore black and clutched a Bible, as if ready for the child's funeral.

She heard the pounding of horses' hooves along with a harsh shout, "Get back!" People scurried from the cobblestone street to the boardwalk, jostling Maelle along with them. She cradled her camera, her focus riveted on the man and boy who remained alone in the street. The crowd, which had been jabbering in nervous excitement, now fell silent, all eyes aimed toward the fast-approaching vehicle.

The moment the horses drew to a stop, two men leapt out of the back of the black enclosed wagon. The men carried a canvas stretcher, which they spread on the street beside the boy. Tenderly yet deftly, they transferred the tiny, unresisting form onto the stretcher. The older man released his hold on the rags as the men lifted the stretcher, but he remained on his knees in the street as if too tired to rise.

The men pushed the stretcher bearing the child into the back of the ambulance and hopped in behind it, closed the doors, and the driver slapped down the reins while calling, "Giddap!" With a clatter of hooves against cobblestone, the horses turned the vehicle in a sharp U and galloped down the street.

The crowd slowly drifted away, muttering in excited tones, leaving only Maelle and the three people who had closely surrounded the boy. The young man, who had been holding the woman in his arms, released her to step into the street and offer his hand to the older man. Maelle waited until the pair stepped back onto the walkway before approaching them.

"Excuse me? Can you tell me what happened to the boy?"

The woman stumbled toward the building and leaned against the slatted siding, her head low. The young man crossed to her, and the older man turned to answer Maelle's question.

"He jumped from the trolley, like he always does—like I've told 'im a dozen times not to do—an' he slipped." Tears glimmered in the man's faded gray eyes. "The trolley took his foot clean off, then just kept goin'. It never stopped."

Apparently this man wasn't a stranger to the child. "You know the boy?"

"His name's Petey . . ." The man's round face twisted into an expression of pained fondness. "He's a scrappy mite. If anyone could come out of somethin' like this with a grin an' a whistle, it'll be Petey."

"And what's your name?"

The man sent her a wary look.

She held out her camera. "I'm hoping to sell the photograph of the accident to the newspaper. A reporter will probably need to ask some questions. Since you witnessed it, it would be best if you gave the information."

The man heaved a sigh. "My name's Ralph Rowley. I own Rowley Market, right here." He gestured to the whitewashed two-story building. "But I don't know about talkin' to some reporter."

Maelle offered a quick, silent prayer for his cooperation. "Mr. Rowley, your explanation, along with the picture I took, could do a lot of good in trying to get children like Petey off the streets. People need to be aware of the dangers these wee ones face."

Sighing, she admitted, "I don't know whether or not someone will even care enough to do an article. It doesn't seem that many are concerned about the plight of the newsboys, but—just in case—would you talk to a reporter?"

The big man gave a slow nod. "If it'll help Petey, an' others like him, I'll talk."

Maelle smiled her thanks. She backed up, patting her camera. "I'm going to go develop my photograph now. Can I come by your store later to find out how Petey's doing?"

The man nodded. "My wife's the one who ran for the ambulance. She'll be stayin' with the boy at the hospital, I'm sure, but she'll send word."

"Thank you." Maelle turned and strode to the back of her wagon. After carefully removing the plate and placing it between layers of burlap, she put the camera away and closed the hatch. Stepping back around to the front, her gaze fell on a scene that brought her up short.

There in the street, with newspapers riffling in the breeze around them, Mr. Rowley and the young couple knelt in a tight circle. With their heads bowed and hands clasped beneath their chins, they obviously were praying for Petey. A lump of longing rose in Maelle's throat, and for a brief moment she considered joining them. But then she remembered she didn't know Petey. She had no connection to the child. She didn't belong in their circle.

As quietly as she could, she climbed onto the driver's bench and picked up the reins. She whispered, "C'mon, Samson." The wagon rolled alongside the silent trio, and Maelle glanced at them again as she passed. Even without a photograph, she knew the image would be forever burned into her memory.

CHAPTER TWENTY-THREE

Molly
Shay's Ford, Missouri
April, 1903

Isabelle opened her eyes and immediately focused on Mr. Rowley's clasped hands. Hands stained with Petey's blood. Tears distorted her vision. "Petey . . . Oh, Petey . . ." The child's still, silent form appeared in her mind. How tiny and helpless he had looked!

An unexpected feeling filled Isabelle's breast, a feeling so intense it threatened to topple her. Love . . . She loved Petey. When had she grown to love that little mop-headed urchin? She didn't know, but in those moments she realized he was important to her—as important to her as anyone had ever been.

Aaron rose, gently lifted her to her feet, and escorted her to the curb. Mr. Rowley stood, too, and followed. He gave her a tender look. "You okay, Isabelle? That wasn't a pretty thing to see."

Isabelle's stomach churned, and she wasn't altogether sure she would hold down her breakfast. But she said staunchly, "I'm fine. But I'm concerned about Petey. Should we go to the hospital? He shouldn't be alone."

"Helen is there now," Mr. Rowley said. "She ran for the ambulance when . . . when it happened." He shook his graying head. "Won't be able to pull her home 'til that child is on his feet again, I'm sure." He winced. "His foot . . . Oh . . ."

Aaron stepped forward and embraced his father. Looking on, Isabelle felt fresh tears sting her eyes. Their shared torment, while heartrending, somehow seemed beautiful. If only she still had a father . . . or a brother . . . to embrace her and offer comfort.

After a long moment, the men separated. Mr. Rowley looked at his hands and grimaced. "I better go wash up." He headed for the store.

Aaron called, "Pa, do you want me to stay here an' help you, or can I take Isabelle to the hospital?" He glanced at her, understanding in his eyes. "I think she'll be happier there with Ma."

Mr. Rowley paused in the doorway, looking back at them. "I can handle the store on my own—people will be patient, considerin' what happened. You go ahead an' take her."

Looking down at Isabelle, Aaron asked, "Do you want to put the Bible away before we go?"

Isabelle clutched the Bible to her breast, hugging it the way she longed to be hugged. "No, I'll take it with me. Let's just hurry."

Aaron placed his hand on her back and turned toward the hospital. They had gone only a few yards when they heard someone call Aaron's name. Turning, they spotted a teenage boy running toward them. He waved a brown envelope in the air.

"Mr. Rowley! Hold up!" The boy panted to a halt beside them and thrust the envelope into Aaron's hand. "Jackson Harders sent it. Said it's for Miss Standler—something about those papers she brought in."

"Thank you." Aaron withdrew a coin from his pocket and offered it to the boy.

The boy grinned, curled his fist around the coin, and shot off down the street.

Aaron held the envelope toward Isabelle. "Well, that was quick."

Isabelle stared at it, her heart pounding.

His brows pulled down. "Don't you want to open it?"

Isabelle licked her lips as confusion filled her. A part of her wanted to rip it open, devour its contents, and discover that the documents were all fake and her life would return to normal. But another part of her—the stronger part, she realized—feared discovering that she could return to Kansas City and her old life.

Taking the envelope, she slipped it inside the cover of her Bible. "I'll look at it later. Right now I want to get to Petey."

Aaron nodded, a soft smile on his face. Although Isabelle turned her gaze forward as they moved quickly in the direction of the hospital, the image of Aaron's smile lingered in her memory. The feeling that had struck as she'd knelt in the street, near the spot where Petey had lain, returned. Only this time it centered around Aaron Rowley.

Isabelle leaned her head against the hard back of the wooden chair and sighed. The room was dark, the shades drawn. A cup of coffee, long grown cold, sat on a little table at her elbow. On the bed, Petey lay silent and motionless, not even the familiar whistle-buzz of his snore keeping her company.

Aaron and Mrs. Rowley had left about an hour earlier. Mrs. Rowley's exhaustion from the long day had finally caught up with her, and Aaron insisted she must go rest. Isabelle's promise to stay near Petey had convinced the older woman she could leave. So now Isabelle sat alone, waiting for Petey to rouse.

She tried to keep her eyes on the child's face rather than the lumps under the blanket. Earlier she had glanced at the place where his foot should have created a bulge, and the smoothness of the plain blue blanket had turned her stomach. Her heart ached at the child's loss. How would he support himself now? Begging? What kind of life would that be? Why, she wondered with a hint of bitterness, had God allowed such a horrible thing to happen to this sweet little boy?

A slight rustle captured her attention. She jerked upright, fingers grasping the edge of the seat, her gaze on Petey's face. The child grimaced, and the blanket shifted slightly, indicating a movement. She looked toward the middle of the bed and saw the lump created by Petey's left leg begin to shift—he was thrashing his good leg, she realized.

Afraid he might bump his injured leg, she jumped up and crossed to the edge of the bed, placing a hand on Petey's forehead. "Shh, darling, lie still."

His eyes still closed, the child moaned, "Hurts . . . Foot hurts . . ."

Isabelle swallowed and placed her hand on his left foot, massaging through the covers while murmuring soothing sounds.

But Petey shook his head violently, his face pinched into an expression of discomfort. "Nooo, t'other one."

Tears spurted into Isabelle's eyes. The doctor had mentioned the probability of phantom pains—a hurt in a limb that no longer existed. But he hadn't told her how to explain it to Petey. She didn't dare touch the leg that had been damaged. When the child tried to sit up, his hands reaching toward the injury, she let out a squawk of protest.

"Nurse!" she called, cradling Petey against her chest. "Come quickly! I need help!"

A woman in a blue dress rushed in. She took one look at Isabelle and ran back out. Isabelle continued to hold Petey, who wailed and thrashed against her, for what seemed hours until a man hurried in. He held a syringe, and without a word he threw back the covers, lifted Petey's nightshirt, and jabbed the needle into the child's hip. Petey cried out, causing Isabelle's heart to constrict, and then the child relaxed into her arms.

Gently Isabelle lowered him onto the pillow. Tears impaired her vision as she smoothed the blanket beneath the little boy's chin. She looked at the man, whose gaze remained on Petey's face. Finally he looked at Isabelle. Despite his abrupt treatment, she saw sympathy in his eyes.

"That'll help him sleep. Sleep is good medicine," he said, his voice kind.

Isabelle swallowed. "He said his foot hurt. What . . . what do I tell him if he wakes and says that again?"

The man touched Petey's head. "Tell him the truth. Children are resilient. He'll take it better than most men, I'd wager." With a brief, sad smile in her direction, he left the room.

Isabelle sat back in her chair, watching Petey's once-more-still form. She closed her eyes and willed herself to sleep.

Fingers of sunlight crept around the edges of the window shade, teasing Isabelle awake. She stretched, grimacing, her back stiff from sitting up all night. Slowly she opened her eyes, blinking as her vision adjusted to the light. Her gaze drifted from the ceiling to the head of Petey's bed and then to Petey himself. His eyes were open, watching her.

She stumbled to the edge of the bed and touched his tangled hair. "Petey. You're awake." Tears tightened her throat, deepening her voice.

He nodded. "Yeah. Been layin' here quiet so's not to bother you. You okay?"

The tears came again. In a hospital bed, one leg cut off above the ankle, there was Petey, asking if she was okay. What a sweet child.

Smoothing his hair, she assured him, "I'm just fine. How . . . how about you?"

He wrinkled his nose. "My foot's really hurtin'. C'n ya pull the covers back? They feel heavy."

Isabelle's chin quivered. "Petey, about your foot . . ."

The child's bright eyes were wide and innocent. How could she bear to tell him his foot was gone? Yet she had to—he had to know. As gently as possible, she explained what the trolley had done. "Petey, do you understand?"

Petey scowled, his little forehead crinkled. "It's cut clean off? The whole foot?"

She nodded, tears stinging. "I'm afraid so."

"But it hurts. I c'n feel it."

Stroking his hair, she nodded. "I know. The doctor said your body doesn't quite understand the foot is gone. That's why it feels like it hurts."

He stared at her, his lips puckering. "But it's really gone?"

Isabelle nodded.

"Lemme see."

Sucking in a breath of fortification, Isabelle folded back the blankets.

Petey propped himself up on his elbows and stared for a long time at the bandaged stump, his big blue eyes unblinking. Finally he sighed and slumped back against the pillow. "Yep. It's gone all right."

She waited for him to cry in anguish or rail in unfairness or scream in anger. But in his familiar little-boy voice, he said, "Think I c'n get a peg leg?"

She jerked back, stunned. "A . . . a what?"

"Peg leg. Seen a man at the docks with one. He strapped it where his foot used to be. He said a fish bit his foot off, but I didn't b'lieve him. Still, that peg leg . . . that was somethin'. Can I get one, too?"

A peg leg. That's all he was concerned about. Get a peg leg, strap it on, and walk again. This child was amazing. Isabelle cupped his pale cheek. "Petey, whatever you want, I'll be sure you get it, I promise you that. I'll get you the finest peg leg ever."

He smiled weakly. "Thanks." Suddenly he scowled, but the expression seemed thoughtful. "You don't gotta worry. I'll be okay, y'know. Jesus said so."

Isabelle's eyes flew wide. "Jesus . . . said so?"

Petey nodded. "He come to me when I was layin' in the street. He said not to worry—I'd be okay. Said I'd be walkin' an' jumpin' in no time. So you don't worry, neither."

Too stunned to reply, Isabelle merely nodded.

Petey's eyes slid closed. "I'm tired." This time, when he drifted off, his whistle-buzz snore filled the room.

CHAPTER TWENTY-FOUR

Mattie
Rocky Crest Ranch
April, 1903

As Matt and Clancy ambled toward the big house together, Matt's stomach growled, causing Clancy to let out an amused snort.

"Don't know why you're so hungry. Hardly worked ya a'tall today. Why, you never left the barn!"

Matt stared at him. "Hardly worked . . . ?" He waved a hand toward the sheep barn. "Shearing an' bundling is hardly workin'?"

Clancy chortled, his face crinkling with mirth. He threw his arm over Matt's shoulders. "Now, no need to get your feathers all a-ruffled. I was joshin' ya. You earned your keep today—that's for certain." He grinned, showing yellowed, crooked teeth. "But we won't have another day like that'n for a year, an' next time you'll know what to expect, so it'll seem easier."

Matt puffed his cheeks and blew. "I can see why you only shear once a year. It's a chore wrestlin' those woollies."

"We only shear once a year so's there's a good coat waitin'," Clancy clarified. Then he chuckled. "Did ya see ol' José with that one cantankerous ewe? I think at one point the ewe was shearin' the hair off José's head instead of the other way around!"

The two men shared a laugh at José's expense as they entered the back door, which led into the kitchen. They found Mr. Harders and his son, Jackson, seated together at the planked trestle table, and Matt's laughter immediately died. Something in the men's faces brought an immediate rush of worry.

Apparently Clancy had the same sense of foreboding, because he put his hands on his wiry hips and said, "All right, let's have it. Someone's either gettin' buried or married—but either way it ain't good news."

Mr. Harders shook his head, a rueful smile playing on his lips. "Clancy . . ." The single word held a gentle admonition. He looked at his son, and Jackson turned to face Matt. Matt felt a cold sweat break out over his body. The bad news—whatever it was—involved him. Was it Jenks? His quivering knees didn't seem sturdy enough to keep him upright. He took two shaky steps forward and clung to the back of a chair.

"What is it?"

Jackson took a deep breath. "Matt, there was an accident in Shay's Ford last Friday. Petey slipped beneath a trolley car. His right foot was severed."

Two opposite emotions swept Matt at the same time—relief that Jenks hadn't caught up with him and remorse for Petey's suffering. Then a third struck—guilt for bringing Petey to Shay's

Ford. He pulled out the chair and sank into it. "Will he be all right?"

"The surgeon is hopeful, but there are no guarantees."

Matt lowered his head, sorrow weighing him down. *Oh, Lord, I shoulda left him in St. Louis. I know Dave was mean to him, but even if he had a few welts, at least he'd be whole.* A hand clamped onto his shoulder. He looked up into Clancy's concerned face.

"Don't you be thinkin' you're the one who brung harm to that boy." The crusty tone warmed Matt's heart. "No way you could've seen this comin'. It's just . . . one of them things."

Matt nodded, but inside he rebelled. It wasn't just "one of them things"—it was wrong. A little boy should have two good legs for running and playing. And a little boy shouldn't ride on a trolley, unattended. Petey needed a home. A permanent home.

"Who'll be takin' care of him when he's out of the hospital?"

"The Rowleys plan to take him in. Their hired girl, Isabelle, has been taking turns with Mrs. Rowley staying at the hospital." Jackson's low voice calmed Matt's racing heart. "When he's released, he won't be selling newspapers anymore."

Jackson removed a piece of paper from his pocket and slid it across the table. Matt realized it was a clipping from a newspaper. Jackson went on. "The newspaper reported the accident. I can only hope this has awakened some people to the real danger faced by our street children. Maybe now they'll be willing to get involved."

Anger billowed in Matt's chest. "Well," he growled, "as far as I'm concerned, they're a few days too late." Pushing out of the chair, he stormed outside.

❧

Molly
Shay's Ford, Missouri
April, 1903

"Gangrene."

When the surgeon who had operated on Petey's leg summoned Isabelle and Aaron into the hallway for an update, she had sensed something was wrong. But the single word stabbed Isabelle's heart with fear. "Is it bad?"

Dr. Carolton frowned as if the question were foolish. "There's no such thing as good gangrene. It's quite serious. If the child were stronger, better nourished, perhaps . . ." The man's voice drifted off, and Isabelle understood his frustration. "I'll have to amputate another few inches higher, to remove the diseased tissue, but I cannot guarantee the child will survive the operation."

Isabelle's legs went weak. Only Aaron's fingers, clamped around her elbow, kept her upright. "And if you don't operate?"

"The infection will certainly kill him."

Isabelle drew in a deep breath, steadying herself. "Then you must operate."

The doctor nodded. "As soon as the operating room is readied, orderlies will return for the boy." He strode away.

Isabelle and Aaron stood silently outside Petey's door. Isabelle's chin quivered, but she clamped her jaw against it. When she had regained control, she said, "I want to return to Petey. He shouldn't be alone."

"Of course." Aaron escorted Isabelle into Petey's room. He took the single chair in the corner, and she sat on the edge of the bed. The child's flushed face, beaded with perspiration, disturbed Isabelle. A foul odor hung in the air, a result of the infection that had taken hold of the little boy's leg.

Leaning his elbows on his knees, Aaron spoke in a husky tone. "Are you going to be all right, Isabelle?"

Isabelle felt a sad smile on her lips. "The morning after the first surgery, Petey asked me the same thing. There he lay, small and fragile, his foot gone, and he asked about me." She released a long sigh. "Aaron, this week has been . . . a growing time, I suppose."

Aaron's brow creased. "How so?"

Their whisper-soft voices, an attempt to avoid disturbing the sick child, gave an intimacy to the sterile setting. Aaron's attentive gaze, his fingers linked as though he were in prayer, brought a flutter to Isabelle's heart.

Rising from the bed, she crossed to the small table in the corner and picked up her Bible. "I've had little to do this week besides read. I've read to Petey, and while he's slept, I've read to myself. There's so much here, Aaron, so much I didn't know. . . ."

Aaron's gaze pinned to hers, his blue-green eyes tender.

"I read Psalm 139, the one you told me about. There's a verse that says God's hand is laid upon me, that He has beset me behind and before. This week, here with Petey, I've finally *sensed* His presence. And . . ." She pinched her brow, struggling to put into words all of the emotion of the past week. "As I've watched over Petey—even when he wasn't aware of my being here—it made me think of God watching me when I wasn't aware of Him."

Aaron offered a slow nod, his eyes shining.

Bolstered by his silent understanding, she continued. "When I read the message from Jackson Harders that said all the documents Randolph had were authentic, I . . . accepted it. I didn't mourn it. And I believe God gave me the strength to accept it."

She lowered her gaze once more to the Bible. Swallowing, she went on. "I've been so unaware of God, but I want to change. I want to *know* Him, the way you and your parents know Him." Raising her head, she met Aaron's gaze. "What . . . what do I do, Aaron, to truly know God?"

To her amazement, tears welled in Aaron's eyes. He clasped her hands, curling them around the Bible. "My dear Isabelle, you've taken the first step. You've said right out loud that you need Him. Now all you have to do is ask His son, Jesus, to come into your heart."

She tipped her head. "It's really that simple?"

Aaron nodded. "For us, it is. Jesus did all the work when He died on the cross to take the place of our sins. When you ask Him into your heart, He'll come. That makes you one of God's children. Then He'll be with you every day on earth, and when you die, you'll go live with Him in heaven."

Yearning made her chest ache. "Oh, I want that, Aaron."

"Then ask."

His sweet voice, deep with emotion, spurred her response. Slipping to her knees, she closed her eyes and pressed the Bible to her heart. "Jesus, come into my heart. Be with me from this day forward."

When she opened her eyes, she found Aaron kneeling before her, his eyes bright with unshed tears. "Welcome to God's family, Isabelle," he said.

Warm tears splashed down her cheeks, but she laughed. "Oh, Aaron, what wonderful words! For the last weeks I've wondered . . . where do I belong? I am not truly a Standler. I'm not a Gallagher. But now . . . I'm God's child."

Without a word, Aaron reached out and embraced her, pulling her firm against his chest. She nestled there, content, for several seconds. When he released her, there was something in his eyes that sent her heart pattering.

"Isabelle, I have something for you." He rose, lifting her to her feet. Then he slipped his hand inside his shirt and withdrew an envelope. "Jackson sent this for you earlier today. It's a message from your father's lawyer."

Isabelle clapped her hand to her breast. Her heart thumped mightily, and her mouth went dry. Her gaze bounced from the envelope to Aaron's eyes. She placed the Bible on the table, then reached with trembling hands for the envelope. Slowly she withdrew a letter and read aloud.

" 'Mr. Harders, thank you for contacting me concerning the inheritance of Miss Isabelle Standler. Although Miss Standler was never formally adopted by Reginald Standler, he loved the child as his own and planned for her future. An account of—' " Isabelle nearly dropped the paper when she read the dollar amount—" 'was established, which was intended to come into her possession on her twentieth birthday.

" 'In the event of her foster parents' untimely demise, Mr. Standler allowed a provision for early retrieval. Following are instructions on withdrawing these funds. Please advise Miss Standler to contact me, and I shall see that she receives access to the account. Sincerely, Mr. Emery Murray.' "

Isabelle raised her gaze to meet Aaron's.

He shook his head, releasing a low whistle. "So now you know . . . you are Molly Gallagher. But the Standlers loved you as their own."

Isabelle nodded. In her heart, she'd already known these things. Her thoughts raced. She was born Molly Gallagher, but even so the man she loved as Papa had provided for her. She was an orphan but was not penniless. With the fund Papa had established, she had the financial means to return to Kansas City and reestablish her old life.

She looked again at the dollar amount printed on the page, and she suddenly felt as light as air. Lifting her smile to Aaron, she said, "I must lay claim to this fund immediately."

"You . . . you'll be leaving, then?" His voice sounded pinched.

She touched his arm and gave a quick shake of her head. "I must have these funds to pay for Petey's hospital stay. And I must buy him a peg leg. I promised." Aaron's puzzled expression made her smile. "Then we'll use these funds to help the street children. We'll build an orphanage, or a school, or whatever we need." Moving to Petey, she caressed the child's pale cheek. "We'll use the money to fight for the children, Aaron."

CHAPTER TWENTY-FIVE

Maelle
Shay's Ford, Missouri
April, 1903

Cheerful purple crocus and yellow daffodils greeted Maelle from yards that were throwing off their winter brown and turning green beneath the bright spring sunshine. Easter was just around the corner, and even the flowers seemed to recognize it was time for new birth.

From high on the wagon seat, Maelle whistled, observing neat houses with shutters and flower boxes, cobblestone streets, and neatly painted businesses as she rolled toward the hospital. Shay's Ford was a pleasant community, she acknowledged. The kind of place it would be nice to call home.

Her whistle ceased. Home? Maelle's home was as peculiar as her attire—a big box on wooden wheels. If she pressed her memory, she could barely recall her home back in Ireland. A tiny cottage with a mud fireplace, where stew bubbled in a pot and Da's laughter shook the rafters. But try as she might, so much of her early life refused to be remembered. How she longed to recall Ma's sweet smile, Mattie's unruly hair, Molly's dimples. But it was so long ago, and the memories were faded. She wished she had photographs to remind her of the faces and the place. But those kinds of wishes were pointless.

Only one photograph existed of the place that lived in Maelle's memory, and she'd given it to Mattie all those years ago. In her travels across the United States with Richard, aiming the camera at individuals and groups of people, Maelle had often hoped to look through the viewfinder and recognize Mattie or Molly. She had imagined the reunion so many times she had it memorized—she could hear the laughter, feel the hugs, see the distortion of vision due to tears of joy. She had promised Mattie she would never stop looking for him, and she hadn't. Everywhere she went, she looked. And looked. But the search had proved futile.

The search kept her moving from town to town despite the desire to settle down and open a shop where the customers came to her rather than the other way around. But until she found Mattie and Molly, she knew she could never settle down. Her restless feet and seeking heart would press her ever onward. *Let me be findin' me brother and sister, Lord.*

She waited for a horseless carriage to wheeze by before crossing the final intersection that led to the hospital. Leaving Samson nodding in the spring sunshine, she retrieved her camera and headed inside. A woman behind a wooden desk directed her to Petey's room, and she found the door open.

Her heart turned over in sympathy when she entered the simple room. Petey lay, small and unmoving, in the middle of an iron bed. The little boy's face didn't hold much more color than it had the first time she'd seen him crumpled on the road. As she stood watching, his eyelids fluttered open.

"Isabelle?"

She leaned in close so he could see her face. "Nope. I'm Mike. And you're Petey, right?"

Tousled blond hair fell across his wide, unblinking blue eyes. "How'd ja know my name?"

Gingerly, she sat on the edge of the bed and held her camera in her lap. "Jackson Harders told me."

"Oh." The child nodded, nestling against his pillow. "I like Jackson. He's my friend."

Maelle resisted running her hand over the child's hair. "I bet you have lots of friends."

"Yep."

His nonchalant reply gave Maelle's heart a lift. "Maybe I can be your friend, too."

Petey slipped his hands from beneath the covers and linked them on his chest. "Are you a lady?"

She laughed. "Yes, I am."

"Mike's a funny name for a lady."

"I suppose so." She loved this child's openness.

His gaze fell to the camera. "Watcha got?"

"My camera." Maelle gave it a loving pat. "I take pictures with it, and I brought it with me so I could take your picture."

"My pitcher?" The boy's brow pinched. "How come?"

"Well . . . tomorrow some men are coming to Shay's Ford. Powerful men—men who know how to get things changed for the better. Your friend Jackson wants them to help him change some laws so children like you go to school instead of having to sell newspapers all day."

231

Petey nodded slightly. "I know. Aaron an' Isabelle say I'll be goin' to school when I get outta the hospital. I can't sell newspapers no more 'cause I only got one leg."

The child's blithe statement made Maelle's nose sting. "I know. And I'm glad you'll be going to school. But lots of other boys won't unless the laws are changed. So Jackson thought if we had a picture of you to show the men, then they'd know what kind of fine boys they'd be helping by changing the law. So . . . is it okay if I take your picture?"

Petey bit down on his lower lip, surveying her with a steady gaze. "All of me?"

"You mean, do I want a picture of your leg, too?"

He nodded.

She took a deep breath. "It would help."

After a long moment, he gave a slow nod. "Okay."

Maelle carefully pulled the covers back to reveal Petey's small form. She battled tears when she looked at his skinny legs sticking out from beneath the striped nightshirt, one ending with a bare foot and the other ending with a bandaged stump below his knee. The tears nearly blinded her when she put her camera in position and glimpsed Petey's bright smile through the viewfinder.

"What do you think you're doing?"

The sharp tone stilled Maelle's fingers around the bulb. She glanced over her shoulder to find the young, red-haired woman she'd photographed the day of Petey's accident. Turning, she offered a smile of greeting. "You must be Isabelle."

Isabelle swept to the bed and deftly flipped the covers over Petey's hips. "You didn't answer my question. What are you doing?"

Petey caught the woman's hand. "She's takin' my pitcher for Jackson to show to the men. I told her she could."

Isabelle looked at the boy, and her expression grew tender. But when she turned back to Maelle, her green eyes sparked. "Jackson indicated a photographer named Mike Watts would be photographing Petey. Do you work for Mr. Watts?"

Maelle stifled her grin. "Well, not quite." She scratched her head. "I *am* Mike Watts."

Isabelle's eyebrows shot high, and her gaze roved from Maelle's head to her toes and back again. "Mike . . . and that is short for . . ."

"Michael." It was devilish, Maelle knew, yet she enjoyed needling the snippy young woman.

Isabelle pursed her lips and stared at Maelle for several silent seconds while Maelle waited. Then Petey tugged her hand.

"Isabelle? You gonna move so Mike can take my pitcher?"

The woman sucked in a mighty breath, as if holding back an unpleasant barrage. When she released it, the semblance of a smile flitted across her face. "Very well." Folding the covers over the foot of the bed, she stepped aside. "Please proceed quickly. Petey needs his rest. He's been through quite an ordeal."

As if I didn't already know that. Maelle lifted the camera, focused, and squeezed the bulb. "All done."

"Good." Isabelle covered Petey once more, then stood beside the bed like a guard.

Petey said, "Am I gonna get to see the pitcher?"

Maelle tucked the camera beneath her arm and crossed to the bed. "Well, Petey, I can make a copy of it for you and bring it to you, if you'd like. I won't be able to come tomorrow, but I could come Sunday afternoon."

The boy's eyes lit with delight, but Isabelle said, "We are hoping to transport Petey to Rowley Market on Sunday, so that probably wouldn't be a good day to visit."

Maelle looked at Isabelle in surprise. "He's being released so soon? He must be doing well, then."

Isabelle sighed, stroking Petey's hair. "The Lord has certainly answered our prayers."

Maelle found the comment odd. Given Isabelle's cold treatment, she wouldn't have taken the other woman as a Christian. Yet her statement deemed otherwise.

"You can come see me at the Market, though, right?"

Maelle couldn't say no to Petey's hopeful question. "Sure I can! And I'll bring lots of pictures. Have you ever seen the Grand Canyon? Or the Pacific Ocean? Or Pikes Peak?"

Petey's eyes widened. "Pikes Pete?"

Maelle swallowed her amusement. "*Peak*. It's a mountain. A very tall mountain first glimpsed by a man named Zebulon Pike. He didn't actually climb it, but I did."

Petey shook his head, making his hair flop. "I never seen none o' that stuff."

"Well, then, I'll have to show you the pictures before I leave town."

"Really?" His voice became high-pitched with excitement. "You'll really show me?"

"Sure I will. We're friends, aren't we?"

To her surprise, Petey lost his sunny expression. "You ain't teasin' me, are ya? Sometimes people say they'll do somethin', but then they don't. You aren't just sayin' it an' not meanin' it, are ya?"

"Take care o' the wee ones."

Maelle squeezed Petey's thin shoulder, then stepped back, aware of Isabelle's disapproving stare. "I mean every word, Petey. I'll meet you at Rowley Market on Sunday."

Isabelle turned from Petey and pinned Maelle with a regal glare. "May I have a word with you, please? In the hallway."

Maelle shrugged and followed Isabelle.

The woman closed Petey's door before addressing Maelle. "It was kind of you to offer to share your pictures with Petey."

Maelle shifted her camera to her other arm. "He's a great kid."

"Yes, he is. But I'm not sure . . ." For a moment the younger woman seemed to falter, her brow creasing and gaze dropping to the floor. Then she squared her shoulders and faced Maelle again. "I'm not sure spending time with you is a wise idea for Petey."

Maelle frowned. "Why not?"

"Well . . ." Isabelle's gaze drifted from Maelle's braid to her brown boots. "You are hardly . . . conventional. Your motivations may be pure, but . . ." Isabelle's brow crinkled. "Your abnormal appearance leads one to see you as less than respectable. Petey has enough challenges, having been abandoned by his parents, living on the streets, and now facing life as a cripple. He doesn't need any more strikes against him. An open friendship with you might not be in his best interest."

Maelle carefully digested Isabelle's words. "So if I were to dress . . . differently . . . you would have fewer concerns about me spending time with him?"

"I am truly trying not to be judgmental," the younger woman said, "but you must admit, those—those britches . . ." Her face puckered in distaste. "They are quite distracting."

Maelle took a step back. Her heart pounded. She wore the pants for a number of reasons from practical to personal. She'd grown accustomed to people looking at her askance, and she'd never really cared what others thought. Now, for the first time, she wondered if wearing them created more than mild disapproval. Did they create a barrier to relationships?

She'd tried so hard to keep the promise to her da to look out for little ones who needed protection. It was a lot easier to dive into a fight while wearing a sturdy pair of trousers. But she'd made another promise, too—to her heavenly Father to share His love with those she encountered. Would her clothing prevent people from seeing her Father in her?

As much as Maelle hated to admit it, Isabelle had hit a raw nerve. She gave a slow, thoughtful nod. "I'll think about what you said. Thank you for your honesty."

Isabelle tipped her head, her red hair shining in the electric lamps that lit the hallway. "Did I hurt your feelings?"

Maelle felt bruised, but she wouldn't admit it. She forced her lips into a grin and quipped, "I'm right as rain. Don't worry about me."

Maelle returned to her wagon and lowered the hatch. She put the camera safely in its box, then pulled herself onto the driver's seat. As she picked up the reins, she looked down at her trousers and frowned. "Let's go, Samson," she encouraged the big bay. She nibbled her lower lip thoughtfully as the wagon rolled back to Jackson's law office. Guiding Samson to the alley behind the building, she parked in the same spot she'd occupied the previous weeks.

She freed Samson from his rigging and walked him to the livery. She hung a bag of oats around his neck and scratched his ears while he munched. Stepping back from the horse, she brushed her hands on her pant legs. And frowned again.

With a deep sigh, she returned to the wagon and climbed in. *Father, help me . . .* Kneeling beside the drop-down bed, she pulled a trunk from beneath the bunk. It filled the middle of the wagon floor, and she had to wiggle around to its end before she could lift the heavy lid.

Clothing came into view. Trousers. Shirts. Some Richard's, some hers. Her heart doubled its beat as she reached inside with hands that had become unsteady. She moved aside the neat stacks, creating a valley through the center. And there, wrapped in crumpled tissue, she located the source of her trembling hands and palpitating heart.

Lifting it from the tissue, she rose and shook out the folds of pale green muslin. A musty odor rose from the fabric—a scent of neglect. For several seconds she held the garment out, vivid details of that evening assailing her. When the pain became too intense, she crushed the dress to her chest and closed her eyes.

A picture of Richard's sheepish look as he'd given her the dress appeared behind her closed lids. His voice echoed through her mind. *"I know it's not one of those two-piecers the ladies are wearing today, but the lace is real pretty, and the color will go good with your fall-colored hair."* Though his voice was gruff, his expression gentled as he finished, *"You're a right attractive girl, Mike, and it's time to start dressing like a lady."*

Richard had seldom praised her. Those words had meant so much. She savored the memory as she cradled the dress. But then, unbidden, his final words charged through her mind—"Run, Mike! Run for the sheriff!" She'd run, holding up the skirts of that green muslin dress. And when she'd come back, sheriff in tow, Richard lay dead in the alley with a knife in his chest.

She'd worn britches and one of his shirts to his burial. The dress had gone into the trunk and remained there for the past eight years. Never had she planned to put on a dress again. If she hadn't been wearing a dress that evening, Richard might still be alive. She couldn't help him fight while wearing a lacy muslin dress. She wouldn't have gotten the kind of attention that had warranted the fight had she not been wearing a lacy muslin dress.

A tear crept from beneath her lid, sliding down her cheek. Maelle shoved the dress roughly into the trunk and swiped the tear away with the back of her hand. She started to slam the lid, but Isabelle's words made her pause.

Leaving the trunk yawning wide, she turned to her bunk and picked up the Bible a minister had given her when she'd made her way to the front of the sanctuary to ask him how to invite Jesus into her heart. Somewhere in this book she'd read about being a stumbling block.

Her trousers didn't bother her. She had good reason for wearing them. But if her clothing provided a stumbling block to those in the community and kept them from seeing her heart and her Christian witness, then maybe it was time to change. Setting the Bible aside, she looked back at the crumpled dress draped over the edge of the trunk. Her stomach trembled.

"I can't wear that dress, Lord," she moaned aloud, tears threatening once more. She took the two steps needed to reach the trunk, lifted the dress, and folded it with great care. Setting it aside, she retrieved the tattered tissue and spread it as flat as possible on the bunk. She tenderly wrapped the tissue around the dress before returning it to the bottom of the trunk.

She couldn't wear *that* dress. Never again would she wear *that* dress. Her hand drifted to the pocket of her trousers, and her fingers pressed the money clip that held several bills. There were at least three stores in town that sold ready-made garments.

Sucking in a big breath, she spoke aloud. "God, I don't want to be a stumbling block. I want people to see the light of your love in my eyes. Give me the courage to put on the trappings that will enable people to look at my heart."

Chapter Twenty-Six

Mattie
Rocky Crest Ranch
April, 1903

Matt hung his hat on its hook, thumped to his bed, and plopped down on the mattress. The ropes squeaked in protest, but he ignored the sound. With a deep sigh, he plucked up the photograph that rested on the little table beside his bed and fingered the edge, his lips pulled between his teeth.

"You gonna skip supper again?" Clancy leaned against the doorjamb, one thumb caught in the pocket of his trousers. The man's leathered face looked concerned.

Returning his eyes to the photo, Matt grunted a reply. "Maybe."

Clancy took two steps into the room and stood looking down at Matt. "Ever since Jackson's visit, you haven't hardly ate enough to keep body an' soul on good terms. When a man don't eat, it's 'cause his gut's already filled up." Clancy propped his fists on his bony hips. "What's fillin' ya, boy?"

Heaving another sigh that lifted his shoulders, Matt put the photograph on the table and met Clancy's gaze. "I made a promise, Clancy, but now I'm not so sure I can keep it."

Clancy sat on the bed. "What promise is that?"

Matt swallowed. "To help Jackson at that big meetin' he's got planned."

"The one with all them ranchers?"

"That's the one."

"Wal, why can'tcha go? Gerald's approved it. He'll even take ya on in to Shay's Ford. Can't see no problem there."

Matt looked at Clancy. "Problem is, there might be somebody there that I . . . I can't see."

Clancy chuckled. "Somebody gonna be invisible?"

Matt let his head drop, and he blew out a breath. He'd never trusted anybody with the story of his past—not even the Small-woods, who were the best people he'd known up until coming to Rocky Crest Ranch. But if he didn't tell now, he'd end up being in the same room with Jenks tomorrow, and the thought made him break out in a cold sweat. *Oh, Lord, protect me. . . .*

Clancy reached past Matt and picked up the photograph. "Does it have somethin' to do with the family in this here picture? Seems to me you been spendin' a lot of time starin' at it this week."

Matt looked at the photograph pinched between Clancy's gnarled fingers. His chin quivered as longing flooded him. How long until Maelle's promise to find him would be fulfilled? "That family . . ." He swallowed the lump in his throat and took the photograph to cradle it in his palm. "That's my family, Clancy. And I haven't seen any of 'em since I was six, maybe seven years old."

Clancy's brow puckered, and he released a low whistle. "That's a long time."

"Yeah . . ." Matt closed his eyes for a moment, gathering his thoughts. And then, haltingly, in a hoarse voice, he opened his past to Clancy. "My folks died when I was pretty small. Me an' my folks an' my sisters, we was livin' in New York. After the folks died, there wasn't anybody to take care of us kids. So some people—can't rightly remember who—put us on a train and sent us west with a bunch of other kids who didn't have folks."

Clancy's jaw dropped. "Orphan trains? You come from them?"

Matt nodded. "We went to some little town here in Missouri, an' people came to the church to look us over. I got given to a family by the name of Bonham. Good folks—lived in Shallow Creek."

"An' your sisters?"

Pain stabbed Matt's chest. "My baby sister got took by a fancy family." He sent Clancy a brief, self-conscious grin. "Man probably still has a dent in his shin from where I kicked him. Clunked him good, tryin' to keep him from takin' her. But it didn't help."

Looking back at the photograph, Matt touched the image of Maelle. "My other sister went with a man who did photography. Always wondered what happened there. She was dressed like a boy at the time."

Clancy's brows pulled down. "A boy?"

Matt shrugged. "Hard to explain." Shaking his head, he said, "Hope that man didn't get too mad when he figured out he had himself a girl instead of a boy. Hope he was good to her . . ."

"Hoo-doggies, Matthew . . ." Clancy whistled through his teeth. "Wal, I'm glad a good family took you in."

Matt nodded, raising his chin and peering into space. "Oh yeah, really liked those Bonhams. They treated me just like I was one of theirs—sent me to school and everything. Now, Mrs. Bonham, she was pretty strict about how things should be done—real particular, y'know? But never mean or spiteful about none of it. She was a nice lady." His throat tightened. "But when I was nine or so, there was a bad drought. Crops failed, money was scarce, and they couldn't afford to feed their own, let alone an extra. So they took me to an orphanage in Springfield."

"An' just left ya there?"

At Clancy's derisive tone, Matt faced him. "I don't hold a grudge. I knew they didn't want to—the missus carried on somethin' fierce as they left." Remembering Mrs. Bonham's distraught face as the wagon drove away caused an ache in Matt's heart. He pushed the image aside and continued. "I stayed at the orphanage a couple years before a man took me in. He had a ranch in the Missouri River valley, an' that's where I learned cattle ranchin'."

"A cattle ranch in Missouri . . ." Clancy's voice turned pensive. "But I thought Gerald said you come to us from Texas."

Matt stood and paced to the door. This was the part of the story he'd never told. "I did. I ran off to Texas from that ranch. It . . . it was owned by a fellow named . . . Jenks."

Clancy's head jerked. "Lester Jenks? Big feller, gold tooth in the front?"

Matt nodded. "That's him."

Clancy jolted to his feet. "You got adopted by Lester Jenks? Then why'n tarnation are you here 'stead of—?"

"No!" Matt rubbed the back of his neck, pacing back and forth in the small room. "He didn't adopt me, Clancy. He just *took* me. Took me an' worked me. Just . . . worked me."

Slowly, Clancy lowered himself back to the bed.

Matt leaned against the wall, too tired to remain upright without assistance. "He worked me, Clancy, like you'd work a dog. An' he never paid me. I'd see the other hands line up on pay day, an' I figured I should, too. The first time, he laughed an' told me to run along. The second time, he came around the table, took me by the shirt collar, an' gave me a kick that sent me sprawlin' in the dirt. The third time . . ." Matt's mouth felt dry. He licked his lips. "The third time I could hardly put on a shirt for a week, what with the welts he left on my back. After that, I didn't get in line. 'Course, he found plenty of other reasons to take that ridin' crop to me."

Clancy's jaw clamped so tight the muscles in his cheeks bulged.

"But I kept track of what he owed me. I knew what he paid the other hands, an' I knew how long I'd been there. So one night when . . . when he an' the others headed into town, I sneaked into his office." Matt's legs began to tremble. He sank down on the edge of the bed. "I made up a bill on a piece of paper I found in his desk. Wages for forty-four months. Then I subtracted off the cost of one horse. I found the cash box in his bottom drawer, an' I took what he owed me. I saddled the horse, an' I rode out."

"An' you been on your own ever since?"

"Yes, sir." A smile twitched Matt's cheek. "Wasn't so bad, really. I was tall for my age—most folks figured I was older than I really was, so they weren't opposed to givin' me a job. I knew ranchin', thanks to Jenks. So I worked cattle ranches in Kansas, Oklahoma, an' Texas. Worked my way as far from Missouri as I could get.

"That last one—the Triple E in Spofford, Texas—that's where the boss let us off on Sundays for church. Grateful for that—came to know Jesus. Now He's with me all the time, so no matter where I'm travelin', I'm not alone." He sighed. "Prob'ly woulda stayed at the Triple E, 'cept the boss took sick an' died. His wife had to sell, an' the new owner brought in his own men. Left me lookin' for a job again. I saw Mr. Harders's ad, applied, and"—he flipped his palms outward with a smile—"here I am."

"And you ain't seen your sisters since you were a little boy?"

Matt shifted his head to look at the photograph. "Nope."

"Don't ya want to find 'em?"

"Sure do. But I don't know how. I don't even know what their names are now. Surely not Gallagher anymore . . ."

"Gallagher?" Clancy's tone echoed confusion. "Your name's Tucker."

Matt scratched his chin, grinning. "Well, now, I made that up when I left Jenks. Went from Bonham to Tucker 'cause I was plumb tuckered from him workin' me so hard. Figured it'd be harder for him to track me if I had a different name." His grin faded. "'Course, also makes it harder for my sister to find me."

He blinked hard, looking at the photograph. "My older sister, she made me a promise. Said she'd find me someday. I keep hopin' . . . 'Course, all my movin' around . . . could be she's tried an' just couldn't catch up with me." He paused. "I gotta stay put. But if Jenks sees me at the meetin' tomorrow, he could sic the law on me, accuse me of stealin'. I could end up in jail." Panic welled. "I can't let that man see me."

"Don't worry." Matt had never heard Clancy use such a harsh tone. "You won't be bothered by Jenks. I'll go in tomorrow, give Jackson a hand. Gerald won't mind who goes an' who stays, so long as the chores git done around here. You stay put." He snorted. "It's no secret how Jenks feels about sheep. He won't come out here—not for nothin'. So you're safe long as you stay here."

Matt drew a deep breath and let it out by increments. "Thanks, Clancy."

Clancy's brow creased. "You oughtta talk to Gerald, though. He could maybe—"

"No." Matt shook his head. "I don't want him thinkin' he's hired a thief. The fewer people who know, the better. It'll keep Jenks from gettin' wind of my whereabouts."

"But Jackson bein' a lawyer . . . he might could help ya, Matthew."

But Matt set his jaw. "You know what they do to horse thieves, Clancy."

The older man's face paled.

"Even if Jenks owed that horse an' pay to me, it wouldn't be hard for a man with his money an' power to convince a judge otherwise. You . . . you gotta stay quiet, please?"

Clancy nodded. "Don't you worry none. I won't say nothin'."

"Thanks, Clancy."

"Let's go get us some supper, huh?"

Matt rubbed his stomach, surprised to discover his hunger had returned. Knowing he wouldn't need to face Jenks tomorrow, the weight of dread had lifted. "Sounds good."

Clancy gave Matt's arm a light punch as they walked to the big house together. "You know what I'm hopin', Matt? That ol' Gerald'll get into office, an' them laws'll get changed, an' men like Jenks won't be takin' advantage of no more orphans."

Chapter Twenty-Seven

Maelle
Shay's Ford, Missouri
April, 1903

As Maelle walked into the building Jackson had told her was used for town meetings, she chuckled softly. For one of the first times in her life, she was attired appropriately for an opera house. The flaring gray skirt and trim-fitting shirtwaist felt peculiar after the years of wearing trousers and men's shirts, but no one should look askance at her today.

Balancing the box that held her camera and several blank plates, she walked down the center aisle toward the well-lit stage. Red velvet curtains, hanging from ceiling to floor, bunched at both sides of the stage. The shining wood floor of the stage was empty except for a row of three straight-back chairs behind a simple podium. Her gaze scanned the dim room for the best place to set up her camera. Although electric sconces were placed above shoulder level all along the side walls, none were lit. She hoped someone would light them before things got started or the room would be too dark for photographs.

Stopping at the apron of the stage, she turned to face the shadowy rows of velvet-covered seats. She wanted to be able to photograph the attendees as well as the presenters today, but she didn't want to move around and draw attention away from the proceedings. She tapped her lips, considering her options.

"Mike?"

The single word exclamation startled her so badly she nearly dropped her box. She spun to face the voice, her skirts swirling around her ankles. Jackson stood at the back edge of the stage, gawking in open-mouthed amazement.

She clutched the box like a shield. Her heart pounded as he crossed quickly to the apron and stared down at her, his gaze sweeping from her toes to her eyes. "You look wonderful." The words rasped out. "Just . . . wonderful!"

Her skirts shifted as she took a backward step. Spiders of wariness scurried down her spine. Lifting her chin, she inhaled through her nose and pinned him with a fierce glare. "I had a little chat with Isabelle, and she convinced me that my odd mode of dress might give some people the wrong impression about my character. I only put this on to convince the fine people of Shay's Ford that I'm not a reprobate." She deepened her scowl. "I didn't do it to impress you."

Jackson looked like he was holding back a grin. "I would never have suspected as much."

She lowered her gaze, her trembling arms still hugging the camera's box. A sigh escaped. "I apologize for my snappishness. I . . . I just feel conspicuous, I suppose."

His laugh burst out. She glared at him, and he pursed his lips, stifling the sound. "I'm so sorry. I'm not laughing at you, honestly. It's just that you feel conspicuous in a dress that would blend in with every other woman in town. Yet in your trousers, which stuck out like a crow in a flock of redbirds, you didn't." He chuckled, shaking his head. "I've never met anyone like you, Mike."

Heat filled her cheeks, and she looked to the side. "It's a matter of feeling comfortable." Her voice seemed oddly intimate in the empty, echoing room. "I've worn trousers since I was very young. And I feel . . . safe . . . in them. In this dress . . ." She brought her gaze around, meeting Jackson's once more. Tears filled her eyes, but she blinked them away. "I don't feel like me."

Jackson squatted, resting his elbows on his thighs and linking his fingers together. "So be yourself. If you're more comfortable in trousers, wear them. Don't let Isabelle tell you what to do." He smirked. "She likes to tell everyone what to do. Aaron's working on her penchant for bossiness."

Maelle felt a grin grow on her lips. "I'm pleased to hear it." But then she sobered. "However, she made a valid point, and I certainly don't want my attire to be a stumbling block that keeps others from seeing my true character. I want people to see Jesus in me. If they're put off by my clothes, they won't see my heart. So . . ." She took in another deep breath. "The pants will be set aside. At least while I'm in polite company."

Jackson smiled, his dark eyes shining in approval. "Mike, do you have plans for this evening?"

She shifted the box a bit. It was growing heavy. "Why?"

Still hunkered a mere few feet away, he said, "There's a restaurant in a hotel on the edge of town. It has a view over the

Mississippi so you can watch barges and paddleboats coming in to dock. Very relaxing. Would you like to join me there this evening?"

Another dozen spiders raced up her spine, causing her breath to come in little spurts. "Is it me or the dress you're asking out to dinner?"

He jerked to his feet. "I . . . I . . ."

"That's what I thought." She turned and headed down the aisle toward the back of the room.

An echoing thud told her he'd hopped off the stage. "Mike, wait!" A hand curled over her shoulder, bringing her to a halt. "Please, don't run away from me."

Ducking from his grasp, she fixed him with a fierce glare. "I'm not running away."

"Are you sure?"

Maelle took two steps backward, putting distance between them. "I'm not *running* away. I'm just *getting* away."

"But why?"

"Suddenly you ask me to dinner, pay me compliments. Well, that makes me uneasy. I don't know whether you're asking me—Mike—to dinner, or if it's just the dress giving you ideas."

Jackson frowned. "Now, wait just a minute. I—"

"I put on this dress so my trousers wouldn't be a distraction to the people in this town. I didn't put it on to invite attention from men. So keep your invitation, Jackson Harders, and leave me alone!"

Storming between two rows of seats, she charged to the side aisle. She made her way to the front of the room, stopping at the left side of the stage. A quick glance confirmed her opinion that she would have a view of the entire room and the stage from this location. After setting up her tripod, she plunked her camera into place. Once it was secure, she stepped behind it and made a show of perusing the room for the best views. Out of the corner of her eye, she watched Jackson stomp up the middle aisle, catch the stage lip with his hands, and lift himself onto the platform. He disappeared behind the curtains.

The moment he was out of sight, she lowered her head and closed her eyes. Tears pressed behind her lids, but she held them at bay. Tears were for sissies. No one could ever call Mike Watts a sissy. She'd always been the toughest kid in every town she entered. She'd fielded punches and verbal assaults and always came through unscathed.

So why did Jackson's invitation to dinner leave such a bruise on her heart? Because she expected better of him. She'd thought he was different—that the external didn't matter to him like it did others. But then he saw her in a dress, got all bug-eyed, and nearly tripped over himself asking her to spend the evening with him.

"Why, Jackson, did you have to remind me of those other men?" The words were a groan that nearly wrenched her heart from her chest.

"What other men?"

Her hand flew up to press against her pounding heart. Jackson stood in the center of the stage, one hand in his trousers pocket, his weight resting on one leg. The tenderness in his brown-black eyes brought a new sting of tears.

She focused on her camera, fiddling unnecessarily with the lens. "What are you doing, sneaking up on me like that?" Her body quivered from head to toe, and she hated herself for appearing so weak.

The squeak of floorboards warned her of his approach. Maelle's heart doubled its tempo, and she whirled around, ready to demand he leave her alone.

But he only sat on the edge of the stage, several feet away, his legs dangling. "I didn't intend to sneak up on you. I actually stomped pretty hard just so you would hear me coming."

"Well . . ." She shifted the camera a few inches to the right and peered through the viewfinder. Anything to keep herself occupied and avoid making eye contact. "I didn't hear you. And I think it's rude to listen in on someone's private conversation."

"But you asked me the question," he reminded her.

A hint of teasing underscored his tone, but Maelle refused to let him dissuade her from her anger. The anger kept the hurt at bay. "I was thinking out loud. I wasn't talking to you."

Jackson leaned sideways, resting his palm on the stage floor. "Mike, I didn't intend to offend you by asking you to dinner, but I suspect that's what I did. I apologize."

She pinched her brow and examined his face. His expression remained open, kind, with no trace of insincerity. Yet she still wondered . . . She jabbed her finger in his direction. "I find it interesting that you never asked me to dinner when I was wearing pants." Lifting her chin, she challenged, "So why now?"

Jackson shrugged, holding out both hands in surrender. "Because you have to eat?"

The twinkle in his eyes undid her. She snorted, then giggled, covering her mouth with her hand. His chuckle joined hers, and they enjoyed a moment of shared mirth.

Then he turned serious again, tipping his head and looking directly into her eyes. "Truly, Mike, I know I scared you, and I didn't mean to. I'm not even sure why you found my invitation so frightening." Leaning forward slightly, he added softly, "If you'd like to talk about it, I've got two good ears for listening."

"There's nothing to talk about."

He raised his eyebrows at her quick answer, but he didn't push her as he rose to his feet. "All right. But the invitation to listen remains open, whenever you're ready to talk."

She didn't answer.

One side of his lips raised in a smile. "The invitation to dinner also still stands. They serve a pounded beef steak covered in grilled mushrooms that I highly recommend."

Maelle's stomach rolled over, her tongue creeping out involuntarily to lick her lips. Then she squared her shoulders and shook her head. "Thank you, but no."

Jackson frowned. "Are you still afraid of me?"

Afraid? Of Jackson in his three-piece suit and silk jabot, the stage lights slanting across his face and highlighting his chiseled features? The shadows on his face brought a reminder of other faces, other shadows, but Maelle fought the bad feelings. Swallowing, she replied firmly. "No, I'm not afraid of *you*. But I can't go."

He tipped his head, his expression turning boyish. "Why not? You have to eat. Why not eat with me?"

Maelle sighed. She might as well be honest with him or he might not give up. "Jackson, I've never eaten in a nice restaurant like you described. My uncle and I ate our meals in saloons or cooked over a campfire. Sometimes we'd go into some small diner where the same person who cooked the food slapped the plates onto the table. But what you're talking about is a place with waiters and tablecloths and probably some words in the menu that I can't even read. I wouldn't fit in a place like that."

He raised one brow, deliberately giving her an up-and-down glance that directed her attention back to her dress.

She felt a blush building. "Just because I put on a skirt and ruffled shirtwaist doesn't mean I suddenly know how to behave in a fancy-pants restaurant. I'd probably stab the entire steak with the fork and nibble around it and embarrass you to no end." She shook her head. "No. I can't go."

Jackson folded his arms across his chest. "So let me make sure I understand. You are refusing my dinner invitation because of a lack of etiquette?"

The unfamiliar word threw her for a moment. "If etiquette means manners, then, yes. I'm refusing because of that."

"Well, that's easy to fix, Mike. Manners can be learned."

Maelle scowled. "Jackson, I'm not going into a fancy restaurant for the purpose of practicing manners. I'd need them before I went."

"Of course you would." He beamed at her. "And I know exactly how you can learn them."

She lifted her shoulders in a silent gesture of inquiry.

"From Isabelle."

❧

"I hold to my personal opinion that by hiring youngsters and teaching them a trade, we do the young person a favor. When they reach adulthood, they will have a means of providing for themselves. I can see nothing detrimental in that."

An answering murmur rose from several areas in the room. Maelle snapped a picture of the man who had been most vocal about allowing employers to hire whomever they chose, regardless of the age of the worker. Although the man's fashionable suit and slicked-back hair gave the appearance of a reputable businessman, there was something about him that made her believe he was untrustworthy.

Another man, several seats back, raised his hand and called, "If you make these laws, how will they be enforced? We all"— he swept his arm, indicating the gathered ranchers—"reside outside of city limits. Even if the legislation is passed, what are the guarantees the laws will be followed?"

Maelle looked again at the man with the slicked-back hair. His smirk gave her the clear impression he would do whatever he wanted to do, regardless of laws.

Jackson held the podium with both hands, his shoulders square, as he replied. "As with any law, it is only as good as the people who choose to obey it. You're right that it will be easier to enforce in the cities, in the factories."

Maelle noticed the glimmer of a gold tooth as the man with slicked-back hair openly grinned.

"But"—Jackson's tone turned stern—"not impossible. And the children deserve our best efforts to secure their futures."

As Jackson continued to implore the group to consider the potential positive ramifications for all children receiving an education and growing into productive citizens, Maelle looked at Mr. Gerald Harders. The rancher was an older, stockier version of Jackson—the family resemblance was easily seen. But the man lacked Jackson's zeal. She wondered why he didn't stand behind the podium, expounding on the need for child labor laws, instead of allowing Jackson to speak for him.

She shot another picture, capturing Jackson leaning forward, his hand outstretched, his face reflecting passion. Just as he had that day in the park, his exuberant persuasion brought applause. He finished the session by encouraging the men to complete a pledge card, committing financial or personal support toward electing Gerald Harders to the Missouri House of Representatives, where he would fight for laws dictating the end of child labor.

Maelle cushioned the slides between layers of burlap as an older, weather-beaten man and Aaron Rowley roamed the room, collecting cards. Jackson and his father also left the stage to mingle with the guests, talking quietly one-on-one with ranchers. A man approached her, a notepad and pencil in his hands. She recognized him as a reporter from the newspaper.

She straightened from arranging the slides and asked, "How soon will the paper need the photographs I took?"

He flipped the pages of his notepad. "I'll turn in my article this evening. My boss may want it in tomorrow's edition. It'll be more effective the closer it comes to the one about the little urchin who lost his foot under the trolley."

Maelle glanced at the large pendulum clock on the back wall of the room. If she hurried, she could have the photographs turned in by early evening. "I'll make sure the photographs will be ready by tonight."

"Good. I'll tell the boss." He pointed at the box of slides. "Would you like me to carry that for you?"

"No, thank you. I can take care of it."

He gave a nod and strode away.

Maelle returned to her tripod and released the camera from its perch. She turned to place it in the box with the slides, but her progress was halted by a man stepping into her pathway. Her blood chilled when she glimpsed the flash of a gold tooth.

Chapter Twenty-Eight

Mattie
Rocky Crest Ranch
April, 1903

Shucked down to his long johns and holey socks, Matt paced the cabin floor, his head swiveling with every turn as he kept his eyes on the door. Clancy and Mr. Harders had set out just after dawn broke this morning, and he knew they'd be back sometime tonight. Curiosity about how the day had gone, and whether Jackson had drummed up support for his cause, and whether Clancy had seen Jenks, and whether Mr. Harders had an update on Petey had kept him awake well past bedtime. He knew he wouldn't sleep until he'd had a chance to talk to Clancy, so he waited.

The moon was high and bright in the black sky when the doorknob finally turned and the hinges' creak announced Clancy's entrance. The older man crept in, boots in hand, shoulders hunched. He nearly threw his boots over his head when he spotted Matt in the middle of the floor.

"Land sakes, boy, what're ya doin' up in the middle of the night? You pret' near scared the life outta me!"

Despite the late hour and the worries that had kept him awake, Matt released a chuckle. Folding his arms across his chest, he drawled, "Only other time I saw a man sneak into a room like you just done, he had a farm girl by the hand."

Clancy harrumphed, dropping his boots with a clatter. "As if any woman worth her salt'd be seen with the likes of me." He shook his head, drawing in a deep breath. "Wal, now that we've established I'm not sneakin' in with some farm girl, what're you doin' paradin' around here in yer underdrawers?"

Matt scratched his chin. "I just wondered how things went. If you'd seen . . ."

Clancy raised one bushy eyebrow. "Jenks?"

Matt nodded, his throat dry.

"Yep. I seen him." With a snort, Clancy crossed to the little table in the center of the room and yanked out one of the chairs. After seating himself, he sent Matt a knowing look. "That man don't exactly try to endear himself to folks, y' know?"

Matt knew. Jenks probably figured his money covered a lot of sins. Sitting across from Clancy, he said, "He didn't offer support?"

"He didn't fill out no pledge card. An' his carpin' about how kids'll learn a good trade if they take jobs while they're still young'uns kept a whole passel of others from offerin' support." Clancy's derisive tone echoed Matt's feelings about Lester Jenks. "An' not only that, I had to keep him from accostin' a lady newspaper reporter."

Matt's mouth fell open.

Clancy nodded. "That's right. Pushed this lady right into a corner. Scared her into droppin' her camera, an' then he didn't even apologize—just said it was her own clumsiness what caused it to fall." He shook his head, clicking his tongue against his teeth. "Felt right sorry for her. Nobody deserves to be treated thataway. That man's bad news, Matt. You was right to get away from him."

Having been on the receiving end of Jenks's ill treatment, Matt's heart turned over in sympathy for the unknown woman. "That lady . . . is she okay now?"

"Oh yeah. Jackson—he seen it, too, an' he said he'd be sure her camera got replaced. Seems Jackson had invited her there to take pitchers, so he felt responsible." A low chuckle rumbled in Clancy's chest. "He shore let ol' Jenks know how he felt about his shenanigans, too. Don't reckon Jenks'll show his face around Shay's Ford again too soon."

Matt couldn't express any regret for that, yet he wished it hadn't taken something so extreme to make Jackson turn on the man. He said, "I hope Jenks won't cause trouble for Jackson or Mr. Harders now. He's used to getting what he wants."

"Reckon he is," Clancy agreed, stifling a yawn, "but the way I figure, that lady could turn him in for lascivious behavior. He'd be wise to just slink away an' not come back."

"Besides Jenks stirrin' up trouble, did everything else go all right?"

"Oh yeah." Clancy propped his elbow on the table edge and then rested his whiskery chin in his hand. "Got some pledges for money for Gerald's campaign. Some fellers said they'd donate to the orphans' school Jackson's friend is plannin'."

"Orphan school?"

Clancy squinted at him. "Didn't nobody tell you 'bout that? Jackson helped Isabelle—the one who's been takin' care o' Petey—claim her inheritance, an' she's usin' it to start a live-in orphan school. Bought some land outside of Shay's Ford, an' she's plannin' to put up a dormitory with a schoolroom, a carpenter's shop, an' some stables. That way kids'll learn to read an' write an' get a trade."

Clancy pointed a bony finger in Matt's direction, his chin tucked low. "Real ambitious little gal—an' real educated. Says she'll be the teacher out there, but I reckon she'll need some other workers, too. Cain't imagine a little thing like her handlin' it all by her lonesome. Jackson's been helpin' her 'cause he hopes other cities'll do the same once they see it's a good way to keep those abandoned kids off the street an' give 'em a good start in life." A yawn split the man's face after the final word.

Matt had other questions he wanted to ask, but Clancy looked about ready to tumble from the chair, so he simply smiled. "Go on to bed. We can talk more tomorrow."

Clancy gave Matt's shoulder a hearty thump, then shuffled to his room and closed the door. Matt blew out the lamp and went to his room, but in spite of the late hour and his weariness, he remained awake. Thoughts of the orphans' home played at the edges of his mind, holding sleep at bay.

CHAPTER TWENTY-NINE

Maelle
Shay's Ford, Missouri
April, 1903

Dressed in a flannel shirt and her usual tan trousers, Maelle curled on her side on her bunk and stared at the flickering light cast by her lantern. Her eyes burned, but she waited as long as possible between blinks, fearful the shadows might overtake her the moment her eyes slipped closed. The city had long since gone to sleep, but she was restless. Every noise—the call of a night bird, the fierce yowl of a tomcat, the whistle of the wind—seemed magnified. And malicious.

Not since that night in Littleville, New Mexico, had she experienced such fear. Remembered moments from Richard's last day on earth bounced back and forth with moments from today's encounter with the gold-toothed man, becoming a confusing jumble in her mind.

A green-sprigged muslin dress on her girlish form; a dove gray shirtwaist hugging her womanly bodice; two drunken men in rough clothing grabbing her arm, sneering in her face, their breath foul as they paid lewd compliments; a man in a fancy suit running his fingers over her arm, leaning close, his heavy-lidded appraisal offensive as he murmured unwanted invitations. Then a dark alleyway, sounds of saloon music and men's laughter filling the air; a well-lit opera house, squeaks of chair seats and men's low-toned voices providing background noise; Richard's yell, "Run for the sheriff, Mike!"; the Harders' hired man's demand, "Take your hands offa that lady, Jenks!" . . . The flash of a silver knife blade; the flash of a gold tooth. Richard crumpled on the dust-laden ground, lifeless; her camera shattered on the rose-printed carpet, useless.

Such different events, yet so much the same.

Maelle swallowed the lump in her throat, pressing her fists tightly beneath her chin. Both times she'd received unwarranted attention. Both times she'd lost something precious.

The sting of tears forced her to blink several times. Her heart ached afresh at losing Richard, and it ached anew at the loss of her camera. Nothing would bring Richard back, but Jackson had offered to replace her camera. She appreciated the gesture, but it wouldn't be the same. Carrying her old camera—Richard's camera—was like having a piece of her past with her. It represented security and stability. A new camera would take photographs, but it could never be as meaningful as the one she had inherited from Richard.

Inheritance . . . She turned the knob on the lantern, raising the wick. The interior of the wagon immediately brightened, dispelling shadows and giving her a small measure of reassurance. She located the cigar box that held her only tie to her life as Maelle Gallagher and carried it to the bunk. After sitting, she placed the box in her lap and lifted the lid. The once-bright pink ribbon had faded to a dingy peach, decorated here and there with rusty-looking splotches. But the writing on the envelopes that held her parent's love letters was the same—her father's name in her mother's script.

Maelle didn't bother to untie the ribbon. Just holding the stack was enough for now—creating a sense of her parents' presence. She closed her eyes, hugging the letters to her chest, her chin quivering.

"Oh, Da, if you'd been there today, that man would never have touched me." Her words groaned out, the remembered panic causing her heart to pound erratically. "You would have protected me."

You were protected.

Her eyes popped open with the thought. The letters still snug against her heart, she considered this new idea. Had she been protected? Her lips parted with the realization that, even though Da wasn't there, she'd been given assistance. The Harders' hired man had pulled that rich rancher away from her. Jackson had given the man a tongue-lashing and sent him away.

Bits and pieces of a Scripture recited from the pulpit only last Sunday flitted through Maelle's mind: *"In him will I trust . . . my refuge . . . thou savest me from violence . . ."* As she remembered those words, peace washed over her. Lowering her head, she whispered, "Oh, Father, forgive me. How could I forget your presence? I allowed my fear today to take my focus from you. Neither Da nor Richard is here—but you are. You always will be."

Tears crept from beneath her closed lids, running in warm rivulets down her cheeks. "Thank you for sending help today—

for not allowing that man to hurt me. And, Father, please let me set the memories aside so I can have peace. That day in Littleville has a . . . a hold on me. . . ." She held her breath, pushing down the wave of panic that threatened once more to rise in her breast. "I want to be whole again, Lord. Please. . . ."

With her arms clasped across her chest and her eyes tightly closed, Maelle absorbed the warmth and comfort that overcame her. In time, her grip loosened as her muscles relaxed, peace finding its way around the edges of her heart. At long last she opened her eyes, surprised to find the lantern had burned out. The wagon was bathed in darkness, yet the deep shadows held no threats.

❧

With a cigar box tucked under one arm and her free hand holding her skirts out of her way, Maelle walked through the front door of Rowley Market. A cowbell hung above the door clanged out a warning, and Mr. Rowley immediately appeared from between tall shelves.

"Can I help you?"

Maelle held up the cigar box. "I told Petey I'd come by and share some photographs with him. Is he up to company?"

The big man's eyes sparkled. "Oh, Petey's been keepin' himself awake, waitin' for you. He's in my daughter's old room—go through that door an' up the stairs. Second room on the left. Door'll be open." He returned to his tasks.

Maelle moved quickly past the tall counter at the back of the store, smiling at the middle-aged woman who stood behind it counting coins into a tin box. She passed through a wide doorway and located an enclosed staircase immediately on the left. At the top, she found herself in a large room that was obviously the Rowleys' kitchen and sitting room.

For a moment she stared, openly envious, at the functional kitchen and the spaciousness of the room. She could probably fit a dozen wagons in the sitting area alone! *Lord, when will I be able to give up my meandering ways and settle into a home that isn't on wheels?* Then, remembering the purpose of her visit, she forced her feet to move through the hallway on her right. The second door was open, as Mr. Rowley had indicated, and she spotted Petey propped up on a pile of bed pillows in a large bed. She charged through the door.

"Hello, Petey! I'm sorry I'm late. I—" She came to a halt when she realized Petey wasn't alone. Her steps faltered, her smile fading. "And hello, Isabelle."

The younger woman rose from her chair in the corner of the room and pinned Maelle with a glare. "He's been sitting here patiently for nearly twenty minutes, wondering if you forgot about him. If you make a promise to a child, you should keep it."

Angry words pressed in Maelle's throat. How dare this little snip take her to task? But rising above the anger was a rush of guilt so strong her knees nearly buckled. Isabelle's words rang in her mind, bringing back memories of another little boy, another promise made nearly twenty years ago. Did Mattie ever wonder if she'd forgotten about him? Did he resent her for not keeping her promise to find him?

Swallowing, she focused on Petey. The child looked at her out of the corner of his eyes, his chin quivering. Ignoring Isabelle, Maelle sat on the edge of the feather bed and put her hand over Petey's much smaller one. "Did you really think I forgot you?"

Petey shrugged, his gaze dropping. "Sort of." The words were mumbled so softly, she almost didn't catch them.

"I'm sorry I was late. My camera got broken, and your friend Jackson wanted to buy me a new one. We went to every store in town, and it took longer than I thought it would. But I didn't forget you, Petey. I came as fast as I could. And I brought Pikes Peak with me." She held out the cigar box.

Petey smiled. "The big mountain?"

Maelle opened the lid. "Do you want to see it now?"

The child nodded, but he looked up at Isabelle. "Is it okay if I look at the pitchers?"

Maelle met Isabelle's frosty glare. For a moment, Maelle feared the woman would demand she leave. But Isabelle offered a small, abrupt nod and said, "Yes, you may." Angling her chin, she fixed Maelle with a challenging expression. "And I shall look, too."

Maelle ducked her head, hiding her grin. If Isabelle wanted to intimidate her, she would have to do a lot more than look down her nose. Maelle was an expert wrestler, bully-buster, and champion of the underdog. Those snooty looks might grate on her nerves, but they wouldn't chase her away. She set the cigar box on the bed next to her hip and invited, "Well, sit down, then. You're in for a treat. I'm a very good photographer."

With a sweeping of her black skirts, Isabelle seated herself gracefully on the other side of Petey's bed. They spent a half hour examining each photo in turn, with Maelle telling little stories about some of the pictures. Petey laughed especially hard when Maelle confessed she tripped over a rock and accidentally sat on a cactus when backing up to get a better view of the Great Salt Lake.

She fought her own giggles at his unbridled mirth. "It's not that funny!" Truthfully, the situation had never seemed as amusing as it did now, seen through the eyes of this little boy.

Petey covered his mouth with both hands, his eyes sparkling merrily beneath his mop of blond hair. "You got prickles in your backside? How'd ya get 'em out?"

Maelle glanced at Isabelle. The other woman looked as though she'd swallowed a pickle, her lips were pursed so tight. Instead of giving Petey an accurate answer, she said, "It wasn't easy. But the picture was worth it. Isn't it pretty?"

Petey's attention returned to the photograph. The mountains rising in the background, reflected in the flat pool of water, was one of Maelle's favorites. He puckered his brow. "Did ya do any fishin' while you was there?"

Maelle chuckled. "No. Fish can't survive in that lake. It's too salty."

The child's eyes grew wide. "Then, what's it good for?"

Giving him a gentle smile, she said, "It's beautiful to look at."

He looked once more at the picture in Maelle's hand and nodded. "Guess you're right." He stretched, bumping the box into Maelle's knees. "Thanks for showin' me the pitchers, Mike."

Maelle rose, picking up her box. "You're welcome, Petey. I'm glad you liked them."

He adjusted the covers across his chest. "An' I bet you take real good ones of people, too. Will you take one of me and Isabelle?"

Maelle looked at Isabelle, who remained perched on the bed with her hands folded in her lap, her back straight as a poker. "Maybe . . . If Isabelle likes."

The younger woman's fine brows rose. "Can I assume from your reply to Petey that you were successful in securing an adequate camera?"

"There wasn't anything in town that was suitable, but we found one in the Sears and Roebuck catalog." Maelle stifled the sigh that longed for release. "So now I have to wait for it to be shipped, and I don't have anything to do in the meantime." She chuckled ruefully. "I'm not accustomed to doing nothing."

Isabelle pinched her chin between her thumb and fingers, her expression thoughtful. "Do you have neat penmanship?"

"Penmanship?" Maelle peered at Isabelle. "What does that have to do with anything?"

Isabelle rose and rounded the bed with a graceful sweep of her full skirts. She clasped her hands at her waist and tipped her head to the side. "I am in need of a . . . secretary of sorts."

Work for Isabelle? Maelle took a step backward. "I'm not so sure I—"

"Has Jackson spoken to you of the orphans' home being erected north of town?"

The abrupt question stirred Maelle's curiosity. "No, he hasn't."

Isabelle glanced toward the bed. Petey's eyes were closed, his lips slack. She looked to the hallway, giving a nod of her head that communicated her desire for Maelle to follow her. When Isabelle had closed Petey's door, she spoke in a soft tone.

"In a few weeks, there will be a ground-breaking ceremony for a school for orphaned and destitute children. The school will provide room and board, a proper education, and opportunities to give the children skills that will meet their financial needs when they graduate from the program."

"Sounds like a good idea."

"Oh yes." Isabelle's voice, though whisper soft, held fervor. "It is reprehensible that children are left unattended day and night, living on the streets and facing hardships. Our Petey would probably have two good legs right now had a school like this been available to him. My hope is that no other child in Shay's Ford shall ever suffer the way little Petey has."

Maelle folded her arms. "Well, I'm in favor of a school like you're describing. But where does a secretary fit in?"

"As I said, ground-breaking is only a few weeks away. I have sufficient funds to construct the appropriate buildings and begin its operation, but there will be a need for consistent financial support to keep the school in service for the long term." Isabelle pursed her lips for a moment. "There are many wealthy businessmen in Missouri who contribute to worthy causes. I believe this cause is one of the worthiest, as it involves the future well-being of children. But these businessmen won't know about the opportunity unless they are informed."

"So you need someone to inform them," Maelle stated for clarification.

"Yes. I require assistance in penning letters inviting businessmen to commit to a monthly contribution. Time is of the essence, and I simply do not have enough hours between helping in the market and seeing to Petey's needs while he recovers."

Maelle lifted her shoulders in a slight shrug. "Can't you go to the newspaper office and have some fliers printed up to send out?"

Isabelle's fine brows pinched together, and she clicked her tongue against her teeth. "A printed flier might present the information, but it is highly impersonal. A handwritten invitation to contribute is much more likely to garner a favorable response, don't you think?" A sly smile teased the corner of her lips. "I know the wealthy enough to understand that they like to believe they are the only ones being asked to participate in a specific cause. Then they can gloat a bit, adding to their feeling of importance." She touched Maelle's sleeve. "Believe me, Miss Mike, a handwritten invitation is the only acceptable means of communication."

Maelle glanced at Isabelle's hand. Her fingernails were chipped, her skin red and chapped. The working-girl hands didn't match the cultured voice and regal carriage of this young woman. She met Isabelle's gaze. "How did you get involved in this project?"

Isabelle peered at Maelle for long moments, her vibrant green eyes wide and unblinking, as if probing for hidden motivations. Finally she lifted her hand and gestured toward the sitting area of the apartment. "If we're going to visit, we should be more comfortable."

The two women sat in opposite horsehair chairs in front of an open window layered in yellowed lace panels. The bottom edge of the layers billowed and fell in an off-beat rhythm, teased by the fresh-scented breeze.

Isabelle placed her hands in her lap and fixed Maelle with a steady gaze. "If you are going to become involved in the school, perhaps it is best for you to know the details." She took a deep breath, as if gearing for battle.

Maelle said softly, "Isabelle, you aren't obligated to divulge any private matters to me."

A slight smile curved her lips. "Thank you. But if you hear the entire story, you might be willing to do more than write letters."

Maelle leaned back and crossed her ankles. "I'm not a wealthy business owner, so I probably won't be able to make a commitment for finances."

Isabelle laughed airily. "Oh no, I have no intentions of requesting your financial support. But"—she raised a graceful finger—"I will make a request, once the story has been told. So please be patient, and I will do my utmost to be succinct."

Maelle bit the insides of her cheeks to keep from laughing. In her brief acquaintanceship with Isabelle, she had learned the young woman was rarely succinct.

"You see, several months ago my brother evicted me from our home in the Kansas City area. Our parents were killed in an accident, and he was executor of our father's will. He never made any pretense of loving me . . ." For a moment Isabelle's haughty tone faltered, pain creasing her brow. But she quickly recovered and continued fluently. "He saw an opportunity to finally be rid of my presence. The eviction resulted in my fiancé rejecting me, as well."

Looking at Isabelle, Maelle would never have guessed such heartache existed beneath the surface. Perhaps some of the young woman's arrogance was a shield of protection. "Kansas City is on the opposite side of the state. How'd you end up in Shay's Ford?"

"I accepted a position as house servant to a family here. However, after several weeks of employment, I heeded the toll of a chapel bell."

A tickle crept through Maelle's scalp. The chapel bell had beckoned to her, as well. Another connection with Isabelle . . .

"At chapel service, I met the Rowleys, who offered me the opportunity to live in their spare room and work for them." She smiled sadly. "The proposition, although humble, was preferable to the conditions in the Drumfeld household, so I accepted. Then one night Petey"—the first genuine smile Maelle had seen on the woman's face appeared, transforming her countenance—"slipped into my bed, uninvited, and I found myself involved in helping street children.

"Thanks to the Rowleys, and a Bible given to me before I left my home, I also met God and became a part of His family." She closed her eyes for a moment, drawing in a breath through her nose, an expression of contentment on her face. Opening her eyes, she continued. "Initially, I hoped to claim my inheritance in order to return to Kansas City and my place in society, but after becoming a child of God, living in the Chesterfield district didn't seem important any longer. So instead, my inheritance is being used to establish the"—she squared her shoulders, lifting her chin—"Reginald Standler Home for Orphaned and Destitute Children."

Standler. A fierce tingle attacked Maelle's scalp. She scratched her head. "Is Reginald your brother?"

"Oh no. Reginald was my papa, a wonderful, loving, giving man. I'm sure he would approve of my use of the funds he left for me." Her fire-colored brows rose, her eyes wide and guileless. "I never would have considered taking on such a project had God not led me to this place, to these people. I am certain it is my God-ordained purpose."

Maelle thought about the weeks she had spent in Shay's Ford. Never in all of her years of travel had she remained so long in one town. Then there was that tell-tale tingle in her scalp that plagued her so often here . . . Was it God's plan that she be involved in the school, too? She leaned forward. "I'll be glad to help you with those letters you need written."

Isabelle tilted her head, her eyes flashing. "Thank you. And my second request concerns your skill with a camera."

Maelle raised her brows, waiting silently.

"I would very much like to have a pictorial record of the school's construction. Could you be persuaded to remain in Shay's Ford until the completion of the buildings?"

CHAPTER THIRTY

Mattie
Rocky Crest Ranch
April, 1903

W hat'n tarnation . . ."

At Clancy's exclamation, Matt paused in drawing the razor down his cheek and faced his friend. "What's wrong?"

The older man held up a piece of paper. "Got this here letter in yesterday's mail, but it's a might confusin'. My readin' . . . wal, I reckon it ain't what it could be." He scratched his chin, his jaw thrust forward. "Could you maybe look at it an' tell me what ya think?"

Matt set down his razor and crossed the floor to Clancy. He glanced at the handwritten note and felt a chill when he saw the signature at the bottom: Lester Jenks. He shifted his attention to the beginning and read slowly.

Clancy stood at Matt's side, muttering, "Accusin' me of assault? I didn't do nothin' more'n pull him away from that lady photographer. Didn't hurt him. Not like I wanted to . . ."

The letter completed, Matt handed the paper back to Clancy, who scowled at it. "It sounds as though Jenks is threatening to file charges against you, Clancy."

"What kinda charges can he make? He's the one what was botherin' that lady. An' he's the one what busted her camera. Me an' Jackson, we was tryin' to help. Shorely the law'd recognize that."

Matt heard the worry in Clancy's tone, and as much as he wanted to reassure the man, he had witnessed Jenks's power over others. He feared Jenks would do exactly what he'd threatened and Clancy would lose the battle. He pointed at the letter and offered a small glimmer of hope. "Says there he's willin' to talk to you about it first. Do you . . . do you reckon he'll come here?" His belly seemed to turn a dozen somersaults as he waited for Clancy's answer.

Clancy frowned at the letter. "It don't say, but if he's wantin' to speak to me, he'll hafta come here. I ain't a-goin' to him. I got a job to see to." Suddenly his eyes widened. "If he was to come here, then . . ."

Matt nodded. If Jenks came here, Jenks would see Matt. Maybe recognize him. The somersaults doubled their speed in his middle.

Clancy clamped a wiry hand around Matt's upper arm. "Don't you be frettin' now, Matthew. I'll talk to Gerald, an' Gerald'll talk to Jackson, an' we'll git this here matter all straightened out without that man comin' here."

Matt wanted to believe Clancy, but he felt certain Jenks wouldn't let the Harders or Clancy have the upper hand. He wouldn't tell Clancy that, however. No sense in distressing his friend. The soap on his face had dried, making his skin feel tight, but he forced a smile. "Aw, don't worry about me, Clancy. You just worry about you—gettin' that matter worked out so you're clear of any charges. If he comes around here, I'll just stay in the barn with the sheep. Don't reckon he'd come out there."

Clancy snorted. "Course not. Might get his hands dirty." He shook his head, folding the letter and stuffing it in his shirt pocket. "Don't have much respect for a feller who never does any work hisself, just points and gives orders. Man like that . . . filin' charges against me . . ." His muttering continued as he ambled out the door toward the big house.

Matt washed the dried soap from his face without finishing his shave. Maybe he'd grow a beard. He'd never cared much for the feel of facial hair—made him itch—but if it would keep Jenks from recognizing him, it just might be worth it.

✍

Maelle
Shay's Ford, Missouri

Maelle stood before the tiny mirror fastened to the wall of the wagon, hairbrush raised, when a knock on the back of the wagon intruded into her thoughts.

"Who is it?"

"Jackson Harders, Mike."

Setting the brush aside, she dropped the hatch and smiled at Jackson. "Don't tell me Isabelle sent you with another list of addresses." She let her fingers dangle and shook her hand back and forth. "My hand is worn out from letter writing!"

Jackson didn't return her smile, and a feeling of trepidation washed over her. She crouched on the hatch, bringing her eyes to his level. "What's wrong? Is it Petey?" Although the little boy was doing much better—had even managed several steps on wooden crutches—his frailty was a continuing concern for all who knew him.

Jackson shook his head. "No. Petey's fine. It's . . ." He held up an envelope. "I got this in the mail yesterday, but I didn't look at it until late. It's addressed to me, but I think you need to see it." He handed it over.

Maelle shifted to sit on the wagon hatch. Heavy strands of hair swung into her face, and she caught them and pushed them over her shoulder. She noticed Jackson observe the motion, and for some reason heat rose in her cheeks. But she ignored the curious feeling of embarrassment and opened the envelope. By the time she'd finished reading the short note, more heat filled her face, but she knew this time anger was the cause.

"Who does he think he is, accusing you of—" she sought the words on the page—"libelous intent to defame his character." Waving the offending letter, she exclaimed, "The man has no character! All you did was stand up for me when he . . . he . . ." She swallowed, remembering the fear of that moment when he'd run his smooth, cool fingers up the length of her arm. Shoving the letter back into Jackson's hands, she stated, "He has no grounds."

"He thinks he does," Jackson said grimly, pointing at her with the letter, "and he's determined to take this as far as he can." A crease appeared between his eyes. "This kind of hearing creates very unfavorable publicity."

"Do you think it will harm your case for ending child labor?"

The morning breeze caught a rippling strand of hair and carried it under her chin. Jackson seemed mesmerized by the waving lock. Maelle pushed to her feet and retrieved a piece of string. Her back to Jackson, she confined her hair in a tail at the nape of her neck, then returned to the hatch.

Jackson replied as if she'd never moved, but his voice sounded tight. "There's a real possibility this could carry over and create problems since the alleged attack on his character took place at a meeting centering on the child labor issue." He sighed deeply, the brocade vest taut against his chest with the initial intake of breath. "I don't want to put you through an unpleasant encounter, Mike, but it might be necessary for you to make a formal complaint against Jenks to show valid cause for my actions."

Maelle sucked in her lower lip and stared at her clenched fists in her lap, considering Jackson's words. She had involved herself in this fight by giving Jackson photographs and penning dozens of letters. She cared deeply about the plight of children trapped in dangerous, demanding occupations, but the thought of having to face the gold-toothed man who had coldheartedly treated her like a common strumpet made her want to close up her wagon and drive away as fast as she could.

"Mike?" Jackson placed his warm hand over her fists. When she raised her gaze to meet his, he continued. "I hope to work this out without involving the court system, but if Jenks ends up taking this before a judge, will you testify as to the reason for my verbal assault?"

Somewhere at the back of Maelle's brain it registered that a man held her hands. Yet no fear filled her. She offered a slight nod. "I'll do whatever's necessary, Jackson. We can't let him keep this legislation from being passed."

His hand slipped away. "Thank you."

Odd, unrecognizable emotions swirled through Maelle's chest. Why had the touch of his hand on hers not created the same reaction as Jenks's touch? She hopped off the edge of the hatch and closed it. Her fingers trembled slightly as she dropped the pins into place. She pressed her palms together as she faced Jackson and assumed a flippant tone. "Well, I'm stuck here until my camera arrives anyway. And I told Isabelle I would photograph the groundbreaking of the orphans' home, so I might as well make myself useful while I'm still in town." Flinging her arms outward, she concluded, "And speaking of useful . . . I'm sure Isabelle has more letters for me to write."

She hurried away without giving him a chance to respond. Her boots thumped purposefully against the boardwalk as she walked in the widest stride her skirts would allow. She found it frustrating that she had to take smaller steps in a full-cut skirt than she had in trim-fitting trousers. But with trousers there were no layers of fabric to wrap around her ankles. Walking in skirts slowed one's stride. A slower pace allowed racing thoughts to catch up and be acknowledged.

A warmth flooded her cheeks again when she remembered her response to Jackson's simple touch. The last time he'd touched her—the hug in his office—she'd nearly knocked herself to the floor trying to get away. But this time there'd been no rush to escape. Instead, she'd sat meekly, her hands beneath his wide palm, allowing the contact to continue. For a fleeting moment she wished Jackson had tried hugging her, just so she could know if she still found it repulsive. The yearning to be held took her by surprise. When had the idea of having a man's arms around her become desired rather than distasteful?

She pushed the strange thoughts aside as she stepped through the open doorway of Rowley Market and moved directly to the back of the store.

Petey, perched on a high stool beside the counter, broke into a huge smile when he spotted her. "Hi, Mike!"

Maelle glanced around the quiet store. "Where are the others? Did they leave you all alone?"

Petey giggled. "I'm mindin' things. I'm s'posed to ring the bell if anybody comes to buy somethin'." He gestured toward a tarnished brass bell standing on the counter, then crinkled his face in concentration as he began a recitation. "Papa Rowley's in the storeroom. Mama Rowley's takin' a nap. She's got a bad headache. Aaron went to the church to do some cleanin'. An' Isabelle went upstairs to check on Mama Rowley."

Maelle propped an elbow on the counter. "Well, I guess I'll wait here for Isabelle, if you don't mind."

"I don't mind." Petey imitated her position by resting his elbow on the wooden surface. "You got your camera yet?"

"Nope, not yet."

The boy sighed. "Sure am wantin' to have my pitcher took. Isabelle says we'll all get in it—me, an' Mama an' Papa Rowley, an' Aaron an' Isabelle. It'll be like a family pitcher."

A sad smile tugged at Maelle's cheeks. While it was gratifying that this small waif had found his place to belong, his simple words stirred a longing to revisit the photograph she'd given to Mattie. To remember when she was part of a family. "That sounds like a good idea. And I'll have to make sure to come back through Shay's Ford again in a year or two and take another picture to show how you've grown."

Petey sat up straight, his eyebrows high. "You're leavin'?"

"I'm afraid so, Petey." Maelle discovered she truly was sorry to think of leaving this community. Her lengthy stay had stirred her long-held desire to settle in one place. Yet she knew she could never settle down until she'd finally located her brother and sister. "I'm a traveling photographer. I have to travel on."

Without warning, Petey launched himself from the stool into Maelle's arms. She staggered backward a step with the unexpected weight, but she caught him and scooped him close.

He wrapped both skinny arms around her neck and held tight. "I sure wish you wouldn't go, Mike." His breath teased her ear, his voice quavering with emotion.

Maelle swallowed the tears that rose in her throat. "Oh, Petey . . ." She inhaled the scent of the boy, relishing the feel of his body in her arms. Only a few minutes ago she'd longed for someone to hold her. Holding Petey was just as good as being held, she decided. His hands on her neck released the string that confined her hair, and thick strands cascaded around her shoulders as she lowered him to the stool.

Tipping forward to bring her face only inches from his, she said, "I promise to come back, Petey. You're my friend, and I'll want to check on you."

With the resilience of a child, he brightened. "An' see my new peg leg? I should be gettin' it afore too long."

Maelle chuckled. "And see your peg leg. Just think . . . you'll be running when I come back next time!"

Petey flashed a bright, endearing grin.

A clatter on the stairs alerted them to someone's approach. Isabelle winged around the corner, her face flushed. "Petey, I'm sorry I took so long. Are you—" Her gaze found Maelle, and she stopped so abruptly it looked like she'd come into contact with a brick wall. Her eyes widened and her jaw dropped. "Mike . . . Oh my . . ."

Maelle frowned, glancing at Petey.

Isabelle glided forward, her hand reaching. She caught a strand of Maelle's hair and let it drift through her fingers. "You have lovely hair. Such a rich color—the burnished red of an oak leaf in late October. Are those waves natural? With it always twisted into a braid, I didn't realize . . ."

She took hold of Maelle's shoulders and turned her around, and then Maelle felt Isabelle's fingers stroke the length of her unfettered waves. The gentle touch sent a tremor through her entire body. Isabelle's finger must have caught on the second stroke, because she felt a slight tug, reminding her of Da's habit of giving a little pull on her curls to tease her. A lump formed in her throat.

"It's just hair," she said, stepping out of Isabelle's reach. She searched the floor for the piece of string.

Isabelle clasped her hands beneath her chin. "It reminds me so much of my mama's hair, although hers wasn't as thick as yours, nor as long. She used to allow me to brush it out and then fashion it into a knot on the back of her head."

Isabelle's blithe comment sent Maelle backward in time to Ireland, to a tiny cottage, to a fireside stool and the remembrance of her mother seated in front of flickering flames, twisting pink ribbon through her own waist-length braid of shimmering red . . .

Her scalp tingled at the memory, and she shook her head, dispelling the image. "I prefer a braid." She quickly plaited her hair and tied the end securely.

The expression of longing in Isabelle's green eyes faded. She squared her narrow shoulders and said briskly, "Well, then, are you prepared to write letters?"

"Yes. How many more are there?"

A gleam appeared in Isabelle's eyes. "Enough to keep you quite occupied this morning."

Maelle released an exaggerated groan that made Petey giggle. She headed to the table tucked in the corner of Isabelle's tiny bedroom, uncapped the ink pot, and began the message she now knew by heart. *Dear Sir . . .*

CHAPTER THIRTY-ONE

Mattie
Rocky Crest Ranch
April, 1903

Matt, his belly full from breakfast, rounded the back corner of the big house on his way to the horse barn. He and Russ would spend the morning taking the ewes to the north pasture for feeding. An approaching surrey caught his attention, and he paused, tilting his hat brim to block the sun.

He recognized Jackson in the driver's seat, and he lifted his hand in a wave. Jackson pulled the surrey beside Matt and peered down at him with a serious expression. "Matt, could you find Clancy and bring him to the house? We need to talk."

Jackson had skipped a polite good morning, and that made Matt worry. Something must be wrong. "Sure, I know where he is. Everything okay?"

"No." Jackson rubbed the back of his neck. Lifting the reins, he said, "Hurry, would you, Matt?" He clicked his tongue, and the bay obediently heaved forward.

Matt waited until the surrey turned toward the house before he trotted in the direction of the sheep barn. He found Clancy in the first stall, rake in hand, clearing soiled straw. But he dropped the rake immediately when Matt told him Jackson was at the house looking for him.

"Gotta be about that letter from Jenks," he growled, his arms pumping as he headed for the wide opening. "Gerald tol' me Jackson'd take care of it."

Matt thumped along beside Clancy. "Jackson didn't look too happy. Do you reckon he isn't gonna be able to fix it?"

Clancy shot a quick glare in Matt's direction. "Course he c'n fix it. He knows the law, an' the law won't hold nothin' against me fer doin' the right thing."

Matt put his arm around Clancy's shoulders. "You're right, Clancy. It'll all work out."

They reached the back door, and Clancy paused for a moment, rubbing his chin. "I'd say come in, but—"

"Nah." Matt backed up. "I got work to do. You can tell me at lunch how it went."

Clancy bobbed his head in a brusque nod, opened the door, and stepped through.

Matt headed to his duties, but even while he watched the dogs herd the sheep to a grazing area, his thoughts remained back at the big house. How would Jackson keep Jenks from following through on filing charges against Clancy? What would Mr. Harders do if Jenks managed to send Clancy to jail? The two men were more than boss and employee; they were good friends. The other two hands, José and Parker, were closer to Matt's age and had only been on the ranch a few years. Mr. Harders and Clancy had worked together for more than Matt's lifetime.

Matt jerked in the saddle, forcing away the unpleasant thought. "Need to quit thinkin' the worst'll happen," he muttered, smoothing his gloved hand along Russ's shiny neck. "The Bible says things work for good if a person's committed to God and doin' right. Clancy surely fits that. It'll be okay." Saying the words aloud offered an element of peace, and the rest of the morning passed quickly.

When he met up with the others for lunch, Clancy's sullen expression washed away the morning's calm. "Clancy? You okay?"

Mr. Harders passed a tin plate of corn muffins. "We've had a rough morning, Matt. Lester Jenks is not only filing trumped-up charges, he's made an offer on the land a young woman from town wanted to purchase to establish an orphans' home." He heaved a sigh. "I must admit, I'm not eager to have him as a neighbor."

Matt put a muffin on his plate even though his appetite suddenly fled. His hands shook as he passed the plate to Clancy.

Clancy snorted, jerking the plate from Matt's hands. "That man's nothin' but a peck of trouble!"

Mr. Harders set his mouth in a grim line. "You're right, Clancy, but I'm afraid he has an upper hand in this situation."

Clancy shoved the plate on to José without taking a muffin and sent Matt a disbelieving look. "He's got some fellers gonna say he was just offerin' to help that lady carry her camera—that I started a squabble 'cause I wanted to carry it myself!"

Matt gawked at Mr. Harders. "Can he do that?"

The boss shrugged, scooping beans and ham onto his plate. "He's already done it. According to Jackson, each of the men who supposedly witnessed the altercation between Clancy and Jenks have borrowed money from Jenks in the past. They owe him, and he's calling up their debts by requesting their support."

"But that's not right!" Matt automatically ladled a scoop of beans onto his plate when Mr. Harders handed him the pot, but he didn't pick up his spoon to eat. "Somebody's gotta stop him. He can't just keep doing harm to folks!"

Silence fell after Matt's outburst. José and Parker ate quietly, their furtive glances flitting around the table. Clancy's plate remained empty, his fists clenched in his lap. Mr. Harders held his fork, but he didn't stab it into the mound of beans on his plate. He met Matt's gaze. "You feel pretty strongly about this."

Matt's thudding heart proved his boss's words.

"Want to tell me why?"

Matt could feel Clancy's eyes on him, but he didn't look at his cabin mate. His gaze on his plate, he forced through clenched teeth, "Just . . . ain't right."

Mr. Harders pulled his lips to one side, making his mustache twitch. He pinned Matt with narrowed eyes. "I agree with you, son. Jackson's going to do everything he can to help Isabelle purchase that land and to disprove Jenks's charges. He's also facing a lawsuit brought by Jenks."

Matt's jaw dropped open. "A lawsuit? What for?"

"For defamation of character."

"Man's got no character," Clancy muttered.

Matt agreed.

"So there's a lot at stake. But I'm hopeful. And I'd appreciate it if all of you would join me in praying"—his fervent expression touched each man at the table—"that when Jenks comes here next week to discuss his claims, we'll be able to work things out without involving the court."

Suddenly the air seemed to be sucked from Matt's chest. He gasped for breath. "He . . . he's comin' here?"

"On Tuesday." Mr. Harders frowned. "Matt, are you all right?"

Sweat broke out across Matt's back. His scarred back. He pushed his chair away from the table, the legs screeching against the floor. "No, sir. I gotta be excused." He dashed out the back door, careened around the corner of the house, and bent over the bushes while his stomach emptied its meager contents. A hand touched his back, and he jerked upright, his eyes closed, gulping air.

"Matt?" Clancy's voice.

"I'm sorry, Clancy." He wiped his mouth with the back of his hand and turned slowly to face his friend. The ground seemed to tip, and he grabbed the cool rock wall of the house for support. "I wanna help you out, but . . . I can't be here when Jenks comes. If he recognizes me . . ."

Clancy nodded, his lined eyes sad. "I know, Matthew. If'n you need to ride on, I'll 'splain things to Gerald after yore gone. He won't hold a grudge against ya. He's a fair man."

Matt nodded miserably. He knew Mr. Harders was a fair man, and it pained him to let his boss down, but how could he stay?

Oh, Lord, I wanted a home here so bad. . . .

CHAPTER THIRTY-TWO

Maelle
Shay's Ford, Missouri
April, 1903

From the high seat of the wagon, Maelle flipped the reins and encouraged, "All right, Samson, let's go get that picture taken." She smiled as Samson pulled the wagon over the cobblestone street toward Rowley Market. Not only was the day beautiful, with a scented breeze pleasing her nose and the bright sun warming her hair, her new camera had arrived. It now sat in a specially made carrying case in the back of the wagon.

Jackson had purchased an Eastman Century View camera, the best model available from the catalog. Maelle had spent most of the morning reading the instructional book to familiarize herself with its use. Her old camera had used dry plates, but this model made use of non-curling film, which Maelle hoped would be easier to store and use. The portrait of Petey and his surrogate family—her first one on the new camera—would let her know whether or not she could successfully use the new, modern equipment.

She tugged the reins, drawing Samson to a stop outside the market. The entire Rowley family waited on the boardwalk. Aaron held Petey in his arms, and the boy lifted his hand from Aaron's broad shoulder to wave at Maelle.

"Mike! You came! Mama Rowley wants us to take our pitcher out here in front of the market. Can we do that?"

Maelle climbed down from the wagon and crossed to the family. "Sure. We can take the picture wherever you like."

Mrs. Rowley touched the cameo pinned in the center of a flurry of ruffles beneath her double chin. "Just don't seem natural, standing in front of some painted backdrop. We want our photograph to show us like we really are, just humble shopkeepers."

Maelle smiled. She'd never seen Helen Rowley minding the store in a white ruffly blouse and black pleated shirt, nor did Mr. Rowley and Aaron wear suit coats to stock shelves. But she had to admit, they made a handsome family, right down to Petey, who wore a Little Lord Fauntleroy suit with the right pant leg folded back and pinned out of the way. He had more ruffles beneath his chin than Mrs. Rowley.

She flicked the brim of his hat. "Aren't you fine-lookin' in your suit!"

The boy grimaced. "Mama Rowley made me wear it. Ruther be in my shirt an' britches."

The Rowleys joined Maelle in a laugh at Petey's expense. Aaron lowered him to the ground, and the child positioned his crutches beneath his armpits. Petey's bright eyes flashed as he looked around. "Where's Isabelle? I want her in the pitcher, too."

"I'll get her," Aaron said, and headed inside.

A small crowd gathered to watch as Maelle set up her tripod at the curb. Accustomed to an audience, she ignored the whispers and stares as she measured how far away from the market's window she would need to position the family to keep them out of the awning's shadow yet still ensure the market's front would be evident in the final photograph.

In her mind's eye, she envisioned a balanced placement of subjects and decided to put Petey in the center, the two men behind him, and the women on the outside of the group. Their faces—the focal part of the image—would form a rough M.

"Over here," she directed, pointing to spots on the walkway, "and here." Ralph and Helen Rowley obediently stepped into position. "Okay, Petey, you'll be in the middle." The boy brought his crutches forward and swung his body after. She made him giggle by catching him under the arms and moving him over a few inches. Just as she released him, Aaron and Isabelle stepped outside.

Isabelle held a small, leather-bound book. "May I hold my Bible in the picture?"

Maelle barely glanced at it. "Certainly. Now, Aaron, you'll be next to Petey, and—"

"No!" Petey's face reflected dismay. "I want Isabelle by me. Please?"

Maelle frowned. Placing Isabelle on the inside would disrupt the balance. But looking into Petey's face, she couldn't deny his request. She sighed. "All right. Mr. and Mrs. Rowley, please switch places." They did so, with Mrs. Rowley clucking and adjusting her ruffles. Then Maelle turned to Isabelle. "Beside Petey, please, and Aaron can stand on the outside."

Petey grinned. "Thank you, Mike!" He beamed up at Isabelle, and she returned the smile. Something in the younger woman's profile—the curve of her jaw, the sweep of her vibrant red hair, the gentleness in her green eyes—sent a prickle of awareness across Maelle's scalp. She shook her head to dispel the feeling.

She stepped back and surveyed the arrangement, her brows low. A lumpy shadow intruded next to Aaron's feet, formed by the heads of several onlookers who blocked the sun's rays. "Could you folks move back?" She watched the walkway, frowning. "A little more, please." The area around Aaron's feet cleared. "There, that'll do. Thank you."

Satisfied, she stepped behind the camera and peered through the viewfinder. One eye squinted shut, she zeroed in on each subject with the open eye, shifting her gaze from left to right across Mr. Rowley to Mrs. Rowley to little Petey to Isabelle's hands cupping the Bible . . . and she froze.

Her scalp came alive, as if struck by lightning. Her ears buzzed with the intensity of the reaction. A memory flashed in her mind—her own hands, young and smooth, holding out a worn black Bible to a tall man. The echo of her childish voice whispered through her mind: *"Will you take me family's Bible . . . for Molly?"*

She jerked upright, staring over the top of the camera at Isabelle, at her exquisite profile as she smiled down at Petey. Her hands began to tremble as Isabelle's image flashed in and out, competing with another image. A black-and-white image. Printed on paper. Of another woman, in another place—another country—holding a baby in her lap and smiling in just the way Isabelle was now smiling. *Oh, Heavenly Father, why did I not notice before?*

Her breathing erratic, Maelle stepped to the side of the camera. She feared her quivering legs might collapse. But somehow she stumbled forward three feet, her gaze bouncing between the book in Isabelle's hands and Isabelle's face. *Could it be?* Hope rose in her heart as she forced her tongue to form a single word: "M–Molly?"

❧

Mattie
Rocky Crest Ranch

Matt buttoned his shirt, his gaze on the photograph lying on the little table beside the bed. He sighed deeply, his heart heavy. "Maelle," he spoke aloud, "I don't make things easy for you, do I?"

Although he needed to return to the sheep barn—he'd been given permission to change shirts after catching his sleeve on a piece of barbed wire and ripping it nearly in two—he took an extra minute to sit on the edge of the lumpy mattress and pick up the photograph of his family. Staring at the faces printed in black and white, he tried to bring them to life in his memory. But too many years had passed.

What might Maelle look like now, he wondered as he traced his rough fingertip down the length of the child-Maelle's tumbling curls. He shifted his focus to baby Molly. He remembered the baby had flaming red hair and eyes as green as a clover leaf. Did he recall his da saying the baby was as beautiful as their mother, or did he only imagine it?

At least he could confirm for himself his mother's beauty. He held the evidence in his hand, and he spent several minutes staring at the image of Brigid Gallagher.

Another sigh escaped, laden with regret. How different his life would be had Ma and Da not perished in that fire . . . No orphan's home, no train ride, no separation from Maelle and Molly, no Jenks . . .

Worry hit hard with the remembrance of Jenks's planned visit to the ranch tomorrow. He couldn't stay, not with Jenks coming. He pressed the photograph to his chest, closing his eyes as a familiar question rose in his heart in the form of a prayer. "How will Maelle ever find me, Lord, if I keep pickin' up stakes an' movin' on?"

Matt slapped the photograph onto the table and stood up. Despite his need to stay put, he had no choice. If Jenks was coming, he must be far away. Clancy had said Mr. Harders would understand. He headed out of the cabin, determination straightening his shoulders. He'd perform his very best for his boss during his final hours at Rocky Crest Ranch.

Maelle
Shay's Ford, Missouri

Isabelle tilted her head, her brows coming down in puzzlement. "What did you call me?"

Maelle licked her dry lips, searching Isabelle's face. The younger woman's confusion was evident. Embarrassment flooded her. Her years of wishing, praying, hoping had made her see things that didn't exist. She shook her head. "Nothing. I didn't say anything." She turned to go back to her camera.

A small hand on her arm stopped her. She stared at the hand—Isabelle's work-roughened hand. The fingers slim and feminine despite the dry skin and rough nails. Her gaze lifted to Isabelle's face, and Isabelle's deep green eyes bored into Maelle's.

"Did . . . did you call me . . . Molly?"

Hardly daring to breathe, Maelle forced her head to offer a nod of admission.

"How do you know her—Molly?"

Maelle closed her eyes, tears stinging. She didn't know her. Not anymore. Not like she should—not the way sisters should know one another. But oh, how she longed to. "I don't know her. I thought . . . I saw . . . She's my . . ." She shook her head again, twisting her face into a grimace. "It doesn't matter."

Isabelle's eyes implored. "Please tell me. If you know Molly, then, maybe . . . maybe you also know—" she lifted the Bible and flipped the cover open—"Maelle and Matthew?"

Maelle stare at the exposed page. A family register bearing her and her siblings' names in her father's penmanship. Her knees buckled, and the world spun. Somehow she managed to remain upright. Her hands groped and found Isabelle's—Molly's—arms. She clung, her mind whirling with the realization that she held her flesh-and-blood sister in her trembling fingers. Real. Not imagined.

Oh, Father, thank you! Only you could have reunited us.

"Mike?" Isabelle's cheeks flushed red in her pale face and her tone became insistent. "How do you know Molly?"

"I know her because she's my wee sister, the baby I carried from the burning tenement, the tiny lass I was forced to hand to a fancy family although I begged them not to take her from me. I know her because I am Maelle Gallagher."

Isabelle's eyes grew wider as Maelle spoke, her jaw dropping into an expression of astonishment. Maelle released her sister's arms to cup her face. The face that was as beautiful as her mother's had been. She finished in a rasping whisper. "And I've been longing for you my whole life long."

"My . . . Maelle . . . ?" On the quavering note of wonder, Isabelle fell into Maelle's embrace. Maelle wrapped her arms around her sister, unable to hold her closely enough. The Bible in Isabelle's hand pressed against Maelle's spine, providing the presence of their parents to the encirclement and reminding Maelle of God's answer to prayer. For long moments they simply clung, with tears flowing.

But then a small voice interrupted. "What're ya doin', Mike? I thought you was gonna take our pitcher."

With a laugh, Maelle pulled back. She tapped the top of Petey's hat. "I am. But you'll have to let me catch my breath. I've just had a surprise."

Isabelle snuffled, rubbing her hand beneath her nose. "I can't possibly have my picture taken now. I must look a sight!"

Maelle touched her sister's cheek. "You're as lovely as our mother was. Our da always said our mother was more lovely than springtime."

Isabelle smiled and clasped Maelle's hand. "Oh, I want to know about our mother and . . . da. You will tell me, won't you?"

"I can do more than that." Maelle smiled through her tears. "I can show you letters written by our mother to Da, in her very own words." Her voice caught. "I've held on to them in the hopes that one day I'd be sharing them with you."

"And our brother, Matthew?" Isabelle's eyes lit with eagerness. "Will you introduce me to him, as well?"

A stab of sorrow pierced Maelle. "Isabelle . . . about Mattie . . ."

"Are we gonna take a pitcher or not?" Petey's cranky voice intruded once more. The little boy shifted impatiently. "My armpits is hurtin'! Let's hurry up!"

"Oh, Petey," Mrs. Rowley scolded, her voice quivering with emotion, "let these sisters have their moment. The picture can wait." Her eyes glistened with tears as she leaned down and touched the little boy's shoulder. "It's a special blessing we've just witnessed, seeing Isabelle find her sister."

Petey shrugged. "Wasn't that hard to find her. Mike was standin' right on the boardwalk."

The adults laughed, washing away the tears. Maelle hugged Isabelle once more—briefly, firmly, wholeheartedly—and set her aside. "We'll have plenty of time to catch up. Let's take the picture."

CHAPTER THIRTY-THREE

Molly
Shay's Ford, Missouri
April, 1903

Isabelle closed the market door and turned the lock. Pressing her face to the glass, she squinted through the dim light, watching Mike—her sister, Maelle—climb into the wagon's seat, lift the reins, and drive away through the gloaming. Only when she could no longer hear the click of the horse's hooves against the cobblestone did she turn and lean against the door, closing her eyes and releasing a deep sigh of contentment.

Her long afternoon and evening with Maelle had revealed so much. She recognized anew the advantages she'd been given. Comparing her childhood to Maelle's had brought a rush of guilt, but her sister hadn't allowed it to take hold.

"Be grateful you were loved. It's what I wanted for you," Maelle had told her, holding tight to her hands. "It must be what God wanted for you, too."

Isabelle had argued, "God wanted me separated from you and our brother?"

"God knew you would need the education and the financial means to provide help to children who need it," Maelle had insisted. "He had a plan for you, Isabelle. Now see it through."

Isabelle walked slowly through the dark market toward her little bedroom, reflecting on her sister's strength and surety. When Isabelle had expressed dismay at the lost years, Maelle had proclaimed they mustn't look back and think "what if." Isabelle had set the questions aside while Maelle was present, but now she found it difficult not to let her mind ponder. What if the children had been allowed to stay together? What if she'd had Maelle and Matthew in her life instead of Randolph? What if—

A creak on the stairs stopped her thoughts. She spun, her gaze locating a shadowy figure moving toward her. "Who is it?"

"It's me—Aaron."

"Aaron." She waited for him to approach. In the muted light, his blue-green eyes appeared almost black. "You startled me."

"I'm sorry." The words came out in a soft whisper. He was so close his breath brushed her cheek. "Did Mike leave?"

"Yes." Isabelle hugged herself. "I think we could have talked all night." She laughed lightly. "It is the oddest thing, Aaron. When I first met Maelle, I didn't like her. She was so . . . different. I suppose she made me uncomfortable, because she is such a free spirit and I was raised to follow convention. But the moment I realized she was my sister, something inside of me opened up to her. And now, after only one evening together, I feel as though I love her."

Aaron's gentle smile let her know he understood.

"She really is amazing." Isabelle shook her head in wonder. "Do you know the only home she's had since she was a little girl is that wagon? She's not lived in a house or attended school . . ." She blew out a delicate breath. "The stories she can tell of her travels . . ."

"You have lots of lost years to catch up on."

"Yes." A lightness filled her breast. "But we'll have time. She says she'll be staying in Shay's Ford and opening a photography studio here. She doesn't want to be far from me again."

"Good."

"But that means she'll no longer be searching for our brother, Matthew."

A long pause followed, during which Isabelle sensed that Aaron shared her heartache. Finally she said, "It's late. Why are you still up?"

"I was waitin' for you to—" He stopped for a moment, pressing his lips together. His hand found her arm. "I wanted to talk to you. Can we go . . . sit?"

Isabelle nodded, and he guided her with a hand on her back through the dark store to the stairway. A lantern glowed somewhere above, casting enough light for her to make her way safely up the stairs. But her limbs still quivered as if she were uncertain of her footing. A keen awareness of Aaron's presence made the fine hairs on the back of her neck stand up. The spot on her back where his hand had rested still tingled, as if he'd left an impression in her flesh. The feeling both puzzled and pleased her.

When they turned the corner at the top of the staircase to go into the sitting room, Isabelle crossed directly to the sofa and sat on its edge. Aaron hesitated, seeming to examine each piece of furniture before seating himself on the other half of the sofa. Except at the dinner table, they'd not sat in such close proximity. Isabelle was certain her face glowed more brightly than the lamp on the table beside her.

Aaron linked his fingers and placed them in his lap before shifting his body slightly to face her. "The groundbreaking ceremony for the school is next weekend."

For some reason, the words caused disappointment to wash over her. But what had she expected him to discuss? Giving herself a mental shake, she said, "That's right." She frowned, worry striking. "You don't think that man . . . Mr. Jenks . . . will convince the owners to sell to him instead of me?"

Aaron shook his head. "Jackson said you've shaken hands on the deal an' made a partial payment. That's bindin'. If he were to break the deal, people in town wouldn't trust him anymore."

She blew out a breath of relief, her fingers at her throat. "Thank goodness."

"Don't worry. Jackson'll take care of Jenks."

Isabelle smiled, lowering her hand to her lap. "No worries. But I'm hoping for a good turnout from town and the surrounding communities. I've already heard from several businessmen who have committed to assisting with funding. Surely the school will be a success."

"I have no doubt." Although the topic was impersonal, Aaron's warm tone lent the essence of intimacy. "And I'm sure proud of how you're reachin' out to the orphans."

Isabelle lowered her chin, pleasure at his simple compliment rendering her speechless.

He continued. "I've been talking to Pa and Reverend Shankle, but I wanted to ask you . . ."

When his voice trailed off, Isabelle lifted her gaze to meet his eyes. "Yes?" The single word quavered.

"I wondered . . . if you might have need of . . . a man around the place." Suddenly the hesitation disappeared. His words poured out as if dumped from a barrel. "It's outside of the city limits, where any unscrupulous person could come by, but a man on the property would offer protection. The buildings'll need maintenance and repairs, and a man should do those things. Plus the boys will need to be taught more than reading and writing. They need to learn to use tools an' to plant crops an' . . . man stuff. Things you can't teach them. And—" he took a deep breath, as though running out of steam—"there may be need for a firm hand now and then. Kids'll be kids, you know, and sometimes they need correction. I'm not so sure you're up to that."

Isabelle wanted to argue with him—to state quite adamantly that she was perfectly capable of handling the school on her own—yet she knew he was right. She had never learned to wield a hammer or plow a field. The boys would have need for such lessons. She had gotten so caught up in the planning of the school, she hadn't considered its actual day-to-day running. Certainly she would need a staff. Not only a man to provide protection and maintenance, but someone to cook and clean, as well as teachers versed in subjects beyond the rudimentary. Her shoulders slumped as she realized how much more was needed than she could give.

She released a sigh of resignation. "Did Reverend Shankle or your father have a suggestion?"

"Actually . . ." The hesitation returned, causing Isabelle's pulse to race. "I had a suggestion, which Pa and Reverend Shankle approved. Now I just need to know what you think."

He swallowed, the gulp audible in the quiet room. "Remember the day in the hospital, when you got the letter from your foster father's lawyer? When you found out he'd left you that sum of money?"

Isabelle nodded.

"You said . . . you said we would fight for the children together." There was another pause, while she stared into his unblinking eyes. "Did you mean that?"

Isabelle's tongue felt stuck to the roof of her mouth. She managed another nod. Of course she'd meant it. She knew their hearts were united in desire to help the orphans and street children. Now she realized her heart desired to be united with Aaron in other ways, as well.

"Then . . ." He swallowed again. "Then, what would you think of my living at the school, too . . . help you run it?"

A part of her wanted to cry out an exultant *yes!* She knew Aaron, trusted Aaron, believed wholeheartedly his presence would be of benefit to the children in many ways. Yet she held the reply inside, a niggle of apprehension silencing the response.

Living here at the market with Aaron's family, spending time with him each day, she had come to admire him. How different he was from Glenn Heaton. Her money meant little to Aaron— he was concerned about Isabelle the person. She believed with her whole soul that Aaron was an honorable man. In fact, she loved him. But how difficult it would be to spend each day working side by side with him and keep those feelings hidden. In fact, it would be impossible. She couldn't do it.

Aaron waited for an answer. She licked her lips and spoke evenly. "I'm quite sure you would be a tremendous benefit to the school, Aaron, and I'm honored you would consider giving up your duties at the church and the market to assist me. But . . . but I'm not sure it's . . . wise."

His sweet face drooped with disappointment, piercing Isabelle's heart. He turned his head, staring across the dimly lit room toward the windows. "I understand." A huge sigh lifted his shoulders, and he stood abruptly. Barely glancing at her, he said, "Would you like me to help you hire some workers?"

His defeated tone brought Isabelle to her feet. "Aaron, it isn't that I don't want your help, it's just—"

He held up his hand. "Isabelle, I said I understand. I should have known someone like you would never be—"

Isabelle held her breath, anticipating the completion of his thought, but he clamped his jaw and held back whatever he'd planned to say. With her heart beating so hard she felt it in the top of her head, she ventured in a bold whisper, "Would never be . . . interested . . . in you?"

The muscles in his jaw twitched. His gaze straight ahead, he gave a brusque nod. "I know I'm just a shopkeeper's son, nobody special. But I care about you. And the kids. I just thought . . . I hoped . . ." Once more, his thought went unfinished.

Isabelle's fingers trembled as she placed them lightly on Aaron's forearm. "You hoped . . . ?" *Tell me, Aaron. Tell me you love me, please. . . .*

As if in response to her silent plea, he turned and faced her. Lamplight flickered in his irises. He searched her face while her breath came in little spurts. He must have found what he sought, because he tipped his head toward her and admitted, "I hoped you cared enough about me to want to work together . . . as a team."

"A . . . a team?"

His lips parted, and he took her hand. "As husband and wife, Isabelle."

The softly uttered statement filled Isabelle with a rush of emotion—joy, gratitude, fulfillment. She closed her eyes, absorbing the wonder of the moment—*He loves me!*—and then opened them again to lift her smile to him. "You truly want that?"

His voice turned husky. "More than anything."

"Then ask me." She tugged his hand. "Please ask me."

Aaron caught her shoulders and gently pressed her onto the sofa. Then, as she watched in wide-eyed awe, he knelt before her. Taking her hand, he carried it briefly to his lips to deliver a soft brush across her knuckles. She held her breath as he met her gaze, his expression tender.

"Isabelle Standler, will you do me the honor of becoming my wife?"

Although in her daydreams she had prolonged the moment, now that the scene played in reality, eagerness brought an immediate response. "I would like nothing better than to become Mrs. Aaron Rowley."

He opened his arms, and she melted into his embrace. His large hand cupped the back of her head, holding her securely against his shoulder. Warm tears ran from her eyes to soak his shirt, and she felt his tears wetting the top of her head where his cheek rested. Her eyes closed, she memorized every detail—the feel of his calloused hand on her hair and his firm shoulder beneath her cheek; the lingering scent of supper's lamb stew combined with Aaron's own musky scent filling her nostrils—a homey, comforting aroma; the steady thrum of his heart matching the pounding she felt in her own chest.

Aaron's hands slipped to her shoulders, and then his thumbs brushed her cheeks, wiping away her tears. He used his sleeve to clear the moisture from his own face before taking her hands and lifting her to her feet. Their hands still joined, he smiled and said, "I suppose you'll want Mike to take our wedding picture."

"Yes. The moment her studio is completed."

Aaron's forehead creased for a moment. "Shouldn't we wait until your year of mourning is over?"

Isabelle found no reason to hesitate. "Perhaps it breaks with convention, but I believe my parents would approve. Mama and Papa always wanted my happiness. From what Maelle has told me, so did the Gallaghers." Tears welled again as she said, "And you, Aaron, are my happiness."

CHAPTER THIRTY-FOUR

Mattie
Rocky Crest Ranch
April, 1903

Matt forced the bite of scrambled eggs down his gullet but felt as though it would come right back up. His stomach churned with the knowledge that this was his final day at Rocky Crest. His final day with Clancy and Mr. Harders. His final day of peace. Because today Jenks was coming.

He stabbed his fork into the mound of eggs and made himself swallow another bite. If he was going to travel today, he'd need food in his belly. He wouldn't allow that man to send him away hungry, as he'd done the last time.

It galled him to think about sneaking away, as if he were in disgrace. He remembered slipping away from Jenks's ranch, constantly looking over his shoulder, fearing pursuit. He'd be looking over his shoulder when he rode away today, too, but not out of fear. Out of longing. He'd sure miss Clancy and Mr. Harders. They'd become like family.

He glanced around the table, where everyone ate in silence. None of the cheerful babble to which he'd grown accustomed filled his ears this morning. A cloak of oppression seemed to hang over the room. All because of Jenks.

That man had far too much power. Matt snatched up a biscuit and shoved it into his mouth. *An' you're giving him power over you.* The derisive thought stilled his jaw mid-chew. Could it be true? Did Jenks *hold* power, or did Matt *give* it to him? He swallowed the dry biscuit and turned to stare at Clancy's profile. Clancy had said Mr. Harders would understand if he left, but now Matt wondered if it was the best thing to do. Should he let Jenks run him off?

"Mr. Harders?"

The older man jumped at Matt's voice. He set down his fork. "Yes, son?"

His gentle tone brought a lump to Matt's throat. How could he possibly leave and disappoint this man who'd placed so much confidence in him? "I wondered . . . when you're expectin' that visitor today."

Mr. Harders' lips formed a grim line. "Jackson planned to meet the stage this morning and drive Jenks to the ranch. They should arrive shortly after noon."

Matt's mouth went dry. Only a few hours from now . . . He yanked up his mug and gulped several swallows of coffee before speaking again. "I wondered if . . . maybe . . . I could stick around when you meet with him."

Clancy gawked at him, slack-jawed.

Matt managed a lopsided grin. "Might be I have a reason or two to visit with that man, too."

Mr. Harders stared hard at Matt, his brows low. "If you want to sit in on the meeting, you're welcome."

"Thanks." Matt pushed back his chair. "But I reckon I better head to the pasture. Want to have my work done before Jenks gets here." He gave Clancy's shoulder a squeeze, slapped his hat on his head, and strode out the door.

✺

Matt sat on a chair in the corner, elbow on the armrest, his fingers pinching his chin. So far Jenks had hardly glanced in his direction, which suited Matt just fine. It gave him an opportunity to observe the man who'd stolen his childhood. A chance to pray and gather strength to face this enemy.

Jenks had aged. His hair bore streaks of gray at the temple, the strands shiny from the oil that held it slicked back from his face. His middle was thicker, his jowls more pronounced. But the gold tooth still flashed. Jenks had always been proud of that gold tooth. Matt got a glimpse of it again as the man stretched his lips into a sneer he aimed across the small parlor table at Mr. Harders.

"Whether I win the court battle or not, the damage will be done. Your son's name will be sullied. Consequently, your name will carry a mar that will follow you straight to the State House. You think you'll still have support when word gets around that one of your hands and your son assaulted an innocent rancher?"

Jackson clenched his fists, pressing them to the wood trim of his chair's armrest. "You're hardly innocent, Jenks, and you know it. That lady photographer will testify to your intent."

He snorted arrogantly. "I offered an invitation to dinner. An invitation many other women have gladly accepted. Any number of them will testify to my *intention* with them, which was merely to entertain. Your friend's word will be meaningless."

He pointed at Clancy, who stood silently beside Mr. Harders' chair. "And that man will be ruined. No judge in his right mind will take the word of a beaten-down sheepherder over mine." His smirk returned, his eyes narrowing. "He's been with you a long time, Gerald—as many years as your son. He's been with you through the hard times, like burying your wife and daughter back in '84, and good times, like Jackson's graduation from law school. Surely you want to repay him for his years of faithful service by getting these charges dropped before it goes any further."

"What exactly do you want, Jenks?" Mr. Harders nearly snarled the words.

"You already know. I want you and Jackson to stop this nonsense about the child labor laws. You both know it won't go anywhere. Factories will continue to hire the labor force they can afford to pay. Parents will still send their children out to work to add to the family's income. You can't change it, Gerald, so why fight it?"

"And why are you fightin' it so hard?" Matt rose from his chair slowly, by inches, his heart pounding but his voice strong. He waited until Jenks shifted his gaze to face him. He read no recognition in the man's scowl. Stepping around the end of the sofa, Matt said, "If Mr. Harders has no chance of makin' a change in those laws, why do you even care if he keeps on fightin'?"

Jenks's eyes narrowed until they were malevolent slits. "You're insolent." He glared at Mr. Harders. "Do you always let your hands speak to guests in such a disrespectful manner?"

Mr. Harders leaned back, his expression bland. "This is a free country, Lester. Every man is entitled to his opinion and his say."

Jenks glowered, but he clamped his lips together.

Matt took a step closer. "So what's your reason? Why're you fightin' against these laws?"

Another snort blasted from the man. "I'm just trying to save Harders here the humiliation of a defeat that's sure to come. He's wasting his time and money on something that will never happen!"

"It's his time and money. Shouldn't he be able to spend it like he wants to?"

"Bah!" Jenks waved a beefy hand, a ruby ring on his pinky finger catching the light. "It's foolishness." Resting his elbows on his knees, he stared into Mr. Harders' face. "Drop it now, Gerald, and save yourself and those you hold dear a lot of heartache."

Mr. Harders opened his mouth, but Matt interrupted. "Mr. Harders, I'm guessin' Jenks here has a more selfish reason for wantin' to keep those laws from bein' passed. I'm guessin' right now, on his ranch, he's got a youngster or two he's workin'. Workin' harder than he works his other hands, an' without a penny of pay. And he wants to keep working 'em. That's all he cares about."

Suddenly Jenks straightened, his mouth dropping. "You . . ." He jolted to his feet. "What's your name, boy?"

Mr. Harders rose, too, angling his body slightly to shield Matt. "Lester, this young man is Matthew Tucker."

"Matthew . . ." Jenks nodded slowly, realization dawning. "But not Tucker, is it, boy?"

Matt's chest felt tight, but he answered in a calm tone. "It is now."

"But it wasn't always."

"No, sir. It wasn't always."

Shoving his finger toward Matt, Jenks whirled on Mr. Harders. "This man stole a horse and a fistful of cash from me! I demand he be given to me to be taken in for prosecution!"

Mr. Harders stared at Matt in surprise. "Matthew?"

Clancy stepped forward. "You gotta hear it all, Gerald. Matt here didn't steal nothin' that wasn't owed him." His gnarled hand curled around Matt's shoulder. "Tell him, Matthew. Tell him what Jenks done to you."

Jenks blustered, "I did nothing but take him in, give him a home. I taught him a trade so—"

"So you could work me," Matt inserted quietly. Every muscle in his body quivered, yet he felt strength fill his bones. Turning to Mr. Harders, he said, "Jenks took me in, all right. He took me from an orphanage in Springfield. He kept me for close to four years, but he never paid me a wage. Instead, he worked me mercilessly an'—"

"You were paid in room and board," Jenks roared. "You ungrateful—" He clenched his fists, leaning toward Matt. "It's only by my generosity you know anything about ranching! How dare you accuse me of wrongdoing?" Suddenly his shoulders relaxed. He lowered himself onto the sofa, crossing his legs and sliding his thumbs beneath the edge of his brocade vest. He looked every bit the cultured gentleman as he formed a sly smile. "But why should I argue with the likes of you, a no-good

313

thieving orphan? You've got no proof of maltreatment. It's your word against mine."

Matt swallowed hard. *Lord, give me strength.* Looking directly into Jenks's eyes, he said, "I do have proof."

Jenks's hands slid to his lap as Matt began to unbutton his shirt. Matt glanced at Clancy. The older man's chin quivered. Clancy no doubt suspected what Matt was about to reveal. But it took more courage than he knew he possessed to slip his shirt away from his shoulders and turn his back to the men in the room.

A gasp split the air—Jackson's. The low-toned "Dear Lord in heaven . . ." came from Mr. Harders. Matt felt certain Clancy held his breath.

Matt slipped his shirt back into place and turned to face Jenks once more. "I carry the mark of your 'generosity' with me. You think your rancher friends will have any respect for you when they know what you did to me? When they know what you probably continue to do to the boys you've got working your ranch? How many are there, Jenks, on your ranch right now?"

"That's none of your business!"

Matt matched Jenks's volume and tone. "How many?"

A fierce scowl provided all the answer Matt needed. Matt nodded at his boss. "He's still doin' it, Mr. Harders. He's got orphaned boys workin' for him, an' he's likely keepin' 'em in line with his riding crop or a handmade bullwhip, just like he did me."

Mr. Harders put his arm around Matt's shoulders. "Jenks, decent men don't turn a blind eye to the abuse of children."

Jackson took two steps to stand beside his father. "What might happen to your reputation, Jenks, should word get out?"

Clancy moved to Matt's other side, forming a unified front. "If you got any sense at all, Jenks, you'll back off on tryin' to buy any land around here. You'll put them boys on a stagecoach an' send 'em to Shay's Ford to that new school what'll be built by Miss Isabelle, so's they can have a decent life." His tone turned menacing. "Fact is, if no boys show up sayin' you sent 'em, I'll be comin' after them. An' I'll make sure yo're sorry it was necessary fer me to come."

Jenks rose, glowering at Mr. Harders. "Are you going to stand there and allow your hired hand to threaten me?"

Mr. Harders replied calmly. "I didn't hear a threat, Lester. I heard a promise. And, based on my long-time relationship with Clancy, I can assure you he keeps his promises."

Matt added, "I'd do as he says."

Jenks looked from one man to the next, his expression incredulous. "Anyone could have left those marks on his back. He can't prove it was me!"

"And you can't prove it wasn't," Jackson returned. "So no matter how you look at it, your reputation will be sullied. Win or lose, people will never look at you the same way."

Jenks's face glowed red as his own words were turned back on him. His jaw flapped uselessly for a few seconds, and then he clamped his teeth together. He stormed past the men to the parlor's doorway. Without turning around, he grated, "Jackson, take me to Shay's Ford. I'm finished here."

"That you be," Clancy agreed, giving Matt a sad smile.

Jenks clomped out the door, and Jackson followed.

Mr. Harders turned to Matt. His eyes reflected sorrow. "Matt, I wish there was some way—"

Matt shook his head. "Can't change what's been done, Mr. Harders. All we can do is move forward. But if we can get those boys off Jenks's ranch and give 'em a chance to grow up with a little bit of peace and happiness, it'll all be worth it."

Clancy blew out a noisy breath. "Hoo-doggies, Matthew, don't know how you stood up to that man after what he done, but I gotta tell ya, I'm right proud of ya, son."

Matt chuckled, rubbing a finger under his nose. "Well, I admit, Clancy, I'm right proud of me, too." *Thank you, Lord, for givin' me the strength to face my nightmare.*

CHAPTER THIRTY-FIVE

Maelle
Shay's Ford, Missouri
May, 1903

Maelle banged the hammer two more times, securing the cloth backdrop to the wall. Hopping down from the ladder, she propped the hammer on her shoulder and admired her handiwork. The backdrop painted with a white pillar and shadowy lines to resemble draped linen had always been her favorite of the four Richard had used.

The other three lay, rolled, behind the counter. Eventually she would need to rig a bracket so the backdrops could be changed out easily, but for now she needed the pillared one in place.

Maelle turned a slow circle, examining every detail of the room that now served as her studio. In front of the window, two stuffed chairs flanked a low table that held albums of samples of her work. Across the room, an elbow-high cabinet held her cigar boxes, Richard's picture albums, and a money box. A door in the corner led to the small room that would serve as her darkroom. Everything was ready. All she needed now was customers.

She was eager to put out the *Open For Business* sign Jackson had given her, but she had to wait. She wanted her first customers to be a specific bride and groom whose photograph would be taken in front of the pillared backdrop. Only a week until the wedding. She could wait that long.

A smile grew on her lips as she thought about the newly married couple she'd be shooting in front of that backdrop. Her heart tripped happily as she contemplated the ceremony being planned by Isabelle and Aaron. Isabelle had asked her to be her attendant. Her baby sister, all grown up and getting married . . .

Her mind wandered to all the years that were lost to them, but she pushed those thoughts aside. This was not a time for sorrow. It was a time of celebration, of new beginnings—the beginning of her business; the beginning of a relationship with Isabelle; the beginning of Isabelle and Aaron's life as man and wife; the beginning of the Reginald Standler Home for Orphaned and Destitute Children, where Aaron and Isabelle would serve as caretakers and teachers.

Maelle winged a silent prayer of thanks heavenward for all the wonderful things happening for her, her sister, and the homeless children of Shay's Ford. Only one small storm cloud hovered on the horizon. Mattie . . . Maelle sat in one of the chairs and peered out at the street. Now that she'd found Molly, the need for Mattie was stronger than it had ever been. *Lord, will our family be reunited someday?*

The door opened, and she rose as Jackson strode in. She met him in the middle of the room and swung her arms wide. "Well, what do you think?"

His gaze roved around the room, and then he turned his smile on her. "You've been busy."

She shrugged, his warm smile creating a patter in her heart. Brushing the dust from her pant legs, she grinned at him. "All I've done for the past week is work in here. It's come together well." She crooked her finger. "Come on, I'll give you the grand tour." She showed him every detail of the studio and darkroom, and even let him peek at the room in the back that would serve as her living quarters.

"I know it's small, but it's at least four times the size of my wagon. I'll be fine until I save up enough to buy myself a little house."

He caught her hand. "About that little house . . ."

Something in his tone made Maelle's heart pound. "Yes?"

"Let's go back to the studio and sit down. I'd like to talk to you."

Jackson followed her to the sunlit studio. She sat, and Jackson scooted the second chair closer. When he sat down, their trouser-covered knees brushed. She chose not to move away.

"Maelle . . ."

How good that name sounded after years of being Mike! She closed her eyes, savoring the sound.

". . . you know Aaron and Isabelle will be married a week from Saturday."

She let her eyes slide open and fixed him with a steady gaze. "Yes. I'm glad I have things pretty well settled here now so I can help Isabelle with the last-minute arrangements. Deciding to get married the same day as the groundbreaking ceremony has given her a great deal to accomplish."

"I know she'll appreciate your help." His hand stretched out to touch her knee. "So many things are changing . . . for Aaron and Isabelle."

"And for me," she offered quietly, very aware of the gentle weight of his fingers on her knee.

"Yes." He drew in a deep breath. "I know you're happy to have your sister back, and to have this studio."

"Two lifelong dreams."

A nod acknowledged her words. His fingers quivered for a moment. "I'm experiencing a change, as well."

Maelle tipped her head, bringing her brows down. "Oh?"

His hand slipped away as he sat up straight. She felt the absence of the simple touch. "Yes." Rising from the chair, he paced around the room, seeming to examine the ceiling. His gaze aimed heavenward, his voice came in a strangled rasp. "This battle for the children must be taken as far as it can go, and my father . . . He has finally confessed he isn't up to it. His heart lies on the ranch. I suppose I suspected as much, but I didn't want to admit it. I hoped . . ."

Maelle's heart lodged in her throat. She pushed herself to her feet and stood on wobbly legs. "Jackson, you aren't giving up, are you?"

Quickly he brought his gaze around to meet hers. "Giving up? Oh, no. I'll not give up until the laws have been changed. But it means someone else must run for the House of Representatives. Someone with the determination to see the changes made. Maelle . . . that someone else is me."

Suddenly, she realized what he was telling her. He would be leaving Shay's Ford. With the realization, she felt a wave of disappointment. Taking a forward step, she held her hand toward him.

He clung to her fingers with a desperation that brought tears to Maelle's eyes. "It's difficult for me to leave . . . you."

She read the hidden message in his eyes. Meeting his gaze, she hoped he read her heart's response. She chose her words carefully. "I'll miss you, but I understand why you've got to go. The children need your voice, Jackson. If anyone can bring about the needed changes, it will be you."

"Thank you."

His brown eyes held her captive, and she forgot to breathe as he gently tugged her into an embrace. Maelle didn't feel any need to pull away. Her heart rejoiced as she found the freedom to wrap her arms around his middle, to splay her fingers on his firm back and hold tight. *Thank you, Lord, for the healing you've begun.*

After long moments he took hold of her upper arms and set her in front of him. She folded her arms across her chest and assumed a casual pose that belied the wild thumping of her heart. "When will you leave?"

"I'll be here for the groundbreaking ceremony. Isabelle has asked me to say a few words. Then I'll attend Isabelle and Aaron's wedding that evening. Aaron has asked me to stand up with him. But the following Monday, I'll begin traveling around the state, petitioning support not only for my campaign but also the issue of child labor laws."

Maelle swayed. A little more than a week . . .

"If I'm elected, which is the goal, I will need to relocate temporarily to Jefferson City."

"How temporarily?"

"The duration of my term." He shrugged. "One term is two years. And if I'm reelected . . ."

No further explanation was needed. Maelle forced a smile. "You know my prayers will go with you."

His hands curled around her upper arms. "And I'll be praying for you, every day, that somehow your brother will find his way to you. In fact . . ." He pressed his lips together, regret tingeing his features. "I should have offered before. My focus has been on this legislation. But I'd like to send out some feelers—give you some legal assistance in tracking him down, if you'll allow me to help."

"Oh, Jackson . . ." Maelle melted against him, clinging, appreciation for this caring man welling up to fill her chest. "Thank you."

He held her close, his chin against her hair, his hands caressing her back. Delicious shivers ran up and down her spine. She remained in his embrace, savoring the pleasure of his nearness, as time ticked slowly by and a bit of the pain in her heart washed away.

"There is something else I wanted to ask you."

She could feel his voice vibrating in his chest. She smiled, unwilling to move. "Yes?"

He pulled loose. "It's about my house." He glanced around, his forehead creasing. "You've done so much work here, and if you want to stay, I'll certainly understand."

She tugged his hands. "What are you talking about?"

"I wondered if you might consider moving in and being caretaker of my house while I'm gone."

Her eyes widened. "Live . . . in your house?"

"When I come back through this area, I'll stay at the ranch with my father. You won't have to worry about impropriety."

His assurance only endeared him to her more. "Oh, Jackson, a *real house* . . ." She shifted her gaze to the window, imagining the privilege of living in a house with a sitting room, a separate bedroom, a real bathroom, and a fully functional kitchen, where she could cook over a stove and then sit at a table to eat. She allowed her imagination to take wing.

Jackson touched her arm, bringing her back to reality. "Maelle? There might be an additional responsibility."

She waited expectantly.

"You see, the newest hand from my father's ranch rescued two orphaned youngsters from a cattle rancher. You know the man: Lester Jenks."

Maelle scowled. She remembered Lester Jenks. Thankfully her prayers had been answered concerning the need to testify against the man in court. He had inexplicably dropped his charges against Jackson and the hand from his father's ranch and had withdrawn his offer to purchase the land north of town. God certainly worked miracles.

"Right now, the boys are staying at Father's ranch, but they need to attend school. If they have a place to stay here in the city, they can go to school in Shay's Ford until the one Isabelle plans to open is complete."

"And you want them to stay in your house?"

Jackson shrugged. "It's a large house, so I have the room. But if it would be too much for you, I can ask Aaron and Isabelle to move into my home with the boys."

Maelle thought out loud. "But when the orphans' home is complete, they will be living out there. So that would leave your house uncared for again."

"I don't want you to feel responsible, and you don't have to answer now," Jackson said. "Think about it, pray about it, and you can let me know by the groundbreaking. My father will be bringing the boys along to the ceremony, so you can meet them then."

Maelle nodded in agreement.

"Well . . ." Jackson backed toward the door. "I better let you finish up here. I'll see you in church tomorrow?"

"Of course." With a grin, she added, "And I'll be wearing a dress, not these trousers."

Jackson lifted his shoulders in a shrug, his eyes twinkling. "Suit yourself. I happen to think you're cute as a button in trousers."

Clapping her hands to her cheeks, she admonished, "Get on with you!"

He laughed and strode out the door.

She moved beside the large window, looking out at the street. A feeling of contentment filled her. Knowing she would remain here, no longer a wanderer but a citizen of one community, brought a rush of joy. *Thank you, Lord, for letting me find a place to call home.*

She gathered up her tools and carried them to the room that held her bedroll and belongings. Thinking of Jackson's offer to allow her the use of his house while he traveled, she threw her arms wide and exclaimed, "A house to myself!"

But not completely to herself . . . She was soon to become surrogate mother to two boys. Once again, she'd be following her father's request to take care of the wee ones. *Oh, Lord, you work in mysterious ways.*

CHAPTER THIRTY-SIX

Molly
Shay's Ford, Missouri
May, 1903

Isabelle placed her hands on Aaron's shoulders and allowed him to lift her to the ground. Her hand shielding her eyes from the bright morning sun, she glanced down the line of wagons and buggies parked haphazardly along the road. A dust cloud marred the landscape between the school site and the town, providing evidence that more vehicles headed in her direction.

A glance toward the crowd near the platform Aaron and Jackson had constructed in the shade of three tall maples indicated most of the buggies had carried more than one person. Clusters of men, most in business suits with fashionable homburgs covering their heads, milled across the ground. Isabelle blew out a delicate breath. Maelle's letter writing had certainly been successful. Her stomach tilted in nervous excitement.

Aaron whistled through his teeth, looking around. "Lots of people here already."

"Just as we hoped." With a regret-laden sigh, Isabelle added, "But I do wish your parents had come with us." Deciding Petey wasn't up to two celebrations in one day, Mr. Rowley had stayed at the market to keep an eye on the boy. Mrs. Rowley was spending the day in the kitchen, preparing pastries for Aaron and Isabelle's wedding party.

Aaron touched her arm. "I know, sweetheart. But they'll be prayin' for you as you make your speech."

The reminder that her soon-to-be parents-in-law would lift her in prayer somewhat calmed her jumping stomach. She pressed her gloved hands to the abundance of ruffles marching from her neckline to her velvet cummerbund and took a deep breath, further bringing herself under control. When she pulled her hands away, she grimaced. Her white gloves held a coating of dust.

A few firm claps removed most of the gray speckles. Then, grasping the skirt of her new suit, she gave the folds of fabric a vicious shake, dispelling more dust. She smoothed the skirt back into place, admiring the color. After months of wearing black, it cheered her to don a less somber color.

The suit, with its matching skirt and jacket of deep green worsted, would serve as her wedding dress this afternoon. Mrs. Rowley had questioned the wisdom of wearing it to the groundbreaking ceremony, but Isabelle had wanted to look her best for both occasions. She reasoned there would be time in between the events to give it a thorough brushing.

Confident she had managed to rid herself of most of the road dust, she looked up at Aaron. "Do you see Maelle?"

Aaron stood on tiptoe and peered past the horse's rump, his brows low. Then he gave a nod. "Yes. She's with Jackson, beside the platform." He chuckled. "She's wearing her trousers."

"She warned me she would be. She can't climb in and out of the wagon quickly in a dress. But"—she crossed her arms over her chest and assumed a tart tone—"she will be wearing a dress for the wedding."

Isabelle looked across the grassy landscape to the spot where Jackson and Maelle stood, heads together, obviously deep in conversation. She hid a smile. Although neither Jackson nor her sister had intimated a romance might be blooming, she suspected they harbored fond feelings for each other. She had come to respect Jackson during the weeks of their acquaintance, and it wouldn't displease her to have him as a part of the family. She'd then have a brother-in-law. It wasn't exactly the same as having her brother, but—

"Oh." Aaron interrupted her thoughts. "Maelle wanted to use the wagon bed to set up her camera so she'd have a better view of the ceremony. I'm going to take the wagon over and ask her where she wants it. Do you want to ride with me?"

Isabelle placed a finger against her lips in thought, then shook her head. "No. I'll walk over to speak to Jackson." She drew in a breath that straightened her shoulders. "That way I can greet those who've chosen to come out today."

Aaron beamed his approval. "That's my brave girl. All right, then." He delivered a kiss to her forehead before pulling himself back onto the wagon seat and picking up the reins.

Isabelle made her way across the ground, weaving between groups of men, nodding, smiling, pointing out the stakes connected with twine that showed where the three-story dormitory, school, and stables would soon be erected. When she reached Jackson and Maelle, Jackson bestowed a kiss on her cheek in greeting.

Maelle offered a hug and then held Isabelle's hands out from her sides. "You look wonderful! That color is perfect with your hair." She slipped her arm around Isabelle's waist and grinned at Jackson. "Have you ever seen a more beautiful bride?"

Jackson smiled. "You look ravishing, Isabelle." Then he raised one brow at Maelle. "And I'm sure your dress is equally fetching."

Isabelle answered, "It certainly is! Hers matches mine in color, but—"

"But has no ruffles on the blouse," Maelle inserted, wrinkling her nose.

Isabelle laughed and gave the end of her sister's thick braid a gentle tug. "But her hair will be swept up into an elegant twist and—"

"—hidden underneath a ridiculous hat half-covered with a bird's nest," Maelle finished, making Isabelle and Jackson both laugh. She had argued adamantly against wearing the millinery, but Isabelle had insisted it was her wedding day and therefore she should have the final say. Maelle had eventually given in.

Now she released an exaggerated sigh. "At least she isn't making me wear one with a pheasant's wings stitched on its sides. I might have flown away!" Maelle put her hands alongside her head and flapped her fingers. The three shared a laugh.

"Mike!" Aaron's voice captured their attention. "Where do you want the wagon?"

"I'll show you." She gave Isabelle another quick hug before trotting to the wagon.

"This is a big day for you." Jackson turned his attention to Isabelle. "Are you nervous?"

"Not at all about the wedding. I love Aaron so much. I'm eager to become his wife. But . . ." Isabelle quirked her lips into a weak smile. "About the speaking, I am a little nervous. Although I attended many ladies' meetings with my mother, I was always in the audience, never the one entertaining the audience." She clutched at his fingers. "You are speaking first, aren't you?"

"Yes." He patted her hand and released it. "But you needn't worry. Just share from your heart, and you'll be fine. Now, come here." He led her to the center of the platform, where a large cloth-draped object waited. He lifted the edge of the cloth and let her peek underneath.

She clapped her hands in delight. "Oh, it's perfect!" Aaron had teased her about purchasing a plaque to mount on a building before the building was constructed, but she had insisted the dedication plaque must be the first purchase made for the new school.

Jackson dropped the cloth. "You can unveil it during your speech." He glanced at his pocket watch. "Which will take place in less than ten minutes."

Instantly the flutters returned in her stomach. "Oh my . . ."

He gave her shoulder a brief squeeze. "Don't worry. You'll be fine." Then he scowled, looking toward the road. "But I'm getting concerned. My father isn't here yet."

"Do you want to wait?"

Jackson smirked. "Oh, no, there will be no postponing of the event. We'll start right on time." Reversing toward the edge of the platform, he said, "I'm going to check with Maelle, and I'll be right back. Just relax."

Jackson stepped off the platform and strode across the grass. As if sensing the time to begin was near, the milling throng began gathering around the platform, their conversations creating a rumble that covered the gentle whisper of the wind through the maple leaves. Isabelle stood beside the cloth-covered plaque, her linked hands pressed to her ribcage, her head down, inwardly praying.

Thank you, Lord, that this school is becoming a reality. Thank you that my sister is here to share this day with me. Thank you for those who have chosen to support the school. Bless the children who will one day live here. Give me strength and courage, Father, to speak this afternoon . . . Lost in her prayer, she jumped when someone touched her shoulder.

Jackson stood beside her, a smile lighting his face. "It's time. Are you ready?"

To her surprise, she discovered the nervousness had fled. "Yes, I am."

Jackson moved to the front edge of the platform and raised both arms. "Gentlemen!" The murmur faded and Jackson propped his hands on his hips, his smile broad. "Welcome! I'm so pleased you chose to join us this morning for the groundbreaking of a school and home that will benefit the orphaned children of Shay's Ford and the fine state of Missouri."

A cheer went up from the crowd. Jackson allowed it to die on its own. "I'll not tell you about the school itself. I'll leave that to the lovely lady standing behind me—" he shot Isabelle a quick grin—"but let me tell you about the children whose lives will be positively influenced, thanks to your generosity in making this school possible. . . ."

☙

Mattie

Clancy bumped his boss with his elbow and said, "Looks like things've already started, Gerald."

Matt leaned sideways in the back seat of the carriage to peer past Clancy. Despite the churning dust, he made out Jackson's head and shoulders above a crowd of onlookers. Even from this distance, it was obvious he was addressing the group.

Gerald flicked the reins. "I feared we'd be late when we had to change horses," he said, his tone rueful, "but we didn't have a choice."

Clancy gave an emphatic nod. "If'n we'd've left poor Rosie in the riggin', she'd've thrown that shoe fer sure, the way it was fittin'. An' then we'd've been stuck along the roadside an' not've gotten here at all."

The boy sitting on Matt's left shifted forward and tapped Clancy's shoulder. "When we get back to the ranch, will ya show us how to shoe Rosie?"

Clancy turned clear around, his smile bright. "Why, shore I will, Tommy. That's a good thing fer you to know."

Of the two boys sent from Jenks' ranch, Tommy was the most interested in learning the aspects of ranching. Freckle-faced Chester, however, openly admitted he looked forward to spending his day in a schoolroom. After this weekend, Matt knew Chester would get his wish. Jackson had made arrangements for both boys to live with a woman from town until the new orphans' school was completed. He'd miss the boys—he'd grown attached to them in their brief time at Rocky Crest—yet he knew they would benefit from a real education.

Matt scrunched his face against the dust as Mr. Harders drew back on the reins and brought the horse to a stop behind the row of parked conveyances. Immediately the boys leapt out of the carriage and took off at a run.

"Boys!" Mr. Harders called. They whirled and returned. He grasped their shoulders. "Remember to be on your best behavior. These men are here to offer funding for the school where you'll be living in a few months. Let them see what fine boys they're helping."

"Yes, sir," the pair chorused. When Mr. Harders released them, they walked politely in front of the three men to join the group clustered in the dappled shade of the trees.

Matt could hear Jackson speaking as they approached. ". . . and I'm pleased to introduce to you the woman whose caring heart and benevolent nature has made this day possible. Please welcome Miss Isabelle Standler."

Matt joined the others in applause as an attractive young woman with shimmering red hair stepped to the front of the platform. She looked vaguely familiar, and Matt wondered where he'd seen her before. She raised her glove-covered hands in a silent plea to end the clapping, and the crowd obediently quieted.

"God has richly blessed me," the young woman began. "I had the privilege of being raised in affluence. As a child, I never wanted for material goods. All of my needs were met promptly, without hesitation, and I was provided with many luxuries, as well."

Clancy tipped his head toward Matt and whispered, "A body could figure that from her dress. Purty fancy, huh?"

Matt flashed a quick grin in response, then turned his attention back to the woman.

"I might have continued in the manner in which I was raised had it not been for the untimely death of my parents in an accident last December. Their deaths made me an orphan, and I shall never forget the despair and uncertainty of those first days, knowing I would never again have the pleasure of calling anyone Mama and Papa."

Tears glittered in the woman's eyes, bringing out the vivid green of her irises. Matt's heart swelled with sympathy. He understood too well the despair she mentioned.

"Just days after their deaths, I learned a disturbing truth. Rather than being orphaned at the age of eighteen, I discovered—through paperwork hidden in my papa's safe—that I had been orphaned many years previously, when I was still a baby. I learned, much to my heartache, that the man and woman I called Papa and Mama were not my true parents. Indeed, I had not been born to the Standler family as I'd always believed, but I had been taken in as infant."

A murmur broke out across the crowd. Matt leaned forward, straining to hear the woman's soft voice over the jumble of voices.

"I was not born to affluence. Rather, I had a humble beginning, born to an immigrant couple named Angus and Brigid Gallagher."

Chapter Thirty-Seven

Clancy drew such a sharp breath, two men turned around to stare. His bony hand grasped Matt's arm, and Matt clamped his hand over Clancy's. Matt's knees nearly gave way as the meaning of the woman's statement dawned on him. She continued, oblivious to the fact that she'd just turned his world upside down.

"I was born Molly Gallagher. And had it not been for Reginald and Rebecca Standler's willingness to accept an orphaned baby into their home, I might have grown up like the children Jackson described for you earlier. I might have spent my days on the streets, selling newspapers to survive. No child deserves such a cold, harsh upbringing."

Her green-eyed gaze swept across the audience. Matt held his breath as it skimmed past him, unaware. "Since coming to Shay's Ford, I have encountered, face-to-face, the difficulties of being without a home, without a family. The children I've met are amazingly resilient, amazingly able, far beyond their years. Yet they are sacrificing something precious to be self-sufficient—they are sacrificing their childhoods and their opportunity for education. I believe they deserve more than a day-to-day existence, and I applaud you for sharing my belief.

"Although I was never formally adopted by the Standlers, my papa loved me enough to provide for my future. Since the inheritance he left me has made it possible to purchase this land and the materials to construct the buildings, it gives me great pleasure to dedicate the project to his memory."

Matt rose on tiptoe to watch his baby sister move quickly to an object draped with a white cloth in the center of the platform. A deft flip of her wrist removed the cloth, revealing a brass plate. With a huge smile, she announced, "The Reginald Standler Home for Orphaned and Destitute Children." She blinked rapidly and said in a tear-choked voice, "May the children who enter this home feel as welcomed and loved as I was made to feel by my dear foster parents."

Wild cheers, whistles, and applause broke out. It continued, unfettered, for several minutes. But Matt didn't join in. His trembling hands were incapable of connecting. His quivering legs threatened to collapse. His heart pounded so hard he feared it might leave his chest. Standing fewer than twelve feet away was his baby sister, Molly, holding on to Jackson Harders' arm and beaming at the raucous crowd.

What if he'd given in to his fears and run away from Jenks? He'd be miles down the road, far away from his sister. Gratitude competed with the shock of finding Molly, and tears stung so sharply his nose burned. *Oh, Lord, you brought me to her. Thank you!*

Eventually things quieted, and Jackson led Molly from the shaded platform into the bright sunshine. The crowd surged after the pair. Clancy herded Matt along, his whiskery face wearing a grin so broad it nearly split his face in two. When the group formed a circle around Jackson and Molly, Clancy planted his hands on Matt's back and gave a firm shove that propelled him from the rear of the group to the front, where he had a clear view of Jackson Harders placing a shovel in Molly's small hands.

Green ribbons tied to the shovel's handle danced around Molly's wrists as she pressed the blade against the grass. She smiled at the crowd before putting her petite foot on the blade's shoulder. With a tiny grunt, she leaned her weight against the shovel, and the blade bit into the ground. Her lower lip between her teeth, she gave the shovel handle a jerk that turned the spot of soil. She laughed, her eyes shining, as another cheer broke out.

She passed the shovel to Jackson, who gave a bow before jamming the blade into the ground and turning a sizable chunk of sod. Molly patted her palms together, and then she shifted her gaze above the crowd. Raising one hand, she waved to someone. Her sweet voice called out, "You've taken a sufficient number of photographs! Come and break ground, Maelle!"

Matt jerked his head so hard his neck hurt and he nearly lost his hat.

Maelle?!

Maelle

With a laugh, Maelle grabbed the edge of the wagon and leapt over the side. Her boots hit the ground, sending up a puff of dust. The crowd parted, allowing her passage, and she joined Isabelle and Jackson. Her piece of sod matched Jackson's in depth and size, earning a rousing shout of approval from the onlookers.

Laughing, she enveloped Isabelle in a hug. Behind her, Jackson's voice rang out. "That concludes our ceremony, gentlemen. Thank you for coming, and may God bless you!"

The crowd dispersed, the men moving toward their waiting vehicles, except for a tall cowboy, who remained as if rooted in place just a few feet from the three grayish brown clumps of overturned sod. Although his hat brim shaded the upper half of his face, Maelle made out two thin rivulets of moisture running toward his quivering chin.

Isabelle stepped from her sister's embrace to dash to Aaron, and Maelle heard Jackson say her name, but she couldn't take her gaze from the cowboy. Something in his stiffly held shoulders and clenched fists, his chiseled cheeks stained with tears, spoke of a deep emotion. A tingle raced across her scalp. The artist in her desired to capture the man's posture on film so she could examine it later, understand its impact. Yet she couldn't move.

She stared as his hand rose to remove his hat. Tawny brown eyes met hers. Thick locks of reddish-brown hair, tousled by the wind, fell across his forehead.

She gasped. *Oh, heavenly Father, can it be . . . ?*

She took one hesitant step forward, her jaw dropping, her body straining toward him. She searched his face, her hands pressed to her thumping heart, and she uttered the question she had longed to ask for so long, "Would you still be havin' your tie to home?"

The cowboy crushed his hat against his thigh. His Adam's apple bobbed, and he offered a slow nod. "I look at the photograph every night before I go to bed, hopin' I might be seein' you in my dreams."

Maelle's knees buckled, and she clasped her throat with both hands. "Mattie!" Did she speak his name or only think it?

From behind her, she heard Isabelle's puzzled query. "Mattie? You mean . . . our brother?"

Before Maelle could respond, Isabelle raced past her and threw herself into Mattie's arms. Maelle watched Mattie scoop their little sister from the ground, Isabelle laughing as she clung to his neck. Her chest ached with the effort of containing her joy as she witnessed the reunion between the two people she loved more than anyone else in the world.

Mattie swung Isabelle in a circle, trampling his hat beneath his boots, then set her back on the grass. His head lifted, his tear-wet gaze meeting Maelle's. He held out one arm in invitation, and she staggered forward, her feet clumsy. A cry of delight left her lips as her brother crushed her to his chest in a hug that stole her breath. A strangled sob found its way from her throat, and she allowed her tears to flow. Tears of joy the likes of which she'd never shed before.

She wriggled loose enough to stand on her toes and kiss her brother's damp cheeks and forehead, just as she'd done the last day she'd been with him. He pressed his lips to the top of her head, murmuring, "You're real. I can't believe you're real."

Maelle understood his wonder. To be in his arms was a gift she feared she'd never receive. The awe of the moment filled her and overflowed.

The world faded away, and all that existed was Maelle, Mattie, and Molly, floating on a plane of happy abandon. They clung, their arms entangled, alternately laughing and crying. Then they separated to all talk at once.

"How did you find me?"

"Did you know we were here?"

"Have you just arrived in Shay's Ford?"

Laughter rang again, the answers unnecessary.

"Maelle . . ." Mattie's hand convulsed on Maelle's back. His voice—a voice so much deeper than the childish voice from their past—quavered with emotion. "You're so beautiful . . . Still in trousers . . . Your hair long again . . ." He shifted his attention to Isabelle. "You're all grown up an' as tiny an' lovely as our own mother. Lookin' at you is like seein' her all over again, Molly."

Maelle corrected gently, "Her foster parents named her Isabelle."

Isabelle shook her head wildly, making her silky red curls bounce. "He can call me Molly if he wants to." She beamed upward, her slender fingers reaching to touch Mattie's cheek. "All my life I've longed for a big brother who loved me, and now here you are!" Fresh tears rained down Isabelle's face.

They melted once more into a three-way hug. Maelle's heart praised, *You've answered me prayers, dear Father. You've brought me Molly and Mattie. I thank you, Lord. I thank you . . .*

"Maelle?"

Maelle jumped at the sound of Jackson's voice. He stood a few feet away with his father, Aaron, Clancy, and two young boys. Unwilling to relinquish Mattie, she tucked herself beneath her brother's arm before answering. "Yes?"

Jackson held out his pocket watch. "I hate to intrude, but we've got to get back to town or Aaron and Isabelle will be late to their own wedding."

"Wedding?" Mattie gawked at Isabelle, who beamed at him from beneath his other arm. "You're gettin' married?"

"Today," she confirmed. "Maelle is my attendant."

Mattie shook his head. "Married . . . My baby sister . . ."

"To Aaron Rowley." Isabelle gestured him forward. Then she pressed her hand to Mattie's chest. "And you must come." Catching Maelle's hand, she joined the three of them together. "Will you walk me down the aisle, Mattie?"

వ

Her hand tucked into the bend of Jackson's elbow, Maelle walked slowly along the city's boardwalk. He tempered his stride to match hers, slowed by the full skirt of her dress. For once she didn't rue the slower pace. She was in no hurry to leave his side.

Streetlamps cast a golden glow, lighting their path, and their shadows provided company as they made their way to Maelle's studio. The empty streets and darkened places of business lent an intimacy to the setting. She and Jackson might have been the only two people in the world.

Only minutes ago she had bid farewell to her sister and brother. After hugs and kisses, Isabelle and Aaron had departed in a gaily decorated buggy to a hotel at the river's edge, where they would spend their first night together as husband and wife. Shortly afterward, Mattie had climbed into the Harders' carriage. Remembering their last leave-taking, Maelle had clung to him extra hard, but he'd whispered in her ear that he would see her soon. The realization that he would only be a few miles away, at Rocky Crest Ranch, made the good-bye bearable.

She turned her head to admire her escort. In the soft light, Jackson's dark hair became the color of midnight, his chiseled features more pronounced and masculine. She owed him so much. What if he hadn't convinced her to stay and photograph the meeting at the opera house? She would still be alone—rolling across the landscape in her wagon, hiding from relationships in a pair of men's trousers, longing to find her sister and brother.

God had used Jackson to begin healing in her heart and to answer her lifelong prayer to reunite with her siblings. Her fingers tightened on his firm arm, sending him a silent thank-you. Somehow, he must have understood the meaning behind her touch, because he turned his head and smiled down at her. Odd how they seemed to communicate without words. Maelle pondered the strange ability as they stopped in front of her studio and she removed the skeleton key from her reticule.

Jackson plucked it from her fingers and unlocked the door for her, then held it open for her entry. She giggled as she stepped across the threshold.

He dropped the key into her hand, his head tipped in puzzlement. "What's funny?"

"You treat me like a lady."

Confusion creased his features. "And you find that humorous?"

She offered a shrug. "Not humorous, just surprising." She admitted something she'd never said out loud before. "Men have never treated me like a lady, Jackson."

He met her gaze directly, his expression sincere. "You are one of the finest ladies I've ever known."

Uncertain how to respond, she turned mischievous. Grasping her skirt, she dipped into a curtsy. "Thank you, kind sir."

He caught her arm and drew her upright. Cupping her cheek, he said, "I'm not playing, Maelle. Even in a pair of trousers and a worn-out shirt, you are every bit a lady. Will you remember I said so?"

Looking into his face, his expression fervent yet tender, Maelle knew she would never forget his words. Or the look in his eyes. She gave a nod, and his hand slipped away.

"Good." He ran his hand through his hair.

Even in the minimal light coming through the uncovered window, she could make out the ridges left behind by his fingers. She wished she had the courage to touch his hair just once, but she knew doing it now would be folly. The air fairly crackled with tension.

"Well, I suppose I should—" she began.

"Maelle, I find myself—" he began.

They both stopped. She waved her hand at him. "Go ahead."

He dropped his gaze, seeming to examine the toes of his shoes for long moments before lifting his head and looking into her eyes. "I find myself wanting to say . . . more. To make promises. To extract promises. But . . ."

She nodded, reading the unspoken words. "It's all right, Jackson." Taking a step forward, she rested her fingers on his forearm. "God has plans, and He's given you the task of helping children few others care to help. If you didn't see the work through, you'd never be happy with yourself. You must go. It's your fight, so go do battle."

He placed his hand over hers, his fingers warm and strong. "I appreciate your confidence in me."

"It's well placed," she assured him. "And I'll eagerly await reports on your progress when you travel through." She tipped her head, her heart pattering hopefully. "You *will* travel through, won't you?"

"Of course. And the first time I come back, you and I will go to dinner at the restaurant on the river. You can wear your trousers and stab your steak. It won't bother me a bit."

His lighthearted banter made her laugh. "That sounds fine."

"Until then . . ." His hand slipped away, but he made no move to go. "Maelle, I wish—"

She placed her fingers against his lips. "No, Jackson. No wishes. Just prayers. You see, God has plans beyond your work with the children, but He also has a perfect time. I know that better than ever now."

He kissed her fingertips before taking a wide backward step to the door. Then he remained there, one hand on the doorknob, one hand half reaching toward her. "But do you believe the time will come for us?"

Maelle closed her eyes, reliving the moments when she, her sister, and her brother shared an embrace under the Missouri sun. Opening her eyes, she curved her lips into a smile. "I think the time will come."

Jackson's fingertips grazed her cheek—a whisper touch that spoke more eloquently than words could. His gaze held her captive, his dark eyes conveying longing and . . . something more. And then, with a gentle nod, he slipped out the door.

A NOTE FROM THE AUTHOR

It is estimated that one million Americans are descendants of the 150,000 children who were sent from crowded cities in the East to new homes in the West between 1854 and 1929 on what were eventually termed "orphan trains." I am proud to say I am among those descendants. Not by blood, but by heart.

In 1968, my paternal grandfather married a woman I already loved. Helen Haak had been my babysitter from the time I was born until our family moved from Hillsboro to Garden City, Kansas, in mid-1963. So many of my favorite childhood memories involve this sweet-faced woman whose arms seemed designed to bestow hugs.

Taking care of children was nothing new to Helen. Although she desperately wanted children of her own, she was unable to carry a baby to term. So she became a surrogate mother to children whose parents were unable or unwilling to care for them, fostering more than a dozen. She could reach out to these children with empathy since she knew the pain of being parentless. When she was still a toddler, her mother passed away and her father chose to relinquish her. Helen rode an orphan train and was taken in by a foster family.

Hers, unfortunately, wasn't a happy-ever-after story. Like many of the train riders, she was never formally adopted, and she grew up feeling as though she didn't quite fit in. Yet, rather than wallowing in bitterness, she chose to open her heart to other people's children.

I can only hope she found a measure of acceptance from the love of those for whom she cared. I do know there was never a happier little girl than I the day my dear "Tantie" (my childish attempt at the German word *tante*, meaning "aunt") married my grandpa and officially became my grandma. Although she passed away in 1979, Helen lives on in my memory as my grandmother—not by blood, but by heart.

So, Tantie, grandmother of my heart, this story is my gift to you. Thank you for the love you freely poured into me. It is reciprocated a hundred times over.

Kim Vogel Sawyer

Acknowledgments

At an American Christian Fiction Writers' conference in September of 2003, three other authors and I planned an anthology project—four novellas under the title *Ties to Home*, which would tell the stories of four orphan-train riders reuniting in adulthood. The anthology project was declined, but the idea wouldn't leave me alone. I asked these three ladies if they would be opposed to my using the initial idea with different characters for a single, full-length story. They graciously offered their blessings, and away I went. It delights me to no end to thank Lena Nelson Dooly, Susan K. Downs, and Lisa Harris for their excitement when the idea was presented and their words of encouragement as I forged forward alone. Your belief in the story made me believe in it, too. Thank you!

And Susan, extra thanks and a super-sized hug for the research materials you willingly shared. What a blessing your friendship is to me!

None of my stories would find their way from my thinker to the computer without the support of my family. Thank you, Don, and my beautiful daughters, for sharing this journey with me.

I owe a huge thank-you to my parents, Ralph and Helen Vogel, for indulging my curiosity about things past and always encouraging my imagination. A child never had two better parents than the ones God gave me.

As always, my critique group deserves praise for their great suggestions. I wouldn't survive without Eileen, Ramona, Staci, Margie, Crystal, and Donna. Thanks, ladies, for your continued efforts on my behalf. (Jill and Ramona, thanks for the advice on the Irish brogue—what a huge help you were!)

Prayer support is invaluable, and I'm so grateful for my prayer warriors—Kathy, the choir at First Southern, Don and Ann, Rose, Carla, Cynthia, Connie . . . You bless me every day.

Special thanks to my agent, Tamela, for believing "someday" would come.

I am always grateful for the support from my editor, Charlene, and the staff at Bethany House. What a great bunch of people you are!

Looking back, there are a number of authors who have inspired me either through their novels or through their words in e-mail or in person. I'd like to thank Deborah Raney, Tracie Peterson, Brandilyn Collins, Joyce Livingston, Judith Miller, and Janette Oke for reaching out to a nervous, wannabe author and making her feel as though she could find her place in this writing business. I appreciate you more than words can say.

Finally, and most importantly, thanks be to *God*. He alone brings dreams to reality and makes them sweeter than the dreamer imagined. May any praise or glory be reflected directly back to You.

KIM VOGEL SAWYER is fond of C words like children, cats, and chocolate. She is the author of eleven novels, including the bestselling *Waiting for Summer's Return*. She is active in her church, where she teaches adult Sunday school and participates in both voice and bell choirs. In her spare time, she enjoys drama, quilting, and calligraphy. Kim and her husband, Don, reside in Kansas and have three daughters and four grandchildren.